Praise

"I am totally besotted with this cleverly amusing author, her irreverent humor had me barking with glee." **DJ's Book Reviews**

"As always Charlotte Fallowfield has made me howl with laughter and had me reaching for tissues to wipe away the tears streaming out of my eyes from the amount of laughter!" **Two Bookish Brits**

"Welcome to Dilbury, where life is never dull." Hell, ain't that the god's honest truth! I am soooo excited to be back in my favourite quaint British countryside village! I love Dilbury!! Love it! Love it! Love it!" **Read & Share Book Reviews**

"This was yet another brilliantly written, hilarious, amazing book by Charlotte Fallowfield. Having read so many books by her, I'd come to expect a certain flair and she didn't disappoint. This book was jam packed with pure brilliance. The series has always been a better version of Bridget Jones to me. I love me some Bridget, but Abbie, Georgie, Charlie...Bridget has nothing on them." **Gothic Angel Book Reviews**

"I can't get enough of the *"Dilbury Village"* series. My hope is that Ms. Fallowfield will continue to write about this charming and quaint little town and the endearing characters who live there for the unforeseeable future. Each time I pick up one of these books, I feel like I'm getting the chance to spend time with some of my oldest and dearest friends." **Wrapped Up in Reading**

About the Author

Charlotte released Until We Collide, her debut romantic comedy novel, in February 2016. It became an Amazon UK, and international, #1 bestselling contemporary romance, romantic comedy, and humorous novel.

She likes to use many of her own life experiences in her novels, it helps that she's a total clutz and walking disaster.

Charlotte lives in the beautiful Welsh countryside with her significant other, and two much loved tuxedo pets, Mr. Pumpkin, feline of mass destruction, and Waffle, the boisterous cockerpoo.

She has a myriad of titles under her belt, under two pen names, and is proud to be both an independent, and traditionally published, author.

Her website the most comprehensive information about her, as well as her current and up and coming releases.

charlottefallowfield.co.uk

Laughter's the journey ~ Love's the destination

The Best Medicine

(Dilbury Village #3)

By

Charlotte Fallowfield

Imprint

ISBN-13: 978-1797560298

KDP Edition 1

This is a work of fiction. Any similarity between the characters and situations within its pages and places or persons, living or dead, is unintentional and co-incidental.

I am a British author and write in British English, unless writing from an American point of view, where I will use American spellings and slang.

Copy Editing by Karen J & Jasmine Z
Proofreading by Tracy G

Image Copyright © 2018

Cover Art by Kelly Dennis at Book Cover by Design
Charlotte Fallowfield Branding by Hang Le Designs
Illustrated Map by Holly Francesca at www.hollyfrancesca.co.uk
Book Content Pictures Designed in Bookbrush & Canva

Foreword

The Best Medicine is book three in the Dilbury Village series, which will comprise of a number of standalone novels set in the quaint English village.

charlottefallowfield.co.uk

Dedication

To everyone dreaming of their happy ever afters.

Table of Contents

Dilbury Village Map

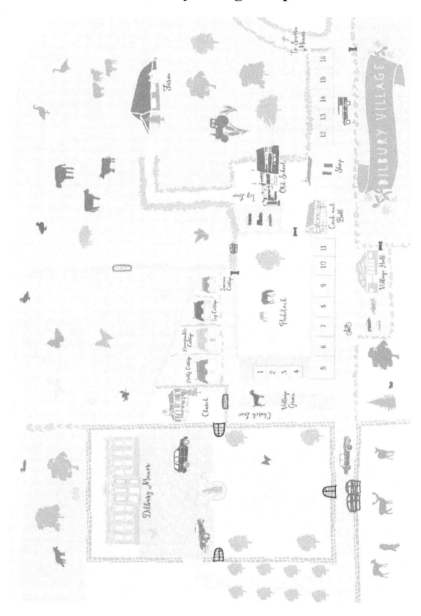

Holly Cottage – Abbie – Accountant
Honeysuckle Cottage – Daphne – Retired, then
Quinn – Wedding Planner
Ivy Cottage – Georgie – Dog Groomer
Jasmine Cottage – Charlie – Author

Chapter One

'WHERE THE HELL DID they put my shot glasses?' I huffed, as I tried to shift boxes to see their contents. This was why you needed to be organised when you moved house, and I was anything but. I'd made sure my favourite tipple of peach schnapps was the first thing I'd located when I'd moved in yesterday. In fact, it was on the kitchen worktop before the toaster. But could I find my glasses, or my kettle come to that?

I gave up and tipped a good glug into the glass measuring jug I'd found. Quite why I had a measuring jug I had no idea. I was as scared of cooking as most people were of spiders. My diet was atrocious, and not helped by the fact that I sat on my arse all day writing, eating when I was hungry instead of at set times. Just one of the hazards of being an author. It was like disappearing into the twilight zone. One minute the sun was shining and I was starting a new chapter, the next it was midnight and I'd not eaten because I'd been so engrossed in my characters' lives. I was living vicariously through them.

Living in Cheltenham town centre had been perfect at times like those. I could either call one of the many places I had on speed dial to bring dinner to my door at any hour, or slip out to the nearest burger joint while I took a break and people watched. I loved doing that. Strangers I'd watched and snippets of conversations I'd heard had inspired so many characters and situations in my novels. However, as much as I'd loved the hustle and bustle of the town, it was also one of the reasons I'd decided to move to Dilbury. I'd done the clubbing scene in my twenties, and I was finding it hard to concentrate on writing with the constant noise. What's more, I was worried that my fast metabolism, which had allowed me to get away with eating what I wanted while doing no exercise, was soon going to wave a white flag in surrender, and my hips and arse would suddenly balloon and stop me from fitting into my trusty writing chair.

Hitting thirty the previous January had really made me reassess my life. I couldn't afford a house in the Cotswolds, but in Shropshire, particularly villages like Dilbury that were close to the Welsh border, houses were far more affordable. I'd moved here with the intention of enjoying some peace and quiet, of getting more exercise in the fresh air, and getting away from the myriad of convenience foods at my fingertips so that I could learn to cook and eat more healthily.

'Epic fail so far, Charlie,' I scolded myself as I tried to hide the evidence of last night's Chinese delivery by squashing more of the annoyingly squeaky white polystyrene pasta shapes, which the movers had packed around my breakables, on top of the rubbish in the kitchen bin.

The Internet was a curse sometimes. The previous day, moving in day, I'd stopped at the local village shop and picked up a supply of healthy-looking produce to do a stir-fry. Of course, I had no idea how to stir-fry, unless it really was as simple as it sounded and just involved stirring food around in a frying pan, but I doubted cooking could be that easy, or there wouldn't be so many restaurants and takeaways. After I'd stared at the courgette for five minutes, with it only inspiring ideas for the next sex scene in my current work in progress, I'd given up on the idea of a stir-fry. I'd gone online to discover, in under thirty seconds, that there was a Chinese takeaway and a pizza place in the next village, both of which would deliver within twenty minutes. That was a hell of a lot faster than I could work out how to cook a damn stir-fry.

After quickly phoning the local Chinese before the guilt kicked in, I'd placed the courgette on the floor behind Mrs. Tibbles, my four-year-old tabby cat, who was happily eating the freshly-diced chicken I'd just purchased and purring like a pneumatic drill. It had given me a few minutes of amusement when she'd turned, spotted the courgette lurking behind her, and leapt about three feet in the air as her tail expanded and she hissed in surprise.

If anyone ever needed a courgette shredded in record time, Mrs. Tibbles was the cat for the job. In seconds, she'd attacked it with her front claws and teeth, then laid next to it and dragged it into her furry embrace, using her back paws to maul it to death. When she'd finished, she'd stalked off, leaving strips of courgette all over my beautiful oak floor as she'd continued to try and decide where in the new house her favourite sleeping spot was going to be. The giggle I'd had at her surprise was almost worth the extortionate cost of the damn courgette and chicken. No wonder I'd never eaten well. Fast, convenient food was far less expensive and had never ended up in hundreds of tiny strips all over my kitchen floor, or in Mrs. Tibbles' belly.

I drank some of the schnapps from the jug and wandered over to the bi-fold glass doors that ran across the back of my kitchen-diner, gazing at the view. It didn't suck to look out and see such an amazing vista down the garden and over the fields towards the river, instead of looking out at the rooftops of the town centre. I sighed in contentment. I had a feeling I was really going to like it here. The cottage was the perfect size for me. I was lucky that the previous owners had spent a lot of money on it before being offered a job overseas, which had necessitated a fast sale at a ridiculously low price. The timing had been perfect and I'd snapped their hands off.

I'd started working as a financial advisor almost immediately after leaving university and had pulled in an absurd salary, some of which I'd been saving up for the day when I would want to get out of my cramped one-bedroomed flat and quit my job to write full-time. My author income fluctuated month to month, but the knowledge that I didn't have a mortgage to pay and that I had a buffer of a year's decent salary gave me the confidence and freedom to focus on trying to get my work traditionally published. If I could, it meant that I could earn enough to never have to consider applying for a "normal" job again. Writing was my passion. I lived and breathed it, and I knew there wasn't a better way to spend the rest of my days. It didn't feel like a job when I was lost in my own writing world.

I couldn't have found a more perfect cottage if I'd created it in my own vivid imagination. It had been modernised to my taste while keeping the character I liked, and there was no need for me to do anything but slowly unpack my boxes. A beautiful white shaker kitchen with oak butcher-block worktops, sage green painted walls, and oak floorboards complimented the brilliant white butler's sink. A glass and oak dining table with cream leather scroll chairs completed the look. From the kitchen, there was a door to a small utility room with a downstairs cloakroom on the side of the house. On the other side of the hall was my lounge, which had a huge open log fire, and also benefitted from glass bi-fold doors to the rear. A glass wall behind the oak staircase in the middle of the house let light flood into the small hall.

Upstairs, in the eaves of the thatched roof, was a small bathroom opposite the stairs, and a decent-sized master bedroom with its own en-suite shower room. The guest room doubled as my office. I'd had a custom-built study bed made, which was a huge desk where my notebooks, pens, and MacBook sat, but could be pulled down, everything in-situ, and turned into a double bed in seconds if I had visitors. The views from upstairs, even through the small windows, were even better than down here.

Something in my left field of vision suddenly drew my attention. My eyes wandered over to the corner of the garden, and I frowned as I spotted movement.

'Hello there. It looks like your reputation has already reached the villagers of Dilbury, Charlie,' I chuckled to myself, as I took another sip of the warming schnapps. Two women were lying down in the field, barely concealed by the winter-bare hedge at the bottom of my garden.

I was used to the looks I got from neighbours when they discovered I wrote "illicit material." But truth be told, it was great that it was becoming far more socially acceptable to say you were an author of steamy novels. I'd often toasted the success of E.L. James for helping me gain the courage to try writing in that genre without worrying that I'd be chased down the street with pitchforks for admitting that I did. That said, I was in quite possibly one of the sleepiest villages in England, complete with its own stately home owned by a Lord. Maybe news of the erotic romance revolution hadn't reached its aged population. Though, looking at the women who were currently failing to inconspicuously spy on me, they didn't look like the blue-rinse brigade I'd seen on my few trips to view the house. I'd been warned that the average age of the villagers was pushing seventy, but these women looked my age.

I sniffed the air, my nose wrinkling in disgust at the scent of cow dung that was somehow making it inside, even with the windows shut. Wow, that was definitely one downside to living in the country. I watched as I saw a tractor approaching from the field on the right, manure spraying out from the contraption hooked onto the back and arcing up and over the hedge. My eyes flicked back to the women, who appeared to be arguing as they pulled their jumpers up over their noses. Part of me was ready to fling open the doors and warn them that they were about to be showered with cow manure, but the evil part of me triumphed. Maybe it would teach them not to be so rude. If they'd just knocked on the door, I'd have happily invited them in and answered any questions they wanted to ask.

Their high-pitched screams as they were suddenly pelted with the sludgy mess made me laugh so hard that I had to walk away from the glass doors. I didn't want them to realise that I'd seen them and feel embarrassed.

I accidentally kicked a box on the floor and heard the chime of glass on glass, and rejoiced that I'd found my shot glasses. I paused for a moment, biting my lower lip. Maybe I should go and introduce myself, invite them over for drinks. Anyone prepared to go to those lengths to see me must be slightly crazy, and that was something I'd been accused of many a time. I'd never really had any girlfriends to speak of, as my previous career in finance had meant I'd worked mainly with men. It might be fun to get to know the neighbours and hopefully develop the sort of friendship that my heroines always had with their best friends.

I hurried to the cloakroom and quickly raked my fingers through my long blonde waves, trying to make myself look halfway presentable. Working from home each day meant that I rarely wore makeup, but I was lucky enough to have thick, dark lashes that framed my brown eyes so well, it looked as if I was wearing mascara. I'd pass muster, I'd never tried to be someone I wasn't. I grabbed my keys and hurried out of the front door, groaning at the pungent smell that filled the air. Did people in the country ever get used to it? It wasn't until I was walking up my front path that I realised these women might not even be my neighbours, as I knew there were public footpaths all around Dilbury. They might have come from any direction and disappeared home already.

Shrill screams puncturing the air made me quicken my pace up the lane to follow the sound, which seemed to be coming from behind Ivy Cottage, the one closest to mine. I walked up the drive and spotted a log cabin to the left, against the hedge. In front of it, the two women were standing in their underwear, hosing each other down. I giggled as I leaned on the wide gate and watched them. It seemed I'd found my spies, and one of them actually lived next door.

'I hate you, Abbie Carter!' the redhead shouted.

'Oh, shut up,' the other one laughed.

'Hello?' I called, making them aware of my presence. 'Is everything ok?'

They both turned to face me, looking aghast to be caught in such an embarrassing situation.

'Are you kidding me?' the redhead muttered, shooting a glare at her friend.

'Sorry to interrupt your … whatever it is you're doing in your wet underwear,' I said as I waved a finger at them, 'but from the screams, I thought you might need some help.'

'We're awesome, thanks,' the brunette called, crossing her arms over her chest.

'Just hosing off cow manure.' The redhead put her hands on her hips as she tossed her wet hair back over her shoulder and stood in a pose that would rival any of the girls on America's Next Top Model. She was stunning.

'We were walking the dog in the field when the muck spreader went past,' the attractive brunette added.

'Really? I thought it was that you were lying like army commandos as you spied on me through my hedge.' I shot them a grin and laughed as they glared at each other.

'I *really* hate you right now, Abbie,' the redhead hissed. 'It was her idea,' she added, flicking an accusing thumb at her friend.

'Don't worry, my reputation precedes me. I'm used to people wanting to see the "hussy" next door. I'm Charlotte, by the way, but most people call me Charlie.' I smiled as I leaned over the gate and offered them my hand. The redhead made the first move.

'Georgie Basset. So sorry, it was my stupid best friend's idea. I wanted to come and knock on your door like normal people would,' she said with a grimace as she shook my hand.

'I wasn't feeling glamorous and I didn't want you to see me looking a mess, but now you've ended up seeing us in our wet underwear, stinking of cow shit. Abbie Carter, and I really am sorry,' the brunette said as she shook my hand too.

'Don't be. You've just inspired a whole "hot lesbians in the country" novel,' I teased.

'*Not* lesbians,' they both stated firmly.

'Why don't you go and change, then come over for a drink? I've no idea where the kettle is, but I've got my shot glasses and some alcohol out.'

'A girl with my own priorities,' Georgie laughed.

'We're actually supposed to be heading back to Daphne's, next door,' Abbie reminded her. 'Her husband just died and we were having afternoon tea with her. Why don't you give us ten minutes and head over there instead? She has whiskey, as well as hot drinks.'

'I won't be intruding?' I asked, not sure it was the best time to meet one of my neighbours if she was grieving.

'Trust me, she's eager to meet you too. And from what we learned this afternoon, she'll be grilling you for sex tips when she's ready to get back on the horse. She's not as innocent as she looks. Plus, as the village gossip, your book sales in Dilbury will soon go through the roof.'

'Excellent!' I nodded. Well, that sold me. 'Ok, I'll go rummage out a bottle of wine for her. See you in a while.'

'Bye,' they both called in unison as I turned to head back up the drive.

'Owww,' I heard one of them moan.

'Great way to impress the sexy new neighbour, dripping wet in my unmatching underwear and stinking of shit. I'm so going to get you back for this,' hissed the other, making me smile to myself. They sounded like they'd be fun to get to know.

I rapped sharply on the solid stable door of Honeysuckle Cottage, and was startled when Abbie flung it open faster than I'd expected.

'You came. We weren't sure if you would after we embarrassed ourselves earlier.'

'You made me laugh for the first time since I started packing up to move house, of course I came,' I grinned, brandishing the bottle of wine and giving it a wiggle for her to see.

'Well, invite her in, Abbie, you're letting all the heat out,' a voice softly scolded. Abbie rolled her eyes with a sigh and flicked her head, gesturing for me to step inside.

The cottage appeared to be the same layout as mine, without the modern glass back wall. Where my beams had been painted white, these were dark brown, bordering on black. I followed Abbie through to the warm, old-fashioned living room. It was just how you'd expect a pensioner's lounge to be, even down to those weird knitted doily-looking things on the backs of the chairs. But it had a real homely feel, with the roaring fire, green patterned floral carpet, and tall floor lamps with large pink shades. Georgie smiled at me from one of the chintz armchairs by the fire, and I saw an elderly white-haired lady sitting on the matching patterned sofa, her knitting needles clacking away loudly, moving at such a fast tempo they were a blur.

'Hello, dear, don't be shy, come on in. I'd stand and give you a kiss, but my knees are playing up today. I'm Daphne, Daphne Jones.' The warm smile on her kind, wrinkled old face made me give her one in return. She seemed sweet and reminded me of my grandma.

'I'm Charlie, Charlie Faulkner, but I guess you already knew that.' I walked over and leaned down to place a kiss on her cheek. 'Thank you so much for inviting me over, and I'm so sorry for your recent loss.'

'Thank you.' She let out a heavy sigh, then patted the sofa next to her, indicating for me to take a seat.

'I was sitting there, that's where I always sit,' Abbie protested.

'Well, now it's where Charlie's sitting. Don't be petulant, Abbie, it doesn't suit you. Besides, I know everything about the two of you. I have a new and interesting neighbour to become acquainted with.'

'So, now we're not interesting anymore? Honestly, I could rapidly go off you,' Abbie retorted, flashing a scowl in her direction that made me bounce my eyes between them and wonder what I'd just walked in on. I'd never have spoken to Grandma like that, she'd have clipped me around the ear. I was surprised to hear Daphne tittering as she carried on knitting.

'Don't mind us, Charlie. I've known this feisty one since she was born, like a daughter to me she is. A very annoying daughter sometimes, but a daughter all the same. Georgie too, though we've only known each other a few years. Sit, sit,' she ordered in a bossy tone as she noticed I was still standing. 'We like to pick at each other, it's our thing, when we aren't busy laughing. These two girls are wonderful friends, they've seen me through a tough month and not treated me with kid gloves, and that's what I need. Life goes on, it's for the living.'

'You are allowed to cry on us too, Daphne,' Georgie said with a serious face as I sat down, and Abbie smiled at me as she plopped down in the other armchair by the fire.

'He wouldn't want me to cry, girls, unless it was with laughter. My David always loved hearing me laugh with you both, said it kept me young at heart and reminded him of the young girl he fell in love with. He'd want me to enjoy the rest of my days, not spend them mourning him. You know one of his favourite quotes was from Thomas Jefferson. "I like the dreams of the future better than the history of the past,"' she said with a wistful sigh, a tear appearing in the corner of her eye. She quickly wiped it away and smiled again. 'Anyway, enough about me. Why doesn't someone go and put the kettle on and we can all warm up with a nice whiskey coffee while Charlie tells us all about these sexy men she writes about in her books.'

'You want to hear about my writing?' I spluttered. Grandma would have had a heart attack if she'd found out I was writing the sort of material I was.

'No need to be bashful,' Daphne smiled, patting my knee with one hand. 'I can't get enough of those BSM books.'

'BSM,' Abbie giggled, and Georgie let out a weird snort of amusement that didn't seem to fit with her character at all.

'Did I say it wrong? Isn't it BSM?' Daphne asked, not stopping her knitting for a second.

'BSM is British School of Motoring, hardly a sexy topic. I think you mean BDSM,' Abbie told her between more laughter. I stared at them all wide-eyed, not quite sure I believed the frank, unfiltered conversation I was hearing in front of an old lady.

'Ah yes, I always forget the "D." Why do I forget that each time? What does it stand for again?'

'Well, the "D" is for domination,' I said slowly, not sure what weird universe I'd woken up in this morning, where I was potentially discussing the world of bondage with my aging neighbour.

'Oh yes,' Daphne nodded with a wide smile. 'How could I forget domination? Who doesn't love a bit of domination in the bedroom?'

'Oh my God,' Georgie snorted, shaking her head as I tried not to laugh myself. 'Seriously, Charlie, tell me you have a boyfriend and have hot and kinky sex like your heroines do, as Daphne and the Dilbury old-age pensioners have a better sex life than Abbie and I do. We can't be outdone by them.'

'Actually, I'm single, have been for quite a few years now. I seem to keep picking the wrong guys, so figured it was safer to stay single.'

'I hear you,' Georgie nodded as she leaned over to high five me.

'So, how do you write such realistic and steamy sex scenes? I started one of your books as soon as I heard you'd moved in, and I have to say, that first steamy scene, with the dirty-mouthed Frenchman, nearly necessitated a trip to accident and emergency for the fitting of a pacemaker. I haven't had such a vivid and exciting dream in a long time.'

'Oh my God, you're reading one of my books?' I gasped, my cheeks colouring up with embarrassment as I desperately tried to remember just how graphic that book was. Once I'd written one, it was like wiping the blackboard clear of all the chalk scribblings on it. I had to forget the last one to come up with the next new story and characters.

'Don't underestimate her,' Abbie said as she stood up with a wide grin. 'She looks like butter wouldn't melt in her mouth, but underneath that sweet granny exterior she likes to portray is a sex-crazed nympho with a mouth that would make a sailor blush.'

'Abbie Carter,' Daphne scolded, as she peered at her over the top of her glasses. 'Don't scare the poor girl off before I've grilled her.'

'I'm putting the kettle on and I've a feeling we'll need extra whiskey in Charlie's coffee, judging by the shocked look on her face. Welcome to Dilbury, where life is never dull.'

'I'm beginning to get that,' I laughed as I shook my head, wondering what on earth I'd let myself in for.

'What the hell?' I exclaimed, as I opened my front door to what looked like the most enormous slice of pepperoni pizza I'd ever seen, with a pair of jean-clad legs and scuffed black army boots sticking out of the bottom of it. A pair of arms were outstretched, holding out a green, red, and white pizza box for me to take, the delicious herby smell of it making my stomach rumble.

'Pizza on wheels,' mumbled the pizza's male voice.

'Seriously? That's the best slogan they could come up with?' I laughed.

'Seriously,' sighed the guy from somewhere inside his outfit.

'How did you get here? I can't even see your eyes, surely you didn't drive?'

'I have to put the suit on when I get off the bike, it's all part of the customer experience,' he replied, making me laugh even harder as I imagined him desperately wanting to air quote the words "customer experience" to highlight his indignation.

'There have to be better jobs, surely?' I asked, as I took the box off him and put it on the small console table in the hall, then grabbed my wallet.

'You'd think, wouldn't you? I can't say it was my dream, when I left university, to one day dress in a sweaty, flammable suit and scare the crap out of customers when I deliver their dinner.'

'You have a *degree*? Why on earth are you delivering *pizza*?' I asked, completely astonished at the revelation, as I peeled a tenner out of my wallet.

'My mum's sick. She doesn't have anyone else to take care of her. I couldn't afford a carer for her twenty-four-seven, so figured it was easier to do it myself and get someone to look after her for a few hours every night while I did some part-time work.'

'Surely you're paying more to a carer than you're actually earning?' I asked in amazement. The pizza shrugged, its pointy tip wobbling back and forth as if the guy was nodding his confirmation.

'Yes, but I'd go stir-crazy looking after her around the clock. It does me good to get out, even if I'm not getting any fresh air in this damn suit,' he chuckled. I laughed as well, warming to his rich timbre and honest admissions.

'Well, I think what you're doing is amazing. She must be so proud to have a son that puts her welfare first.'

'I wish. Most days she has no idea who I even am. Anyway, you didn't order pizza with a side of self-pity. Sorry, it's not very professional to talk about myself. That'll be nine pound ninety-nine please.'

'Please don't apologise, it must be really hard for you. I'm not surprised you need to get out and talk to someone. I have a pizza addiction, so if it helps, you can always offload when you deliver to me. Though I *am* supposed to be cutting way back, I'm too fat as it is,' I grimaced, still trying to work out where his eyes were. It was weird having a conversation with someone you couldn't even see, especially when looking at them dressed as a pizza made you hungry enough to be tempted to take a bite out of them.

'You're not fat. I think you have an amazing figure,' he said sincerely, making me blush as I handed over my ten-pound note.

'Thanks. Don't worry about the one pence change.'

'Thanks, Mrs. Faulkner,' he replied.

'It's Miss Faulkner, but I prefer Charlie. We're likely to get on first name terms if I can't control my cravings. Thanks for delivering, I'm sure I'll see you again.'

'Thanks for listening, Charlie. Enjoy your pizza. See you.'

'See you.'

Pizzaman, as I'd decided to nickname him, turned around, and I giggled as he shuffled his way up the path and struggled to get the bottom section of his costume through the gate, softly cursing before he turned sideways and did a crab-like walk out. He shut the gate behind him and gave me a wave as he disappeared behind the hedge. I went to close the door, but hesitated and bit my lip. I felt sorry for him. As if having a parent who didn't even know you were their son or what you were sacrificing to take care of them wasn't enough, his employers made him dress up in a ridiculous costume. He was probably only getting minimum wage as well. I quickly pulled a five-pound note out of my wallet and ran up the front path in my socks. I threw the gate open and stepped into the lane to find a guy desperately trying to fit the folded pizza costume into a small box on the back of a bright green, red, and white moped that could have been plucked straight from the streets of Italy. His black helmet was balanced on top of a well-worn black leather jacket that had been thrown over the seat.

'Ermmm, hey, I forgot to give you a tip,' I said. He took a startled jump and gasped before he turned to face me. I was pleasantly surprised. I'd expected a spotty, greasy-haired, sulky-faced twenty-something. Instead, I was looking at a seriously cute guy who was probably in his mid-thirties. He had cropped dark brown hair, deep green eyes, and a classically good-looking face, with some freckles over the bridge of his nose. Dressed in a white t-shirt and black loose-fit jeans, he looked like the kind of guy I might give a once over in a nightclub. He wasn't drop dead, "snap my neck from the whiplash I'd get from checking him out" gorgeous, but he was far from being unattractive. Dressed like that, he had a whole "James Dean" vibe about him. He ran a hand through his hair as he frowned at me.

'There's no need to tip.'

'Maybe not, but I like to. Here, take this,' I offered, holding out the five-pound note. 'Don't worry about change.'

'I can't take that, it's too much. You could have another half a pizza for that.'

'Despite my love for the food, even I couldn't eat a pizza and a half. Please, take it. I really appreciate having a delivery tonight. I'm not the best cook and I just moved in and have no idea where anything is in my kitchen. You really saved my bacon, so to speak.'

'Are you sure?' he asked.

'I wouldn't offer if I wasn't,' I nodded, waving it at him. He reluctantly took it from me, his cheeks flushing slightly with embarrassment.

'Thanks, Charlie, that's really kind of you. Well, I'd better get going, I'm sure more orders will have come in while I've been chatting. See you again.'

'You can count on it,' I replied. I gave him a smile, then went back through the gate and shut it, watching him shrug on his jacket and strap his helmet on. 'I never got your name,' I called as he straddled the tiny moped.

'Kitt,' he answered, sounding puzzled, as if no customer had ever asked him the question.

'See you around, Kitt.'

He waved over his shoulder as he kicked the stand away and started the engine. I headed back to my front door, only to gasp when I saw that I'd left it open. Mrs. Tibbles was peeking around it, her eyes as wide as saucers as she scanned the front garden. She only looked like that after a hefty dose of catnip spaced her out.

'Oh God, you could have run off,' I exclaimed, as I dashed in and quickly slammed the door behind me, my heart racing at the thought of losing her. She'd been an indoor cat all of her life, and had more than likely never even seen a blade of grass before. Yet another tick on the list I'd made of reasons to move. I wanted to be able to let her out to run wild now and then, like animals should.

She'd spent most of yesterday sitting in front of the lounge glass doors, watching all of the wildlife and occasionally chattering her jaw, making a weird-sounding noise that I'd never heard from her before as her tail quivered. And last night, she'd started meowing and pawing at the glass as if she was begging me to let her out. She scurried into the kitchen with a meow of disappointment that she still hadn't been allowed out to explore her first ever garden. Though I suspected that the second she made it out, she'd be so scared she'd hare back in and cower behind the sofa. It was going to be a gradual process to coax her to go out, but not until we were fully settled and I'd finished unpacking.

I threw myself onto the sofa with the pizza box on my knees as I turned on my TV. I dug into my tasty, calorie-laden meal with enthusiasm while I washed it down with a glass of wine. Pizza really was a cure all. It was the best medicine for all moods.

It hadn't been a bad day, all things considered. I seemed to have made three new friends in my neighbours, not to mention having great pizza on tap, delivered by the cute Kitt. And best of all, I couldn't hear a thing. No drunken people shouting in the street below me. No beeping from the buttons being pressed on the cash machine in the next building. No annoying noise of the TV or arguments through the paper-thin walls that separated my flat from the one next door. No smashing of empty glass bottles, or clanging as they bounced off the large metal waste bins as they were thrown out at closing time. Best of all, no being woken up by the sounds of the street cleaners at some ungodly hour.

In fact, the only sounds I'd heard so far tonight as I sat here was the occasional screech of an owl. Even the inky darkness, lit only by thousands of stars that I'd never seen above Cheltenham, was oddly comforting and not at all oppressive as I'd worried it might be. It was so much nicer than the harsh glow of street lamps outside my flat windows.

Yes, moving to Dilbury was turning out to be a very wise decision indeed.

Chapter Two

Valentine's Night
One Month Later – February

'DAMN,' I UTTERED WHEN I finally looked up from my computer to check the clock on the wall. There was a permanent reminder of the time on my Mac, but it never seemed to register, I always looked up at the clock on the wall. And, as usual, I was running late. We were having a singletons' Valentine's Day commiseration meal at Abbie's tonight. I was really touched at how quickly the tight-knit threesome had welcomed me into their group.

I scurried over to my bedroom, grateful I'd laid my outfit out in advance, only to curse when I found Mrs. Tibbles curled up on top of it, kneading it with her claws as she purred.

'Seriously, Tibbs? You can pick a sleeping spot anywhere in the house and you choose my favourite little black dress?' I huffed. She barely opened her eyes to fix me with a disapproving look before closing them again. 'Come on, off, I need to wear that. Seriously, Tibbs, shift it,' I warned her. I ended up risking my hands, which I really ought to insure when I had to carry out dangerous pastimes like moving a sleeping Mrs. Tibbles, and quickly slid her off the dress and onto my duvet, only just retracting my hands as a warning swipe came at me. Why wasn't there a "let sleeping cats lie" adage?" They were far more vicious than dogs when disturbed.

I dressed and put on some eyeliner, a touch of blusher, and lip-gloss in record time, then ran out of the bedroom, pulling on my high heels as I headed to the stairs. I should have known that wasn't the greatest of plans with my luck. I winced as my ankle turned and I felt myself toppling forwards.

'No,' I shrieked, desperately trying to stop my descent by thrusting my hands out.

I landed with a thud and an "oomph," a sharp pain radiating through my right wrist and cheekbone, before I slid head first down the stairs to the half landing and did an odd roly-poly onto my side. My entire body was trembling from the shock as dizziness and nausea hit me. Somehow, I managed to stand on my one foot that wasn't throbbing, clutching my painful wrist to my chest. My vision swimming slightly, I stepped forwards, but missed the top step of the next flight and fell backwards, this time bouncing all the way to the bottom of the stairs, various expletives leaving my lips as my bottom and back took the brunt of each blow. I landed in a puddled heap in the hallway and lay there for a few minutes, slightly dazed, closing my eyes as I tried to work out which part of my body hurt the most. A meow and whiff of fishy cat breath forced me to open my eyes to find Mrs. Tibbles had come to check on me, and was currently licking all of the blusher off my right cheek.

'Thanks, Tibbs,' I uttered. I managed to get myself up to a seated position, and knowing I was still too dizzy to even attempt standing, I did a slow bum shuffle across the hall to reach for the phone. I needed medical attention. I had a horrible feeling I'd broken my wrist, and my ankle wasn't feeling too great either, not to mention all of the bruises I was going to have. I called for an ambulance, not wanting to ruin any of my friends' evening, and just sat with my back against the front door as Mrs. Tibbles rubbed herself against me, leaving a trail of cat hair all over my dress. '*Now* you're in a loving mood,' I sighed, as I used my good hand to tickle under her chin, wondering why she always picked the worst moments to show her affection for me. I closed my eyes to focus on anything but the pain I was in and to stop the room from spinning.

I felt like I'd been waiting forever for the ambulance to come when the shrill ring of my home phone sitting in my lap roused me from my attempts at meditating the pain away. Turns out I needed to add sucking at meditation to my sucking list, which sounded a lot ruder than it actually was when I said it to myself. To date, it had only ever had cooking on it, but now it had a companion.

I picked up the phone and winced as I answered it, my shoulder blades screaming at me to stop moving.

'Bugger, bugger, bugger,' I moaned.

'Well, that's a new way to answer the phone,' Abbie said with a laugh. 'Is that how you used to do it down in the Cotswolds?'

'Sorry, Abbie, I'm in pain. I stupidly decided to try and ski down the stairs, and now I'm waiting for an ambulance. My wrist is killing me.'

'You skied down the stairs? My God. In salopettes, goggles, and everything? Eddie the Eagle style?'

'No,' I laughed, the movement making me wince again. 'I was being sarcastic. I was rushing, as usual, and slid down them rather ungracefully, with language that Daphne would probably have given me one of her stern headmistress stares for.'

'And you rang an ambulance? You could have just called me.'

'You're busy cooking for Daphne and Georgie, I didn't want to bother you. I was going to call you before the ambulance got here.'

'Actually, neither of them are coming for dinner now, they had better offers, but Heath's here.'

'Oooh, the sexy gardener I've yet to meet?' That perked up my spirits. I'd heard nothing but good reports about him. Maybe I'd be back from the hospital in time to check him out and have a late dinner.

'The one and only, and I was thinking it would be a great night to set the two of you up.'

'I thought he liked you?'

'Once maybe, but that was ages ago. Are you really ok? I can come and wait with you.'

'I'll be fine, trust me. I've yet to fill you in on my list of medical disasters. This is nothing.'

'The ambulance has just gone past. I'll come to the hospital to sit with you.'

'Abbie, honestly, I'll be fine. Enjoy your night with Heath. Don't ruin his evening just because I'm a klutz.'

'Will you message me later, let me know how you're getting on then?'

'As soon as I can, I'll send you an update. Sorry to let you down,' I grimaced.

'Take care, Charlie.'

'You too, have fun with Heath!' I called before hanging up. Typical. My timing just sucked.

'Charlie Faulkner?' The deep male voice saying my name soothed me. It felt like I'd been sitting there for hours, and for once my imagination actually matched reality. As I took a frustrated look at the clock above the accident and emergency reception desk, I noticed I'd been sitting here in agony on a hard, plastic chair for over five hours. Last time I'd checked, it was one a.m. and I was surrounded by drunks and people with an array of gross injuries that they seemed only too willing to share with me in graphic detail, complete with visuals. I obviously had a "come share with me" face tonight, hence the reason for closing my eyes in the hope they'd leave me in peace. 'Charlie Faulkner, please,' the voice repeated with a hint of frustration.

'Here,' I called as I raised my left hand, an automatic reflex to the school register name calling, and snapped my eyes open when it dawned on me that it might finally be my turn.

'Follow me, please.'

'Hmmm,' I murmured, as I drank in the exceedingly handsome man in scrubs standing at the entrance to the assessment bays with a stethoscope hanging around his neck. Wow. Now there was a man I'd get whiplash from ogling if he walked past me in the street. With his mocha brown hair, sparkling green eyes, and utterly kissable lips, combined with a dark and broody aura, he reminded me of my go-to muse for the heroes in my novels, Brazilian model Pedro Soltz. I licked my lower lip as my eyelashes automatically started to flirt with him. I had no control over them when a hot guy was around. Automatic batting.

'Are you coming?' he asked.

'If only,' I sighed, images of us frantically tearing at each other's clothes under the X-ray machine playing in my mind while I forced myself up and tried to sexily slink my way over to him. It didn't really work with a gammy foot and no high heels. At a mere five-foot-four, I needed my heels with a tall, swoon-worthy doctor. Instead, I hobbled over, my usual sassy and sexy sway more a limp akin to the hunchback of Notre Dame.

'I beg your pardon?' he asked as he blinked a few times, his annoying "immune to Charlie's sex appeal" shield up and deflecting my charm offensive.

'I said "very slowly,"' I replied with a smile, forgetting about my bruised cheek and ending the smile with a stretched-out, high-pitched "argh" as the pain kicked in. Jesus, I sounded like Mrs. Tibbles in the moments before she coughed and vomited a fur ball onto the floor.

'Do you need a wheelchair?'

'Not unless you're planning on giving me a good workout,' I replied, seeing the name Dr. Guy Fitton on his name badge.

'Workout?' he asked, his handsome face still deadly serious.

'That corridor looks like it goes on for miles, so it depends on how far you plan on making me walk as to whether I need a wheelchair.'

'Oh right, just in this first bay please,' he said flatly. Hmmm, hotness factor ten, sense of humour zero. That ruined his appeal a bit, regardless of him ranking up there in my all-time hot fantasy list. Who didn't have dreams about romance blossoming with a sexy and obviously intelligent doctor? He just exuded alpha-male as he stood there in his scrubs with that serious face.

'Do doctors normally perform triage?' I asked as I headed inside and he followed.

'Not normally, no,' he replied, sounding surprised that I knew the term. Sadly, it wasn't my first visit to the A&E department. I was fairly confident I could accurately assess most patients' injuries, my medical knowledge was so extensive. 'We're short-handed tonight. The paramedics noted on your file that you weren't in need of critical care, with no open wounds, so I'm sorry if you've been waiting a long time. I see your main concern is your right wrist and right ankle. Please take a seat and tell me what happened, then describe your pain for me.' He spoke quickly, like most A&E personnel did due to having too many people to attend to, which in my experience often led to a less-than-desirable bedside manner, regardless of great physical care.

I kept my gaze on his face as I spoke and talked him through what had happened, but he kept those gorgeous eyes out of view as he made notes and nodded from time to time, interrupting me with the odd question. I gasped as he gently started touching and examining my hand. I'd written about it so many times, but I'd never experienced that elusive crackle when you supposedly touched your soul mate. It happened again when he crouched in front of me and lifted my foot up, placing it on his knee as he checked it. My mouth drained of saliva, a wave of sexual need flooding my body as I willed him to look up at me and say something in that posh public schoolboy accent of his. Damn, did I have the hots for Dr. Fitton.

'… so I think that would be best,' he said.

'I'm sorry, what was that? I was distracted.' By your firm thighs and that dark hair on your forearm, nicely set off by a masculine watch. Men's hands and a nice watch always did it for me.

'I'm sending you for X-rays, in case of any breaks. I'll go and call for a porter and a wheelchair as it's a long walk.' He spun on his heel and headed out of the bay, bumping into another hot male doctor with blond hair and the most stunning blue eyes.

'Wow, it's like I'm in an episode of *Grey's Anatomy* right now. Do they employ any non-sexy doctors?' I murmured as I watched them talk, and Dr. Fitton's serious face relaxed as he laughed and slapped the other doctor on the back. I cocked my head to scan him from head to toe, more than liking what I was seeing. I blushed as his friend caught me staring and smiled at me, before making his excuses and disappearing in one direction, Dr. Fitton the other.

Another hour and a half later, I was back in a room with him as he brought up my X-rays on the wall-mounted computer screen.

'Hmmm,' he nodded as he studied them.

'Hmmm?' I questioned, as I checked out his high and tight backside.

'No sign of any break or fracture on your ankle, likely a bad sprain. We'll get it strapped up and give you some crutches until you can put weight on it. Now the wrist, I can't be one hundred percent sure due to the extensive swelling, so I'll have you put in a cast to be on the safe side.'

'A cast?' I gasped in horror. 'But I'm an author, I need my hands.'

'You might still be able to type and write, but it will hamper your efforts, I'm afraid. Right, I'll send someone in to sort you out, but I'm discharging you as soon as you're done. You'll get a letter to come back to the clinic when it's time to remove the cast and re-check your X-ray in around four weeks, and we'll decide if we need to do anything else then.'

Before I had a chance to ask him any more questions, he was gone, leaving a waft of seductive aftershave in his wake, and me with a newly awakened sense of longing for a man. I sighed at both my predicament and the sudden loss of my new sexual fantasy.

'Just up here,' I told the driver of the ambulance, pointing to where Church Lane branched off to the right to run down past Abbie, Daphne, and Georgie's cottages to mine.

In my haste to leave the house when the ambulance arrived, I'd forgotten my wallet and phone, which made calling someone for a lift or arranging a taxi all the more awkward. I was in luck that the ambulance crew who brought me in were about to head out on a non-emergency call to a house the next village over and were able to give me a lift home.

'For the love of God,' exclaimed the driver as he slammed on the brakes, all of us jerking forwards and my muscles screaming their protest. 'What the hell is that?'

'Ermmm, that would be my neighbour Georgie, in an embarrassing Dalmatian onesie.' I giggled as I looked up to see her standing in the lane with her paws in the air. For a woman who took as much pride in her appearance as Georgie did, always looking immaculately groomed, I could only imagine how embarrassing it was for her to be seen in that outfit without her staple mascara on.

I thanked the paramedics for the lift and for helping me out of the ambulance, and tried to hop on my good foot and single crutch up to Abbie's gate to find out why Georgie was out here at this time in the morning. We all loved our lie-ins.

'My God, what have you done?' Georgie asked, her impossibly blue, Indian Ocean-hued eyes wide with surprise.

'Being my usual accident-prone self. Sprained ankle and a possible fractured wrist. What on earth are you doing up at this time?' I asked.

'You've missed all of the drama. Abbie and Heath got drunk and he slept on the sofa, but answered the door in just his boxers when Miller turned up. Miller got the wrong end of the stick, punched him, had an argument with Abbie, and left,' she told me, gesticulating wildly as she did. 'Come on in. Daphne's inside and Abbie's going to cook breakfast for us all.'

'That sounds so good,' I groaned. I was starving, having missed my meal last night.

'Here, link arms with me, you don't look too stable teetering on that one leg like a new-born flamingo.'

We made it into Abbie's kitchen in one piece, and Daphne and Georgie helped me into a chair, then sat down to grill me further when Abbie walked in and gasped.

'Charlie, are you ok?'

'You should see the other guy!' I teased her with a wink.

'Is it broken?'

'It was too swollen to be sure if it was fractured, so I'll have to wear this for a while, but enough of the injury talk. I think I'm in love,' I stated with a happy grin as I thought of Dr. Fitton. 'I met *the* hottest doctor ever at accident and emergency.'

'Tyler Jackson,' Georgie and Abbie sighed in unison.

'Who's Tyler Jackson?' I asked. 'This was Dr. Fitton, and my *God*, he really was a fit one. If I hadn't got my hand in this damn cast, I'd be tapping out a whole new "sexy ER doctor" novel about him on my MacBook right now!'

'Damn it,' Abbie moaned, as she pulled some mugs off the shelf and put them on the kitchen island. 'I was going to set you up with Heath, Daphne's nephew.'

'Oh, Charlie, he's looking super hot today, all buff and toned,' Georgie nodded, making her little Dalmatian ears waggle. 'Sorry, Daphne, is this grossing you out?'

'No, but *that* is,' she retorted, pulling a face as she pointed at the kitchen doorway. Everyone's jaws went slack as we looked over. Standing in a black t-shirt, so small that it exposed his toned stomach and nearly cut off the circulation in his arms as it tried to stretch around his biceps, was who I could only assume to be Heath. Even with the silver words "Textually Active" on his extremely unmanly top, there was no denying he was hot, but it was far too late for me to even think about finding him attractive. My head was already full of Dr. Fitton.

'I swear, if you breathe a word of this, I'll make up gossip about you all and feed it to Sheila Vickers.' Everyone burst out laughing as he pointed at us and gave us a warning scowl. I'd already had the honour of meeting the local shopkeeper, who was definitely a few biscuits short of a packet.

Abbie handed over the coffees and started rummaging in the fridge for breakfast supplies as Heath joined us at the table and we were introduced. Even at this ridiculous hour, everyone was on fine form, the laughter around the table warming my heart. This was what I'd been missing by being so insular back in Cheltenham. No one spoke to each other there. I had no idea what my neighbours were called, what they did, or any of their life story. Dilbury was the complete opposite and I liked it. No, like was too tame a word for how settled and at home I felt here. I loved it.

A loud fart rang out an impending stench warning. I gagged and hauled my top up to cover the lower part of my face, Georgie and Daphne doing the same, while Heath smothered his nose with his hands.

'Sumo!' everyone moaned, then started laughing. Abbie's old bulldog was known for his flatulence. Thank goodness Mrs. Tibbles didn't have that problem.

By the time Heath helped me into my house, and insisted on feeding Mrs. Tibbles before seeing me upstairs to my bedroom, I was exhausted.

I curled up in bed, a hot water bottle comforting my bruised lower back, and smiled as Mrs. Tibbles came to curl up next to me, pulling a face of distaste as she licked my plaster cast. I gave her a scratch behind the ears with my good hand and finally closed my eyes.

I planned on sleeping the day away and ringing Kitt for another pizza delivery. I was traumatised and had a cast that restricted my cooking ability, after all.

My dreams were filled with the hot doctor, giving me lots of material for a sexy new book, which I planned to start tapping out as soon as this cast was off.

Chapter Three

Hot Stuff
One Month Later – March

'I'M SICK OF THIS damn plaster cast,' I moaned to Tibbs as I fed her some dinner after a struggle to open the can of cat food. From now on, I'd forget trying to save money by buying tins of cat food and just buy her the fancy cuts in foil tubs that she loved so much. How people managed to do things when they had double casts on was beyond me. I mean, wiping my bottom with my left hand was a challenge, what did you do with both hands out of action? I shuddered at the thought of it.

I opened the fridge and stuck my head inside, letting out a sigh as I tried to decide what I could attempt to cook. I'd lived on microwave meals and takeout since the accident. My healthy eating plan had yet to happen, and I knew it was high time I tried cooking. I had a hob and oven I hadn't even used since I'd moved in. Sadly, the fridge let me down, badly. I had cheese, butter, and milk. That was it. I cringed at my failings and inspected the kitchen cupboards, which were nearly as bare. I had loads of packets of chocolate chip cookies, my snack of choice when I was writing, but that was hardly a great option for a dinner substitute. I'd even run out of bread, so I couldn't have any toast. I looked out of the window to see it was drizzling, and while I didn't fancy walking to the shop and getting wet, neither did I want to get in the car just to drive around the corner.

'Yes!' I rejoiced, hoisting the solitary pack of chicken-flavoured Super Noodles up in the air with a triumphant flourish. Ok, not exactly haute cuisine, but they were quick and tasty, and involved using a saucepan, a spoon, and my hob. Surely that counted as cooking?

I flicked on the kettle, put the rectangular dry noodles in the pan, and emptied the sachet of flavouring on top of them. While I waited for the water to boil, I sighed. I was bored. So incredibly bored. I couldn't write, as my plaster cast was getting in the way. Trying to type one handed, with my non-dominant hand no less, was far too frustrating when I was used to touch typing at speed with two, so I'd had to go cold turkey. There needed to be an "Authors Anonymous" for those of us that were suffering severe withdrawals from writing. The struggle was real. I'd watched so much TV, my eyes had turned square. When I'd run out of things to watch that held my interest, I'd read lots of my author friends' books, but that just left me even more depressed about not being able to get on with writing my own.

My ankle was much better, but I wasn't ready to even think about going out for long walks, let alone taking up jogging, which had been an inkling of an idea I'd had when I'd been pondering the benefits of keeping fit. Anyway, jogging didn't look fun. Women all sweaty faced, arses and tits bouncing, risking black eyes from boob fling back, not to mention the stress on underdeveloped lungs and underused muscles. I'd need a personal trainer when I was better, someone to whip me into shape and give me nutritional advice. Until then, I was going to continue to be a couch potato and eat Super Noodles and takeout.

I measured out the boiling water in my measuring jug, remembering why I had one and what it was used for, other than as an emergency schnapps glass. I tipped the measured dose of hot water onto the noodles and placed the saucepan on the hob, fiddling with some buttons and hoping I'd managed to turn it on. I was starving. Mrs. Tibbles decided to weave around my ankles, rubbing her cheeks against my calves as she purred. I smiled down at her. Sometimes she was the most loving cat, but it was rare. She had the temperament of a cantankerous old moggie most of the time.

'Did I turn on the hob?' I asked myself as I waited for the water to come back up to a boil. It seemed to be taking an age. I lifted the saucepan off and set it on another of the solid raised black plates, frowning to see that the one I'd thought was on wasn't even glowing red yet. Without a second thought, I put three fingers onto it, then screamed as there was a loud sizzling noise and my fingertips heated up. 'What the hell?' I yelped as I whipped my hand back and nursed it.

Why wasn't the hob red if it was on? My old glass one in Cheltenham glowed with an unmistakable warning that if you touched it, you were going to cook your fingers. I quickly turned the stupid thing off and rushed to the kitchen sink to turn on the cold tap. Thrusting my fingers underneath, I was careful not to get my plaster cast wet.

'Owww,' I moaned as my fingertips painfully pulsated. Well, that well and truly ruined my cooking plans. I was going to get Kitt over with a pizza and go online to find a replacement induction hob that made it clear it was actually working. Not that I was going to be in any rush to try cooking again, if this was the sort of thing that happened when I did.

I answered the door an hour later with my hand in a plastic bag full of ice cubes that I'd managed to parcel tape to my plaster cast to try and stop the burning pain.

31

'What on earth have you done now, Charlie?' Kitt exclaimed as he spotted my bizarre makeshift remedy. I shook my head and filled him in. He was a really nice guy. We'd spent many a time standing on the doorstep chatting when he'd dropped off my deliveries.

'Honestly, I swear it's more painful than if I'd accidently chopped off the ends of my fingers,' I complained.

'I think you ought to go to hospital.'

'They haven't blistered, I'll be fine.'

'When did you last check? It takes a while for a blister to develop and if it has, you need to get them looked at.'

'You think?' I asked with a frown. He nodded and I sighed.

'Go check them now, I'll wait. I'm assuming you can't drive with your hand in that cast, so I can drop you off at the hospital on my way home. You were my last delivery for the night,' he told me. That was no coincidence. I'd started timing my orders so he could drop them off on the way home. I enjoyed our chats. It was nice to have a male friend without the pressure of feeling like he was trying to worm his way into my knickers.

'I don't think I'd fit on your moped,' I laughed, then took a soft gasp of surprise. 'Where's your pepperoni slice Pizzaman outfit?'

'In the bin, thank God,' he chuckled with a shake of his head. 'I convinced them that it wasn't a great sales tool. They also sold the moped when I said we could all deliver to more customers during our hours if they paid us mileage to use our own cars. Go on, go and check your hand. If you need it looked at, I'll drive you in and you can eat your pizza on the way.'

'Thanks, Kitt, that's really kind of you.' I gave him a grateful smile as I took the delicious smelling box off him. 'Come in, I need to shut the door quickly before Mrs. Tibbles makes a bid for freedom.'

'Mrs. Tibbles?' he asked, as he stepped inside and pushed the door closed behind him.

'My cat. She's never been outside, which is why I always join you on the doorstep for a chat. I'm waiting for some sunny days so I can open the back doors and supervise her first adventure into the unknown. Follow me. I taped this bag on so tightly that I might need a hand taking it off, or I'm liable to lose a finger using the scissors left-handed.'

'Kind of accident-prone, huh?' he asked as we headed into the kitchen.

'You could say that,' I laughed, setting my pizza on the side and rummaging in the drawer. 'Here you are, do you mind?' I asked, offering them to him.

He made short work of snipping through the tape while I rested the bag in the kitchen sink. When I pulled my hand out, we both winced. I had three huge white blisters puffed up on my fingertips, which were full of fluid.

'Ok, you definitely need to go to hospital. If one of those bursts, you'll be at risk of an infection. Do you have your bag and keys handy?' he asked as he grabbed my pizza.

'I can't put you to all of that trouble,' I objected. He'd only come to deliver my dinner.

'I live on Falcon's Way, right opposite the hospital.'

'Well, ok then,' I relented, giving him a grateful smile. He gave me one in return, a pair of cute dimples appearing in his cheeks. He soaked one of my tea towels in cold water and wrung it out as I stuffed my phone and wallet in my handbag. When I said I was ready, he carefully wrapped the tea towel around my fingers, the coldness of it very soothing. As his fingers brushed mine, I kind of wished I'd felt that surge of electricity I had when I'd touched Dr. Fitton, as Kitt was so sweet. I was a firm believer that you needed great chemistry for great love. It was an idea that I based my living on, and all my fictional characters experienced it. He grabbed my pizza and pulled the door shut behind me as we made our way into the lane, where a little white Fiat 500 was sitting.

'Sorry about the girlie car,' he grimaced as he ran around to open the passenger door for me. 'It's Mum's. She hadn't had it long before I realised it wasn't safe for her to drive. So I sold my old car, which was due to be replaced anyway, and use hers instead.'

He settled me in, leaning over me to buckle up my seat belt, and I felt myself breathing him in. As well as the scent of herbs that they sprinkled on their pizzas, his aftershave made him smell of a fresh ocean. It was nice. He opened my pizza box for me and handed me a few napkins from the side pocket in the door, telling me not to be shy about tucking in. I took a gigantic bite and quickly chewed and swallowed it before he climbed in and started the engine.

'Do you mind me asking what happened to your mum?' I took a more ladylike and delicate bite of pizza as he started to head up the lane. People had a tendency to judge me when they saw the amount I could stuff into my mouth in one go.

'Rapid onset dementia,' he sighed, rubbing his left hand over his face before returning it to rest on the gearstick. 'It seemed like it came on overnight, but looking back, the warning signs were there. I should have visited her more often, maybe I'd have picked up on it sooner, but I was living in Newcastle-upon-Tyne at the time.'

'You can't blame yourself. It's not like there's a cure if she'd been diagnosed earlier, is it?'

'No,' he admitted. 'But it doesn't stop me from feeling guilty as hell for not being there to support her sooner or spending as much time with her before she forgot I even existed.'

'I'm so sorry, Kitt.' He nodded, but clenched his jaw and kept his focus on pulling out onto the main road. He seemed lost in his thoughts as he headed to Shrewsbury, so I stayed quiet and just continued eating. The silence might have been awkward. It should have been awkward. I mean, I was sitting in Pizzaman's car after he'd shared something pretty personal. But it wasn't. It was a comfortable silence, like we both understood that no words were going to make him feel any better about his situation.

'You really like pizza, huh?' he asked with a slight laugh as I closed the empty box with a contented sigh and noticed we were nearly at the hospital.

'Just a bit, what gave it away? That I can polish off a large pizza all on my own?' I flashed him a grin.

'That, the frequent orders, and the noises you were making as you ate.'

'Oh God no,' I groaned, quickly closing my eyes as my cheeks flushed. Andy, my ex, had told me that I made sexual noises when I was enjoying my food.

'Don't worry,' he laughed, flashing me a smile. 'It's just been a while since I've heard any sexy moans like that.'

'You're not seeing anyone?' I asked.

'Not since I moved here. It's not like I have a lot of free time, and saying "Hey, I'm Kitt, a thirty-something who still lives with my mum, who likes to sit in the lounge in a self-inflatable rubber dinghy," isn't exactly the best sales pitch.'

'A rubber dinghy?' I made a concerted effort not to laugh, but he did anyway.

'Yes. She's convinced that the blue lounge carpet is the ocean and she's going to drown or be mauled by sharks, so she was refusing to go in there. I wanted her to be comfortable and not sit on a hard chair in the dining room, so I brought a self-inflating dinghy and filled it with comfy cushions. Now she'll go and sit in it. Sometimes I cover her with the duvet as she likes to sleep in it and I sleep on the sofa to watch over her.' He indicated left at the roundabout to turn into the hospital.

'You're a special man, Kitt,' I said sincerely. 'One day, a woman will realise that and snap you up.'

34

'Thanks,' he replied with a tight-lipped smile. 'But it's not fair to anyone to date them while I have my hands full with Mum, she has to be my priority.'

'You can't put your life on hold,' I reminded him, thinking he sounded too good to be true. 'You deserve some happiness, too.'

'She is my life, Charlie,' he said as he pulled into the car park, sounding as if he really meant it and didn't begrudge it. 'She put hers on hold to raise me when my dad left us, it's my turn to return the favour. She has a shortened life expectancy with the disease. Offering her my full support for her remaining years is the least I can do.'

'And here I was feeling sorry for myself with my burnt fingers, I feel ashamed,' I admitted.

'God, please don't,' he replied, flashing a smile in my direction. 'I'm coming across as a real attention seeker, telling you all of this. Truth is, I don't get much adult conversation that doesn't involve pizza, and it feels good to talk to someone. Ok, shove the box on the floor and I'll undo your belt for you and come around to open your door.'

'Don't make yourself late,' I told him as I saw him quickly check his watch.

'I'm ok for a while. I'll see you inside, make sure you're settled.'

He was true to his word and offered to sit with me after filling in the paperwork for me, seeing how I couldn't even hold a pen to do it. I noticed the receptionist casting a few furtive glances our way, then blushing and looking back down at her computer when I caught her.

'You have an admirer,' I giggled as I elbowed him and nodded in her direction. He just scoffed and stretched out his legs, crossing them at the ankles as he folded his arms across his chest. He was a seriously good-looking guy, with a decent body from what I could see. It was a shame he was keeping himself off the market when women were obviously interested. 'Now, I need to ask a favour, and I warn you it might not be pretty.'

'You want me to check your gross blisters again?' he asked as he held my gaze.

'No, my teeth. I can't risk seeing McFitty again if I have oregano stuck between my teeth. Now, I'll probably look like a horse with an overcrowded mouth, too many teeth is one of my flaws. Do you mind?' I didn't give him the chance to object as I grinned at him and bared them, and quite possibly a whole load of pink gums at the same time, as I tilted my head from side to side. He laughed and shook his head.

'I pronounce you oregano, and all other herbs, free. And who the hell is Mc … what did you call him?' he asked.

'McFitty, my nickname for Dr. Fitton,' I replied, hushing him with a finger to my lips. 'Only the sexiest doctor I ever laid eyes on, and I've seen enough doctors to be confident in my claim. I have a *serious* crush on him and don't want him to see me looking anything but my best.'

'You're in a plaster cast with an "I Love Cats" tea towel wrapped around your fingers,' he reminded me.

'Damn it,' I uttered, hastily unravelling the tea towel. If I was lucky enough to see him, I didn't want him thinking I was a crazy cat lady. Which of course I was. But he didn't need to know that, not yet anyway.

'You're a very attractive woman, Charlie. I doubt a tea towel will affect him seeing you as one.'

'Well, thanks, but I'm not taking any chances. I've got it so bad for him.'

'I'll get going then,' Kitt said, abruptly standing up and straightening the black jumper he was wearing over a white t-shirt, with his trademark black jeans and boots. 'You won't want him seeing you sitting with another guy, in case he gets the wrong impression.'

'Kitt, thank you so much. I really appreciate the lift. I'll find a way to repay you. Oh God, pay you, I haven't paid you for the pizza.'

'On the house,' he smiled. 'You've tipped me enough over the last few months for me to offer you a free pizza in your hour of need.'

'Thank you,' I repeated sincerely. I'd have to find a way to make it up to him.

'Good luck, hope you don't lose those fingers,' he teased.

'Me too,' I gasped, looking down as I gave them a wiggle to make sure they were still in working order. How would I write books with no fingers?

'See you soon, Charlie.' He shoved his hands into the front pockets of his jeans as he smiled at me.

'Yes, see you soon, Kitt. Hope your mum isn't too much trouble tonight.'

'God, me too,' he sighed, before he turned and headed out. The receptionist cocked her head to check out his backside, which made me have a quick look too. With his hands in his pockets, it had the effect of pulling his jeans tightly around a nicely toned backside that I'd not noticed before.

'Hello, Pizzaman, you've been hiding that from me,' I observed as he walked out of sight. I was quickly distracted by my name being called, and let out a sigh of disappointment as I saw it was a nurse, not McFitty.

She didn't seem convinced that I hadn't actually deliberately stuck my fingers on a red hot, or rather hot but not red, hob and proceeded to bandage the three fingers until they looked like fat white sausages, which looked even more ridiculous offset against my plaster cast. I was told to go to the doctor's the following day to get them looked at and they'd change the dressings and advise what to do next, but it was likely I'd need to keep them covered for another few weeks. Well, that definitely put my cooking plans on the back burner. I giggled at my inadvertent pun and thanked her for her time, then headed out of the door, bumping straight into Dr. Fitton.

'Oh, I'm so sorry,' I gasped, using the opportunity to test out one of his biceps as I clung to him with my left hand. Hmmm, it seemed the sexy doctor worked out in his free time.

'No problem,' he answered, with a smile that told me he wasn't impressed. He gently prised my clinging fingers from his arm and stalked away up the corridor as I watched, my heart thudding with excitement and disappointment. He hadn't even recognised me. I knew it was crazy to imagine he would. After all, I was probably one of hundreds of women he treated every day, a thought that brought on a wave of irrational jealousy. But I'd memorised his face from our first meeting. I guess it was just wishful thinking that he'd have done the same and been dreaming of me since then.

I sighed and called Andy, Dilbury's resident taxi driver, to ask if he could come and get me. I was looking forward to getting home and curling up in bed with Mrs. Tibbles. Life at the moment really sucked.

Chapter Four

Look Sexy
One Month Later – A Sunday in April

'SERIOUSLY?' I EXCLAIMED AS I leaned over to pour us both another cup of tea. Abbie had called me earlier to ask if I'd keep Daphne company. Usually Abbie and Georgie took it in turns to cook Sunday lunch and invite Daphne over, but after an apparent disaster at the latest wedding Abbie was a bridesmaid at, where Miller had turned up with another woman, she'd booked a last-minute holiday to Mexico and had dashed off to the airport with Georgie. They'd asked me to go with them, which I'd actually have loved to do, but after so many weeks of being unable to type, I had too much to do. That said, I'd never begrudge spending a few hours with one of the most hip eighty-year-olds I'd ever met.

'Miller has a twin sister,' Daphne repeated. 'Who knew? He certainly kept that close to his chest.'

'With his history, I'm not surprised. He probably didn't want to say he'd been searching for her until he knew for sure he'd found her. He's been let down so much in his life. I really hope she's nice and won't take advantage of him and his money.'

'I feel so sorry for poor Abbie. It must have been such a shock to see him there with another woman, not knowing the truth. Then that horror Fi-Fi involving her in a scene at a wedding again. I'm not surprised she needed to get away and clear her head. I just hope she sees sense when she comes home and gets back together with him. I've rarely seen two people who are so meant to be.' She sighed and sipped from her cup.

I'd not officially met Miller, as he and Abbie had split up before I'd arrived in Dilbury. I'd seen him in passing when he'd come all the way from New York to comfort Abbie when her dog, Mr. Sumo passed away last month, which said a lot about his character. Other than that, all I knew was that he was good-looking, with a very kind face. And I knew how badly Abbie missed him.

'Anyway, how about you, dear? Any news on McFitty?'

'No,' I giggled, amused that she used the new name we were all calling him. 'Short of causing myself a deliberate personal injury in an effort to see more of him, how would I? All I know about him is that he works at the hospital.'

'Then you need to spend more time at the hospital. The more he sees you, the greater the chance of him noticing how attractive you are.'

'Thank you, Daphne. But how do I spend more time at the hospital without him thinking I need psychiatric care due to the amount of injuries I go in with?'

'There's plenty of pensioners in the village that have regular hospital appointments, me included. You could offer your services out of the goodness of your heart.' She winked at me, making me smile. 'It would be a win-win. They'd save money on the taxi fare and you'd get to hang around and maybe see McFitty a little more often.'

'They say absence makes the heart grow fonder, and familiarity breeds contempt,' I reminded her as I supped from my cup, wishing I'd brought over a pack of my cookies to drown my sorrows with.

'Nonsense. A man never knows what's missing from his life until we take the initiative and show him,' she stated firmly.

'I pity any man you set your sights on, Daphne. He stands no chance of escape,' I laughed.

'If David was still here, you could have asked him. He'd never have plucked up the courage to ask me out if I hadn't made sure he saw me at every opportunity and made my interest in him clear.'

'Forward thinking even in your day, you're incredible. Do you think you'll ever fall in love again?' I wrote about characters who only ever had one great love in their lifetime and wondered if that was actually true. I couldn't even write that from personal experience, I wasn't sure I'd even been in love. In lust, yes, but love?

'I don't know, dear,' she sighed, taking another sip of tea with a distant look in her wise old eyes. 'He was the love of my life, and I'm not sure anyone can compete with the years of history I had with him. That said, there's nothing to say that I might not fall in love again, even if it's not so deeply. I don't want to spend the rest of my years being lonely. Oh, I know I have you girls,' she added quickly as she saw me open my mouth to say we'd always be there for her if she needed company. 'But it's not the same as having a man at your side, someone to hold your hand and tell you how beautiful you are when all you see in the mirror are the lines of history etched on your face, a reminder of what's gone and how little is left to come.'

'What about Mr. Bentley? You're spending more time together.'

'We are,' she nodded, with an adorable blush. 'We're very good friends.'

'That's all?'

'Sometimes great love starts with friendship, Charlie. We all dream of that instant, all-consuming need and passion for someone, and to have that returned, but it's rare to find that and have it last a lifetime. When the passion fades, great friendship is what will see you through the rest of your years.'

'Did you have that passion with David all of your life?'

'I did,' she smiled. She stayed silent for a while, obviously reflecting on her past, so I gave her the space to lose herself in her memories as I finished my tea. 'But maybe it's time for me to think about having an amazing friend at my side and let nature take its course. If love follows, that would be wonderful, but at my age, I'd rather have his friendship than start looking for love elsewhere.'

'I really hope love comes again for you, both of you,' I stated sincerely.

'Thank you. And instead of hoping for it to come for you, you can get your diary out, or one of those fancy phones that seems to hold everyone's lives in it nowadays, and put in my next hospital appointment in May. I'll phone my friends and get some more dates off them and pass them on. The more times you go, the more chance you have of seeing him.'

'You're one in a million, Daphne,' I smiled with a shake of my head as I put the date she repeated into my calendar.

'Nonsense, dear,' she rebuffed with a scoff. 'There is no one like me, I'm unique.' Her eyes twinkled with merriment as I laughed and nodded.

'You're right there.'

'Oh my,' she exclaimed, as we both jumped when there was a sharp, loud knock on her front door. 'Whoever can that be?'

'Maybe it's Mr. Bentley, wondering if you're up for some Sunday afternoon delight, a bit of the old horizontal mambo,' I suggested with a waggle of my eyebrows, which made her chuckle.

'Be a dear and go and see who it is. If it's salesmen or Jehovah Witnesses, tell them you just found me dead on the floor and you're waiting for the undertaker. That should get rid of them.'

'Daphne.' I shook my head in amusement as I went and did as she asked. Opening her door, I was surprised to see Miller standing on her doorstep with whom I assumed was his sister, Quinn. She had his warm brown eyes.

'Oh, hey. Charlie, right?' Miller said as he ran a hand through his blond hair. I nodded, not sure what to say. 'Sorry, I … I'm looking for Abbie. Is she here?'

'Ermmm,' I grimaced, not sure it was my place to tell him she'd fled the country. 'Daphne, I think you're needed.'

'Who is it, Charlie?' she called.

'Miller and his sister.'

'Well, well. Don't leave them on the doorstep, bring them in and flick the kettle on again while you're up.'

'You heard the lady.' I swept my arm to gesture them in and returned the warm smile that Quinn gave me. She wasn't what I'd expected. She had platinum hair with multi-coloured tips, in a sharp bob to the jawline on one side and shaved on the other. She looked like someone I'd have seen out in the trendy bars in Cheltenham, not the sort of woman who frequented Dilbury, that was for sure. Then again, how would I know what to expect?

'Thanks.' Miller gave me a wan smile as he stepped inside. The signs of a sleepless night showed on his face, judging by the dark bruises under his eyes and an unshaven jaw.

'Thanks,' Quinn agreed, with a noticeable American accent.

'No problem. What can I get you to drink?'

'Black coffee, please,' Miller nodded. 'Quinn?'

'I'm good, thanks.'

I left them to go into the lounge and see Daphne to get the bad news, and went and made Daphne and Miller's drinks. I decided it would be best if I went home and gave them some privacy. I felt like I was intruding as I hardly knew the poor guy. I cleared my throat before padding into the lounge, carrying the tray. Miller was standing with his back to me, looking out at Daphne's immaculately kept garden. Having a nephew to do it for you certainly paid off. Maybe I needed to think about hiring Heath too. At this rate, my neglected garden was going to either turn into an overgrown jungle or a tired-looking wasteland.

'Here you go, Daphne. I think it's best I give you some peace to talk in private.'

'Actually, dear, I was about to suggest the same thing, but I have a favour to ask, and before you say yes, it's a big one.'

'You know I'll help with whatever I can, as long as it's not cooking dinner for you all. I'd probably poison everyone. I have about five different takeout places' numbers memorised if that helps?' I offered, and Quinn laughed and nodded.

'I hear you. When you live in New York, surrounded by places to eat, where's the incentive to cook?'

'It's not cooking, but honestly, girls. You'll never find husbands with that attitude,' Daphne scoffed.

'Daphne Jones!' I exclaimed. 'I thought you were more modern thinking than to come out with a phrase like that. It's the twenty-first century, there's nothing wrong with a man doing the cooking.'

'In my limited experience, there is,' she replied, screwing up her face as if she was recalling an awful meal.

41

'Well, that's what happens when you only date men your age. If you found yourself a toy boy who'd been brought up to learn those skills, you might change your mind. So, relieved as I am to hear it's not cooking, what's the favour?'

'I'd like to spend some time alone with Miller. We need a long chat and he needs a good night's sleep before he heads back home, so he's going to stay in my spare room tonight.'

'Daphne,' Miller began to protest.

'Don't argue with me, I've made up my mind. You don't want to make an old lady who's on the verge of death upset, do you?'

'You're not on the verge of death,' I laughed. 'You're in better shape than some women half your age. Honestly, you're such a drama queen, you should be in amateur dramatics.' Daphne giggled. She was a crafty old fox, she knew exactly how to play a room. I so wanted to be like her when I grew up.

'Now, Charlie, be a dear and offer Quinn a room for the night. My other spare room is full of boxes of David's things, which I must get around to sorting one day.'

'I agree that it would be best if Miller spent the night here with you, but there's no need for Charlie to put herself out on my account. I can stay in a hotel, I'm sure I saw a sign for one nearby?'

'Nonsense, Charlie spends too much time on her own, living with her characters. It will do her good to have some real-life company, won't it, dear?' Daphne said, giving me a look that said non-compliance wouldn't be tolerated.

'Daphne, don't steamroll the woman into putting my sister up. I can sort a room at Severn Manor for her,' Miller said, his back still to us.

'She's not steamrolling. Besides, Severn Manor is usually booked well in advance. How do you feel about a wild night out instead of a boring night in with me and my cat, Quinn?' I asked, turning to face my new roommate.

'I'm the queen of wild, are you sure you know what you're getting yourself into?' she responded with a grin.

'Bring it on,' I grinned back. I hadn't been out in ages. It was the perfect excuse and she looked like she'd be fun.

'Lord help Shrewsbury,' Daphne uttered. 'I'm sure Miller would like his sister back in one piece, Charlie.'

'What are you trying to say?' I asked indignantly.

'Quinn, get your fancy phone out and save the number 999 in it, as a night out with this one will end up with you needing to dial it, it's almost a guarantee.' Daphne gave me a look as I went to protest, then sighed and shrugged. She was probably right.

'9, 9, 9,' Quinn repeated as she did as she was told. 'Is that a cab company?'

'Emergency services.' She looked at me wide-eyed. 'I'm sort of accident-prone sober, so mix in alcohol and who knows what could happen.'

'There's no "sort of" about it,' Daphne scoffed. 'Well, come on then, off you go. See you both in the morning, not too early mind, I like my lie-ins.'

I loitered as Miller turned around to hug Quinn goodbye, and the reason for him keeping his back to us became clear. The poor guy had anguish written all over his face. I suspected the minute we left, he was going to break down on Daphne's shoulder. From what I'd heard about him, he was some huge mogul in America, running a billion-dollar gaming corporation. But I guess any man could weep if the right woman broke his heart.

'There's no way I'm gonna fit in any of your clothes, Charlie,' Quinn rightly observed as we looked in my wardrobe for something suitable for her to wear on a night out, as she had limited supplies in her small suitcase. Mrs. Tibbles eyed the newcomer with interest from the bed, the tip of her tail flexing back and forth. 'I'm too tall.'

'Or I'm too short,' I nodded, turning to face her. 'What are you wearing under that jumper?'

'What's a jumper?' she asked, looking confused.

'This,' I replied, tugging it. 'What do you guys call it?'

'A sweater. I'm gonna have to learn a whole new language if Miller and Abbie get back together.'

'*When* they get back together. I'm sure they will, she just needed a time out. So, what's under your sweater?'

'A shirt, why?'

'Let me see it, I have an idea.'

'Ok,' she said, not sounding convinced. She pulled it over her head to reveal a black silk shirt. When I told her to pull it out, it hung down to rest mid-thigh.

'Perfect,' I clapped. 'I'm hoping that you don't have an issue with baring a bit of leg, or in your case a lot of leg?'

'No, why?'

'Because you can ditch your jeans and wear the shirt as a dress with a belt, and wear those black biker boots you already have on. I've got a chunky black belt with metal studs on it somewhere, which should go with it perfectly.' I pulled it out of my wardrobe with a flourish and handed it to her.

'Awesome,' she nodded, taking it off me.

'Hmmm, you're going to look sexy in that, and there's no way I'm being out-sexied on a night out,' I said, making her laugh.

An hour later, Andy, his eyes on stalks, was driving us into Shrewsbury. I suspected that he was more used to taking the pensioners into town than a couple of women dolled up for a night out. Quinn was rocking the sexy biker chick look, while I'd put on my black suede, over-the-knee, high-heeled boots with a short black jumper dress that had a low-cut back. I was lucky that my boobs hadn't yet started the old-age migration south to hibernate in the bush, never to return north. I could still rock it braless when I needed to. Even Quinn had admitted we looked hot as we'd finished doing our eyes and checked ourselves out in the mirror.

'Cheers, Andy, we'll probably call you later,' I told him as I paid him and shut the door. 'Right, I don't know how you do it in New York, but here we take advantage of an empty stomach. You can get leathered on a few cheap jugs or shots, then hit a club legless and save paying their extortionate drink prices. When we're done, we can hit up the kebab shop on the way back and pray we don't barf in the taxi on the way home, or Andy will bar me from using him again. Sound good?'

'I didn't understand half of what you said, but I'm up for an adventure,' she grinned. I high fived her and we headed to the nearest cocktail bar on a mission. I'd got sick of doing this a couple of times a week back in Cheltenham, but after a period of abstinence, I was actually looking forward to a night of carefree fun. It helped that, so far, we were getting on great, setting aside the odd language lesson we were having to give each other.

'So, what do you do in New York?' I asked her as we bagged a table and a couple of high stools and set our pitchers of cocktails down.

'I'm a wedding planner, which is pretty weird considering I don't believe in marriage or happy ever afters,' she snorted.

'How on earth did you get involved in doing that then?'

'I don't know how much you know about me and Miller, but we were abandoned by our parents, then accidentally separated. We were both brought up in the foster system, but with different families. I had so little control over my life as a kid that the moment I had the ability to make my own decisions, taking back control was the first one I made. So I'm a planner. It freaks me out if I don't plan everything and try and picture the outcome.'

'You're here with me, spur of the moment with a stranger,' I reminded her, deciding off the cuff that this was a girl who wouldn't want mollycoddling or to be on the receiving end of sympathy, after her calm and factual assessment of her pretty shitty life as a child.

'Nights out are different. Sober or drunk, I still have some control. I know men are likely to come on to me, so if I go out knowing that, I can control the outcome by projecting a "get lost" vibe and rejecting them before they get too close. And if they push it when I'm not in the mood, well, I'm a black belt in Krav Maga.'

'Seriously?' I exclaimed. 'Wow, you're like Lara Croft or something, without the long brown hair. Beautiful and deadly. So, no man in your life?'

'I don't think I'm destined to be in a relationship,' she shrugged. 'When you've been rejected as often I have, closing your heart is the only way to stop anyone from getting to you. It's the only way to make sure no one can shatter it from the inside out.'

'I get that, but surely that's lonely?' I said, thinking how much I could empathise with her. I'd certainly not experienced the degree of hurt she had in her life, but I totally got where she was coming from.

'I never said I was an angel,' she winked. 'Just because I don't want a relationship again doesn't mean I'm not up for some short-term fun.'

'Gah, that's what I need to learn. I can't seem to enjoy a fling and walk away. I let them in, then they stomp all over my heart. It's a shame you don't live here, I could learn so much from you.'

'Or maybe I could learn something from you. As a little kid, I never imagined I'd be single with no significant relationship to show for my thirty-year life.'

'I'm so glad Miller found you, you have a significant relationship now.'

'Huh, I guess I do,' she smiled, then surprised me by shooting her palm out to the side in a "stop" gesture without even looking away from me. 'Not interested, buddy.'

'But–' a male voice began to protest.

'*Not. Interested.* Beat it before I beat you,' she warned. I watched in astonishment as he did as he was told, then burst out laughing.

'How did you even see him coming?'

'It's like an innate sixth sense that's taken years to perfect,' she grinned, and I lifted my jug and clanked it against hers.

'Cheers, Quinn. I think this is going to be a fun night.'

'Ok, explain this "cheers" to me, as we use it like you just did, but you also said it to the cabbie too, and I seriously hope he wasn't drinking.'

We were out of breath as another song finished and we paused our dancing for a moment. I needed something to quench my thirst, and nodded when she jerked her thumb in the direction of the bar with the same idea. We'd been dancing for ages, and laughing as she taught me how to fend off come-ons from the guys that were swarming around us like flies on Farmer Davies' manure. For a small town, Shrewsbury had some decent clubs, even on a Sunday night.

'Oh. My. God,' I gasped, grinding to a halt as we made our way across the dance floor.

'What?'

'McFitty, in the flesh, without his stethoscope. And for once, I look hot and haven't injured myself.'

'Which one?' Quinn asked. I'd already filled her in, wondering if she had any special American flirting tips to share with me that hadn't made their way over to the U.K. Sadly, it seemed flirting was the same in all languages. My skills had never let me down before, the automatic bat of my lashes and pout of my lips was normally enough, but it appeared Dr. Fitton was immune to my powers.

'Brown hair, blue jeans, and white shirt, leaning on the bar laughing.' I noticed that he was with the hot blond doctor I'd seen the night I'd got my plaster cast put on.

'Hmmm,' she purred. 'I can see why he has your panties in a bunch. He's hot, his friend too. So, what now? You gonna go over and introduce yourself?'

'No,' I scoffed. 'This is England, you wait for the man to come to you. I'm not totally crazy, even though he probably thinks I am. Oh crap, he's looking over.'

'Come on, act confident and look sexy. I'll show you how it's done.' Quinn stalked off ahead of me.

'Wait,' I hissed, tossing my hair back over my shoulders and doing my best sultry catwalk strut to catch her up. He frowned as he caught my eye, which threw me. What was that about? Was he frowning in an "Oh crap, the crazy woman's here" or a "Where the hell do I know that sexy woman from" way? I let out a girlish shriek as I suddenly felt myself falling, so transfixed on his gorgeous eyes that I totally missed the set of three steps that Quinn had managed to navigate, despite the amount we'd had to drink.

I landed heavily on one knee, which made a stomach churning crunch, and then the other one soon after, followed swiftly by my outstretched hands. I ended up on my side on the sticky floor, not even the copious amounts of alcohol we'd consumed forming any sort of pain buffer.

'God, Charlie, are you alright?' Quinn gasped as she shot over to offer me her hand.

'No,' I moaned, blinking back some tears of both pain and humiliation.

'Come on, see if you can stand up,' she coaxed as she pulled me upright. My right leg buckled and I cried out in agony as I fell against her. 'Is there a doctor in here?' she yelled, before flashing me a discreet wink. 'May as well make the most of a bad situation.'

'Quinn, no, please,' I begged, but it was too late. McFitty and McNotQuiteSoFitty, as I was going to call his friend, were already hurrying over. Not that he wasn't hot, but I'd already ranked Guy Fitton in gold medal position.

'Are you guys doctors? My friend just had a real nasty fall, I think she's busted up her leg,' she told them.

'We are,' McFitty replied, nearly making me swoon as he slipped an arm around my waist and ordered me to put mine around his shoulders. His friend ordered a suspiciously underage-looking couple to vacate their table and the comfortable love seats they were snogging in, which they did, obviously not wanting to argue with two strapping older guys. I was carefully set down on the still warm seat and winced, while Quinn gave me a grin and raised her eyebrows. I hissed as Guy unzipped my boot and slid it off, in a reverse Cinderella and the glass slipper move. Seconds later, I was gripping the leather of the seat, not sure whether feeling his strong hands sliding up my bare leg to probe my throbbing knee was painful or erotic. I decided that I'd turned into a temporary masochist, as it was a combination of both. 'Hmmm,' he murmured, giving me a déjà vu of our last proper meeting.

'Hmmm?' I questioned, as I tried not to succumb to the tears I wanted to shed. I wasn't sure if they were from the shock of the fall, the humiliation of him seeing me at my clumsiest, or the sheer agony of my excruciatingly painful knee.

'I don't want to try manipulating it as it's swelling already. Tyler, can you call for an ambulance, she'll need an X-ray.'

'On it,' his friend nodded as he pulled out his phone. Tyler? It seemed like he was the doctor Abbie and Georgie had been swooning over. Hang on, had he said ambulance? I was going to the hospital?

'Oh no,' I groaned. 'Not again.'

'She needs to go to the ER?' Quinn asked.

'ER?' McFitty questioned, distracted as he gently rested my foot on his knee.

'Over here it's A&E, Quinn,' I corrected. 'Daphne warned you that you'd need to ring 999 on a night out with me, though technically you're not dialling them. I can't believe I'm going back there so soon.'

'You've been seen recently?' Dr. Fitton asked as he raised his gaze to mine.

'Ermmm, yes. By you, for a twisted ankle and suspected fractured wrist after I fell down my stairs. Then by a nurse, with second degree burns on my fingertips after touching my electric hob to see if it was on. Yes, I know, stupid of me.' I rolled my eyes as he gave me an incredulous look. 'I bumped into you in the corridor as I came out with my fingers mummified,' I reminded him, searching his reflective green eyes for any kind of recognition, but finding nothing other than some stunning gold flecks that made his eyes sparkle. He was so handsome it took my breath away.

'Sorry, I see so many patients that it's hard to put a face to a case,' he replied, shattering any illusions that he'd imagined me in the downright filthy ways I had him far too many times to count.

'Charlie Faulkner.' I decided to be brave and introduce myself, and held my hand out.

'Guy Fitton, but I guess you knew that,' he replied, curling his warm hand around mine. Damn it. His sleeves were rolled up, and I found nothing sexier than seeing a watch on a strong forearm with a smattering of dark hair. I tried to swallow, but all of a sudden my mouth had gone dry. 'Well, Charlie, you need this X-rayed before someone decides how to treat you. What do you do? You might need to stay off this for a while.'

'I'm an author, so standing isn't really an issue most of the time.'

'What do you write?' he asked. Quinn made me blush as she pulled a face at me, waggling her eyebrows suggestively, then gave me a quick thumbs-up while Tyler's back was turned as he spoke into his mobile.

'Romance novels, of the … *hot* variety.'

'Ah, Fifty Shades type stuff?' He grinned and gave me a knowing look.

'Yep, that type of stuff. You'd be amazed at my mental capacity for kink and explicit erotica.' The words left my mouth before I had a chance to filter them, and my mouth dropped in shock as he choked. Quinn turned away, her shoulders shaking in silent laughter. I wasn't sure who was more embarrassed, me or the now pink-faced Guy Fitton. Luckily, we were saved by Tyler.

'There was a unit outside like normal, paramedics are on their way in.'

'Great,' Guy and I said at the same time as he gently set my foot on the floor and quickly stood up. Quinn came and sat on the armrest of the chair, squeezing my shoulder as Guy and Tyler waved over the paramedics and gave a summary of what had happened. In a flash, I was loaded onto the stretcher, covered in a soft white blanket, strapped in, and wheeled out of the nightclub, with barely time to say thank you to either doctor for helping me.

'When you said a wild night, I didn't think we'd be ending it in the hospital,' Quinn laughed as the doors of the ambulance were closed.

'And we never even had our kebab.'

'Tell me you at least have bread, butter, and cheese at your house and I'll forgive you.'

'I do, though God knows what time we'll get back to eat it. I was in A&E for over six hours with my ankle and wrist injury. But on the plus side, something to look forward to, I have cookies. And they're ones with proper chocolate, not your horrible American crap.'

'Hey,' she protested.

'I wish you lived closer, Quinn. I've had such fun, despite this.' I gestured in the area of my knee, pretty thankful I couldn't see the damage that was causing me so much pain.

'Me too. When your leg is healed, I'll return the favour and take you out in New York.' She laughed as I squealed with delight.

It sucked she'd be going home. I loved Abbie and Georgie dearly, they were great friends, but a night at the village hall doing drunk karaoke was the liveliest they got. Luckily, I'd managed to avoid it so far, though I was sure my excuses for not going would run out soon. It wasn't that I wanted to go clubbing on a regular basis, but it would be nice to know I had someone to do it with if the mood took me.

At least I'd seen McFitty. And he'd spoken to me for a few seconds. That was progress.

Chapter Five

Any Excuse
One Month Later – A Friday in May

WHEN KNOCKING ON DAPHNE'S front door for the third time didn't seem to get me any response, I bent over and pushed open the flap on her letterbox.

'Hello? Daphne, are you ok?' I hollered through the black rectangular slot. I frowned as I heard a thud, then a load of footsteps and mumbling. 'Daphne? If you don't answer me, I'm going to use my emergency key and come and check you're ok.'

'I'm fine dear, just give me a moment,' she called, sounding flustered. Just before the letterbox snapped shut, nearly taking off the tips of my fingers, I was sure I heard some girlish giggling and a masculine chuckle.

I did my best to keep a straight face when she opened the door and let Mr. Bentley out before letting me in, but when she closed the door, I couldn't stop the smile from spreading.

'I see you and Mr. Bentley have moved out of the friend zone into the friends with benefits one.'

'And why exactly do you have a surprised look on your face, Charlie?' she retorted as her hands smoothed her ruffled hair back into place. 'Just because my body isn't as able doesn't mean the mind isn't willing. You youngsters think that when someone hits fifty, their desire magically vanishes.'

'Good to know that I might still get to act on it when I'm eighty, as my mind's willing and my body's able, but no one seems to want to take advantage of it.'

'And that's exactly why you're taking me to my appointment, dear,' she reminded me.

'One we'll be late for if you don't bust some more moves and get in my car.'

She grabbed her handbag and gave me a nod to say that she was ready. I helped her down the steps and locked up for her, then we walked along the side path in front of her cottage and headed out of the side gate onto the drive.

'What on earth is that?' she asked, giving my car a disapproving once over.

'A Mazda. Why, what's wrong?'

'For a start, I'm not sure why it has wheels, as it appears to be sitting on the floor.'

'It's a sports car, Daphne, they're all like that, with low profile tyres.'

'And how exactly am I supposed to get in and out of it at my age?'

'Getting in and out didn't seem to stop Mr. Bentley earlier,' I chuckled as I walked around to open the passenger door. 'Come on, stop with the disapproving looks and I'll help you.'

'Honestly,' she huffed as she skirted around it, the look not subsiding from her face. 'If I'd known I was going to be dragged along the road into town, I might not have suggested you take me.'

'Well, if I drove a Range Rover, you'd complain it was too high. I know I have the hots for the guy, but I'm not so desperate that I'm going to change my car to one more old-age-pensioner friendly on the off chance I might see him more often. Come on, take my hands and I'll help lower you in.'

With much muttering and banged heads and knees, I finally managed to get Daphne inside and made a mental note that it would be a lot easier to retract the roof to get her in and out in the future. Five minutes later, we were purring through Dilbury on our way to Shrewsbury, Daphne clutching her handbag as if she was scared that by putting it on the floor, she wouldn't be able to bend down low enough to retrieve it again. Once we left the speed restriction through the village, I put my foot down a little and Daphne screamed as she let go of the bag and clutched her seat, making me swerve from the shock of her shrill cry.

'Don't *do* that while I'm driving,' I warned her.

'Well, slow down.'

'I'm doing fifty miles an hour in a sixty, how slow do you want me to go?'

'Fifty, are you sure?' she asked, craning her neck to check my speedometer.

'Yes, I'm sure. It feels faster as you're closer to the road.'

'Remind me to wear incontinence knickers next time, as it feels like you're doing one hundred miles an hour,' she muttered.

'Are you telling me you just wet yourself in my car?' I groaned.

'No, but judging by the way you're driving, I'm surprised I haven't.'

'There's nothing wrong with my driving.'

'On that we'll agree to disagree.'

'I could just pull over and make you walk the rest of the way,' I warned her. 'So, which department is your appointment in?'

'Hmmm?' she asked.

'Which department? It's a big hospital. If I know where you're going, I can try and park as close as possible to the right entrance.'

'Oh, right. Ermmm, orthopaedics,' she replied after a brief hesitation.

'What are you seeing them for?'

'Rheumatoid arthritis.'

'Really? I thought that the rheumatology department dealt with that.'

'Oh, silly me, of course they do. This is for my osteoarthritis, I might need a new hip soon.'

'Hmmm, I wonder why that's suddenly developed wear and tear.' I flashed her a knowing look and winked, and she giggled and blushed. 'Well, we should just make it for your two-thirty appointment.'

'Lovely.'

By the time we parked and I retracted the roof, then enlisted the help of the parking attendant to extract Daphne from my car, it was nearly half past two. While she was still amazingly mobile for her age, she didn't have the speed needed to get into the main reception by two-thirty, let alone on to wherever the orthopaedic department was located.

'Be a dear, Charlie, and go and get me a wheelchair,' she suggested when we discovered it was a long walk up one of the corridors. 'We'll get there faster if you push me and run.'

'When did running become part of the deal?' I gave her an amazed look as I shook my head and sat her down on one of the chairs in the entrance. So much for a quick and easy scouting mission, this was turning into hard work. I quickly returned with one and flipped on the brake as I settled her into it and put her feet on the resting plates. Moments later, I was weaving in and out of the pedestrian traffic like a professional wheelchair pusher.

'Go for it, Charlie,' Daphne ordered, hooking her arm through the handles of her handbag and gripping the arms of the wheelchair as we turned the corner and found the corridor ahead was clear. I took a deep breath and pushed as I started to trot, then jog, then went into my version of a full out run. I laughed as Daphne let out a "Yippee" and a whoop, her fine hair lifting with the wind tunnel we were creating as we shot up the corridor, the widest smile I'd ever seen on her face.

'Brace yourself,' I warned, as I spotted the overhead sign that indicated the department we were after was fast approaching on the right. It turned out that stopping a wheelchair that was intent on forward momentum was a lot harder than getting it going. Despite clawing back some time with my corridor dash, when we made it to the reception desk of the department, we were ten minutes late.

'Yes?' asked the receptionist, barely glancing up at us.

'Daphne Jones. Sorry I'm late, but I have a two-thirty to see Dr. Fitton, please.'

'What?' I gasped. She hadn't mentioned she was seeing him.

'Who are you seeing?' the receptionist asked, frowning as she lifted her head from the mountains of paperwork in front of her.

'Dr. Fitton.'

'There's no Dr. Fitton on duty today.'

'Are you sure? It definitely said his name on my letter.'

'Ruth,' the receptionist hollered over her shoulder towards the small office behind her. 'Who's Dr. Fitton? Someone says she has an appointment with him.'

'No idea, sorry. He doesn't work in this department,' a voice called back.

'Oh, silly me, it wasn't an orthopaedic appointment today, that's next week. It was optometry. Come on, Charlie, giddy up, we need to motor.'

'Motor? I'm breathless from the last wheelchair dash,' I huffed as I turned her around. 'Are you sure it's an optometry appointment? It seems a bit odd for him to do that and to cover A&E as well.'

'I don't make the rules. Come on, put your foot down.'

'Make your mind up, will you? One minute it's "Charlie, slow down" when I have the ability to speed, and now you're all with the "Charlie, hurry up" when I currently only have three options. Stop, go, or keel over and die.' I rolled my eyes as she chuckled, then started running back up the corridor towards the main reception to try and locate optometry. By the time we made it to that reception desk, we were nearly half an hour late. I was a hot mess and on the verge of needing admission to the respiratory care department.

'Daphne Jones to see Dr. Fitton, please.'

'I'm sorry, doctor who?' the receptionist asked, making me giggle between pants for air.

'Dr. Fitton. Fit. Ton. Doctor Guy Fitton,' Daphne said slowly.

'Hmmm, he's not on this service. What were you seeing him about?' she asked. I was beginning to wonder, too.

'Well, obviously I thought it was my eyes, or I wouldn't have come to see you, dear. You'll have to excuse me, I'm very old so I'm not with it most of the time,' Daphne sighed, making my eyebrows raise at the comment. She was as sharp as a button. 'Can you look him up and tell me what department he works in, please? Even better if I could have his phone number, I could save you the trouble and call him directly to let him know I'm running late.'

'We don't give out phone numbers for confidentiality reasons, but I'll find out where he works,' she said as she turned around and rolled her chair across the floor to tap into her computer.

'Ok, what's going on?' I asked.

'I must have got confused, maybe I'm seeing him about one of my other ailments.'

'Hmmm,' I said as I gave her a suspicious look. She was up to something. She broke my gaze and looked down as she fiddled with her handbag straps, while the receptionist spoke on the phone and I managed to regulate my breathing.

'Sorry to keep you waiting.' The receptionist gave Daphne a kind smile, then shot me a sympathetic look. 'I think your grandmother *has* got a little confused. Dr. Fitton is one of our specialists in accident and emergency, he doesn't see out-patients. I can't find any other doctor with a similar name. Can I take her full name and date of birth? I can search and see who she was supposed to be seeing.'

'Oh my, oh,' Daphne cried as she threw herself back, slumping over the side of the chair as she dramatically clutched her chest. 'I think … I'm having … a heart attack. Quick, Charlie, thank goodness they have an emergency department on site.'

'Sorry,' I grimaced at the stunned receptionist as I realised Daphne's game. I spun her chair around, everyone in the waiting room throwing concerned looks our way as she moaned loudly. I pushed her out of the department as quickly as I could, pulling up as soon as we turned a corner and were out of sight. She immediately shuffled herself upright and glanced up at me, looking like the cat that got the cream.

'Daphne Jones, I'm on to you. Do you even *have* a hospital appointment today?' I demanded. She pulled a face and shrugged. 'You little minx!'

'Well, now we know for sure where he works.'

'All this to confirm what was pretty obvious to assume, seeing how he treated me in A&E and I saw him there the next time I was admitted?'

'Of course not,' she scoffed. 'I don't like being cooped up in my house all day on my own. I wanted to get out, somewhere where I don't see memories of David everywhere I look.'

'You only have to ask if you want to go out for the day, any of us would be happy to take you somewhere,' I said, softening my tone.

'I know that, but just because I'm eighty doesn't mean I want to visit boring garden centres. Inside I'm still a young girl with a list of dreams I haven't fulfilled yet.'

'Let me guess, a wheelchair race was on your bucket list?' I smiled.

'Well, that was the closest I'll ever get to one. And I always regretted not going into acting when I was younger. What would you have rated my heart attack on a scale of one to ten?'

'You're incorrigible,' I gasped. 'What if you have a heart attack for real and I think you're messing with me?'

'There's nothing wrong with my heart. Strong as an ox, my doctor tells me. Come on then, I think I've had my fill of being mischievous for the next few weeks. Now I've been rumbled, and you know for sure where he works, we can go and get a coffee in the League of Friends café. He has a stressful job, I bet he gets coffee all the time, so we might see him in there.'

'Ok, we'll go and get coffee, but I bet there is a special doctors-only lounge with fancy percolated stuff. We won't see him in the café.'

'Maybe, maybe not, but on the plus side, they do the best carrot cake in all of Shropshire.'

'Come on then,' I sighed, looking around to get my bearings before moving off. 'So, tell me about this bucket list? Is there anything else we can tick off today?'

'Not unless you fancy a Zimmer frame race?' she winked, making me laugh and shake my head.

I parked her up at a vacant table and went to place an order for two coffees and two slices of carrot cake. The elderly dears behind the counter set about preparing the order on a tray. I looked out at the main corridor, amazed at the amount of people moving through the hospital. I wondered what all of their stories were. I'd spent a fair bit of time in hospitals over the years, but it was easy to forget just how many people were ill at any given moment. In fact, it was really depressing. My heart stalled and skipped a beat as I saw the object of my infatuation striding up the corridor, his head down as his thumbs moved speedily over his phone. He was going to walk right past me.

'McFitty,' I breathed, willing him to hear my dulcet tone and look up and meet my gaze.

'What's that, dearie?' asked one of the ladies behind the counter. 'You want a McVitie? I don't think we have any. Jean, Jean? Do we have any McVitie's biscuits?'

'No, no McVitie's. We have Hobnobs.'

'That's ok, the carrot cake will be fine,' I said, not tearing my eyes off him as he got closer. I'd heard of white coat syndrome, and looking at him right then, I could understand how your blood pressure could be affected, as mine was rocketing to see how gorgeous he looked in his scrubs. There was something about an intelligent man in control, and in a uniform of sorts, that I found so sexy. I needed to do something or I'd miss my opportunity. 'Can you just give me a moment?' I said to no one in particular at the counter, and took a deep breath as I stepped out into the corridor, putting myself directly into his path. 'We really need to stop meeting like this,' I quipped.

He looked up with a frown, seconds away from colliding with me.

'Sorry, I wasn't looking where I was going,' he said. Before I had a chance to say anything in response, he side-stepped me and carried on walking. My jaw dropped as I spun to watch him heading up the corridor away from me. Seriously? He *still* didn't recognise me?

'Dearie, do you still want this order?'

'Yes please, and can you stick an extra slice of carrot cake on it, too?' I called as I kept my eyes on him until he disappeared out of sight. I needed the calories to soothe away yet another rejection.

'Was that him, dear?' Daphne asked as I carried the tray over.

'Yes,' I sighed.

'Well, I can see why you're smitten. He's quite the dish, but he has the air of a cad about him.'

'A cad?' I asked, still stunned. I knew I wasn't the most beautiful girl in the world, but I was confident enough to know that I had a certain amount of sex appeal, and I'd never had trouble attracting a man I was interested in before. But Dr. Fitton seemed completely immune to my charms.

'A cad, a rogue. He looks like a man who knows he's good-looking and uses it to his advantage. I'd be wary of a man like that.'

'You don't know him,' I reminded her as I ripped open a sachet of sugar and tipped it into my coffee.

'And neither do you. But I've always been good at reading people. Just be cautious with that one, Charlie. He's surrounded by pretty nurses all day.'

'Most men are surrounded by pretty girls while they're at work, it doesn't mean that they all stray.'

'Very true. I'm sure there's lots of lovely doctors that work here that are faithful, but I'm telling you that my gut says he's not to be trusted,' she stated firmly, as I forked a large chunk of the calorie-laden goodness into my mouth and groaned with pleasure.

'How can you say that after one look at someone?' I mumbled, then winced as Daphne gave me a gentle cuff around the back of the head.

'It's a gift. Now don't speak with your mouth full. How many times must I tell you and Abbie that it's not ladylike. And eating your weight in carrot cake isn't going to make you feel better about him ignoring you.'

'Maybe not, but I'm going to give it a damn good try,' I told her, wondering if I could buy the rest of the slices to take away.

'Well, don't be too long about it, I'm tired after all that excitement. I need a nap and then I have things I need to do at home.'

'Hmmm … Mr. Bentley? Owww,' I moaned as she cuffed me again, then smiled as she tucked into her cake with a smile on her own face. She really was unique. I'd never met anyone else like her, and I wasn't sure I ever would.

'She's so naughty,' Georgie laughed as I finished filling them in on my day with Daphne over our monthly Friday night meal at The Fox.

'We need to get this bucket list from her and make sure she ticks off all of the items. I had no idea she even had one,' Abbie said as she blew out a deep breath. She pulled a face and groaned as she palmed her stomach. 'I've eaten too much.'

'Me too,' I agreed as I pushed away the plate that had contained my sticky toffee pudding, before I was tempted to pick it up and lick off all the sauce stubbornly clinging to it. 'Thank God I've got a stretch body on, it has loads of give.'

'I'm seriously considering pregnancy trousers for when we come out to eat. I just can't resist a pudding, even though I know I'll be full by the time I've finished my main meal,' Abbie said.

'Anyway, I'm not quite sure how tonight turned into an "all about Charlie" night. We were supposed to be talking about what you've both decided about the men who actually want to be in your lives. Honestly, I'd give anything to be in the position where McFitty was begging me to see him.'

'Weston's hardly begging,' Georgie scoffed. 'I have more enthusiasm in my tone when I say, "Yes, of course I'd love to come in for my annual smear test."'

'But he rang you, Georgie. I don't even get an acknowledgement that my non-guy remembers me. You're a lot further on in your potential relationship than I am. But I think it's Abbie that we need to focus on tonight. He was so devastated when he found you'd run away.'

'Don't,' she sighed. 'I hate that we've hurt each other so badly, but I have a plan to win him back and convince him that I still love him. All I need to do now is book my flight and hope that he agrees to see me.'

'He'll agree,' I said, using my knuckles to gently rub my eyes.

'Seriously, a bit of wheelchair pushing has made you so tired you're falling asleep on us?' Georgie teased.

'Sorry. I've been writing so much, trying to make up for the time I lost when I couldn't. My eyes are obviously irritated.'

'You need to get some decent nights' sleep as well. I woke up when I thought I heard a noise in the back garden last night, it must have been at least three a.m., and when I looked out, I could see the glow from your office window lighting up your back patio.'

'You can't sleep while the voices are talking,' I protested. I shifted in my seat, wondering just how much weight I'd put on as these jeans were seriously uncomfortable in the crotch area tonight.

'Don't say things like that around McFitty,' Abbie laughed. 'If he thinks you're listening to voices, he'll have you admitted to the psychiatric ward. So, when's the next book out?'

'There's one at the end of this month, but I don't know about the next one. It's written and edited already, but …' I hesitated, wondering if I would jinx things by telling them.

'But?' Abbie prodded.

'I finally found an agent to represent me,' I smiled.

'Oh my God, that's amazing,' Georgie said, reaching over to squeeze my arm. 'How will that affect your pending work?'

'Well, that's the thing. She's submitted the book that was due to be out in August to one of the big publishers. We're talking full worldwide marketing, possible film rights, flying me to book signings around the world, and giving me advances on works to come.'

'Wow,' Abbie exclaimed, looking suitably impressed. 'That's incredible, well done. We need to order some bubbly.'

'Hey, steady on,' I laughed. 'A publisher still has to say yes, and they might not.'

'Well, they should, Charlie. You deserve recognition. We love your books and we're not saying that just because we're your friends,' Georgie added, Abbie nodding her agreement.

'Ok, I'll make a deal with you. If I get a contract out of it, I'll buy the bubbly and a celebratory slap-up meal for us, Daphne too. How does that sound?'

'As long as you're buying and not cooking it, I'm in,' Abbie said, giggling as I swatted her arm and laughed. I stood up and tugged my jeans at the knees to relieve some of the uncomfortable pressure, then sat back down again.

'You've had ants in your pants all night. Are you ok?' Georgie asked.

'I need you to date Weston. I'm piling on the pounds and need someone to whip me into shape. I moved to Dilbury to get fit, not get fat.'

'You're not fat,' Abbie scoffed with a roll of her eyes. 'You have amazing curves. You're like a little Latin package of hotness.'

'Then please go and tell Dr. Fitton that, as I feel invisible around him,' I moaned, rubbing my tired eyes again.

'If he doesn't see you, Charlie, then he's not worth the time of day,' Georgie said. 'Come on. If there are no voices talking, I think it will do you good to get home and have an early night.'

'Yes, at your age, you need your sleep,' Abbie teased.

'You cheeky minx,' I laughed. 'I'm only two years older than you are.'

'But I'll always be two years younger,' she replied, sticking her tongue out at me, then screamed when I flicked her with my napkin.

So, McFitty might not be in my life, but I had three amazing friends in it. And I'd had another really fun day. Life wasn't so bad.

Chapter Six

Eye Eye
The Next Day – Saturday

'HMMM,' I MOANED, POINTING my toes and stretching when my morning alarm went off. I'd slept so well. I loved waking up after a good night's sleep, especially when I was warm and toasty. 'Morning, Tibbs,' I smiled as I felt her bat my face with her paw. I sat up and rubbed my eyes, then let out a terrified scream.

'Oh my God, I've gone blind,' I wailed. I couldn't see. Not a thing. I'd seriously gone blind overnight. I started to hyperventilate as I desperately fumbled on the bedside cabinet for my mobile, forgetting for a moment in my literal blind panic that it was no use to me if I couldn't see what I was doing on it. 'No,' I whimpered, feeling my eyes fill with tears.

Losing any sense would be awful, but I needed my eyes to write. I inhaled sharply as common sense kicked in. I hadn't opened my eyelids, they were shut. I could feel them covering my eyes, that was why I couldn't see anything. Any momentary relief I'd felt soon left me and panic kicked in again when I made a concerted effort to try and open them, but still remained in darkness with them firmly shut. I needed my home phone, I could call Abbie to come over by using my speed dial, but that was over in my office. I stumbled out of bed and screamed again as Mrs. Tibbles let out an ungodly cry, then hissed at me. I must have accidentally stepped on her tail.

'I'm sorry, but that will teach you for getting under my damn feet,' I cried. 'Like it's not dangerous enough when I can actually see.'

She growled and I heard her padding across the carpet, then the gentle rhythmic thumping of her taking one step at a time to head down to the kitchen. I decided that trying to navigate the house while I was blind wasn't a great move, so I dropped onto all fours and crawled. I was thankful I had a cat who slept in my bed, as it meant I kept my door ajar overnight. Keeping the bathroom wall and door against my left-hand side so I wouldn't end up rolling down the stairs, I crawled across the landing.

'I'm never going to make it through this alive,' I grunted when I bashed my head on the office door. Seriously, how did blind swimmers not do that when they got to the other end of the pool? I eased myself up, located the handle, and made a wobbly and tentative beeline for the desk, walking straight into the corner of it and swearing again. I knocked over my pen pots, the noise making me jump. It was like losing my sight had heightened all of my other senses. I was like Daredevil! He didn't need his sight to do anything, but I wasn't sure my skills extended to fighting crime in a tight red leather suit, especially not when I was carrying a few extra pounds in weight. Plus, leather was so in and out of trend. No one wanted to be an untrendy blind superhero.

'Get back on point, Charlie, now's not the time for your vivid imagination,' I warned myself as I patted around the desk for the landline handset. 'Ha, got you.'

I felt my way around the buttons, got a dial tone, and then pressed one for Abbie's number. It was rare for her to work on a Saturday, whereas Georgie was usually busy with her doggie clients, especially owners who couldn't make appointments for them mid-week.

'Hello?' Abbie mumbled, her tone sleepy.

'Abbie, please come, something awful has happened. I can't see.'

'Charlie? You can't see what?'

'Anything. Anything at all! I thought I'd gone blind, but I realised my eyes were shut.'

'Well, opening them would be a good start,' she yawned.

'Oh, of course, silly me. Go back to sleep, crisis averted. How stupid of me not to try opening my eyes when I woke up, the way I've done every day for the last thirty-one years of my life,' I almost screeched, my voice rising as I got more frustrated.

'You're serious? You really can't see anything?'

'No. I mean yes, I'm serious, and no, I can't see. It's like my eyelids have been superglued shut. I'm scared, Abbie. Please come.'

'Ok, stay where you are. With your track record, adding blindness is asking for trouble,' she said, her voice quickly changing to her efficient accountant's tone. 'I'll throw on some clothes and come and let myself in. Where are you?'

'My office,' I sniffed, feeling the need to start crying, but worrying where the tears would go if they couldn't leak out. The last thing I needed was my eyelids bulging out with a lake of salty tears unable to escape.

'Ok, sit straight down on the floor and don't move a muscle, understood?'

'Yes,' I whimpered, then did as I was told.

'I'm going to hang up and I'll be with you shortly. If I can't see what's wrong, sorry, poor choice of words in the circumstances, I'll drive you to the hospital, ok?'

'Ok. Hurry, Abbie, I'm seriously scared.'

She ended the call. I put the phone in my lap, then reached up to feel my eyelids and gasped. They didn't feel normal, they were hot and puffed up really badly, and so damn itchy. I curled my fingers into my palms to resist the temptation to rub or scratch, not wanting to make matters worse. It wasn't long before I heard the front door open and close and Abbie running up the stairs.

'Oh my God,' she exclaimed. 'Are you allergic to shellfish? Your eyes are so swollen, no wonder you can't see. I bet it was those prawns you had last night. You're having an anaphylactic reaction.'

'The next morning? With my breathing not impaired? I don't think so. How bad are they?'

'Well, you can't open them, so even without the benefit of seeing them with my own eyes, I'll go out on a limb and say they're not looking pretty. Do you have any ice packs in your freezer? Putting something cold on them should help.'

'No, but there's some of those pouches of ready mixed cocktails.'

'Oh, which ones?'

'Lemon vodka sorbet.'

'Oh, they're so nice, but I'm not sure alcohol is a great move, Charlie. What if you need urgent medical attention and drugs?'

'I wasn't suggesting drinking them, Abbie. Though, if I have to go to hospital and face Dr. Fitton looking like this,' I gesticulated in the vicinity of my face, 'I might need to drink them to give me courage.'

'Oh right, let me go and get them and I'll put some teaspoons in the fridge as well. They always help when I have puffy eyes after crying.'

She helped me back to bed and arranged the pillows so that I could lie with my head slightly propped up, then dashed off. She returned soon after and told me that she'd got the cocktail packs and had wrapped them in tea towels. She carefully placed them over my eyes.

'Thank you,' I whispered, enjoying the cooling sensation. 'Sorry to drag you out of bed.'

'Don't worry about it. That's the benefit of being good friends with your neighbours, we all look out for each other. I'd say you look like you've had a tearful night, and knowing I looked like that after I ran from Miller, I think it's going to take a few hours for the swelling to go down enough for you to see anything. I'll go and do you some toast and bring you some water, then it might be best for you to have a sleep and we'll see how they look later before deciding if you need to go to hospital, ok?'

'Ok,' I agreed with a heavy sigh.

'Sweet mother of … owww … son of a … shit,' I hissed as I sat on the toilet in my en-suite. Like it wasn't bad enough I was partially sighted, having a pee felt like someone was pouring acid on my lady parts.

'Are you ok?' called Abbie from outside the en-suite door. She'd ended up sitting in bed with me, distracting me from my predicament by making me laugh as she filled me in on how she planned to woo Miller next weekend in New York.

'No. My damn jeans have chafed me.'

'Oh, thigh rash? Nasty.'

'Not there, *there*. You know, down below.'

'I've never heard of anyone getting beaver rash from jeans,' she laughed.

'Honestly, I swear it feels like someone has taken a sander to my privates. I need to pee so badly, but it hurts too much.'

'Maybe your knicker elastic cut you,' she suggested. 'Take a look.'

'How flexible do you think I am?'

'With a mirror,' she tutted.

'I'm not sure I could see anything even with a mirror, not with these squinty eyes.'

'Well, don't ask me. Muff inspections aren't in the "things girlfriends do for each other" handbook.'

'What do I do then?' I huffed. 'I don't know what's wrong and I'm too scared to pee, it kills.'

'I'll go and run a bath.'

'Please, feel free to relax in my Zen-like spa bathroom while I die all alone in agony on the toilet.'

'Not for me. Maybe if you sit in it, the water will neutralise the acidity a bit.'

'Oh my God, you want me to pee in the bath while I'm sitting in it?' I shuddered at the grossness of it.

'Well, you can always stay in there for the rest of the day, letting out a drop at a time and then moaning about it for an hour before trying again.'

'God damn it, sometimes my life sucks!' I shouted in frustration. 'Run the damn bath, but this is like *Fight Club*. The first rule of me peeing in the bath is no one talks about me peeing in the bath. Got it?'

'Got it,' she called with a giggle.

'Charlie Faulkner?'

I sighed with relief as I turned to see a female nurse holding a clipboard. 'Oh, thank God, it's not him.'

'Do you want me to come in with you? If you don't, that's fine, I'll wait here.'

'I'd rather you come, just stay at the head-end, ok?' I suggested.

'You have no worries on that front,' she confirmed with a vigorous nod.

I stood up, and Abbie grabbed my arm to guide me. The idea of coming to A&E with my eyes still hideously puffed and a vagina that looked like it had caught the worst ever case of measles and chickenpox combined hadn't exactly thrilled me. It was going to be bad enough to have anyone looking down there, let alone Dr. Fitton. We followed the nurse into one of the side rooms, me bouncing off the doorframe since I'd put on my sunglasses to try and hide my eyes.

'I'll leave you alone for a moment. Please undress from the waist down, lie on the bed with your ankles together, legs bent, and let your knees flop apart, then cover yourself with the blanket. I'll be back shortly and we'll take a look, shall we?'

'Great,' I replied, feeling my cheeks flush at the mortification of having to lie down with my legs akimbo so a stranger could ogle my mangled lady parts. I heard the door close.

'*We* won't take a look, I'm honouring the head-end deal,' Abbie said. 'I'll help get you settled on the bed if you keep your knickers on, then I can cover you and you can shuffle your knickers off yourself.'

'Thanks, Abbie, sorry to ruin your Saturday.'

'It's ok, it wasn't like I had anything planned. Witnessing your embarrassment is far more entertaining than doing some accounts.'

Five minutes later, feeling like I was about to give birth in this position, I heard the door open.

'Right, let's take a look,' the nurse said. I shut my eyes and felt myself automatically clench as she lifted the blanket. The cool air was actually quite nice, as my beaver had never been so hot. 'Oh. That looks sore.'

'Sore is an understatement. What's wrong?' I asked, as Abbie gently took my hand and squeezed it.

'To be honest, I'm not sure. Have you had sex recently?'

'I wish,' I muttered.

'Sorry, what was that?' she asked.

'No, no sex recently.'

'Well, on first glance I'd have said it was something like herpes.'

'What?' I shrieked, bolting up. 'There's no way it can be herpes.'

'Well, I'm really not sure,' she said as she snapped on some gloves. 'I need to look a bit closer, if you don't mind.'

'Oh my God,' I groaned as her head dipped down again. I flopped back on the bed and shook my head.

'I didn't think you'd had sex for a while?' Abbie asked.

'I haven't, and I've never had herpes, she's made a mistake.' I grimaced as the nurse examined me more closely, then sighed and covered me up again.

'I need to bring a colleague in for a second opinion,' she said, as she removed her gloves and placed them in the medical waste bin. 'Just try and relax and I'll be back as soon as I can, ok?' She didn't wait for my reply before disappearing and closing the door.

'You're sure you didn't use any orgasm enhancements last night?' Abbie asked again. 'It could be an allergic reaction.'

'Well, I'm confident it's an allergic reaction, I just don't know what to. And yes, I'm sure, I've never even tried any cream.'

'Well, don't make a mistake and use eucalyptus rub by mistake,' she chuckled.

'Oh my God, what on earth possessed you to put that down there? It stings like hell if you accidentally put some on a raw nose when you have a cold.' I burst out laughing when she filled me in on the battle of wills she'd had with her arch nemesis Fi-Fi, and was laughing so hard I didn't hear anyone come in.

'Good afternoon. Nurse Walters here has asked for a second opinion. I'm Dr. Fitton, I'm going to need to take a look at your genitals if that's ok, Miss Faulkner.'

My laughter died in an instant and I heard Abbie suck in a gasp as she realised who was standing in front of us.

'Now, I understand there's some blistering. Can you tell me when the symptoms first occurred?' his deep and sexy voice asked, as I cringed and hoped that my sunglasses would mean that he wouldn't recognise me. Hell, with his track record, even without them he probably wouldn't recognise me, but I was still mortified.

'Ermmm, possibly last night, around eight o'clock as I was having dinner with my friends.'

'Any history of food allergies?' he asked as he pulled some gloves from the dispenser on the wall.

'No,' I replied, taking advantage of the fact that he couldn't see my eyes to check him out.

'And when did you last have unprotected sex?' His question made me die a little on the inside.

'Trust me, it's not a sexually transmitted disease,' I said firmly.

'I think it's best you let me make a diagnosis. How long?'

'It's been a while,' I squeaked, my cheeks heating up.

'Can you define a while?'

'Two years,' I mumbled quietly.

'I'm sorry?'

'Yes, me too,' I huffed. He had no idea just how sorry I was about it.

'You too, what?'

'I'm sorry, too.'

'I think we're at cross-purposes here. I didn't catch how long it had been since you last had sex.'

'Oh right, sorry. I thought you were sympathising, because … you know, it's worthy of it.'

'So how long exactly?' he repeated, turning his back as he fiddled in a drawer and extracted something.

'Two years,' I squeaked, beyond embarrassed. I just wanted to be magically teleported out of there.

'Ok, do I have your approval to take a look?' he asked, turning around.

'Oh God,' I grumbled. He was strapping a head torch on. If he found out it was me lying here, it would be bad enough that he'd have seen my vagina before he'd even bought me a drink, but that would never happen now as he'd think either I was so undesirable that no one wanted sex with me or I was frigid.

'Is that a yes?'

'Yes,' I hissed reluctantly, my toes curling up tightly with the shame. My love interest was about to go spelunking around my own personal cave. And we hadn't even been on a first date. 'Someone shoot me now,' I whispered to Abbie as the bright torch was turned on and he moved closer to the car crash that was my privates.

'Now that's what I call diving in head first,' she giggled, squeezing my hand tightly.

'Hmmm,' he murmured. Considering I'd spent all day wanting nothing more than to be able to open my eyes, I couldn't squeeze them shut tightly enough. It wasn't exactly how I'd imagined the first time I felt his breath down there to be. And what was with the "hmmm" every damn time he examined me. 'Well, I'll need to do a swab for formal confirmation, but it's not herpes,' he stated confidently.

'No shit, Sherlock,' I muttered. I didn't need a potholer with a fancy medical degree to tell me that.

'And these blisters are unusually symmetrical,' he advised, making me jump as he ran his gloved fingertip over them. I banged my head on the thin pillow on the bed a few times out of sheer sexual frustration and mortification. 'Do you have any history of allergic dermatitis?'

'Not that I'm aware of.'

66

'No other incidences of blistering, itching, or swelling anywhere on the body?' he asked.

'Your eyes, Charlie,' Abbie exclaimed, making me suck in a breath as she revealed my name.

'I was going to examine those next. I'll just change gloves, if you can take off your sunglasses for me.'

'They're fine, honestly. If you can just give me some cream for whatever's going on south-of-the-border, that would be great.'

'Well, I suspect that the two flare-ups might be related, so I'll have to insist on examining your eyes to make a diagnosis, please,' he said in that oh-so-sexy dominant tone. Or at least it would be if we were anywhere but here. I let out a heavy sigh as I heard the waste bin clang, then him washing his hands and grabbing another pair of gloves. I gritted my teeth as Abbie gently removed my glasses, since I seemed unable, or unwilling, to do it myself.

He moved closer and asked me to close my eyes and shone a bright light over them, before asking me to open them again. He showed no sign of recognising me, yet again. I wasn't sure if I was insulted or relieved.

'Have you come into contact with any metal in either area in the last twenty-four hours?' he asked.

'Not that I can think of …' I mused. 'Oh, actually yes, I use metal eyelash curlers, why?'

'And how about in the vaginal area?'

'No! What would I use eyelash curlers for down there?' The mind boggled. I was surprised to hear Dr. Fitton laugh at the same time as Abbie and the nurse.

'I didn't mean eyelash curlers. I meant any possibility of any metal making contact. What were you wearing yesterday?'

'A body.'

'A what?' he asked, and this time the nurse and Abbie laughed.

'It's like a swimsuit with arms, but far sexier than it sounds. Oh my God, that's it. It has metal poppers on, so you can part them to take a pee, because… well, you know… women can't just flop it out and do it standing up through a hole in their knickers.'

'Quite,' he chuckled, choosing the most inappropriate time to develop a sense of humour with me. 'Well, it appears that you've suddenly developed contact dermatitis. You have an allergy to something in the metal, most likely nickel. Any time it comes in contact with your skin, you'll develop an itchy blistering rash, which is what has happened here.'

'But I've used those eyelash curlers for years. Why now?'

'I can't say, I'm afraid. Sometimes the body views something it's been exposed to for years as a threat–' I zoned out as he gave a detailed rundown of antibodies, histamines, and responses. All I could focus on was that it was curable and I could hopefully get out of here without him even realising it was me. 'You'll get a letter regarding a referral to the allergy testing clinic soon,' he continued. 'I'll give you a few minutes to get dressed, then come back with your prescription, which you can collect from the dispensary. Just follow the instructions on the packet for now and wash your hands carefully after application.' He smiled at me and gestured to Nurse Walters to leave the room with him.

'That was the worst five minutes of my entire life,' I groaned, covering my embarrassed face with my hands.

'Oh, Charlie, of all the luck in the world. But it doesn't seem like he recognised you, does it?'

'No, and on reflection, that actually makes me happier than I ever imagined it would.'

'He's hot, not Tyler hot, but then I always preferred me a blond.'

'Tyler is good-looking,' I agreed, 'but I prefer my men a little darker. Close your eyes unless you want a flash of trauma central,' I warned as I sat up and shuffled my knickers back on.

I stood up and was chatting to Abbie as I pulled up my leggings, having not wanted to risk the pressure of my jeans in such a delicate place when I got dressed earlier today. I'd bent over to do up the laces on my trainers when I heard the door open and close, then a cough.

'I have your written prescription here, Miss Faulkner.'

'Great, thank you,' I replied as I straightened up and turned to face him.

'Have I met you before?' he asked, cocking his head as his eyes did a slow scan of my body from head to toe, then back up again, making my mouth go dry. 'You seem familiar.'

'No, don't think so.' I replied, snatching the prescription out of his grasp. 'Come on, Abbie, time to go.' I shot out of the door before he had a chance to ask anything else or scan me further while I was in such unflattering clothes. I hurried around the corner and let out a sigh of relief as I leaned back against the wall and covered my face with my hands.

'Good God, and here I was thinking you didn't know how to run,' Abbie laughed as she found me.

'Until today I could have set a speed record running towards him. I never imagined I'd want to do it running away.'

'So, what now? Is that it for your aspirations with McFitty? I mean, shouldn't he at least have bought you dinner before getting in there head first?' she teased. I linked arms with her as we started to walk towards the exit.

'You know, I thought exactly the same myself,' I giggled, rolling my eyes, which were thankfully nearly fully open now, though still puffy. 'Oh, damn it, my–'

'Glasses,' came his voice from behind me, making me screw up my face in a grimace. 'You left your glasses, Miss Faulkner, and I thought you looked familiar. A quick scan of your records reveals that I seem to have treated you a few times.'

'Well, saying I'm accident-prone is an understatement, you've seen the size of my file.' I reluctantly released Abbie's arm and turned to face him.

'I've seen bigger.'

'Isn't that supposed to be my line?' I cursed myself for never knowing when to rein in my sexual quips, but he surprised me by laughing again as he held out my glasses for me to take.

'Hmmm, I definitely remember you now. What was it, an extreme mental capacity for kink? You're the author, aren't you?'

'Yes,' I said slowly, taking my glasses from him. Our fingers brushed, which sent a shiver down my spine. I wondered why he suddenly remembered me then and he hadn't before.

'Maybe I'll see you again in town one night when I'm off duty, you can tell me more about it then.' He frowned as his pager started beeping. 'Sorry, got to run. Try and stay out of A&E for at least a few weeks, will you? Your file is going to need its own transport if it gets any bigger.'

'I'll try, but … hey, it's me.'

'Quite,' he nodded, flashing me a smile and nodding to Abbie. He spun on his heels and quickly jogged away, disappearing around the corner as I stood rooted to the spot, slightly stunned.

'Hello, Miss Faulkner, I do believe that the hot doctor is starting to warm up to you.'

'Don't be silly, he was just being polite,' I said as I turned around, not wanting to make a big deal out of a few comments.

'There was nothing polite about the way he was checking out your backside when he walked in to find you bending over.'

'He was?' I asked, as she took my arm again and we started walking.

'Mmmm-hmmm,' she nodded, grinning at me. 'And I saw the slow once over, too.'

'Why now? He's virtually blanked me most of the times I've met him.'

'Well, you obviously have one hell of a magical beaver, one look and he's fallen under its spell. Thank God I stayed up top, or I might be rethinking my plans with Miller.'

'Shut up,' I laughed, shoulder bumping her. 'It wasn't the beaver.'

'With some men, it's *always* the beaver,' she laughed.

I smiled at her, then frowned. With some men, it *was* all about that, but I didn't want a guy who was only interested in sex. I was thirty-one, I was ready to fall in love and think about settling down. It wasn't all about sex anymore, not that it ever had been for me.

We left the hospital with me feeling more confused than if McFitty had treated me like he had all the other times.

'Hurrah,' I cried when I heard the knock on the door, scaring Mrs. Tibbles, who was sleeping on the sofa next to me. I quickly gave her head a ruffle and ran to the front door, grabbing my wallet off the hall console on the way. 'Is that you, Pizzaman?' I called.

'It is, but I could say yes now even if it wasn't, couldn't I?'

'Yes, maybe, but I know your voice too well, Kitt. Can you close your eyes?'

'Last time I checked, yes,' he laughed.

'I meant, I want you to close your eyes. And keep them closed, I'm not a pretty sight,' I warned him, as my hand hovered over the door handle.

'Some girls look even better without makeup.'

'Is this where you say, "sadly you're not one of them?"' I laughed.

'No, you're one of the lucky ones. You always look stunning, even without it. Are you opening the door or what? It's not like you to wait three seconds to open the door for pizza, let alone three minutes.'

'Don't say I didn't warn you,' I told him, as I checked that Tibbs wasn't poised to make a bid for freedom. I threw the door open, shot out, and pulled it almost closed behind me, making sure I didn't lock myself out. 'Oh my God, that smells so good.'

'It always smells good. Oh no, what happened?' His hand shot up to sweep my hair away from my eyes. 'What's made you cry so much?'

'I could have cried. You won't *believe* what happened today.' I handed him his money, with the usual tip that he'd stopped arguing about around twenty deliveries ago. He shoved it in his pocket as I took the pizza box from him.

'Thanks, Charlie. Don't tell me you've been to A&E again?' he chuckled as he leaned against the oak beam that held up my thatched canopy over the front door.

'How on earth did you guess?' I grinned and quickly opened the box and offered him first slice, but he shook his head. 'Do you have time to hear all about it?' I mumbled through my first bite, groaning with pleasure. Instead of just Authors Anonymous, they needed a PAAA. Pizza *and* Authors Anonymous. I'd need daily meetings.

'You know I do, you always make sure you time your call with my clocking-off time.' His dimpled grin came out as he shook his head.

'I enjoy our chats. Come in if you want,' I offered as I virtually inhaled the rest of the slice, knowing what his response would be.

'It's not appropriate. You're the customer and I'm Pizzaman.'

'Kitt.' I rolled my eyes at him, but flicked my head over to the bench under my kitchen window. The only time it was ever used was when Kitt and I chatted. We sat down and I filled him in on my latest encounter with Dr. Fitton, leaving out some of the more embarrassing finer details. 'Anyway, Abbie reckons he's thawing. What do you think?'

'I think he's an idiot if he hasn't already thawed.'

'Well, I think after about another five or six medical emergencies, I'll have completely wooed him.'

'Isn't it a bit weird for a woman to woo a man? Shouldn't it be the other way around?'

'You sound just like Daphne,' I chuckled. 'Such old-fashioned virtues. Women are allowed to woo nowadays, you know. Some even propose.'

'Well, I guess I can get on board with a woman showing her interest, but not proposing. That I don't agree with at all. A man should propose, it's a matter of pride. So, it could get serious with you and the doctor, you think?'

'Steady on,' I said as I wiped my mouth and shoved the napkin into the empty pizza box. 'He recognised me, that's all. That's hardly serious.'

'He's seen parts of you naked,' Kitt reminded me as he suddenly reached out his hand and cupped my face.

'What are you doing?' I asked, taken aback. He swept his thumb over the corner of my lip.

'Pizza sauce, you missed some,' he replied. He lifted his thumb to his mouth and sucked off the aromatic mixture. He opened his mouth as if he was going to say something, but shook his head and glanced at his watch instead, then shot to his feet. 'Damn it, I didn't realise it was this late. I need to go.'

'How is your mum?' I asked as I shoved the box onto the bench and stood up too.

'No change,' he sighed, running a hand over his face.

'I'm sorry to hear that. And I'm sorry if I kept you, you look tired.'

'It's been a difficult week,' he shrugged. 'But never apologise, talking to you isn't a chore. I look forward to our conversations. I guess I'll see you soon, Charlie.'

'You know it, take care driving back.'

He flashed me another smile and headed off up the path, his hands tucked deep in his jeans pockets, his shoulders slumped with the weight of the responsibility he carried on them. I was about to go in when I changed my mind, ran up the path, and hung over the gate.

'Kitt,' I called, just as he was about to shut the door on his car. He leaned out and looked back at me, his eyebrows raised in question. 'You're not just the delivery guy to me. You're a friend, ok?'

'No more Pizzaman references?' he asked as his face lit up.

'Don't be silly,' I scoffed. 'You'll always be Pizzaman to me. See you.'

'See you, Charlie,' he replied with a smile and a shake of his head.

I disposed of the evidence of my pizza weakness in the bin around the side of the house, then headed back in and locked up. Mrs. Tibbles quickly took up residence on my lap when I sat down and we enjoyed some rare quality time watching television together. After all of the drama today, I wasn't in the mood to write. There was always tomorrow.

Chapter Seven

Pull The Other One
One Month Later – A Wednesday in June

I FLICKED THROUGH SOME magazines in the waiting room, noticing how nervous everyone seemed. I was lucky, I'd never been nervous about coming to the dentist. But then I'd had so much work done, all thanks to overcrowding as a result of my genetics, that visits were old hat to me. After you'd had your gums sliced open to remove four wisdom teeth and four molars in your teens, and your face had ballooned up like a chipmunk carrying his supply of food for hibernation, having a tooth pulled or filled was as easy as melting butter on a hot day.

'Charlie Faulkner for Mr. Wankowksi,' called the dental assistant. I put the magazine down and followed her through to Mr. Wankowski's room, tittering to myself. It seemed I was the only person who found his name funny and wondered when I'd be able to hear or say it without laughing.

'Good morning, Charlie,' he greeted with a smile and a handshake. He was always friendly, but for some reason, I didn't have as much confidence in him as I had his predecessor. I'd only met Mr. Wankowski twice before, and for something as invasive as potential root canal treatment, I'd have preferred someone whose skills I was more familiar with. However, when it was a choice between being stuck with him or this agonising tooth pain, it was no contest. 'So, this is an emergency appointment because you have bad tooth pain?'

'Bad is an understatement. Right now, I'd pay you to pull it out,' I told him as I settled back into his chair and slid on the protective glasses. 'The pain was so bad last night I was crying, and I even thought about taking a pair of pliers to it.'

'Well, I've just studied your X-rays and they show a nerve infection, so I'm not surprised you're in pain. In about five minutes, it will be a distant memory,' he told me in a reassuring tone.

The relief as my face went numb from the injection was almost as good as having a relaxing massage and facial at a spa. Even the noise of the drill whirring away, and the slight smell of burning as it ground the inside of my tooth away, didn't faze me.

'Wuddy hell,' I gasped as the hygienist managed to suck the end of my tongue into the saliva extracting machine.

'Oops, sorry,' she grimaced, quickly turning it off and freeing me as I flashed her a disapproving scowl. How hard was it to angle that damn thing into the corner of my mouth? I'd never had my tongue vacuumed up before. 'How about you take a rinse?'

I sat up, then picked up the bright pink water and went to take a sip, but with my lips numb, I missed my mouth and poured most of it all over the waterproof apron I was wearing. Hastily blotting myself dry, I tried again, holding a finger in my lips and using it as a guide for the rinse. This time, I managed to get it in and sloshed it about, but made another mess as I tried to spit into the bowl and instead dribbled it all down my chin. Having a bruised and numb tongue and numb lips didn't exactly make it easy to empty a mouthful of water into a tiny bowl, and I succeeded in spraying the next mouthful all over the assistant. I mumbled a "Sorry" at her, though inside I was rejoicing. I'd never come out of the dentist with a tongue-related injury, until she'd let loose with that super-sonic vacuum cleaner in my mouth.

I gave her a "don't mess up the suction this time" warning look as Mr. Wankowski went back in and she followed. I closed my eyes as he got to work trying to clear out the pulp, muttering that he couldn't find the third root. How hard could it be? He had X-rays, and it wasn't like it was a large search area. He was poking and prodding like an archaeologist on a dig, and I howled as he slipped and stabbed his excavation tool into my lip.

'Oh, sorry Charlie. My bad. Have another rinse, will you?'

My bad? My bad?! Thank God he wasn't performing an eyelift and had just mistakenly gouged my eye out, followed by a "my bad" comment.

Half an hour later, I was feeling pretty sorry for myself with my newly split lip and swollen cheek. I also had possible whiplash from his overly enthusiastic jerking of my head as he'd tried to pull off the metal band he'd put around my tooth while he put the temporary filling in, not to mention another incident of the nurse getting my tongue stuck to the suction tube.

I wasn't feeling in any fit state to eat, let alone cook, but I was out of fresh chicken for Mrs. Tibbles. If I stood any chance of sleeping off a restless few nights and a sore mouth that was beginning to thaw, Mrs. Tibbles needed chicken. It was like cat heroin to her. After a diced chicken dinner, she was loving and placid. Without it, she was likely to show her indignation by trying to suffocate me as she sat on my head while I tried to sleep in bed, not to mention the face pawing, with her claws out.

I called in at the shop on my way past.

'Afternoon, Mrs. Vickers,' I mumbled as I headed inside to see her sitting at the counter reading.

'Hello, lovely day,' she called.

'It is,' I agreed. The British weather had started picking up a few weeks before and I'd finally been able to let Tibbs out in the back garden. After a few tentative explorations that lasted less than a minute each and had her flying in with her fur on end at the slightest noise, she'd got brave and was driving me insane, howling all of the time to go out. I was going to have to get Heath over to fit a cat flap for her. 'Mrs. Vickers, have you sold out of chicken?' I asked, my voice completely distorted due to my dental-related injuries.

'What's that you want to thicken?' she asked, pushing her glasses up her nose.

'Chicken, not thicken.'

'Well, if you really want to thicken something that badly, we have gelatine somewhere by the baking supplies.'

'Chicken,' I repeated slowly, flapping my arms to try and emphasise the point.

'Oh dear, I think we're out of stock of deodorant. Reg, Reg,' she shouted, 'are we out of deodorant?'

'Yes, love,' he called back over the noise of the TV in the background.

'I don't need deodorant. I want chicken,' I almost shouted, very slowly.

'Well, there's no good getting cross with me because you have a body odour problem that I can't fix,' she scolded. 'And I already told you we have gelatine if you want to thicken something.'

'Oh my God,' I groaned. I pulled my phone out of my handbag and keyed in the words "I want chicken," complete with an appropriate emoji.

'You want chicken? Well, why didn't you say?'

'I did.'

'No, you said you wanted to thicken something. Well, the chicken should be in the chiller.'

'It's not,' I replied, shaking my head.

'You have snot, too? Well, stand back, I don't want to catch your germs. You'll find the tissues next to the deodorant.'

'You just said you didn't have any deodorant, which I don't need anyway. And I also don't need tissues as I haven't got a cold. I want chicken and there's no *bloody* chicken in the chiller.' I was starting to lose my patience. My face was starting to crackle back to life and I just wanted to grab a couple of painkillers and head to bed to try and make up for the last couple of nights tossing and turning.

'There's no thickening the killer? Who's a killer? Reg, I said, Reg. There's been a murder in Dilbury,' she hollered, her eyes wide with surprise.

'A murder?' he shouted, still not moving from his place in front of the television.

'No,' I said firmly as Mrs. Vickers said, 'Yes.'

'There's no killer,' I groaned. My God, it wasn't easy coming in here at the best of times.

'Well, why did you say there was? Honestly, you scared the living daylights out of me. A killer, here in Dilbury? Gave me quite a turn, it did.'

'There's no killer. I'm trying to tell you that there's no *chicken*. In. The. Chiller.'

'I have no idea what you're saying, dear. This is the trouble with all you foreigners moving over here, no one can understand you. Maybe you ought to try speaking English.'

'Jesus. I'm going to kill you and stuff *you* in the chiller in a minute,' I grumbled as I keyed out my predicament and showed it to her. I had visions of me abandoning my usual writing genre to do a factual crime thriller, where the shopkeeper was carved up, then shrink-wrapped and sold as prime steak to the unsuspecting villagers.

'Well, why didn't you say there's no chicken in the chiller. Reg, why's there no chicken in the chiller? Reg?'

'Sold out, love. It's delivery day tomorrow,' he called.

'Poor Mrs. Tibbles,' I sighed. She wasn't going to be happy. Cooked diced chicken was her favourite meal. Plus, if I wanted some sleep, it meant I'd have to shut her out of the bedroom, which would really put her nose out of joint.

'You want some vegetables? Are we out of vegetables as well?' Mrs. Vickers asked.

'I give up,' I huffed, pointing at the village newsletter instead. I had a feeling if I walked out of here without gelatine, tissues, deodorant, or vegetables, my name would be mud, so best to buy something to placate her.

Two Days Later – Friday

76

'Well, how did you manage to break a tooth in half?' Mr. Wankowski asked as I settled back into his chair.

'I didn't do anything. The night you'd done the root canal, I was eating some ice cream and most of the tooth slid out,' I grumbled. To make matters worse, it was the tooth right next to the one he'd worked on. I was convinced his brutal treatment of it had damaged the other one.

'Well, it's beyond repair and there's not a lot of tooth left visible for me to grip. I'm afraid we need to cut your gum open to pull it out. While I've got you anaesthetised, I may as well remove that temporary filling and finish your root canal treatment, if you can bear to have your mouth open that long.'

'Go for it,' I sighed. It was a good job I was selling enough books to cover the cost of all of this. I closed my eyes and tried to imagine I was lying on a Caribbean beach in the sun as he set to work.

Even with my vivid imagination, I wasn't able to zone out. First, there was the drilling, then the ramming of the metal band of torture, followed by lots of forceful jabs as he muttered about still not being able to find the third root, then a triumphant shout as he did and slammed the reamer down inside it. He packed in the filling, then began the same process as last time of trying to remove the band. By the time he was done, I already had face and neck ache, and quite possibly lock jaw, and he still needed to pull the remains of the other tooth.

'Try and relax,' the tongue sucker soothed as she held my shoulders down while Mr. W jerked my head up and down as he tried to pull the tooth out.

'Stubborn little sucker,' he huffed. His assistant stuck her arm on my forehead to try and hold me still as he used his pliers to yank without so much as even a wiggle. 'Ok, I need to try this from another angle, keep her held down,' he ordered.

Seconds later, without giving me any chance to protest, he'd mounted the chair and was straddling me. Now here was a man in desperate need of Mrs. Vickers' deodorant. I was gagging and choking as he continued to try and work the tooth loose with his privates far too close to my face for my liking. I was on the verge of tears when he almost fell off the chair as he finally yanked the bloody remains of my tooth out. I might not have been able to feel my face, but my neck and forehead were killing me as he stitched my gum closed and told me to rinse out the blood in my mouth, which I managed to dribble all over my face again.

'Oops,' I heard him mutter.

'Oops?' I mumbled. Those were words you never wanted to hear from a doctor or dentist who'd just performed a procedure on you.

'Ermmm, I'm missing a bit of metal off my reamer.'

'What?' I spluttered, sitting back up to face him, a load of napkins pressed against my mouth to try and catch the combined drool and blood leaking from my mouth.

He grimaced and held up the reamer he'd used to scoop out the nerve from that last root, then held up a brand new one for me to see how much of the metal was missing. It was significant.

'Did you swallow anything?'

'I don't think so,' I replied, shaking my head.

'Hmmm, it must still be in your tooth then, and I've already filled it. I can either remove the filling and try and get it out, or we can just leave it be. It shouldn't cause you any problems.'

'I just want to go home,' I whined, not sure I was in a fit state to be making any decisions right then. I'd never felt so battered and bruised.

I slowly made my way to the car, feeling sick and light headed. I clutched the wad of napkins to my mouth, noticing the strange looks I was getting as I passed people. Once I was sitting in my car, I looked at myself and started to cry. My face was so swollen and already bruising, I had dried blood smeared all over my one cheek and my chin, and blood splatter all over the neckline of my cream top. And to add insult to injury, I had a big red button mark across my forehead from the dental assistant's shirt cuff pressing down on me. If ever I'd wanted a boyfriend that I could ring to say "Come and get me, I need you," it was right then. Sometimes being single and self-sufficient sucked.

The sound of my mobile ringing woke me up, and I peeled my face off the pillow and swiped to answer it.

'Hello,' I mewled.

'Charlie? Are you ok?'

'Pizzaman?' I mumbled, not sure if I was hearing things.

'Yes, it's me. I'm sorry, I know I shouldn't be ringing you, client confidentiality and all, but I'm calling while I'm at work, so technically I haven't stolen your private number. It's just it's Friday night, and you always have pizza on a Friday night, and I'm about to clock off.'

'I do?' I asked, flopping back down onto the pillow as I held the phone to the side of my face that didn't look like I'd been in a boxing ring and lost. Did I really order pizza every Friday? So much for my healthy eating plan, I was obviously failing miserably.

'Yes,' he chuckled.

'*Every* Friday?' I asked, still not convinced.

'Except the last Friday of the month, and sometimes on a Wednesday too. I was worried as you haven't placed your order. I thought I'd better check if you wanted one before I left.'

'That's so nice of you, but I can't eat. *Ever again*,' I moaned dramatically. 'I've been mouth-butchered by Mr. Wanky and the tongue sucker.'

'You've what?' he exclaimed.

'It's a long story involving a brutal dentist and his sidekick. I can barely open my mouth it's so swollen. I'm in agony and I feel awful.'

'Who's looking after you?' he asked, sounding adorably concerned.

'No one. Unless you count Mrs. Tibbles, who pops her head in to moan at me from time to time. I'm starving, but I can't even chew. I tried a cookie earlier, but I can't fit it through the gap in my lips. My jaw's too sore to open any wider.'

'You can't not eat, Charlie. Can't your friends come and cook something for you?'

'Abbie's in New York, Georgie's on a date with Weston, and I don't want to bother Daphne. I'll be fine. They'll find my shrivelled body in a week or two, if Tibbs hasn't eaten the evidence.'

'Always with a sense of humour,' he chuckled.

'Laugh or cry, and I'm very close to crying right now,' I admitted, my bottom lip trembling. 'Thanks for checking on me, Kitt. That was really sweet of you. I'll be ordering my usual as soon as I gain function of my face again.'

'Ok, well ... just take care, Charlie. I hope you're feeling better soon.'

'Me too,' I huffed.

We ended the call and I pulled the duvet back over my head, trying to ignore the throbbing jaw ache and the grumbling of my ravenous stomach. Instead I willed myself to dream of a sexy Dr. Fitton tending to me, wearing just a pair of tightly fitted boxers.

'Who the hell is that?' I grumbled, as a loud knock at the door disturbed the rather vivid fantasy I was playing out in my head. 'Tibbs!' I scolded as she batted my nose a little too forcefully when my face appeared from under the duvet and I found her sitting on my pillow, waiting for me.

I grabbed a t-shirt and pulled it on as I stumbled over to the bedroom door. If it was sales people, they were about to get a mouthful. The knocking continued as I gingerly made my way downstairs and cracked open the front door and peeked out.

'Kitt?' I blinked at him a few times, totally confused. 'Am I delirious? Did I order a pizza without knowing it?'

'No, no pizza. I didn't like the idea of you being alone and hungry. I wanted to make sure you were ok. Can I come in?'

'I … I guess, but I'm a state,' I warned him, grimacing when I took a quick look at myself in the hall mirror. My hair was sticking on end and matted from tossing around trying to get comfortable in bed, and I still had dried blood on my face, which was so swollen and bruised.

'Jesus,' he gasped as I pulled the door open.

'I warned you.' I tried to smile, but winced and gently palmed my cheek.

'Well, if you're ok to have some company for a while, I brought you painkillers and some chicken soup.' He waved a bag at me as he stood on the doorstep, and I felt my eyes fill up with tears, totally touched at his thoughtfulness.

'That's so sweet of you,' I said quietly as I waved him in, suddenly acutely aware that I was naked under a fairly short t-shirt. 'I'd better go and get changed.'

'No objections on my part if you don't,' he teased with a wink. He stepped in and immediately toed off his army boots. 'How about I go and heat up some soup for you while you get changed?'

'But … you're already late,' I warned as I checked my watch. 'What about your mum?'

'I asked Vicky to stay on with her a bit longer so I could come check in on you. I had a feeling if I didn't, you'd starve to death or die of dehydration from crying yourself to sleep.'

'Kitt, you didn't need to do that.'

'That's what friends do, right? And you said we were friends now,' he reminded me, wincing as he took in my face properly. 'Do you have any peas in the freezer?'

'I think I might. Everyone has an old pack of peas in the freezer, don't they? So, you're going to cook me soup with a side serving of them?'

'No,' he laughed with a shake of his head. 'The peas are to try and help reduce the swelling. Go on, go and get changed and I'll rummage for a saucepan and stuff in your kitchen, if that's ok?'

'Sure, thank you.' I gave his arm a grateful squeeze.

I left him in my kitchen and headed back up to pull on some knickers and a pair of my comfy sweatpants. I brushed my hair and then wrapped a cardigan around myself as I shivered, belting it tightly. I could hear him rummaging around downstairs, humming to himself. It was weird to hear anyone using my kitchen, let alone a man. By the time I'd made

80

it down, he'd already laid out a tray with a bowl and spoon and a glass of water.

'Come here,' he ordered, beckoning me over to the sink. I did as I was told, too tired and grumpy to even ask why. As I reached him, he gently moved my hair away from the carnage that was my face and swept some damp, but warm, kitchen towel across it. I winced and he grimaced as he held my chin with his other hand and carried on wiping. 'Sorry, just trying to clean up this dried blood. The dentist seriously did this to you? You look awful.'

'Thanks.'

'You know what I meant. You look better already with that mess off your face, except you look pale and tired. Here, I put some painkillers next to the water. Why don't you take those and go and sit in your lounge while I heat up your soup.'

'Thank you,' I whispered gratefully, doing as I was told. It had been a long time since I'd felt so rough, even longer since someone had taken care of me. It was a nice feeling not to have to fend for myself for once. Mrs. Tibbles stayed to supervise the newcomer in her kitchen while I went and turned up the heating. I curled up in the corner of the sofa, hugging a cushion to my stomach to comfort myself.

'Here you are,' Kitt smiled as he came through carrying the tray, the smell of the chicken soup making my stomach growl loudly. I was starving, I hadn't eaten anything all day. He chuckled and handed the tray over. 'Careful, it's hot.'

'Help yourself to a drink,' I offered, balancing the tray on the cushion on my lap. 'There's tea or coffee in the canisters by the kettle, or water, soda, or beer in the fridge.'

'I wouldn't mind a coffee, if that's ok?'

'Of course it is, the least I can do after you came and cooked for me.' I blew on my soup to cool it down.

'Hardly cooking, opening a tin and heating it up,' he laughed. 'But thanks.'

He returned a while later with his drink, as I slowly took tiny mouthfuls of the delicious soup, keeping the hot liquid on the opposite side of my battered face and gum.

'Good?' he asked as he sat next to me.

'Mmmm,' I nodded.

'Well, I put another couple of tins in your cupboard. After what you said on the phone, I figured you might not feel like chewing for a few days.'

'Thank you, I'll sort you some money before you go. Talk to me, as I'm not really up for conversation. Tell me how things are going at work and at home,' I suggested as I continued to slurp in a most unladylike fashion.

It was soothing to hear his melodious voice as he filled me in on his week so far. Even Tibbs, who usually treated visitors to her home with disdain, came strutting in to join us. In an uncharacteristic display of friendliness towards a stranger, she jumped onto Kitt's lap and kneaded him, purring as he stroked her with one hand, his other stretched behind me on the back of the sofa while he told me more about his mum.

I set my tray down on the coffee table when I was done and tucked my legs up under me as I sat sideways on the sofa to look at him as he talked. He spoke about his mum with obvious warmth and love in his tone. There was no hint that he begrudged how much she impacted on his life, no sense of anger at how everything revolved around her while his needs were put to one side. He really was incredible. I did my best to listen, but the painkillers were kicking in and with a bellyful of nice hot soup and his soft tone lulling me, I felt myself starting to get drowsy.

A loud snort startled me and I suddenly jerked, snapping my eyes open as I realised that awful noise had been me.

'Oh God, I'm so sorry, Kitt,' I gasped as I quickly bolted upright. It was bad enough I'd just nodded off when he was talking to me, but I'd slid forwards and had been nestled under his arm with my head on his chest. I quickly reached out to try and wipe an unattractive streak of drool from his t-shirt, completely mortified, but he just laughed.

'Come on, it's time I left and you went to bed. I'm so boring, you fell asleep on me,' he chuckled as he bravely scooped up Tibbs from his lap, stood up, and set her down in the warm spot he'd vacated on the sofa.

'I'm sorry. You're not boring, not at all. You know I love talking to you, but I'm so exhausted. I haven't slept well for days,' I said, stifling a yawn, partly not wanting to embarrass him, but partly terrified of hurting my face. 'I've drooled on your t-shirt too.'

'That's ok, it will come out in the wash. Besides, it's not like I wear my best clothes to work anyway.'

'All the same, it's really rude of me when you went to the trouble of coming over to take care of me. I really appreciate it.' My legs gave out on me as I stood. I was actually beyond exhausted. I had a feeling I could sleep for days.

'Ok, you're not climbing the stairs like that,' he scolded with a frown. Before I could protest, he'd swept my feet off the floor and lifted me up into his arms. 'Tell me where I'm going,' he ordered as he strode out of the lounge and made a start upstairs.

'First door on the left,' I squeaked, not sure if I was embarrassed or on the verge of swooning to have a man handle me like that. No one had ever swooped me up like that, the way I'd written about so often. It was so … manly and hot! And he made it seem so effortless, even with my curves. 'Aren't I heavy?'

'Light as a feather,' he grinned down at me. 'I'm going to get you into bed, then sort your face out.'

'Oh hello, that sounded a bit rude.'

'Charlie,' he laughed as he shook his head. 'Always with the humour and double entendres. I meant I'm going to look for something cold to hold on your cheek for a while, then I'll leave you to have a good night's sleep.'

I gave him a half-smile, making sure not to move the bad side of my face. He was making me hungry again. I could smell pizza on him, as well as that scent of the ocean he always seemed to wear. I studied his deep green eyes. They reminded me of Dr. Fitton's, except Kitt's didn't have gold flecks. They were a really deep green that resembled the luminescent sheen of pure emeralds. As he carried me through my bedroom towards my unmade rumpled bed, I decided that he had really kind eyes. He *was* kind. How many guys would have come to look after me like this without expecting something in return? Why oh why couldn't I feel that chemistry I so often wrote about with Kitt? He gently set me down on the bed with a promise to return, then strode out. I waited until I heard him jog down the stairs before I pulled off my sweatpants and cardigan and lay down, pulling the duvet up to my chin as I stifled another yawn.

I was already falling asleep when he came in carrying a tray. He set a glass of water on the bedside table with some more pills, which he told me to take as soon as I woke up, then handed me a hot water bottle to cuddle. He sat on the edge of the bed and gently placed a sandwich bag full of frozen peas on my swollen cheek.

'There, how does that feel?'

'Really nice,' I mumbled.

'Are you going to be ok on your own? If you don't mind me using your number, I can ring you in the morning to see how you are.'

'I'll be fine now, and it would be nice to hear from you tomorrow, you know, just in case Mrs. Tibbles is chewing on my flesh as she didn't get her fresh diced chicken dinner.'

'She has expensive tastes,' he grinned, running a hand over my hair, over and over, making me even sleepier. It was so nice to have someone look after me.

'Hmmm,' I agreed, fighting my eyes closing.

'I'm going to leave you now. You have my number in your recent calls, so call me if you need me, it doesn't matter what time, ok?'

'You're so nice, Kitt. I'm so lucky to have a friend like you,' I mumbled.

'Sweet dreams, Charlie,' he whispered, planting a soft kiss on my forehead.

'Hmmm,' I agreed, pretty sure I was going to as I gave in and let my eyes close.

The Next Day – Saturday

I spent the day pottering around and snoozing, too tired and sore to do anything else. I looked like I'd been in a horrific accident. I managed to have some soggy cereal for breakfast, and heated up more chicken soup for lunch without incident. I'd finally had Heath over a few weeks ago to put in a new glass hob for me, that glowed bright red to tell me which one was on. I still had areas where the ridges of my fingertips were missing from when I'd burnt them, which could be handy if I ever decided to kill off Mrs. Vickers, as the police wouldn't be able to trace me without fingerprints.

I decided to light a fire and snuggle down on the sofa for the night to watch some movies. I had one can of chicken soup left to have for dinner, with two slices of bread that I could soak in it, then I was going to have to venture out to do some shopping tomorrow. Not least for Mrs. Tibbles, who was most unimpressed not to have had her weekend treats and be relegated to cheap, shop-bought cat food pouches.

At least she was happy that she could come and go when she wanted, as Heath had also put a cat flap in the utility door, which worked off Tibbs' microchip. It did confuse her, though, when I locked it overnight to make sure she wasn't out in the dark. She persisted in bashing her head against it for a good five minutes to test whether it would magically open like it normally did. She seemed to have a heightened instinct for hunting prey at dawn and dusk, so that was one good reason to keep her in. I'd soon spotted a pattern in the amount of mice and other furry critters I'd had to chase around the house to rescue and set free again once the sun was going down or rising. It wasn't like she brought me headless prey. She carried them in alive and dropped them at my feet with a "look at the lovely gift I've brought you, human" look on her face. I really hadn't fancied waking up to find various woodland animals on the pillow next to my face, so the cat flap was locked, much to her chagrin.

I scooped up my phone when I heard it ping to find I had a text from an unknown number.

Hi Charlie, it's Kitt. How are you feeling today? I've booked Vicky to come an hour earlier so I can pop by on my way to work to check in on you, if that's ok? Please say if you're not up for company, or if I'm crowding you.

I smiled to myself as I read his message. How could he think he was crowding me? Next to Daphne, Abbie, and Georgie, he was my closest friend since I'd moved here.

It would be lovely to see you. I'll put the kettle on. And don't worry, I know not to touch that to check it's boiled!

You know I was worried for a moment, he replied with a winking face emoji. *See you in a while.*

I debated going upstairs to get changed and put a bit of makeup on to make myself look more presentable, but decided against it. It was only Kitt. He was used to seeing me in my sweats and a t-shirt, bare faced. Now, if Dr. Fitton was on his way, that would be a whole other ball game. I'd have been dashing upstairs to slip into some sexy lingerie under my red silk robe and doing my face and hair. I sighed as I thought of him. My crush hadn't faded at all. If anything, it had only grown. The less I saw of him, the more I wanted him.

'Hey,' I greeted when I answered the door to Kitt a while later.

'Hey,' he smiled back, then winced as he saw the state of my face. 'You look worse than yesterday, if that's even possible.'

'I know,' I agreed, gesturing for him to come inside. 'And I have serious tongue ache, too.'

'Do I want to know why?' he asked, setting down a carrier bag which clunked heavily on the oak floor as he toed off his boots.

'I can't stop poking at the hole where my tooth was,' I huffed, pushing the door shut behind him. 'It's like a sickness. The more I poke, the more my tongue aches and there's this nasty-tasting stuff in there and the stitches are hanging down too, but I just can't seem to stop myself.'

'You don't want to get an infection, Charlie,' he warned, shooting me a concerned look.

'I know. Maybe I need a tongue clamp to keep it in place, stop it wandering where it shouldn't.'

'Maybe,' he laughed. I gasped as Tibbs shot out of the lounge and dove head first into Kitt's bag.

'Mrs. Tibbles,' I scolded, bending down to scoop her up, which prompted a growl as she tried to get out of my grasp. 'What on earth do you think you're doing?'

'Do you always talk to the cat?'

'Bet you think I'm crazy, huh?'

'I would if you said she answered you. She can probably smell the chicken I cooked for her,' Kitt shrugged, scooping the bag up off the floor.

'The what you what?' I blinked at him a few times in surprise.

'You said she was grumpy that the shop was out of chicken, so I picked up a couple of extra breasts when I did the shopping yesterday. I was cooking chicken for me and Mum at lunchtime, so I did two breasts for Mrs. T and diced them up for her. There's also more soup in the bag for you, a variety of tins so you don't get bored of chicken, a loaf of soft white bread, some tins of custard too, and another pack of painkillers in case you run out. Tell me if you need anything else and I can call at the shop tomorrow and bring it over on my way to work again.' He gave me a smile as he ran a hand through his hair.

'I can't believe you went to so much trouble, Kitt.' I gave his arm a gentle squeeze and felt his muscle flex under my grip.

'It was no trouble, I was shopping anyway. How about we feed Mrs. T before she claws you trying to get out of your arms?' he suggested. 'Then, if you haven't eaten, I can do you something before I go?'

'I can heat soup, you know. I'm not quite that bad,' I laughed as I set Tibbs down and headed into the kitchen, both of them hot on my heels.

'I'm more worried about you carving the loaf of bread I got you. I don't fancy having to put your fingertips on ice while I dash you to hospital, or worse, having to take the cat to extract them from her stomach first.'

'Oh God, can you imagine?' I grimaced. He grinned at me as he set the bag on the kitchen counter.

'Dr. Fitton might really think you were crazy then.'

'He doesn't need any encouragement.'

'No sightings of the good doctor lately?'

'No,' I sighed as Kitt started emptying the bag of goodies. 'I've even been loitering around the hospital, taking the OAPs on their appointments in the hope of seeing him, but no such luck. Unless I'm admitted to A&E again, the chances of bumping into him are minimal.'

'If you like him that much, just turn up and ask to see him, then ask him on a date,' Kitt suggested as he opened a Tupperware container to reveal a load of juicy chunks of chicken.

'I can't do that. I might come across as a super confident and sexy woman, but inside I'm still just a scared girl who thinks the guy she likes won't feel the same about her. Besides, I need to grow on him more.' Tibbs stretched up to paw at the kitchen counter, her little nose twitching as she got a whiff of her favourite treat.

'If you need to grow on a guy, I'd say he isn't the right guy for you, Charlie,' Kitt scoffed as Mrs. Tibbles let out a number of pitiful meows.

'Anyone would think I starve her. Honestly, have you ever seen such a fat cat?' I asked him as he leaned against the sink with a serious look on his face. He just didn't get it. A woman like me might flirt and make it known she was interested, but she didn't throw herself at a man. He had to come to her. Besides, no man meeting me under the circumstances Dr. Fitton had each time was going to be in a rush to ask me out.

'She's not fat, she's big boned, sexily curvaceous,' he replied.

'Oh, nicely done. Who trained you in the art of diplomacy with women?' I teased, as I scooped half of the chicken into her clean bowl.

'Mum,' he replied with a quick smile at me. 'She made sure to hammer home manners and respect from an early age.'

'I would love to have met her when she was with it.' I set Tibbs bowl on the floor and smiled as she started to wolf it down, her tail quivering with excitement. 'I'd have told her what an amazing job she did, as you've turned out to be quite the man.'

'Thanks, Charlie,' he said wistfully. 'I'd love for her to have met you, too. She'd have really liked you. Actually, I take that back, I wouldn't have introduced you, as she'd have been nagging me incessantly, wanting to know why I hadn't snapped you up.'

'What is it with parents?' I laughed, shaking my head. 'They don't get that men and women can just be friends, do they? I told my mum about you and she asked when I was going to bring you down to meet them. She said you sounded too good to be true.'

'No one's perfect, Charlie,' he scoffed.

'So, tell me what flaws you have, as so far I don't seem to have seen any.' I leaned against the kitchen worktop as I studied his deep-set frown while he considered his response.

'I'm too soft,' he shrugged. 'I let people walk all over me and I don't stand up for what I want.'

'Why?'

'I guess it doesn't help that I didn't have a dad when I was growing up. Mum taught me to be respectful of others, to be empathetic, and I just never learned to be selfish and put my needs first.'

'It's not selfish to do or go for what you want, Kitt,' I said softly. 'As long as you don't hurt other people in the process, why should you put your needs on hold? You're as entitled to live a happy and meaningful life as anyone else.'

'If I do that, Mum suffers. I can't do what I want, be the man that I want to be, unless I'm neglecting her.'

'Then start by making small steps. Try and have a bit more time to yourself, hang out with friends and have fun once a week.'

'You make it sound easy,' he scoffed, avoiding eye contact as he crouched to give Mrs. Tibbles some affection as she washed her paws and whiskers, no trace of chicken left in her bowl.

'I'm sure it's not,' I agreed. 'Is money so tight that you can't have one night a week off to go and enjoy time with your buddies?'

'No. I just … never mind.' He shook his head as he sighed.

'You just what?' I pushed.

'I don't really have any friends, not here anyway. You're probably the closest thing I have to one,' he admitted. His eyes shot up to meet mine, his cheeks slightly flushed with embarrassment. 'I had to pack up my life in Newcastle to move here, and since then, I've been so busy looking after Mum that I haven't had time to get out and meet people outside of work.'

'Kitt,' I whispered, my heart aching for the responsibility he'd taken on his shoulders, to his own detriment. 'That's no life at all.'

'It is what it is. I don't want to regret not having spent time with her when it's too late. Anyway, I came over to cheer you up, not the other way around. I'd better cut the bread for you and get going or I'll be late.'

'You haven't even had a drink. How about a quick coffee before you go, you look tired,' I observed, as he stood up and ran a hand over his forehead. His green eyes didn't have their usual sparkle and there were signs of dark shadows gathering under them.

'I'll be fine, thanks for the offer though.' He offered me a tight-lipped smile, as if he was straining with the effort of holding in so much more that he wanted to say.

I handed him the bread knife and busied myself putting away the tins he'd kindly brought over, saving a can of mushroom soup to heat up for my dinner. I walked him to the door when he was done and ignored his protests as I slipped him some notes. He stepped outside and bent down to pick something up from the ground, out of sight from where I was standing, but I could hear a crinkle of what sounded like a plastic bag.

'Kitt,' I gasped, as he straightened up and produced a cellophane-encased bouquet of brightly coloured gerberas.

'I thought these might cheer you up,' he said as he handed them over. I took a long, slow inhalation of the blooms. 'They're Mum's favourites and they always make her smile.'

'That's so thoughtful of you, and you always cheer me up. Thanks for being such a great friend.' I took him by surprise with a quick kiss to the cheek, that made his face blush adorably pink.

'Anytime. You know my number if you need anything. Hope you're back on pizza chewing form soon, our takings are going to drop dramatically. You might put us out of business.'

'I swear pizza is the best medicine. It's a total cure all, to make you feel better when you're ill, cheer you up when you're sad, or keep the momentum going when you're on a high. But seriously, do I order *that* often?' I giggled with a shake of my head.

'Let's just say you're up there as one of our best customers,' he called over his shoulder as he made his way up the path.

'Then I hope I can put my mouth back to use soon,' I hollered. 'Ok, that totally didn't sound as I intended,' I cringed as Kitt laughed and I spotted Georgie heading up her path with an astonished look on her face.

Chapter Eight

Girls' Night
One Month Later – A Friday Night in July

'DO I HAVE TO come?' I whined, digging my heels in as Georgie dragged me up my path.

'Yes. You've been closeted away writing for too long, we haven't seen you for ages.'

'But it's karaoke. *Karaoke.* I don't sing.'

'Rubbish, you're one of the most artistic people I've ever met.'

'I write. I don't sing or draw.'

'Well, maybe you should. I mean honestly, you came to Dilbury to change your life. It's been seven months and the only thing that's changed is your location. You still order takeaways, you haven't learned to cook, you don't have a man in your life, and despite you somehow still having an amazing figure with all of the rubbish you eat, you haven't started exercising like you were planning to.' She hustled me out of the gate into the lane and gave me a wilting stare.

'If only I had a friend who was dating a personal trainer,' I said with a hint of sarcasm.

'I barely see anything of Weston as it is. Find your own man to whip you into shape and prevent a pizza-related heart attack.'

'I've found him, he just doesn't seem to have realised that he's found me.'

'Then he's an idiot and you need to set your sights on someone else,' she said firmly as she linked arms with me and we made our way up the lane, me begrudgingly.

'There is no one else. My sights are set. The heart wants what the heart wants and it can't be dissuaded,' I sighed as I thought of McFitty. It had been too long since I'd last seen him. I was getting withdrawal symptoms.

'Well, until he sees the error of his ways and sweeps you off your feet, you're going to have a night of fun with me and Daphne, before your very first experience of the magic that is Dilbury fête.'

'Daphne does karaoke?' I spluttered.

'Oh, Charlie, you have so much to learn when it comes to Daphne Jones. There's nothing she isn't up for. Mr. Bentley picked her up in his car earlier, they were having a quick drink and bite to eat at The Cock first.'

'What about Abbie?' I asked as we passed her cottage and Georgie showed no signs of stopping to knock on her door.

'Not even a house fire would make Abbie leave her kitchen the night before the fête,' Georgie scoffed. 'She's going for an eighth year as winner in three categories against Lady Kirkland.'

'Then shouldn't we be helping her?' I suggested, hoping for a karaoke reprieve. Georgie gave me an incredulous look. 'Not with the cooking, everyone knows it's not my forte. But I can open packets, measure stuff, sample the merchandise.'

'And we're back to you trying to avoid piling on the pounds. Trust me, one minute in Abbie's kitchen, full of the delicious aroma of her sugary baking, and you'd be shovelling in the cookie dough batter so fast your jeans would split and you'd be back to needing to find your own personal trainer. Besides, I've learned the hard way, she's best left to her own devices.'

'She gets a bit tetchy, huh?'

'Tetchy? Tetchy is about seven levels down from what Abbie gets. I even warned Miller he was best staying in New York this weekend. She's terrifying when she's ranting at the oven.'

'I'm so glad they're back together.'

'Me too,' Georgie agreed with a smile. 'So that's three of us out of the four on our lane sorted with a love life, just you to go. We need to come up with a karaoke-related injury that requires you to get urgent medical attention.'

'You could smack me in the face with the microphone?' I suggested.

We made our way up to the village hall, laughing at accident-related song suggestions. The car park was already nearly full, the sound of laughter and chatter drifting out through the open doors and windows. It was a balmy summer's evening, the type of night you'd imagine everyone would be having friends over for a barbeque. The whole village wasn't coming for the quarterly karaoke night, as I'd definitely caught a whiff of burning burgers in the air as we'd made our way here. Georgie insisted on treating me to the entrance fee and first drink from the bar, then we headed into the main hall.

'Cooee, girls, over here,' Daphne called, waving us over to join her at one of the small round bistro tables that had been dotted around the room.

'Don't you want to save these seats for your friends?' I asked as we reached her.

'I am, the two of you. Sit, sit, or I'll be stuck with the boring old farts who are on their way over.'

I shook my head and laughed as she beamed at us when we sat down with her. 'No Mr. Bentley tonight?'

'We had an early dinner and a few drinks. He knows karaoke night is my time with the girls. He's having a few of his friends over for poker.'

'I bet he'll be over to poke her later,' I whisper-giggled to Georgie, then moaned as Daphne cuffed the back of my head. 'Seriously, you have the best hearing of anyone I know, let alone a … however-old-you-are person.'

'I have an excellent hearing aid, and they say you're only as young as the man you feel, and Mr. Bentley's a good few years younger than me.'

'It's the woman you feel,' Georgie giggled.

'Well, in my case, it's the man. And he's all man before you and your smutty mind enquire, Charlie Faulkner.'

'Who said I was going to say anything?' I objected, leaning in to kiss her cheek.

'Well, you obviously need a few more sex tips. I'm getting impatient waiting for this new book of yours.'

'Trust me, much as I love the fact that you're still having sex, I don't want to be hearing about it. I can come up with scenarios all on my own. And I'd probably have finished this book tonight if I hadn't been dragged here against my will.' I shot a look at Georgie, who pulled a face and quickly sipped on her vodka cranberry.

'All work and no play makes Jack a dull boy,' Daphne said.

'From what I hear, Jack's a *very* happy boy,' I tittered, making Georgie splutter her drink and Daphne cuff me again with a giggle of her own.

'Enough with the teasing, I could teach you youngsters a trick or two. Now, do I need to risk more wear and tear of my hip hobbling over to the bar, or is someone going to fetch me another double whiskey?' she asked as she opened her wallet.

'Put it away,' I told her, covering her hand with mine. 'It's on me. Georgie?'

'I've barely started this one.'

'Well, I may as well grab another while I'm at the bar, as it looks like the night is about to start. Double for you?'

'Go on then, twist my arm, but then it's soft drinks. I've got to be up at silly o'clock to go and help Abbie cart everything over to the fête.'

'I'll come and help too, I'm looking forward to my first Dilbury fête. Right, double whiskey and double vodka cranberry coming up.'

Two hours later and even I had to admit I was having fun. I'd decided to stick to cranberry juice without the vodka, Georgie too, neither of us wanting a hangover. Plus Daphne was completely wasted and it was going to require both of us to be sober to somehow manhandle her home. She was currently perched on a stool, gripping the microphone stand as she chair danced, belting out Cyndi Lauper's *Girls Just Want To Have Fun,* as I pondered that she couldn't have chosen a more fitting song. When she started on a Missy Elliot track, I watched in complete astonishment. She wasn't even looking at the monitor as she rapped, she knew the words.

'No dancing,' I hollered, as she tried to get up off her seat.

'Oh my God, she's seriously going to break a hip,' Georgie gasped as Daphne made it to her feet and started to shake her rump amidst a load of applause and hollering.

'Someone needs to tell her it's called hip-hop, not hip-pop,' I laughed. 'She really is about to dislocate it.'

'I think we need to get her home, now.'

We both raced over and cut her off in her prime, flanking her as we held her up and started to make our way across the floor, with her berating us for ruining her big finale. After assuring Mr. Greggs, the village hall caretaker, that we weren't likely to be arrested for taking his little Kawasaki Mule out onto the main road for all of about two hundred yards, he agreed to help us load Daphne into the flat cargo area at the back to save us calling Andy the cabbie out. I climbed up into the back to make sure Daphne didn't try and make a bid for freedom, while Georgie hopped up into the passenger seat. Mr. Greggs took his place in pole position, his cheeks showing signs of an embarrassed blush due to some slightly colourful and tipsy language coming from Daphne. He started the engine and ordered us to hold tight as he made his way over the bumpy car park, Daphne in fits of giggles as she lay watching the stars up above us.

'Honestly, if I come to this event again, I'm limiting your drinks, young lady,' I warned her as she whooped when Mr. Greggs made it onto the main road and put his foot down, looking as if he was committing a cardinal sin. I half expected him to do the sign of a cross on his chest.

'Then I'd just smuggle in my own again,' she hooted.

'You little minx,' I laughed, snatching her handbag up to find an empty flask in there, which smelled suspiciously like whiskey. 'I knew you were too drunk for the amount of shorts we'd got for you.'

'Girls just wanna have fun,' she yelled, waving her hands in the air.

'I'm going to be arrested for disturbing the peace,' groaned Mr. Greggs as he hooked a right to head down Church Lane, running his hand over his head as Georgie giggled.

'You know what they say about bald men?' Daphne shouted.

'Do we want to?' I asked, cringing on Mr. Greggs' behalf for whatever was about to come out of her mouth.

'Their head's a solar panel for a sex machine,' she chortled. I burst out laughing and Georgie buried her face in her hands as Mr. Greggs' face went even pinker.

'Well, you won't be testing out that claim, or we'll have Mr. Bentley threatening him with a dual at dawn. We're getting you to bed to sleep this off. Alone.'

'You're no fun tonight,' Daphne huffed, grabbing her chest as Mr. Greggs turned right to head down our bumpy lane. I quickly did the same, not wanting to risk a couple of black eyes.

'You've had plenty of fun for one night. Besides, if we weren't enough fun, you'd be hanging out with people your own age.'

'Never got why she hangs out with you youngsters,' Mr. Greggs tutted with a disapproving shake of his head.

'They remind me of my daughter. I miss her, so much,' Daphne sighed, her eyes glistening as a shaft of silvery moonlight reflected off them.

'Now I know how drunk you are,' Georgie called over her shoulder. 'I'm no fan of Roger, but last time I checked, he was still a son and not a daughter.'

'Not ... *Roger*. Evelyn. My *beautiful* Evelyn.'

'You don't have a daughter called Evelyn, Daphne,' I said gently, reaching for her hand as her bottom lip started to wobble.

'Not ... not anymore. She died in childbirth. I remember it like it was yesterday. I miss her terribly,' Daphne sniffed, some tears trickling from her eyes to meander down the wrinkles on her face. I shot a look at Georgie, who pulled a face and shook her head. Obviously this was news to her as well.

'I'm so sorry to hear that,' I said as I squeezed her hand in mine. 'You've never mentioned her before, Daphne.'

'I'm not allowed to. *Sssshhhh*, I'm not supposed to talk about it. Don't you go telling anyone, promise me? Promise me you won't say anything to anyone?' she begged, her face quickly changing to one of fear as she held my gaze.

'Of course we won't, but you know that you can talk to us about it whenever you want, right?' I said, wondering why on earth she couldn't discuss it. If she'd buried it as a way of not upsetting her husband, then surely she could talk freely about it now that David had died.

'No talking about it. Forget I said anything, please?' she pleaded as Mr. Greggs pulled onto her drive.

'Ok,' I nodded as I bent over to kiss her cheek, feeling puzzled. 'Your secret's safe with us.' I looked at Georgie again, to find her frowning, as confused as I was at this revelation.

Mr. Greggs pulled down the guard at the back of his utility vehicle and I hopped out, and the three of us stood looking at Daphne lying there, trying to work out the most dignified way of getting her out.

'I think I'll have to use the tilt hydraulics to lift the top end of the cargo bed,' he said. 'It will tip up and she'll slide out. You'll need to catch her, stop her landing on the ground.'

'How about you show Georgie what to do and you and I catch Daphne? We might need a bit of muscle.'

'Mr. Bentley has plenty of muscle,' Daphne giggled, the giggle turning into an unexpected cackle, which was quickly followed by a round of uncontrollable laughter. Well, she was definitely drunk, to go from laughter to almost tears and back to laughter in the space of a minute.

'Did you know she had a daughter?' Georgie asked him quietly.

'Whole village did, lovely girl she was, pretty as a picture. There was some talk about the scandal, as she was pregnant and unmarried, but we never found out who the father was. After she died, Daphne and David said it was easier to deal with if they weren't reminded of her, so folk stopped bringing her up. Truth be told, it's the first time I've heard mention of her for over thirty years.'

'How sad,' I said, swallowing a ball of emotion as I looked at Daphne, who was laughing away to herself as she gazed up at the sky. Maybe *that* was why she loved hanging out with us, it really did remind her of her relationship with Evelyn. 'What happened to the baby? Did it die, too?'

'No one knows or dared to ask,' Mr. Greggs replied. 'She was so upset about Evelyn that no one talked about it, just how she wanted it.'

'She doesn't even have any pictures of her up in her house,' Georgie said, shaking her head.

'Different people cope with grief in different ways,' I shrugged. 'Who are we to say what's right or wrong. Come on, let's get her into her bed. We might need your help with that as well, Mr. Greggs.'

'Good God, the missus will kill me if she hears I've been out gallivanting with two young women, let alone been inside Daphne Jones' bedroom,' he groaned, shaking his head.

'Well, if you don't mention what you heard here tonight, we won't say anything either,' Georgie reassured him. 'Come on, show me what button I need to press.'

I couldn't stop giggling as Mr. Greggs and I crouched like baseball catchers, waiting for the mule to tip up enough to slide a hysterical Daphne out.

'Woohoo, I'm flying,' she shouted as her head started to lift, the truck shuddering and making a groaning noise as the hydraulics worked their magic.

'Hold on to your skirt,' I warned her, hoping she wasn't so progressive that she'd ventured out with no knickers on, as Mr. Greggs was about to get a flash of octogenarian beaver if that was the case.

'I'm closing my eyes,' he said quickly.

'No, you're not. You won't see her to catch her and she could break something,' I warned him. 'Daphne, hold your skirt, you're about to shoot feet first out of the truck.'

'I'm holding my handbag.'

'Forget the bag, hold your skirt, please. I won't tell you again.'

'Oooh, bossy Charlie's come out to play. I bet you're a secret dominatrix, aren't you?' she said, completely ignoring my advice.

'I'm thinking that covering my ears might be a better move,' Mr. Greggs grunted, seconds before Daphne whooped with joy as she shot down the flatbed, her skirt gathering up around her waist. I'd never been so happy to see such an unsexy pair of large, matronly, flesh-coloured knickers, as we launched ourselves forwards to stop her from hurtling to the ground.

'Told you, Charlie. Never a dull moment in Dilbury,' Georgie laughed as we struggled to get Daphne into an upright position and manoeuvre her towards her gate. 'I think I'd better sleep over here tonight and keep an eye on her.'

'I think that might be best,' I agreed, as Mr. Greggs yelped when Daphne's free hand found its way to his bottom and gave it a squeeze.

The Next Day – Fête Day

'Abbie, seriously, I think we need to call the first aiders over,' I gasped. She'd been farting all morning, except farting was a polite way of describing the noises she'd been emitting, along with some blue language. It had been funny to start with, but seeing her doubled up in pain was starting to worry me.

'It … will … pass,' she whimpered, letting out another series of horrendous noises. Passing definitely didn't seem to be the problem. She'd expelled more gas than an active volcano this morning.

'Sing,' Daphne said firmly to Georgie.

'How's that going to help her?' she exclaimed.

'I'm telling you to sing, not Abbie. We can't serve people food while she's playing a symphony of trumps in the background. You have a lovely voice, Georgie, drown her out.'

'Talk about putting me on the spot,' Georgie complained.

'Yes, come on Georgie, sing,' I urged as Abbie fell to the floor, trying to drown out the noises escaping her bottom with a series of curses.

'Yes, Georgie, come on, sing for us.'

I turned around, wondering who the deep and sexy voice belonged to, and bounced my eyes between the good-looking guy and Georgie, who looked completely stunned.

'Weston? What are you … I had no idea you'd be coming today,' she uttered. So this was Weston. Wow, the girls sure had great taste in men.

'I thought I'd surprise you, but by the noises coming from the tent, it sounds like I picked a bad time.'

'Georgie, for goodness sake, sing,' Daphne repeated. 'Drown her out.'

'Oh my God,' I giggled, hastily covering my ears. The sounds coming from behind us were horrific, and everyone in the queue was starting to take notice. I soon had to drop my hands to clutch my sides as I roared with laughter when Daphne leapt to her feet and started singing Kelis's *Milkshake,* complete with some hilarious dance moves and pelvic thrusts that I'd had the pleasure of witnessing for the first time the previous night. Georgie just watched, dumbfounded, and the same look appeared on her boyfriend's face, his mouth ajar.

'Help me,' Abbie mewled from behind us.

'Charlie, you serve while Daphne entertains. Weston, go and grab a beer and I'll be with you in a while. Abbie needs me.'

'Can I do anything?' Weston asked, while I reluctantly moved behind the table, closer to the danger zone. Sugar-free gummi bears may be sweet going in, but they didn't smell sweet coming out.

'Honestly, that's really sweet and I'm sure you could with your skill set,' Georgie replied, 'but this is kind of a sensitive deal and I think it would embarrass Abbie if you came back here.'

'I won't be far. You call me if you need me, no matter what, ok?' Weston ordered.

'Clear,' Georgie nodded.

'Wow, hot and bossy, I like him already,' I murmured.

'Find your own, he's taken,' Georgie grinned, quickly turning her attention to Abbie as I waved the next customer forwards and shot Daphne an amazed look as she launched into Missy Elliot's *Get Ur Freak On*. Who on earth had given her such eclectic music taste?

'That's five pounds please, Mr. Spalding,' I said as I bagged up his jam and cookies.

'What on earth is going on back there?' he asked.

'Abbie's just practicing the trumpet, she's thinking of joining the village band,' I said.

'Well, she needs a lot more practice judging from that,' he scoffed as he moved away.

'I'm actually thinking her stopping would be an even better idea,' I said under my breath as I desperately tried not to inhale the toxic smell filling the tent. I carried on serving, noticing that Daphne was drawing quite a crowd, which sort of defeated the object of her trying not to bring any attention to Abbie's predicament.

'Charlie, move everyone back. Now!' Georgie barked. 'We need privacy.' I turned my head, wondering what was going on, and saw her grab one of the spare tablecloths, opening it out to shield Abbie from our sight. 'Go, Abbie.'

'I can't shit in a box on the front lawn of Lord Kirkland's manor,' Abbie wailed. 'Not after last year. It will be known as turdgate the sequel. Just when you thought it was safe, Abbie strikes again.'

'You don't have a choice. No one can see you but me. Do it. Daphne, seriously?' Georgie uttered as Daphne started Europe's *The Final Countdown*, rapping out the drum sections with some serving tongs and miming air guitar between, as my shoulders shook from the effort of not giving in to a fit of laughter.

'Give us about half an hour, everyone. Abbie's brewing up another batch of sauce for the last of the scones,' I suggested as I quickly skipped around the table to herd everyone away from the tent and gulp down some welcome fresh air. Georgie called me back inside and asked me to run home and get some moist toilet wipes, which she kept in her cloakroom, so I started running across Lord Kirkland's lawn, making it as far as the koi pond before I had to slow down to a jog. I was panting by the time I made it to Georgie's house and seriously considering giving up pizza, I was so out of breath. I swiped up the packet of wipes and began the long trek back. I really did need to get fit if I couldn't even manage running home and back in one go. I handed over the wipes, hardly daring to ask what had happened, before turning to start packing away the remaining food items on Georgie's instructions.

'Charlie, can you find Weston for me and ask him to come and help me get Abbie home?'

'No need, here he comes,' I pointed. 'Wow, he even walks sexily. Look at that swagger. Does he have a brother?'

'Honestly, I've no idea,' she replied.

'Ok, from the look on your face, something's wrong, and this time I'm not taking no for an answer,' Weston said. 'Would you?' he asked, holding out the lead of a small dog to me. I had to assume this was Bertie. Georgie had told me all about him. I swear she was as infatuated with this puppy as she was with Weston.

'Why hot,' I nodded. 'Oops, not, I mean not. Not hot. Not that you're not hot. You *are* hot, but I meant why not. I'm Charlie, by the way. No filter. I write sexy books and you kind of get used to getting it all out in the open. Words, that is, not my bits. I don't do naturist breaks. I mean, who wants to see everything on display? It would be like working in a butcher's shop all the time. Nothing would be appetising anymore, would it? Damn it. Can we just erase this meeting and start afresh at lunch tomorrow? Come on, cutie, let's go for a walk before I make things even worse.' I picked Bertie up and quickly disappeared, taking my blushing cheeks with me.

I headed over to the ice cream van parked up on Lord Kirkland's gravel drive and chewed my lower lip as I tried to decide which of the tempting flavours I fancied, as Bertie licked at my jawline.

'Steady boy, you need to ask me out on a date before the French kissing starts,' I warned him.

'Would you say that if a certain doctor tried his luck?' a male voice said from behind me.

'Pizzaman?' I exclaimed, spinning around to find him grinning at me.

'The one and only.'

'What are you doing here?' I asked him, giving him a quick once over. I'd never seen him in anything but his work outfit of black jeans and a white t-shirt, with the occasional jumper on top. Today he was in a pair of knee-length blue cargo jeans, blue Converses, and a very fitted, white short-sleeved Henley-style top that accentuated his muscular physique. I swallowed quickly and dragged my eyes back up to his face as I realised that they were lingering on his toned biceps. I felt like I was seeing him naked for the first time, so much of his upper arm was on display.

'You said the other week that I needed to have more time away from my responsibilities, and as the whole friends thing is a work in progress, I thought I'd come and see my one and only friend and experience the renowned Dilbury fête myself.'

'Well, you have perfect timing. I've been busy all morning helping Abbie, but I'm on a break. What ice cream do you fancy, on me?'

'How about I get them? You seem to have your arms full and Mrs. Tibbles appears to have had a drastic makeover.'

'This is Bertie, Georgie's boyfriend's dog. Here, you hold him. The ice cream is on me, I owe you so much more for looking after me,' I reminded him as I passed Bertie over. He didn't seem to be discriminative with his affections for anyone as he proceeded to wash Kitt's face, making him laugh. I got us a salted caramel ice cream each, and Kitt set Bertie down and held his lead so that we could eat without the risk of our treat being wolfed by the pup.

'I missed you last night. It's rare for you not to order a pizza on a Friday. I would say the healthy eating regime must have started, but seeing the size of these, I'm thinking not,' he observed as he licked at the heavenly ice cream.

'I was all set for a night of writing, then a pizza on the bench with you, but Georgie dragged me out instead.'

'You went into town?'

'No, she introduced me to the quarterly karaoke night at the village hall. It's quite the event around here.'

'I had no idea you sang,' he observed as we went to find a patch of vacant grass to sit down on and soak up the sun.

'Well, everyone sings, don't they? Even if it's just in the shower, badly. Turns out I'm actually not as bad as I thought. It was a really fun night, not least watching the pensioners of Dilbury doing some of the more modern songs. You missed some Daphne classics earlier, in fact,' I told him, filling him in on the morning and making him laugh.

'I like the sound of this Daphne.'

'You might change your mind when I introduce you. How long are you here for?'

'As long as I want. Vicky's with Mum now and then Brenda takes over for the night shift. I wanted to be near enough to go back if I'm needed, and I wasn't sure if I'd outstay my welcome. I did kind of spring myself on you.'

'And I'm glad you did. I'd love to hang out with you without a time limit like normal. Now that I know you're not in a rush, I'm going to take you to The Cock for dinner, my treat and don't object,' I warned, holding my fingers up against his lips as he went to open his mouth. 'You've been so good to me, it's the least I can do.'

'Drinks on me then?' he mumbled.

'Oh dear, you may regret that offer. You have no idea how much vodka I can down in a night,' I laughed, removing my hand to give Bertie the belly rub he was demanding.

'You don't seem worse for wear after your night out.'

'Because I only had two drinks. Daphne got slaughtered and we had to manhandle her home early, in the caretaker's utility truck.'

'I thought she was in her eighties?' Kitt chuckled.

'She is. Trust me, since moving to Dilbury, I've come to understand that age really shouldn't be a hindrance to having fun. She's amazing, I think you're going to love her when you meet her.'

I laughed as Kitt and Bertie jumped when Reverend Potter turned on the microphone of the PA system and called for attention.

'Come on, Abbie,' I said, crossing my fingers as he started to read out the awards. 'Yes!' I shouted, making Bertie bark excitedly as I clapped vigorously to hear she'd kept her titles.

'Wow, you guys take this thing seriously, huh?' Kitt asked.

'Abbie does. Come on, I'll need to help pack up her tent, you can lend a bit of muscle.'

'Who says I have any muscle?'

'I've seen them now,' I grinned, poking a finger into his firm bicep.

'Watch out, I at least expect a woman to buy me dinner before touching me up,' he winked, quickly standing up and brushing grass off his jeans.

'You're safe in my hands, I won't ravish you against your will,' I said, accepting the hand he offered to pull me up.

'Unlucky me then,' he drawled. I shoulder bumped him as I tugged on Bertie's lead and we started making our way over to the tent. We were hampered by a crowd that was gathering around it, the sounds of shrieks and shouting reaching our ears.

'My God, what's going on?' I gasped, as the people in front of us parted like the Red Sea and a God-awful smell made me crinkle my nose, seconds before Lady Kirkland stormed past, looking like someone had thrown a few chocolate milkshakes all over her. I pushed my way through to the tent to find Georgie scolding a smirking Daphne. 'What happened? Lady Kirkland was covered in chocolate or something.'

'That was no chocolate,' Georgie huffed, glaring at Daphne.

'What am I missing here?' I asked as I flitted my eyes between them, while Georgie bent over to scoop up Bertie.

'She had it coming,' Daphne stated firmly.

'No one has *that* coming, Daphne, no one,' Georgie stated, before turning to fill me in. She looked horrified as I roared with laughter and threw Daphne a high five, which she returned, while Kitt stood speechless at the revelation. 'Don't encourage her, Charlie. It would be bad enough behaviour for a teenager, let alone an eighty-year-old.'

'Stop using my age against me, Georgie Basset. Just because I'm old doesn't mean I can't have a bit of fun from time to time. Life is too short to be serious and boring. Now, is someone going to introduce me to this fine young man?' she said, making it clear that the lecture was over.

'Sorry, you threw me with the whole shit shower debacle,' I giggled. 'This is my good friend, Kitt, also fondly known as Pizzaman.'

'Ah, we meet at last.' Georgie smiled and held out her hand. 'I'm Georgie, I live next door.'

'Hi, Georgie, great to finally meet you.' Kitt took her hand and leaned in to kiss her cheek.

'You too. If I'd known how cute you were, I'd have started ordering takeaways myself,' she said, flashing me a look.

'They don't do rabbit food deliveries, Georgie. You're too careful with your diet to order the calorific goodness that Kitt delivers. Kitt, this is my other good friend, Daphne.'

'Pleasure to meet you, Daphne, I've heard so much about you,' Kitt said as he bent over the table to kiss her cheek as well.

'And I've not heard nearly enough about you. Are you single?'

'Ermmm, yes,' he replied cautiously.

'Don't worry, dear, I like myself a toy boy, but I'm not a cradle snatcher,' Daphne reassured him as she gave him the once over. 'He's very good-looking, Charlie.'

'He's not a bull at the cattle market, Daphne,' I laughed, feeling my cheeks colour up. 'And he can hear you.'

'Just saying. Don't know why you're chasing after that doctor of yours when you have a hot, young, single man like this interested in you.'

'Daphne, honestly. He's not interested in me like that, we're just friends. Good friends, aren't we, Kitt?' I asked, batting his arm as I looked at him for some support.

'Yes, just friends,' he agreed.

'I don't get you youngsters sometimes,' Daphne said with an exasperated sigh. 'Well, come on then. If you're not going to smooch in the corner, you can help us pack up.'

'Seriously, you didn't find the Lady Kirkland incident funny?' I asked Georgie as we started lifting the empty boxes.

'Hello, I'm human, of course I did,' she giggled. 'But she can't be allowed to think she can get away with that sort of behaviour. Someone needed to show some disapproval.'

'Honestly, Georgie, I don't think Daphne cares what anyone thinks, and I kind of love that about her.'

'Me too,' she reluctantly agreed. 'Do you think we'll be that much fun when we're her age?'

'No,' I scoffed. 'I plan to be worse.'

'Stop judging,' I warned as I pushed my dessert plate to one side, Kitt shaking his head in amazement.

'I'm not judging, it's great to see a girl with an appetite like yours, I'm just … *in awe* at how much you can tuck away and keep your figure.'

'Practice. Lots and lots of practice,' I grinned, squinting at him as I felt the room spinning. I'd made up for last night's lack of booze, but stupidly I'd done most of it on an empty stomach before our food arrived. 'But I think I'm going to wake up one morning with an arse the size of a hippopatamousse.'

'Hippopotamus,' Kitt chuckled.

'That's what I said.'

'No, it's not. I think I'd better cut you off and get you home.'

'But I'm having fun,' I pouted. He shook his head and folded his arms across his chest.

'Giving me that look won't work. You need lots of water and an early night.'

'Spoilsport,' I huffed. I grabbed the bill out of Tony's hand as he went to put it on the table, making sure Kitt didn't get a chance to take it. 'It's on me, I said it was on me, Kitt, Kitt, you know what, I have no idea what your surname is.'

'Fraser,' he said with a smile. 'I'd have thought you'd have asked about my Christian name before my surname.'

'You're telling me you're not really called Kitt?' I asked as I handed some notes to Tony.

'You've given me a forty-pound tip, Charlie,' he grunted.

'Oops, my bad,' I uttered, pulling a few notes out of his grasp. 'How's that? Still a tip?'

'Yes, but I'm thinking I should have just kept quiet,' he replied with a droll tone as he walked away.

'So, Kitt Fraser, what's your real name?' I asked, as he stood up and offered me his arm.

'That sort of is my real name, but my full name's Christopher.'

'Christopher,' I mused as I grasped his arm and we made our way to the exit. 'You don't seem like a Christopher to me.'

'Well, I assure you that I am, though the nickname Kitt stuck when I was younger.'

'You ate lots of Kit-Kats, huh? A bit of a chocolate fiend? I hear you, Mister.'

'No,' he laughed. 'Kitt's an abbreviation for Christopher.'

'Well, that's silly, it doesn't sound anything like Christopher. Surely you'd be called Christ, Topher, or Fur if someone was going to shorten it.'

'Or simply Chris,' he suggested with another chuckle. 'It is to do with Jesus Christ, though. Actually, they're both derived from connections to him.'

'You'll be telling me next that you were a vicar in your former life?'

'No, not a vicar. Hey, hey, careful,' he warned as I stumbled on one of the pub forecourt flagstones.

'I'm feeling a bit drunk now that we're in the fresh air,' I complained, closing my eyes as everything started spinning.

'Oh God,' I heard Kitt say, seconds before I felt myself falling and everything went dark.

I groaned as I woke up, not sure how I'd ended up in my comfortable bed or why I had such a dry mouth.

'Stop it, Tibbs,' I moaned, batting away her paw as it brushed over my face.

'Come on, drink some more water for me.'

'Oh my God, how drunk am I? You can talk,' I uttered, rolling onto my back as I tried to open my eyes. 'And you have a really gruff voice for a girl, Tibbs.'

'Because it's Kitt, not Tibbs,' came the voice again, laughing. 'Charlie, you need to drink more water.'

'Kitt, it's you? Kitt, not cat?' I giggled, then clutched my head as it hurt with the movement. 'What's going on?'

'You virtually passed out on me. I had to carry you home, then hold your hair back as you were sick in the kitchen sink. I took your shoes off and carried you upstairs and put you to bed, but you need to drink some more water.'

'I was sick?' I croaked, propping myself up on my elbows as I squinted at him, just the soft bedside lamp illuminating his face.

'Yes, but on the plus side, you now have extra room for a big breakfast in the morning. I do a mean fry up.'

'You're staying?' I asked as I accepted the water he offered me.

'I'll sleep on the sofa. I don't like the idea of leaving you when you're this bad.'

'This is nothing, though it's been a long time since I got so drunk,' I admitted. 'What about your mum?'

'I'd paid Brenda for the night, in case you were busy. I was going to go and have a few pints in town, then enjoy an early night and revel in not having to be on call.'

'God, I'm so sorry, now you're looking after me instead of her.'

'It's ok, it's still relatively early. I'll still get a good night's sleep. I'll just feel better if I'm in earshot, in case you're sick again.'

'Well, if you insist on staying, you're not sleeping on my sofa. You can have the spare room, the bed's really comfortable.'

'Then we have a deal. I'll go and get you some more water.' He took the glass off me and headed over to the bedroom door.

'Kitt,' I called as I flopped back down onto my pillows.

'Yes?'

'You're a really good friend, you know that, right?'

'I know that, Charlie,' he replied, then thudded his way down the stairs as I shut my eyes to stop the room from spinning again.

Chapter Nine

Progress
Two Months Later – September

'YOU'RE KIDDING ME,' I cried down the phone as Kristy, my agent, gave me the good news. Good was an understatement. This news was … fantastical.

'It's a great offer, Charlie, and you deserve it. You did a stellar presentation yesterday and your work speaks for itself. It was just a matter of time before I found the right fit for you.'

'Tell me the proposed advance again,' I begged her, bouncing up and down on the spot with excitement. I screamed as she repeated it, then ran around my office like a lunatic as she laughed down the line. Years of hard work had finally paid off. My earnings had been great, far better than I'd ever expected when I'd started writing, and they'd crept up this year with me putting all of my focus into writing and getting more books out. But it still wasn't quite enough to live off and be able to set aside a decent sum into a pension, or to build up a nest egg for a nice holiday each year. I'd been contemplating having to start looking for a job soon, but I wouldn't have to if this worked out.

'I'll email the contract over. I've already made some annotations on it, suggestions that we counter with, in your favour. If they were that quick to write it, it's obvious that they are desperate to sign you. This could be life changing, Charlie. If they launch your latest book and it sells as well as they anticipate with their marketing and publicity behind it, you could be looking at very lucrative future contracts, with worldwide travel for book signing tours.'

'Stop, stop. I'm going to pass out, I'm so giddy,' I squealed.

'Well, take your time to read and digest it, don't come back to me until after the weekend. I really want to make sure you're happy and you've had a chance to think of any questions or concerns, but this is a great offer.'

'Thank you, Kristy, thank you,' I said sincerely.

When she hung up, I clutched the phone to my chest and screamed again, jumping up and down on the spot. I ran into my bedroom, threw myself face down on the bed, and screamed into my pillows as I kicked my legs. This was everything I'd hardly dared to imagine when I'd written my first book. There were so many amazing authors out there who were never noticed or offered a traditional publishing deal. It had been a pipe dream, like buying a lottery ticket "just in case" you were the one in a million who won. But it wasn't a dream anymore. It was real, tangible, almost in my grasp.

'Oh, thank God.'

I screamed again, this time with terror rather than joy, when I heard an unexpected voice behind me. My heart rattled my ribcage as it began to beat out of control. I threw myself onto my back, ready to launch the phone handset at the intruder and hopefully stun them, giving me time to run to the stairs and escape.

'Georgie?!' I gasped, trying to catch my breath and calm down, after I saw it was my friend and not a burglar standing at the entrance to my bedroom, brandishing a poker. 'What the hell? You almost scared me to death.'

'Me?' she exclaimed. 'What about you? I heard the most awful high-pitched screams coming from your house and thought you were being murdered. I raced over to save you. Look, look,' she uttered, waving the metal poker around like a light sabre. 'I was going to try and beat them to death with this. My God, I think I'm about to have a heart attack. I ran here.' She huffed out a heavy breath and came over to plonk herself down on the bed next to me. 'What's wrong? Is Mrs. Tibbles ok?'

'She might have had a heart attack herself from all the commotion. Crikey, my heart is still racing.'

'Mine too, so what's wrong? Did you hurt yourself again?'

'For once, no,' I beamed, the feeling of excitement quickly spreading through my body and calming the fight or flight surge of adrenaline that had hit me when I'd heard her voice. 'It's only happened, Georgie. My agent only went and got me a publishing deal.'

'What?' she cried, her blue eyes wide with amazement as her mouth dropped. 'Seriously?'

'Seriously. The meeting yesterday went so well, they emailed her a contract this morning. They were screams of excitement. Pinch me, I need to be sure I'm not dreaming.' I bit my lower lip as I waited for the sign that this was all real. Things like this didn't happen to Charlie Faulkner. Luck had never been my friend, but if this was real, good luck was about to push bad luck out of the door and slam it in its face. 'Owww,' I moaned, reaching up to rub my arm.

'You said pinch you,' Georgie giggled, throwing her poker down on the floor. Seconds later, she'd thrown herself on top of me like a wrestler as she screeched with excitement, which made me scream with joy again. 'I'm so proud of you, Charlie. You deserve this so much.'

'Thank you, Georgie,' I said as she rolled off me, and we lay side by side on the bed together.

'I guess I owe you girls that slap-up meal I promised.'

'Oh yes, how about we organise it for Christmas? It would be a great excuse for a girls' get together and party. We could make it Abbie's hen party too, as I know she doesn't want anything crazy.'

'I like your thinking,' I nodded. 'I was going to say I'd like to ask Quinn as well, so if it's a hen party, I'm sure Abbie will be down with that.'

'Ok, where should we go? The Fox?' Georgie asked.

'I love The Fox, but it needs to be a bit more special than that, you know, double celebration and all.'

'What are you thinking?' Georgie propped herself up on her elbows as she looked down at me.

'Severn Manor. We could make a day of it in the spa, with massages, facials, mani-pedis, then have a slap-up meal with champagne.'

'Oh, that sounds so good, but expensive.'

'Well, I'll happily pay for the meal for everyone, and I'll treat Abbie to the spa day as her wedding present. That way everyone else only has to pay for their treatments.'

'Oh my God, how much are they going to pay you if you can afford that?' she gasped.

'Stupid money,' I laughed. 'Honestly, Georgie, I wouldn't offer if it was going to stretch me.'

'Wow,' she nodded.

'Wow indeed,' I agreed. I couldn't wait to tell Kitt and my parents, they'd be so excited for me. In fact, later I was going to order a double pizza and Kitt could celebrate with me. I could always think about hiring a personal trainer to come and whip me into shape. 'God, I'm so happy. I know they say money doesn't make you happy, but it's definitely not going to make me miserable, that's for sure.'

'I hope you'll still remember us when you're rich and famous,' Georgie said, bumping my shoulder.

'Sorry, who said that? Do I know you, stranger sitting on my bed?'

'I could go off you rapidly,' she laughed.

'Not now you know I'm rolling in it. I know how shallow you are.'

'Well, I actually came over to say we couldn't be friends anymore as you weren't earning enough money, but I guess we can see how things go.' She grinned at me and I laughed. 'Seriously, Charlie. Don't change, we love you as you are. Outspoken, accident-prone, funny, and loveable Charlie Faulkner.'

'I'll still be me,' I reassured her. 'Just with a bit more money in the bank. My advance is great, and my earnings should go up, but I'm not going to become a millionaire or anything.'

'Don't speak too soon. I bet J.K. Rowling and E.L. James never thought that when they got their first publishing deals either, and look at them now.'

I nodded. It was true. Who would think putting words on paper could change your life immeasurably?

When Georgie left, I made a call to my parents to tell them the good news. Truth be told, while they had been nothing but supportive of my decision to give up work to focus on writing, I had a feeling that they never imagined anything would come of it. I believed that they thought it was something I needed to get out of my system before moving on to a "proper job." I was so proud to prove I had what it took, and to hear the genuine surprise and excitement in both of their voices when they heard the news.

I headed into Shrewsbury and treated myself to a haircut and manicure, and purchased a bottle of my favourite perfume that I'd nearly run out of. On the way home, I called in at the shop to pick up a bottle of champagne and some chicken for Tibbs. I was surprised, and somewhat relieved, to find Joyce Dawson, landlady of The Cock, behind the counter as I set my purchases down.

'Hello, Joyce. What are you doing here?' I asked.

'Just covering while Reg takes Sheila for a check-up,' she said as she scanned my items. 'Going downhill fast, poor woman. It's time he admitted she needs help and that running the shop and post office is too much for her.'

'I'm sorry to hear that, but I agree, she's definitely been getting worse. What do you think they'll do, close the place?'

'In a village this busy?' she scoffed. 'He's looking to sell so they can buy one of those apartments in the old school house down Ivy Lane. Little goldmine this place is. If I wasn't so busy running the pub, I'd think about taking it over. What about you, you must have lots of free time as you only write,' she suggested. I blinked at her a few times, amazed that so many people still thought the life of an author was so easy.

'Actually, I probably do as many hours a day as you do in the pub. It's not just about sitting for a few hours and throwing some random words down. You have to think of interesting stories, create likeable characters, map it out to make sure you keep the pace moving, as well as do the actual typing. And then you write a bit, read it, change it, write some more, and repeat over and over until you have a draft manuscript, which you then rip to shreds and re-write. And that doesn't even include all the time you have to spend on marketing yourself and keeping up a social media presence. It's rare for me to stop working before one a.m.' I told her.

'Well, I never. I had no idea it was so involved,' she nodded, looking suitably impressed.

'Very few people do. I think they all imagine it's easy, that it's really just a hobby, and it's not. It's actually a pretty lonely existence as I have to spend so much time in my office alone while I write.'

'No boyfriend?' she asked as I handed over some cash.

'No,' I replied. I honestly had a feeling that was never going to change.

'There's rumour that the pizza delivery guy stops over on a regular basis,' she said, giving me a knowing look as she handed me my change. 'You'll get yourself a reputation if you're not careful.'

'There's a rumour? It's not exactly regular, Joyce. I think he's stayed twice since I moved in, to take care of me while I was poorly. Besides, it's not like that. He's just a friend.'

'Just a friend,' she repeated, eyeing me suspiciously as my blood started to boil. What business was it of anyone's even if I was getting jiggy with Kitt on a regular basis? How did that warrant me "getting a reputation," for goodness sake? I was single, he was single, where was the scandal in that?

'Just a friend,' I said more firmly. 'I eat a lot of pizza, that's how I got to know him. So maybe you could spread that rumour for me, before I'm painted as the next Dilbury hussy.'

'No need to be touchy, Charlie.'

'Well, I am when it's implied that I have loose morals. Just because I write spicy books doesn't mean that I put it about to get practical knowledge for everything that I write. I have a very vivid imagination. You ought to look a bit closer to home. If anyone deserves to be the subject of warranted gossip, it's your barmaid Rowena, not me.' I grabbed my chicken and champagne and stalked out of the shop before I had a chance to say something I might regret. Honestly. You'd think a quaint little village like Dilbury would be a safe place where everyone got along. The rumour mill here was vicious.

'That's too funny,' Kitt laughed as I filled him in on the talk about us. 'Maybe we ought to give them something to really talk about,' he suggested.

'Like what?' I asked, licking my fingers after pushing the last bite of my pepperoni pizza into my mouth. Kitt was such a novice pizza eater.

I'd been doing all of the talking, as usual, and I'd still managed to finish mine before him.

'We could do a *When Harry Met Sally* kind of deal. Lots of headboard banging, grunts from me, and howls from you,' he chuckled. I laughed and shook my head.

'We could, but only Georgie would get to hear it, and there's no way that it's her that's been spreading gossip. We'd have to go for it in the pub for everyone to witness. You could throw me down on the pool table and we could put on a real show for them all.'

'If I was lucky enough to get that far with a woman like you, there's no way I'd want spectators. I'd keep you all to myself.'

'Thanks, Kitt, that's really sweet,' I grinned, rubbing my shoulder against his.

'So why am I having pizza and champagne with you? You said we were celebrating, but went off on a rant about the villagers talking about us.'

'Oh God, I did, didn't I? Well, you're sitting with an about-to-be-published author,' I said proudly.

'Aren't you already published?' he asked, looking confused. 'I mean, I haven't read one of your books in full, but I downloaded one and made a start.'

'You've read one?' I squeaked, quickly setting my champagne down as I felt my cheeks heat up and a shudder run down my spine. 'Ewww, that's like imagining my dad reading one.'

'Oh thanks, you see me as your dad?' he uttered.

'When it comes to reading … you know … *sexy stuff*. That I've written. I don't want you imagining me doing that stuff. Oh God, what if my dad's read it too and he's imagining? What if he got a … oh no, no, no. Erase that visual fast, Charlie, erase, erase. I need a bottle of bleach for my mind, and I think I just threw up a little in my mouth,' I groaned, completely grossed out.

'Hey, relax,' Kitt laughed. 'I said I made a start. As soon as it started getting steamy, I put it down. It felt kind of weird to read that, since I know you.'

'Are you just saying that to make me feel better?' I asked him, grabbing my flute and knocking back the contents.

'No. You're my best friend, Charlie. It's a bit crap if I have to lie to my best friend, isn't it?'

'It is,' I agreed.

'I'm still not clear why we're celebrating, though, as you're published already,' he said as he set his box down on the coffee table and twisted to face me.

I poured myself another glass of champagne and mirrored his position before explaining the difference and telling him about my offer. His face changed from one of serious contemplation as he absorbed the knowledge to surprise, and then pride to hear what had happened.

'Charlie, that's incredible. You're amazing,' he gasped. I laughed, and seconds later was gathered up in his strong arms and enveloped in the scent of the ocean as he hugged me tightly. I hugged him back and rested my head on his shoulder, revelling in the close contact. It felt so nice to have a man hold me. It had been a long time. Sometimes I really wished I felt that primal attraction to Kitt that I wrote about so often. 'I'm in awe of you. You're such an inspiration,' he murmured, planting a delicate kiss on my temple.

'I wouldn't go that far, but thank you. It means a lot coming from you.'

'Because a pizza guy's opinion matters so much,' he said with a touch of defeat in his voice.

'Hey, don't do that. Don't put yourself down,' I warned him, struggling out of the embrace to fix him with a disapproving scowl. 'I don't care what you do. Your opinion matters to me, ok?'

'You say you don't care, but people do. You've never treated me like I'm a lesser man because I do a job that anyone without an education could do, but I'm sick of people judging me, of thinking that's all I could do with my life. I could be more than this. I was more than this.'

'Kitt, I had no idea you felt that way,' I said as I rubbed his forearm in a reassuring way. 'I assumed you were happy doing this as it fit around your life with your mum. Why didn't you say?'

'Because I feel selfish for complaining,' he shrugged. 'She's deteriorating. At some point, I won't need to do this part-time job and I can focus on being me again, on creating the life that I want for myself. But if I'm free to do that, it means I've lost her. That she's really gone for good, and I'm not ready for that.'

'No one's ever ready for that, I'd imagine.' I let out a sigh and picked up his hand, smothering it in mine. 'You're a good man, Kitt. The best. How many sons would give up their lives so selflessly like that? And to get no thanks for doing it from the one person they need it from the most. I feel awful going on about how excited I am for a new chapter in my life when you're stuck and unable to move on with yours.'

'Charlie, I …' He hesitated and closed his eyes for a fraction of a second, before opening them and shaking his head as he held my gaze. 'I'm sorry. This is the best day of your life and I'm bringing down the mood, going on about my woes.'

'Friends share their ups and downs. I never want you to feel like you have to hide a part of yourself from me. What can I do to make you feel better?' I asked, my heart aching for him. He didn't look like the man I knew. He looked like a little boy who needed his mum to tell him how proud she was of him. He was never going to get that again.

'I'm thinking a strong coffee to wash down this self-pity and the rest of my delicious pizza,' he smiled.

'Coffee I can do,' I nodded. 'Ermmm, when did you sneak in the last couple of slices?' I tipped my head in the direction of his empty box. Had he been scoffing them over my shoulder as we hugged?

'Seriously? Yours wasn't enough for you, you had to finish mine as well?' he laughed.

'I never touched it,' I said, throwing my hands in the air.

'Well, neither did I. How can pizza just vanish?'

'Oh no, she wouldn't,' I uttered as I shot to my feet.

'Enlighten me?' Kitt asked as I scanned the oak floor and spotted a trail of tomato sauce leading out of the lounge door from the coffee table. I skipped over and gasped, putting my hands on my hips.

'Mrs. Tibbles! Let the pizza go and back away from it now,' I warned her as I caught her dragging one of the slices across the hall floor. She just glared at me with a "*you* back away now" expression.

'Your cat took it?' Kitt laughed as he joined me.

'I told you it smelled extra fishy. I should have warned you to put the lid back on the box. Her tail was quivering as she watched you eating it,' I said. 'She loves tuna and prawns.'

I strode over, bent down to grip the end of the slice, and pulled. Tibbs gave me a warning growl as she clamped her jaw tightly around her prize, her eyes taking on a demonic sheen. An all-out tug-of-war commenced, her growls getting more high-pitched the longer we duelled. I whipped my hand away when she swiped at it with her paw, but wasn't quite quick enough as she drew some blood when her claws raked over my skin.

'You little monkey,' I hissed as she quickly disappeared, the pizza vanishing out of sight with her into the kitchen.

'She's vicious,' Kitt exclaimed as he came to check my hand, which had a long ruby line across the top of it.

'Nothing comes between Tibbs and her food. I'm so sorry about your pizza. I'd better put on some gloves to wrestle it from her.'

'Let her have it. It's not like I really want it now that she's wiped the floor with it and slobbered all over it,' he chuckled.

'Well, I wasn't about to put it on a plate and serve it back to you, but she shouldn't be eating it. Tomatoes aren't good for cats. I'll pick off the tuna and prawns for her and bin the rest.'

'I'll do it. You go and clean that cut and put a plaster on it. Can't have this author's million dollar hands damaged, now can we?'

'Million dollar,' I laughed. 'In my dreams.'

'You're one step closer,' he reminded me as we walked into the kitchen to find Tibbs sitting in her dining room bed with two large slices of pizza, purring and picking off the best bits. I shook my head and smiled to myself. If only humans were so easily pleased. Well, I was for once, that was for sure, but what could I do to cheer Kitt up?

I went up to my office when Kitt left and opened the email from Kristy with my proposal, then pressed print. While the printer was shuddering and churning out the various pages, I quickly dialled Georgie.

'Hello,' she answered with a yawn.

'Sorry, did I wake you up? I know it's late.'

'Just caught me as I was climbing into bed. Is everything ok?'

'Great. I just wondered if you'd spare Weston one Saturday soon?'

'Overdosed on pizza tonight, did you? I saw Kitt's car outside.'

'Well yes, but that's not why I need him, not yet anyway. Kitt's having a hard time at the moment, and I'd like to do something to cheer him up.'

'And you're thinking of a threesome with my boyfriend? I'm open minded, Charlie, but even I have my limits.'

'And they say authors have dirty minds,' I teased. 'No, I'd like to book one of those adventure days for Kitt. You know, quad biking, archery, clay pigeon shooting, followed by a few beers down at the pub. He doesn't really have any male friends I can ask to go with him. I thought maybe it would be nice if Weston and Miller went with him, give them all a chance to get to know each other.'

'Are you and Kitt moving past the friend zone?' she asked, her voice perking up.

'No, but Abbie and Miller are getting married and you're getting serious with Weston. We're bound to do things as a group. I'd like to be able to include Kitt now and then, if you don't mind. He's such a nice guy and his life is really restricted with everything he does for his mum. He needs a bit of fun injected into it.'

'Much as I don't want to lose one of my few precious days with Weston, it would do him good to spend time with my friends. Find out when Miller's next home and let me know a date and we'll set it up. We could all go for dinner after at The Fox.'

'Perfect. Thanks, Georgie. Sleep tight.'

'You too,' she yawned as she hung up. Sleep? There was no way I was going to sleep tonight. I was too amped up on excitement. I snatched up the contract, skipped over to my bedroom, and snuggled in to read it in bed.

'Charlie Faulkner, please,' came Dr. Fitton's voice.

'Great,' I said under my breath. I'd wanted nothing better than an excuse to see him again, but not when I was squinting with a bright red and teary eye. I made my way over to him and tripped over the outstretched plaster cast leg of a random patient in the waiting room as I did. I managed to right myself, but not before I let out an unattractive girlish shriek.

'I'm seriously considering dedicating a bed to you here,' McFitty said, one eyebrow raised as I finally made it to stand in front of him.

'You remember me?' I asked, slightly stunned.

'You're hard to forget,' he smiled, flashing some impossibly perfect teeth that wouldn't look out of place in a dental advert.

I was so dazzled by the movie star smile that sent a ripple of attraction through my body, I didn't have a comeback to remind him just how often he actually had forgotten me. Instead, I followed him like an eager puppy into the bay and hopped up onto the bed as instructed. I'd always chuckled when reading historical romances full of "burning loins," but at that moment, I totally got it. Mine were scorching as I drank him in.

'So, you've managed to injure your eye this time?' he asked.

'Yes,' I grimaced, as I tried desperately not to keep winking at him.

'What caused the injury?'

'The duvet.'

'I'm sorry, did you say the duvet?' he asked, looking as surprised as I was when it happened.

'Yes,' I sighed, swinging my feet backwards and forwards as I perched on the edge of the bed and he put on some gloves. 'I was reading in bed, and when I turned over, for some reason my eyelid didn't close as the duvet dragged over my eyeball. It's really stinging and well, you can see how red it is.'

'Ok, I'm going to put some dye on your eye, then take a look if that's ok?'

'I'm hardly going to say no when I've dragged myself here in the middle of the night, am I?'

'No, I'd imagine not,' he chuckled as he rummaged in his supply drawer.

'And it's not like it's embarrassing. I mean, you've already handled my vagina, an eyeball is nothing.'

'Handled your ... oh, you mean when I examined your rash?'

'Yes. Don't worry, you're off the hook. We haven't had amazing sex that you forgot all about,' I reassured him, willing myself to just shut my mouth before I said anything else inappropriate.

'I never have amazing sex and forget about it,' he replied as he turned to face me. His green eyes locked on mine, forcing me to swallow hard. Was he flirting with me? I'd grown so used to his casual indifference, I wasn't sure if I was reading him right.

'Ah, but you haven't had sex with me. I'm so good, I'd blow your mind and leave you incapable of rational thought after.' Jesus, what had come over me? I was never this forward with a man.

'Is that an offer? As it's rather frowned upon at work. Human resources doesn't take kindly to on-the-job extras,' he grinned as he moved towards me like a predator. A sexy, virile, "hot male doctor" predator. 'Shit,' he gasped before quickly backing away, nursing his kneecap.

'Oh God, I'm so sorry,' I grimaced, realising my swinging feet had just connected with his leg. 'Does it hurt?'

'Yes,' he groaned, massaging it.

'It's a good thing you're so tall or I could have got you somewhere a bit more tender.'

'Thank goodness for small mercies,' he agreed, as he straightened up and flexed his knee back and forth. 'How about you keep your legs still while I come and look at your eye?'

'Eye, eye, doctor,' I agreed. 'Sorry, I'm giddy on champagne and excitement. I have no control over what's coming out of my mouth.'

'Good to know. I take it you didn't drive?' he asked as he stepped between my legs, my thighs connecting with his muscular ones and making my breath hitch.

'Andy,' I murmured, drowning in the scent of him. So musky. So ... raw and sexual. 'Andy the taxi driver dropped me off.'

'Good, now tip your head back for me, the drops will sting a little for a moment.'

'Ok.' I swallowed hard again as he placed his thumb below my eye and his fingers above and held it open. I could feel his hot breath on my face as he leaned in and squeezed the medication into my eye, which temporarily distracted me as I hissed.

'Blink for me,' he ordered as he released his hold. I did as I was told, then he moved back in and shone a light into my eye, instructing me to move it up and down and left to right. It was like being at the opticians. You always felt self-conscious having a virtual stranger so close to your face. This was "invasion of personal space" territory. Usually you only let people who were about to kiss you come this close. And I could, I only had to lean forwards a fraction to finally get my lips on McFitty's perfect pout. 'Right,' he said abruptly, quickly stepping away from me.

'No hmmm this time?' I asked, disappointment at the loss of his closeness rattling me.

'No, it's a clear cut, excuse the pun, case,' he advised as he dumped the vial in the bin and proceeded to wash his hands. I watched, transfixed, as he soaped them up and rubbed them over and around each other, imagining how it would feel to have them caressing me like that. 'You've lacerated the surface of your eye. You're very lucky that it's on the white of your eye and not the iris, or I'd be referring you straight to our optometry department for evaluation. I'll prescribe some antibiotic drops and a soothing eye gel. It should heal within the week with no lasting side effects.'

'Great, thanks,' I nodded, feeling relieved it wasn't anything serious.

'What was so distracting?' he asked as he dried his hands on a paper towel.

'What?' I asked, dragging my eyes away from his hands.

'Your reading material in bed. Were you reading one of your own books? Distracted by the steam factor?' he smiled, making me blush.

'Actually no, for once. I just landed a publishing contract. I was reading their offer.'

'Congratulations. What does that mean for you?'

'An amazing advance and the possibility of my worldwide sales rocketing.'

'So I'll be seeing your books come out on film, will I?'

'Gosh, I'd not even thought of that. I guess there's always that possibility, if they did well enough.'

'A lady of means, eh? Your boyfriend will be able to retire.'

'Actually, I don't have a boyfriend. I've been too busy writing to have much of a social life.'

'Hmmm,' he murmured as he studied me, cocking his head. I tucked my hair behind my ear and started nervously swinging my feet again as we held each other's gaze. This was it. This was the moment where he'd ask me if I wanted to go out for dinner with him. It didn't even have to be dinner, I'd be happy with drinks. Hell, I'd be happy with a coffee in the hospital café. He could even skip the coffee and just introduce me to the wonders of his lips. His noisy pager broke the moment and he glanced down and grimaced. 'Sorry, I've got to run. I'll send a nurse in with your prescription. Any problems, straight back to your doctor, ok?'

'Ok,' I agreed, my excitement at the possibility of something happening with him leaving the room along with his delicious scrub-covered backside. Damn it. Foiled again.

Chapter Ten

To Friendship
Three Months Later – A Saturday in December

'SO, WHO BOUGHT IT?' I asked, beyond impatient. The shop had been temporarily closed for weeks. It looked like there were major renovations going on, judging by the huge skip outside and various workmen's vans coming and going.

'Well, if you'd stop interrupting, I'd get to the point of the story,' Daphne said with one of her wilting looks.

'That put you in your place,' Georgie laughed.

'I'm lucky, I haven't earned one of those looks yet,' Quinn grinned. 'And I don't plan on it.'

'Well, that all depends on what you do to my cottage, Quinn Garcia,' Daphne stated. I pulled a face at Quinn, which earned me a cuff from Daphne. 'Am I that bad? I was joking. It will be her cottage soon, she can do what she wants with it. Memories are just that. They aren't tangible. You can't touch them and you shouldn't need to. The best ones stay in your head and your heart, they're always with you. I don't need my cottage staying in a time warp because people are afraid of upsetting me.'

'That's good, because the bulldozer is booked to tear it down the second we exchange contracts,' Quinn said in a serious tone. Georgie and I gasped and shot a concerned look over at Daphne, only to see her smiling.

'Really, girls. You've spent more time with Quinn than I have and you still haven't learned when she's teasing?'

'Of course I'm teasing. Everything in the U.S. is new. Why would I want to erase all those years of history? I mean sure, there'll be some major work to do on it to make it more my style, but I'm not ripping out the bones of the place. It has character and I kinda like that,' Quinn smiled.

'You'd better love that, or you *will* be on the receiving end of one of my looks,' Daphne warned her.

'So, thrilled as I am to have the whole "Quinn's moving to Dilbury" talk, I'm still no clearer on who's bought the shop,' I reminded Daphne.

If anyone needed to know anything, Daphne was the woman. She knew everyone in the village and had a social network to rival Facebook.

'Parlez-vous Français?' she hinted.

'Is that Welsh?' Quinn asked. 'It sounds kinda sexy.'

'She just asked if you speak French, in French. We have a hot and sexy Frenchman moving into the shop?' I asked, my spirits lifting.

'Oh, I love me a man with an accent,' Georgie said wistfully.

'Me too,' Quinn and I sighed at the same time. We high fived each other with a smile. The expression "sister from another mister" could have been tailor-made for the two of us. We'd bonded so fast, and I was thrilled she was going to be moving here and we'd get to spend more time together.

'Then I'm very sorry to disappoint,' Daphne said. '*Her* name is Fleur, French for flower. Fleur Dubois. She trained as a pâtissier in Paris.'

'She makes French pastries?' Georgie asked, her eyes lighting up.

'You're telling me *you* eat cake?' I scoffed. 'With that slim figure?'

'There's cake and there's French pastries, and I'm all over that action. My God, Weston's going to have to work me out big time if I have those on my doorstep.'

'From the noises I heard last night, it sounds like he's already working you extremely hard,' I giggled, making Georgie blush. 'So, no more shop or post office?' I asked Daphne.

'Oh yes, she's converting the upstairs into a self-contained, two-bedroomed apartment, then the downstairs will be open-plan to a certain degree. She's having a custom kitchen and bakery built, with a small area for tables and chairs so she can sell cake and coffee and people can watch her work. She's calling it French Fancie. Then there'll be a new layout for the shop and post office. She's already put out an advertisement for someone to run that side of it for her.'

'How do you know all of this stuff?' I asked, astonished at her investigative skills.

'I talk to everyone and I listen in return. You ought to apply, Quinn. It would be a great way to meet all of the villagers and integrate yourself into village life.'

'I'm going to have my hands full with the renovations in January. Plus, I've already talked to Severn Manor to offer my event planning services exclusively to them. We're having a meeting next week.'

'Wow, you move fast,' I told her.

'I'm still working at the frantic New York pace. I haven't adjusted to the Dilbury tortoise way of life yet.'

'I'll get it,' Georgie said, shooting up when there was a knock on the door. 'It's probably James and Caroline, the photographers.'

'Is it rude for me to network while I'm acting as a bridesmaid?' Quinn asked. 'I had a huge list of wedding connections in New York. It's going to be hard work setting them all up from scratch again here.'

'As long as Abbie's needs come first today, I don't think that would be a problem at all, dear,' Daphne reassured her. 'She wants you settled here as much as Miller does.'

'Loving the hair, by the way,' I added as I eyed Quinn's new do. She'd forgone her usual multi-coloured tips for a deep purple to match our bridesmaid dresses.

'Well, a girl's got to make an effort to be normal now and then.'

'Humph,' Daphne trumpeted, making us both look her way. 'Normal would be getting rid of that ring in your nose. Why a man would find that attractive is beyond me.'

'Well, from what I've seen, it doesn't scare any guys off.' Quinn was a bona fide man magnet, even with that slightly cold, moody, and insular vibe she seemed to give off around strangers. That actually wasn't her at all. I'd already learned that she was as sweet and generous as her brother, but she didn't like people to know it. She wasn't exactly an open book, but from the time I'd spent with her, I'd already realised it was a self-defence mechanism for a woman who'd experienced so much rejection in her life. I had a feeling moving to Dilbury, being surrounded by love from her brother and new sister-in-law, not to mention being part of this circle of great friends, was going to melt her icy defences and heal her from the inside out.

James and Caroline headed upstairs to take some candid and relaxed shots of Abbie as she got ready. I made us all a whiskey coffee on Daphne's orders. As I sat drinking it, soaking up the pre-wedding excitement, I wondered if it would ever be me. The rate I was moving with McFitty, I was going to be Daphne's age before we were at the marrying stage.

It was soon time for all the bridesmaids' photos to be taken in Abbie's lounge, and Quinn chatted the couple up, explaining her possible job role and asking for their business card, which they happily gave her.

'Ok, I'm coming down,' Abbie called, making us all jump to attention. We helped Daphne up and gathered at the bottom of the stairs, letting out a collective gasp as Abbie appeared in her beautiful gown, the widest smile on her face.

'Oh, Abbie,' Daphne exclaimed, blotting her eyes with a handkerchief as Abbie slowly made her way down to join us in the hall. We stood in a circle, all five of us girls holding hands.

'I'm getting married!' she whispered.

'The curse is well and truly lifted,' Georgie nodded, never having looked prouder of her best friend, which was so touching. 'You look just ... wow, Abbie.'

'I've never seen you looking more radiant or beautiful, Abbie Carter,' Daphne murmured, sniffing back some tears.

'Stunning,' I agreed.

'I really don't want to imagine how my brother's going to react when he sees you, as it will scar me for life, but I've got a feeling he's going to be dragging you up to the hotel suite the second you arrive,' Quinn laughed. Abbie blushed and swatted Quinn's arm. 'I'm so happy, Abbie. I've been alone for so long, and now I have an amazing brother and a new sister too!'

'Hey, how about me, Daphne, and Charlie? Are you saying we're not much cop?' Georgie scolded.

'I have no idea what that means. You really need to give me a British expressions prep course,' Quinn said with a confused look on her face.

'She's saying she sees herself as your sister as well. You've become part of this little family here too, Quinn,' Abbie said softly, making Quinn show an uncharacteristic display of emotion as her eyes filled up. She quickly blinked them back, casting a furtive glance at us all to see if we'd noticed.

'You are, you're a lovely girl, Quinn,' I said sincerely.

'Even with that hair and the ring in your nose,' Daphne said, giving it another of her infamous looks of distaste. I had a feeling she wasn't going to give up needling Quinn about it. 'You need to watch Wayne Davies, the farmer's son. He'll be putting a rope through it and leading you to the farmers' market.'

'She'll be off the market soon if I have anything to do with it,' Abbie said. 'I couldn't fix up poor Heath with Georgie or Charlie, so I've got high hopes of setting him up with Quinn.'

'Who is this guy that no one wants? Do I really want you trying to dump him on me?' Quinn asked indignantly. 'Does he look like a slapped ass?'

'Arse,' we all laughed. I had so much to teach her when it came to the English language.

'Hell no,' Georgie said. 'He's super hot, both Abbie and I quite fancied him at one point, but the timing was off and we're parked firmly in the friend zone now.'

'I'd already fallen for McFitty, Dr. Fitton, by the time I met him, but if my crush ever fades, Heath's one stallion I'll be attempting to ride,' I giggled.

'Then let's get to the church and meet this stud, it's been a while since I had a ride,' Quinn grinned.

'Girls, this is my nephew we're talking about,' Daphne groaned as she shook her head. 'Come on, before poor Miller thinks Abbie has changed her mind. The curse isn't lifted until she says the words "I do."'

Everyone headed outside, ready to make their way up the lane to the church for the early evening ceremony. I turned to close Abbie's front door and locked it behind me, slipping the key under the plant pot. I couldn't wait to see Abbie and Miller exchange their vows. No one deserved a happy ending more than they did. I also couldn't wait until we got to Severn Manor and I could let my hair down and party with Quinn. I'd worked so hard the last couple of months, it would be good to have a night off before getting back to finishing my current manuscript.

'Three, two, one, drink,' Quinn counted down, both of us grabbing the first of the shots we'd lined up on the bar and tossing it back before moving on to the next, and then the next.

'Damn, girl,' I whined, screwing up my face as the alcohol burnt the back of my throat and brought tears to my eyes. 'I've never met anyone who could out-shot me.'

'You never met me before,' she laughed. 'Though I kinda wish you had. I could have done with a friend like you growing up.'

'Well, you're stuck with me now, neighbour,' I grinned, clinking my empty shot glass against hers. 'I think you're going to be really happy here.'

'You know, I think you might be right,' she agreed, beckoning the bartender over. 'Line up another three each, will you?'

'Quinn, are you trying to kill me?' I gasped. 'My liver is fast approaching middle age, it only behaves badly once or twice a year.'

'Well, get it used to behaving badly a lot more now that I'm in town. We've got to get you onto the fun programme.'

'And talking of getting some fun, Heath's looking at you again.'

'I know,' she nodded, leaning against the bar but not looking his way.

'How? How do you *do* that?' This girl had eyes in the back of her head.

'I can see his reflection in the mirror behind the bar,' she grinned, flicking her chin towards the long piece of glass that ran behind the vast array of coloured bottles.

'So what are you going to do about it?'

'Nothing,' she shrugged.

'You're telling me you've suddenly become the shy and retiring type?' I scoffed as our glasses were filled again.

'Hey, this is me,' she laughed. 'I'm not going to do anything about it because he's Daphne's nephew. I don't need complicated.'

'Why does it have to be complicated? Heath fancies you, and I've seen some of the sneaky looks you were giving him over dinner, so don't try telling me you don't find him insanely hot.'

'I do, of course I do. I mean, look at him …' She trailed off as she carried out her inspection of him in a seriously sexy fitted three-piece suit, which was so unlike the combats and grubby t-shirts he usually wore to do the gardening and odd jobs in.

'So?' I prodded.

'I don't do relationships, Charlie. I'm never letting another guy get close enough to hurt me again. I'm into short and sweet and I move on before it gets serious. He's not a short and sweet guy. He's long haul, and he's Daphne's nephew. That package of hotness right there is complicated, and we're back to me not doing complicated.'

'So you're never going to settle down with a guy, never going to get married or have a family?' I asked, my heart aching for her as I saw her defences quickly arming themselves.

'Nope. Now, are we drinking or what?' she said, picking up the first shot glass and giving me a look that told me that however friendly we'd become in the last couple of months, she wasn't open for a deeper discussion on her issues. I sighed and nodded. We had time. We all had time to work on her once she moved here next month. And she was naïve to imagine that with our close-knit group, she'd be able to fend us all off when we set our minds to helping her find happiness in Dilbury.

'This time I'm taking you down, Garcia,' I warned her as I lifted my glass.

'Bring it on, Faulkner, bring it on,' she grinned.

'To friendship,' I toasted.

'To friendship,' she replied, moving her glass towards mine.

'Three, two, one, drink,' I yelled as fast as I could before I knocked back the first one, taking her by surprise.

'Hey, that's cheating.' She lifted the glass to her lips, desperately trying to catch me.

'All's fair in drink and friendship,' I laughed, wiping my lips on the back of my hand as I set the last glass down and waited for her to do the same. I got a scowl that Daphne would have been proud of before she shook her head and started laughing.

'You're a piece of work. I'll get you back for that.'

'Yeah, yeah, talk to the rump, Garcia, as this one's on its way to shake its stuff on the dance floor,' I told her as I spun and unsteadily made my way over.

I grinned when I cast a look over my shoulder to see her sigh and follow me. I was glad she was here. Everyone except for Heath was coupled up. I hated being at weddings as a single thirty-something. It was like all heads spun *Exorcist*-style to stare at you, like you were an alien species. Miller had been really sweet and invited Kitt to the evening party, but he wasn't able to make it.

The three guys had got on really well when I'd treated them to a day out, even if Kitt had totally thrashed them both in all things target practice, leading to them setting up the event as a quarterly thing to try and win back their pride. Miller and Kitt had started having a few pints together in The Cock on a Friday night, Kitt either getting a taxi home or crashing out in my spare room. It was great to see him free of some responsibility from time to time, just being a thirty-year-old guy hanging out with his pal.

I didn't regret encouraging the boy's time, but I did kind of miss having him to myself each Friday night. I hadn't realised just how much I looked forward to our few hours together each week.

New Year's Eve

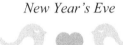

I heard a car pull up and a door shut, and even though it didn't sound like Kitt's car, I quickly pushed a sleeping Tibbs off my lap and ran to the front door. I threw it open and looked out, but my drive was empty.

'Hey, gorgeous.' A masculine voice that sounded like Weston's drifted over the hedge.

'Hey, you. How are you?' Georgie replied.

'Better for kissing you. But I think I need more kisses, just to be sure.'

'Just to be sure.'

I giggled to myself as I heard the unmistakable suction noise of a passionate kiss and padded across the grass to look over the hedge, only to find them locked in an embrace on the front door step.

'I'd shout "Get a room," but it's not like you need to go far,' I yelled to surprise them. I succeeded in making them jump and quickly separate. Weston coughed and bent down to pick up his overnight bag. Georgie tried to discreetly wipe her mouth before she looked over at me, and I gave her a wide grin.

'Hey, Charlie.' Weston saluted me and disappeared inside with Bertie.

'So freakin' hot to watch,' I said, fanning my face. I couldn't remember the last time a guy had kissed me with that intensity.

'Try being on the receiving end, I think he just incinerated my underwear. What are you doing out in the garden at this time?' Georgie asked.

'I got excited when I heard a car pull up, I thought it was Kitt with my pizza delivery.'

'I still find it hilarious that you've ended up such good friends with the pizza delivery guy,' she laughed.

'He's a really nice guy, we've become close through my love of pizza,' I smiled.

'Anyway, why are you having pizza delivered? I thought you'd be out painting the town red with Quinn on New Year's Eve.'

'She decided to go over to New York to see her old friends,' I shrugged. 'She asked me to go with her, but I have a deadline to meet.'

'All work and no play.'

'I know, I know, but now that I'm traditionally published, I've got to keep up my end of the deal.'

'You can come and join Weston and me, we were just going to have a quiet night in,' Georgie offered.

'Nah,' I said, flicking my wrist. 'It's so sweet of you to offer, but you don't see much of each other as it is, go get loved up. Anyway, Kitt's coming down the lane with my pizza and I didn't order enough for all of us, and you know how I hate to share my food.'

'Are you sure?'

'Positive, I've always been tight when it comes to food, especially pizza. How do you think I managed to get all these sexy arse curves?' I winked.

'Well, you know where we are if you change your mind.'

'I won't, but thank you for offering. Happy New Year, Georgie, enjoy your romantic evening.' I blew her a kiss and she blew me one back.

'Happy New Year, Charlie. I have a feeling this is going to be your year. Dr. Fitton is going to see what's been in front of him all this time and sweep you off your feet.'

'One can dream,' I sighed. I'd felt so close to a breakthrough with him the last time I'd seen him, and now I was back to weeks of no sightings. She smiled at me and headed inside. 'Hey, Kitt,' I called as he got out of his car.

'Hey you. What are you doing outside?'

'Well, I raced out when Weston turned up, as I thought it was the pepperoni pizza.'

'So you were more excited about the food than seeing me? Thanks,' he laughed as he turned to dip his head back in the car.

'You know I'm always happy to see you, pizza or no pizza, but I won't lie. Knowing you're coming with my favourite meal always adds that extra level of excitement to your visits,' I teased. He laughed and reappeared, holding two large boxes with a few smaller ones on top. 'You brought treats as well?'

'Yes,' he chuckled. 'As it's a special occasion, I brought spicy potato wedges and New York cheesecake, too.'

'You fiend,' I groaned as he headed through the side gate and over to me. 'What will I ever do if that place closes? I'd be lost without your visits.'

'Are you sure you want me to hang out with you tonight?' he asked, making me slap his arm.

'I wouldn't have asked if I wasn't. I need a night off from writing and if you weren't here, I'd just end up with my head in my laptop. Do you mind if we eat the pizza out here? I know it's kind of crisp, but I lit the fire earlier and didn't realise how hot it had got in there until I came out.'

'Sure,' he agreed, flicking his head over to our bench. 'I love sitting out here. It's so peaceful and you get to see all the stars that I can't see when I'm at home.'

'It was like that in Cheltenham. You don't realise how much air and light pollution there is until you move out to the countryside,' I agreed as we sat down and he set the boxes in between us.

'Do you miss not being in the thick of it all?'

'No way,' I uttered, almost salivating at the smells coming from the boxes. 'How about you? You can hardly compare a market town like Shrewsbury to a huge city like Newcastle.'

'I did miss it to start with,' he nodded, handing over my pizza box, then opening the one containing the potato wedges between us. 'But I did the whole clubbing scene in my twenties, it's not really what I'm looking for now.'

'What are you looking for?'

'What most guys my age are. Settling down and thinking about a family, not that it will happen while I'm looking after Mum.'

'I don't think I've ever asked how old you are,' I mumbled as I set to work on my dinner. I was way past being embarrassed to let Kitt see me scoffing my food, he didn't care.

'Or me you,' he smiled. 'Take a guess.'

'I'll save you a cuff around the ear if you say a figure that's way higher than I am by saying that I think you're around my age, thirty-two next month.'

'I think that instead of a cuff you'd have proposed to me, as I was going to say twenty-seven. You look good for an old bird,' he chuckled.

'Hey,' I protested. 'I could still cuff you, Daphne style. So, have I just insulted you?'

'Not at all, I'm flattered myself as I'm actually thirty-three. I could be your hot sugar daddy.'

'Ewww,' I shuddered, pulling a face.

'Thanks a lot,' he huffed as he looked at me, aghast.

'It's the sugar daddy reference. It's a hot taboo trope in my field, but I just don't see the appeal of daddy role-play. It totally grosses me out.'

'Me too,' he agreed, grabbing a slice of his favourite seafood pizza. We were real creatures of habit.

We sat in happy silence, soaking up the crisp air and unhindered view of the blanket of stars overhead, until we heard a commotion from next door.

'Treat? You call this a treat? Charlie, Charlie!' Georgie's voice screamed. I saw Weston's head bobbing along the top of the hedge as he marched towards her front gate. 'Help me, I'm being kidnapped against my will! Owww, what the hell was that?' she exclaimed after the sound of a sharp slap.

'Screaming is very unladylike behaviour, Georgina,' Weston said, as Kitt and I stood up to see what on earth was going on.

'Oh you ... you ... *brute*. Put me down. Charlie, seriously, do something!'

'I wouldn't be shrieking if he had me over his shoulder like that,' I called back when I saw her hanging down Weston's back with his hand on her backside. He flashed me a grin. 'It's seriously hot. I'm getting images of him just wearing those firefighter trousers and braces, his bare chest and biceps all oiled up,' I giggled. Weston chuckled, and Kitt laughed when Georgie swore at me.

'It's not hot. He's forcing me to go to The Cock,' she moaned as Weston stepped out into the lane.

'Are your neighbours always so brutally honest?' Kitt asked with a look of amazement on his face.

'Not Weston's,' I laughed, swatting his arm. 'She meant The Cock & Bull pub. She won't go inside and I think it's a great idea he's forcing her to go. You have every right to be in there, Georgie,' I shouted as Weston jumped over the stile into the paddock opposite, with her still slung over his shoulder. 'Don't let either of them drive you out.'

'Our friendship is officially over, Charlie,' she hollered back.

'Why's she so upset about going to the pub?' Kitt asked.

'She was engaged, and her fiancé two-timed her with the slutty barmaid Rowena. Georgie's too ashamed to show her face in there now, as that homewrecker still works there.'

'That sucks.'

'It does. I don't get men sometimes. You have a beautiful and intelligent girl like Georgie agree to marry you, and you mess around behind her back?'

'Some guys just want to have their cake and eat it, and they give the rest of us an unfair reputation.'

'You've never cheated on a girlfriend?'

'No. You're either with someone or you're not. If you love someone, there shouldn't be room in your heart to let anyone else in, not even for a quick night of drunken fun. Hey, you're shivering, let's get inside,' he suggested.

'Ok, it has gone a bit chilly,' I agreed. 'But this time guard your pizza, or Tibbs will be off with it again.'

'Does she have a thing for cheesecake as well?'

'She won't live to see the New Year in if she does,' I said as we grabbed our boxes and headed in to the warmth. 'There's a taxidermist a few villages over. I've warned her that if she keeps misbehaving, I'll have her stuffed and mounted in a curled up sleeping position, so I can put her wherever I want and pet her without losing a hand. All the benefits of a pet without the expense of food, litter, and vet bills.'

'You're evil,' he laughed, shaking his head as I grinned at him.

'You're super fidgety,' Kitt complained as I wriggled next to him on the sofa, trying to get comfortable.

'I like to lie down on the sofa to watch TV when I've eaten,' I protested.

'So lie down,' he said, putting a cushion on his lap and patting it.

'Isn't snuggling against the rules in the "friends of the opposite sex" handbook?' I asked, eyeing him curiously.

'There's a handbook?'

'No,' I laughed. 'Well actually, there probably is. Someone's bound to have written one, explaining the lines that shouldn't be crossed in case people get the wrong impression.'

'For God's sake, Charlie, lie down,' he muttered. 'I'm already aware that you're in love with the doctor, it's not like I'm about to read into you watching TV with your head on my lap and think my luck is in.'

'Who said I'm in love? When did I mention *love*?' I exclaimed.

'You're not?' he asked with a frown.

'I don't know him. Trust me, it's all about the lust, definitely not about love. You can't fall in love with someone you don't even know.'

'So how many times have you been in love?' he asked as he patted the cushion.

'I don't think I ever have been. I'm not sure I'd even know if I was,' I said as I tucked up my legs on the sofa and snuggled down with my head on his lap.

'Huh,' he huffed as he stretched his arm along the back of the plump leather sofa back.

'How about you?' I asked, twisting my head to look up at him.

'Once,' he nodded. 'We started dating in college, but it didn't work out.'

'How come?'

'We didn't see much of each other when we went to universities on different sides of the country, and when we graduated and got together more often, we realised we'd grown apart, so agreed to separate.'

'I'm sorry.'

'Don't be,' he smiled down at me. 'It fizzled out, it wasn't a huge, painful break-up that had me turning to drink to drown my sorrows. Does that sound heartless?'

'No. I guess if you know something's not working, you're prepared for the inevitable. You grieve for the loss of the relationship daily over a long period of time, rather than it being a shock and hitting you all at once.'

'Hmmm,' he nodded, with a serious, contemplative look on his face.

'What are you thinking?' I asked after a few minutes of silence.

'I ...' He shook his head and ran a hand over his mouth. 'We're friends, right? Good friends?'

'I'd say we're the best of friends,' I smiled. 'Why?'

'There's things I think and feel about my situation that sometimes make me wonder if I'm becoming cold and heartless, and I'm worried if I tell you, you'll see me differently.'

'What?' I gasped, quickly turning over to save getting a crick in my neck. 'You're one of the most warm-hearted and generous people I know, Kitt. How can you think that?'

'Is it normal to sometimes wish my mum wasn't suffering anymore? That she'd slip away peacefully?' he asked in a pained tone, signs of confusion written all over his face. 'I wouldn't wish this life on anyone, not the way she's living, or me. She has no idea what's really going on around her, she doesn't recognise her friends or her own son. She verbally and physically abuses me when she's having an extra bad day, and it's days like those that I find really hard.'

'Anyone would find that hard, Kitt,' I said softly, picking up his hand and squeezing it tightly. It hurt my heart to think how much he gave of himself for no gratitude. 'I think what you're feeling is perfectly normal. You want your mum back. You're stuck in a toxic relationship, but feel obligated to stay because she *is* your mum and you remember how things used to be. And the fact that you do stay, that you haven't stuck her in permanent care so you can get on and enjoy your life, says just how big your heart really is.'

'You think?' He gave me a pained smile.

'I know,' I said firmly. 'You're not wishing she was dead, you're looking at it through compassionate eyes, wishing her suffering, and yours, was over. It's like your relationship with the girl you loved. Without you being able to sustain it, it's slowly dying. The only difference is you still love your mum. I'm sure when the day comes that she slips away, you're going to be sad, but you'll also feel a huge sense of relief, and there's nothing wrong with that.'

'Thanks,' he said quietly, squeezing my hand back. 'Jesus, talk about a depressing conversation to bring down the start of a New Year.'

'It's not depressing. It's beautiful to see just how far people will go for the ones they love. It's inspiring, actually. You, Kitt Fraser, Pizzaman extraordinaire, are an inspiration. I'm a lucky girl to have a friend like you in my life.'

I struggled up off his lap and planted a kiss on his cheek, then wrapped him up in a tight hug. He hesitated for a moment, then banded his arms around me as well. I closed my eyes and enjoyed feeling the warmth and comfort of being held so tightly. It had been a long time and I'd forgotten how great it felt, like I was cared for and protected, safe.

'I'm the lucky one. How many customers would look past the guy who does a menial job of delivering food and see the man behind him?' He shrugged as he released me and I sat back up.

'There's nothing wrong with what you do, it suits your life right now and is a means to an end. And even if it wasn't, as long as you're happy doing any job, that's all that matters. People put too much emphasis on having to have "a career" or a "decent job." Jobs pay money so you can live, they shouldn't be the main focus of your life.'

'Says the woman who buries herself in work,' he laughed, his mood visibly lifting from one of melancholy to the cheerful guy I'd come to know.

'But to me this isn't work, I love what I do. It inspires me to get up each morning as I'm so excited to get words on paper. The fact it pays me a living is a bonus, obviously. So, if you weren't delivering pizza, which by the way would break my heart if you stopped, what would you be doing?' I asked.

'I'm actually an architect.' A slow smile spread across his face, his eyes lighting up with an enthusiasm and passion I'd never seen before. 'I was working for a large firm in Newcastle, but obviously had to quit to come and take care of Mum.'

'And that job made you happy? It was the one that made you want to leap out of bed every morning, like writing does for me?' I asked as I curled back up on his lap and looked up at him.

'It did,' he nodded. 'I miss it. I miss using my brain and I hate the way people look down on me without knowing what I'm actually capable of. Except you.' He gave me a soft smile of gratitude and ran his hand over my hair, gently tucking some stray strands behind my ear, which sent a shiver down my spine. 'You never treated me like just the delivery guy. You saw me when you didn't even know me. You're the least judgemental person I've ever met, and that's a beautiful character trait to have, Charlie.'

'Don't make me blush,' I giggled, doing just that as I tucked my hands under my heated cheeks. 'I must have recognised another creative thinker, a kindred spirit. Your face just lit up when you said what you used to do. I like seeing you look like that. You've heard my entire life story since we met, but you never told me anything about your passion. Tonight, I'm all ears, and considering you know how much I love to talk, you'll appreciate what a rarity that is,' I said, making him laugh. 'So, come on, the floor is yours. Tell me all about what your job entails and why you love it so much.'

'You're sure I'm not going to bore you?'

'Do I look in a rush to go anywhere?'

'No, you're looking pretty settled.' He laughed as Mrs. Tibbles jumped up onto the sofa and nestled herself on my side as she started to purr and painfully knead me. 'And that definitely settles it, neither of us are going anywhere until she decides we can. They're going to find our skeletons still sitting in the same position sometime next year as we're too scared to move the demon cat.'

'She's not that bad, are you, Tibbs,' I cooed as I bravely rubbed the side of her face. Her loud purr was a rare and welcome sound.

'I bet she's only happy as I let her have some prawns off my pizza, and now she's hoping for some cheesecake.'

'She can keep her grubby little paws off that. Oh no, it's the countdown,' I exclaimed as the chants from ten to zero radiated from the TV behind me. 'God damn it, Tibbs, I'm going to miss the fireworks.'

'I'll record it, we can watch them together when she moves,' Kitt said, picking up the remote from the arm of the sofa. 'Happy New Year, Charlie. Wishing you wealth and happiness, and a serious bucket load of health, as you need all the help you can get.'

'I do,' I laughed. 'Happy New Year, Kitt. If I could reach my champagne, I'd toast to friendship and good luck. I have a feeling that things are going to improve for you this year, because no one deserves a lucky break more than you.'

We smiled at each other as the sound of cheering and fireworks exploded behind us.

Another year full of possibilities and change. I was looking forward to finding out what it would bring. I had a sense that it was going to be momentous.

Chapter Eleven

The Big Thaw
Six Weeks Later – Valentine's Day

'HURRY UP, WILL YOU?' Quinn moaned from the front doorstep as I checked my bag to make sure I had my wallet and keys. 'I'm freezing to death.'

'You lived in New York, with the icy blast of Atlantic winds sweeping through it. A foot of Dilbury snow should feel like summertime to you,' I said, shaking my head as I turned to face her. She was hopping from foot to foot and rubbing her leather-clad hands, completely muffled up with one of Daphne's knitted bobble hats and a matching scarf. She'd even forgone her trademark thick knitted tights and mini skirt for a pair of jeans with her heavy boots. 'Anyway, why am I coming kitchen shopping with you? I'm the last person to be giving advice on kitchens, I don't even use my own.'

'Because Miller and Abbie are away, Georgie is all loved up with Weston, and you're my new BFF, so you're stuck with me.'

'Fine, but we're going to stop at The Cock on the way back and dinner and drinks are on you, now that you have a new fancy salary, Quinn *Wedding Planner* Garcia,' I told her.

'Not yet, I don't,' she replied, a curl of white appearing in front of her mouth as she breathed out. 'I don't start until April.'

'Whatever. Your brother's a gazillionnaire, you can afford dinner,' I teased her as I turned to lock the front door.

'He might have bought me the cottage, but he doesn't throw money my way, you know. He's not extravagant with it.'

'Hmmm, the cars and houses in two countries, private plane, and helicopter beg to differ. He's the kind of guy my readers go crazy over.'

'You think? I'm kinda over the whole "rich guy with issues" books.'

'You'll love my newest one then,' I said. 'I'm so excited, it's abo–' I shrieked as I stepped onto the path and my foot shot out from under me on a patch of ice. 'Quinn!' I squealed as I felt myself tipping backwards, and I reached out a hand to grab her to steady myself. I missed and went down with a thud, landing right on the edge of the raised doorstep with a force that rattled my bones. 'Owww.'

'You ok?' Quinn laughed, offering me her hand.

'No, my legs have gone to jelly and my arse is throbbing,' I complained, wincing as she pulled me up.

'Arse. *Arse.* Arse. *Arse.* Arrrrse,' Quinn repeated in a variety of accents and styles, making me laugh. 'It still doesn't sound right.'

'Whereas "tushy" or "ass" has that air of refined elegance? And don't even start me on fanny pack, that's a whole other level of wrong,' I said, clinging to her arm as we trudged across the treacherous terrain of my path towards the drive. Her boots were so much better equipped to grip than mine were.

'Well, it is wrong when you know what fanny stands for over here, but on the flip side, I nearly choked on my coffee the first time Daphne asked how your pussy was doing. Especially when she asked if the hair had regrown after being shaved and if it had its appetite back,' she grinned, making me laugh again.

'Poor Mrs. Tibbles, she did look a sight with her pink skin on display,' I nodded. She'd been attacked by one of the most vicious farm tomcats, who was known in the village for terrorising everyone's pets. But by all accounts, he'd come out far worse from the ordeal than Tibbs. She'd had an infected bite on her side that had to be shaved and stitched, whereas he'd been taken to the vets missing half an ear, with a swollen and badly bitten tail, numerous bald patches, and a set of claw marks across his nose that were likely to scar. I'd never been prouder of my girl for standing up for herself.

We made it to my car in one piece and I winced as I climbed in and sat down. I'd really hurt my bottom and the base of my spine with that fall. I quickly put on the heated seats for both of us and started the engine. Quinn cranked up the heating, angling all of the vents in reach towards her, and I shook my head.

She'd settled in here so well, having taken up residence in Abbie's spare room while the renovations on Daphne's old cottage were carried out. Each Saturday night, she'd come and stay with me to give Miller and Abbie some alone time. We'd had a few more entertaining girls' nights out, which had led to Andy the taxi driver refusing to accept bookings from us for our return journey. Daphne had given us the feedback, from the Dilbury rumour mill, that we were too raucous and our drunken topics of conversation had interfered with his pacemaker. She'd decided if the conversation was that spicy, she wanted to come on the next night out.

I eased my car out of the drive and slowly made my way up the snowy lane. It was treacherous, and I felt the car sliding a few times. Quinn chuckled to herself when I had to take a couple of runs at getting up the incline from the church to the main road, which didn't look much better than the lane, despite the council sending gritters out every morning and night since we got caught in this cold snap. I loved this weather when I was in my cottage with the fire roaring and I could look out at the beautiful view. Driving in it, in a sports car that wasn't designed for snow, was another matter.

'You ok?' Quinn asked as we made it out of Dilbury, which had never looked more picturesque, coated in a blanket of snow with smoke curling out of all the chimney tops, and headed towards Shrewsbury. 'You keep frowning.'

'I'm trying to concentrate, the road is slippery, and I have a weird sensation in my bottom.'

'You know you're supposed to remove a butt plug, right?'

'It's not a butt plug,' I uttered, swatting her arm as she teased me. 'It's going numb, my ... lady parts are as well.'

'Really?' Her grin morphed into a frown. 'That doesn't sound good, but then you did go down kinda hard. Have you broken something?'

'I don't think you can your break your arse or ... fanny,' I scoffed, shifting in my seat as the weird tingling sensation continued to spread.

'I don't know. You didn't meet my ex,' she chuckled. 'You've probably bruised your coccyx.'

'Did you say that to him after?' We both burst out laughing and she shook her head, but her smile faded quickly and she turned her head to stare out of the passenger window. 'Do you miss him?'

'No.' Her response was too fast and sharp.

'Do you want to talk about it?'

'Not really. I don't do all that emotional chick-bonding crap,' she said brusquely, not looking over at me.

'Did you love him?'

'I'm not capable of love anymore, not for guys anyway. He was ... you know what, I'm not in the mood to talk about him. He's there, I'm here, we're over. Nothing more to say.'

'Ok, I hear you.' If it had been anyone other than Quinn, I wouldn't have taken no for an answer, as it was obvious there was a story there. Much as I'd love to get her to open up though, we were still fairly new friends. I already trusted her, but I got that with her past, my trust would have to be earned before she'd even consider sharing. And she might never want to anyway. Being brought up in foster care, abandoned by the people who were supposed to love and take care of you, was likely to make any kid emotionally withdrawn. She'd been self-sufficient for so long out of necessity. I wasn't offended, I just hurt so much for her. 'Quinn?'

'I don't mean to be a bitch, Charlie, but I said there was nothing more to say.'

'I know, it's just … I don't think I should be driving,' I said as I started to slow the car down on one of the long stretches of road. 'I'm really losing sensation and it's spreading.'

'Pull over, now,' she said firmly, quickly looking over at me. 'You could have slipped a disc or something. We need to get you checked out. How far is your ER?'

'About six miles. I'm sure it's nothing, I've probably just bruised myself badly, but I don't want to risk driving, just in case.'

'If you're losing feeling that fast, it's serious. Pull over, I'll get us there.'

'Have you ever driven over here?' I asked, gradually bringing the car to a halt and putting on my hazard lights.

'No, but I've driven back home. How different can it be?'

'Well, for a start, there's the whole "other side of the road" thing,' I pointed out, wondering if she'd really not noticed that minor detail.

'Oh right. Yeah well, you can just remind me if I do something wrong. Wait for me, I don't want you falling over again. I'll come get you and walk you around.'

I sighed and nodded my agreement. Seriously, I was off to the hospital again? I smiled at the thought that I might see McFitty again, and I quickly angled the rearview mirror to check how I looked. I'd made a bit of an effort as we were going to some of the posh bespoke kitchen showrooms, so that was a bonus.

Five minutes later, Quinn virtually wheel span away from the hedge, the back end of my car sliding.

'Hey, slow down. She doesn't like snow or ice, much like her owner,' I warned her. 'Plus checking your mirrors before you pull out and using an indicator tends to be compulsory around here.' I winced at the crunch of my gears and the potential whiplash as she jerked the car along the road instead of driving smoothly.

'I hate stick shift,' she growled. 'I always drive an automatic.'

'You didn't think that was worth mentioning *before* you got in the driver's seat?' I asked with an eye roll. 'Left foot on the clutch, then change gear. Quinn, seriously,' I gasped as we jerked forwards again. 'Left foot on the clutch. Left foot on the *bloody* clutch.'

'What's the bloody clutch?'

'The left hand pedal. Put your damn foot on the left pedal before you try changing gear, or stick or whatever you call it.' I winced as my head ricocheted off the headrest. 'Left. Foot. On. The. Bloody. Clutch,' I shouted.

'Don't be a … *side seat* driver, I'm doing my best,' she warned.

'How about I tell you when to put your foot on the left pedal and then I'll change gears?' I suggested through gritted teeth as I saw the revs in the danger zone while the engine screamed. 'Foot on the clutch now,' I said as calmly as I could, batting her hand away from the gearstick.

'It's on,' she said, so I moved up to third and she gave me a surprised look as the car gently carried on moving without tossing us around.

'And off,' I said, letting her go a bit further, 'and on,' then waited a beat as I moved into fourth, 'and off.'

'I feel like Mr. Mayagi. "Wax on, wax off,"' she chuckled.

'You'll be giving my car a wax by way of an apology for treating her so badly. Do you think you get it now?'

'I've got it,' she nodded.

We made it off the country road in one piece and turned left onto one of the main roads, and I relaxed a little as we got closer to town. My relaxation was short lived as Quinn decided to forget the whole "we drive on the left" deal once we reached a major roundabout.

'Quinn,' I screamed, gripping the seat and the door handle. 'Wrong way, wrong way!'

'Damn it. Get out of the way, asshole,' Quinn yelled, almost pressing her face up against the windscreen as a car approached, set for a head-on collision. It veered out of the way at the last moment, the driver ranting at us with a furious-looking face and a few rude finger gestures, and I quickly looked in the wing mirror to make sure he'd not skidded off the white snow-covered road into the ditch. My heart sounded like it was beating out a bass drum in my ears. 'Asshole,' Quinn hollered again.

'I'm going to die before I even make it to the hospital. Left, left, ignore the road ahead, that's oncoming traffic. For the love of God, *left* of the metal barriers,' I yelled.

'Don't yell at me, I'm doing the best I can,' she yelled back. 'Get out of the bloody way, you … bloody *asshole*,' she roared as a car zoomed up on our left, nearly taking out my wing, and me in the process.

'He actually had the right of way, as he went the correct way around the roundabout.'

'What's a damn roundabout?' she asked, forgetting the whole clutch in our lesson and jerking the car along the road again.

'That big round thing you just went the wrong way around.'

'That's a roundabout? We call it a traffic circle.'

'You're in England, it's a roundabout or an island.'

'Stupid bloody name.'

'What's with all the bloody? It's a swear word. You don't have to insert it in every sentence to sound more British, you know.'

'I bloody do,' she giggled.

'Whatever. Clutch down. Clutch down,' I cried, almost shedding actual tears of sheer terror.

'How much further? This is *fun* now that I'm getting the hang of it.'

'Our definition of fun is obviously another cultural anomaly,' I stated flatly. We were approaching the hospital and had a mini island to navigate. It was just a small white hump in the road, so I told her to slow down and reminded her to use the clutch as she dropped gears. 'Ok, island coming up, keep left,' I warned, moments before we both smacked our heads on the ceiling of the car.

'What the hell was that? Did I run over someone?' Quinn asked, sitting up to look in the rearview mirror that she hadn't adjusted to suit her.

'No, that would be the island that you just drove straight over.'

'I didn't even see a damn "island."'

'Obviously, as the lump on my head will attest. Ok, take a left at the next roundabout and keep left. Left, left, got it?'

'Right.'

'No, left.'

'I meant left.'

'You said right.'

'I meant I'm going left, left, right?'

'Good God, there's *no* right, it's *all* left. Left, *bloody* left,' I huffed.

'And I meant right, question mark, as in left, *bloody* left, right question mark, all right? As in, you got it?'

'Ah, right,' I said, catching her drift.

'Was that a right full stop, or another instruction to turn right?'

'I give up,' I moaned as the gears crunched and we jerked along again. I resorted to covering my eyes as we approached the "traffic circle" and hoped for the best. 'And indicators aren't optional extras in the U.K., by the way.'

'What the bloody hell is an indicator?'

'Charlie Faulkner please,' called a female nurse.

'Are you coming with me?' I asked Quinn as I gingerly stood up.

'Not if you're going to yell at me again.'

'You did go the wrong way around a one-way car park.'

'Well, it's a stupid country with a stupid driving system,' she muttered petulantly.

'Which is now your home, so you'd better get on board with its rules and systems,' I smiled, linking my arm through hers. 'Come on, don't be so grumpy. You might get to meet McFitty or McNotQuiteSoFitty again. If we see him, you have my full permission to get your flirt on.'

'Nice, I get the doctor you deem not hot enough to warrant the title of McFitty. You're such a great friend.'

We exchanged a look and grinned at each other. We were different in so many ways, but we also seemed to complement each other so well. Like salt and pepper, fish and chips, pie and mash, pepperoni and pizza. I sighed as I realised I was coming up with food analogies. I was starving. We'd missed lunch as we'd been sitting here waiting for so long. Even Quinn had complained of a numb bum.

'Ok, I'll get a doctor to come and assess you,' the nurse said after taking all of my details. 'If you can please remove your jeans and knickers and lie on your left-hand side facing the wall, then cover yourself with the blanket.'

'Take my knickers off?' I asked in surprise.

'Yes, the doctor will need to do a rectal exam to see how much sensation you've lost.'

'A *what*?' I spluttered.

'It's where he shoves a finger up your–'

'Thanks, Quinn, I'm pretty confident a rectal exam is the same in American or British English,' I said quickly, cutting her off. 'Is that really necessary?' I asked the nurse.

'You've got decreased sensation, back and front, after a heavy fall. Yes, it's necessary. Trust me, we've seen everything here. You'll be more embarrassed than the doctor.'

'You're not kidding,' I muttered as she slipped out of the door. 'I'll be even more embarrassed if McFitty's the one to do it.'

'It's a big hospital. What are the chances of you getting him again?' Quinn said, trying to reassure me as I tugged my jeans down.

'With my luck?' I scoffed. 'Close your eyes, the knickers are about to come off.'

'Why knickers?' she said, doing as she was told. 'It makes no sense at all. You nick yourself shaving, why would you want to stick something that nicks you so close to the sensitive fun zone?'

'Fun zone? You're thirty-one, you can't call it by its real name?'

'Says "it" girl. Are you decent yet?'

'No, give me a minute.'

'How about you tell me when it's safe? I don't want to accidentally open my eyes and be scarred for life by a sighting of a possibly hairless British beaver.'

'You know, I think I'd actually choose kitchen shopping over this,' I huffed as I got up on the bed and draped the blanket over myself. 'It's safe, you can open your eyes.'

'You sure? If you're facing the wall and haven't covered yourself properly, I'll be seeing a British chocolate starfish.'

'I don't have a chocolate starfish! We're so progressive in England that we have this thing called toilet paper. I assure you that if you opened your eyes and I wasn't decent, it would be the pinkest starfish you'd ever seen.'

'That's good to know, as I'll be the one witnessing it, Miss Faulkner,' Guy Fitton's voice said, making me groan as my cheeks coloured up.

'Seriously, I get you for one of the most embarrassing examinations of my life? *Again?* Do you specialise in south-of-the-border treatments?'

'I've been known to travel north on occasion,' he chuckled. 'I did treat you for an eye injury last time, if I recall correctly. Hi there, I'm Doctor Fitton.'

'Ah, McFitty in the flesh. We did meet briefly in a nightclub last year. I'm Quinn, neighbour and friend of the injured.'

'Quinn!' I uttered, mortified as he said 'McFitty?' with a puzzled tone and the nurse let out a girlish giggle.

'She thinks you're hot, and I have to agree. Are you dating anyone at the moment?' Quinn asked.

'Ermmm, I think we've got slightly off topic here. Why don't we focus on the patient and her injury,' he suggested. I screwed my eyes up even tighter, and just to be sure I couldn't see his reaction, covered my face with my hands, jumping a little as I heard the snap of the gloves he was putting on, then the unmistakable farting sound of lubricant being squirted out of the tube.

'Kill me now,' I whispered.

'You might want to turn to look the other way to save your friend being embarrassed.'

'There's another level to the embarrassment I'm feeling right now?' I asked.

'I'd say not,' Quinn chuckled as I heard the scrape of a chair on the smooth flooring.

'Ok, Charlie, if you can bring your knees up to your chest … higher... that's great. Now you're going to feel something cold and some pressure. Just try and relax, it shouldn't hurt and won't take long,' he said in his best comforting tone. I automatically jolted forwards as I felt his scouting mission brush past and he placed his other hand on my hip.

'Relax for me and push out as I push in, it will be easier. Relax. Relax ... Relax!'

I bit the heel of my hand as he set to work, me fighting him every step of the way and resisting the urge to shout back, "You try and bloody relax while I do this to you.". This was it, our non-relationship was now doomed. What girl wanted to go on a date with a guy who'd probed her intimate areas before he'd even kissed her? I mean, he might be put off, too. He'd not exactly seen me at my prettiest, with dermatitis rash on my eyes as well as down there, even before this?

'Can you feel my finger?'

'Jesus,' I muttered, my cheeks flaming. 'Yes, I can feel it, but it feels ... weird. I mean, I know it's normal to feel weird when something's ... *there*, but it's extra weird.'

'Extra weird? You're saying it doesn't feel the same as when your partner has been intimate with you back here?'

'Someone pass me my English thesis to do again, as that would be preferable to what's happening here right now,' I groaned, beyond humiliated. 'Yes, extra weird to ... normal. Not that it's normal, you know? I don't go around inviting explorations. There's no "Open for potholing" sign that I stick back there. I've even slapped one guy who ignored the "wrong hole" warning I screamed at him. So no, in summary, vis-à-vis butt examinations, while it doesn't exactly happen on a regular basis, I have a vague recollection that *that* doesn't feel normal.'

'A simple no would have sufficed,' he said, and I heard Quinn giggling to herself. 'Clench for me.'

'If I clench any harder, you're liable to lose a finger,' I warned him. It took a concerted effort to answer his questions as I tried to remember if I'd ever been more embarrassed. I think this actually topped the whole "looking at my lady parts" incident. When he withdrew, removing the tattered shreds of my dignity at the same time, I could have sobbed with relief.

'Well, I'd like to get an MRI of your lower back, so I'll leave some paper towel for you to clean up and go and see how long the waiting list is. You're free to get dressed. I'll be back as soon as I can,' he said, covering me back up with the sheet.

'Ok,' I whimpered, not unfurling from my foetal position or removing my hands until I heard the door open and then the soft click as it closed and they left the room. 'Did that really just happen?' I asked Quinn.

'You said you were a walking medical disaster, but to have him do that? Jeez, I'd have died.'

'I think I have, I can't move. He's going to come back to talk to me and I can't look at him. Go and grab a wheelchair. You can stick me in it and we can make a run for it before he comes back.'

'You're not going anywhere,' Quinn said as I heard her heavy boots walking towards me. 'If he's looking at an MRI, he's worried you've ruptured a disc or something. That's serious, Charlie. Here, the towel to clean up. I'll go out for a few minutes and give you some privacy. I think I saw a vending machine. I'll get us a soda and some candy as I'm starving.'

'Thanks,' I whispered.

I just lay there for a while after she left and took some deep, calming breaths before using the sandpaper-like towels on my delicate behind and getting dressed again. I was washing my hands when he came back into the room and I had to force myself to look at him as he explained that he couldn't get me an MRI scan, so I was on the waiting list and was being admitted until the scan had been done and assessed. In fairness to him, he was nothing but professional, but I could tell from the heat radiating off my face and neck that it was obvious to him how embarrassed I was.

'You really need to admit me? I can't go home and rest and just come back when you're ready for me?'

'Afraid not. The waiting list can change quickly and you'd miss your slot if you couldn't get back fast enough. The worst case scenario is that a disc can rupture or pop out completely, which is a medical emergency that necessitates immediate surgery. Until we've reviewed your scans, we need to keep you here. They're just organising a bed for you. Do you have any questions or concerns?'

I shook my head and listened as he went through the admission procedure and risks if the disc caused cauda equina syndrome. Quinn slipped into the room and grimaced at me as she listened.

'I'll find out if we have a bed ready for you and what ward you'll be on. I understand being suddenly admitted like this is a shock, but you're in the best place here. We'll take good care of you, ok?'

'Ok, thanks.'

'Oh, Charlie,' Quinn sighed as he left the room. She dumped her armful of candy bars and the cans of pop and came to give me a much needed hug. She said she didn't do emotional bonding "crap," but she was in denial. Under that cool self-defence mechanism was a woman with a huge and caring heart. 'I'll wait until I know where they're taking you and I can go back to your place and pack a bag. Tell me what you'd like me to bring back for you?'

'You're going to drive my car? Alone? I'd rather he come and do another rectal exam than give you my car keys!'

'Hey, I did ok. I got you here, didn't I?' she huffed.

'You did, but I'm ringing Andy to drive you back and forth, my car can stay in the car park until I'm ready to go home,' I said firmly, pulling out my phone.

'Happy bloody Valentine's night, eh?' she said, rolling her eyes.

'Valentine's sucks.'

'High five to that. But on the plus side, my diagnosis is McFitty is interested.'

'Shut up,' I laughed, shoving her shoulder.

'I got the interested vibe off him, but do you want my honest opinion?'

'Quinn, you're as blunt as a crappy chef's knife. I think *stopping* you from stating an honest opinion is the real problem.'

'Thanks, I guess.'

'Go on then.'

'He's hot, seriously hot,' she said.

'Well, duh.' I eye-rolled her obvious conclusion.

'But there's something about him that's shady. He was flirting with that nurse in the corridor. I don't think I like him.'

'You don't know him. You've met him once,' I retorted as I sat back down on the bed to wait to be transferred. So what if Quinn and Daphne didn't like him. I did, and it seemed like he was finally starting to thaw.

Chapter Twelve

'YOU'RE NOT PREGNANT?' THE man asked as he ran through a long list of questions.

'No.'

'Any recent tattoos?'

'No.'

'Any metal anywhere in your body?'

'No.'

'Head into the cubicle and get undressed. Put your clothes in this, then put on the gown with the opening at the back. When you're ready, come and wait on one of the chairs in the corridor,' he said as he handed me a black plastic shopping basket.

I did as I was told, cursing to find that I couldn't reach behind me to do up the ties in the small of my back. My curvy backside was hanging out of the patterned hospital gown. As Quinn had packed my favourite fleecy pyjamas, I didn't even have a dressing gown to cover up with. I edged out of the cubicle and looked around to see if anyone was around to offer me a spare gown to slip on, but the area was empty.

I ventured to the open doorway and stuck my head out to look up and down the corridor where I was supposed to take a seat. No one was about, so I quickly scuttled out, back to the wall, and dumped the basket as I tried to pull the gown over each cheek before I made a move to sit on the leather chair. I gave it a quick once over, not wanting to sit on someone else's raw butt print, then perched on the edge, my knees together to protect the remains of my modesty.

I'd had a number of surgeries, but I'd never had an MRI. I'd heard horror stories, that it was coffin-like and suffocating, that it banged so loudly you needed builder-style ear defenders. I wasn't exactly looking forward to it as it was, without the whole "breeze on my naked privates" situation.

'Miss Faulkner,' a lady called. I looked up and saw her standing outside a door a little bit further along on the opposite side of the corridor. I gulped, people were heading my way.

'Can you give me a minute?' I called.

'We're ready for you now. There's a long list of people to be seen, hurry please.'

'I'm never leaving the house in the snow *ever* again,' I muttered to myself as I grabbed my basket with one hand and tried to hold the flaps of the gown together as I stood up. The nurse gave me a curious look as I did a sideways shuffle, my back as close to the wall as possible without painting it with my bare bottom as I went. I drew level with her, and she raised her eyebrows as she stood waiting with the door open. I really wanted the people approaching to go past first or they were likely to get a full moon in their face.

'Miss Faulkner, *please*, we're waiting. We have a very busy schedule.'

'I have a slight situation,' I whispered.

'I can't hear what you're staying.'

'There's a slight situation,' I grimaced, flicking my head over my shoulder. 'I'd rather wait until these people pass.'

'Do you need some toilet wipes?' she asked, far too loudly for my liking.

'Not *that* kind of problem. My bare bottom is hanging out of the back of the gown. I'd really prefer not to flash everyone.'

'Where are your knickers?'

'In the basket.'

'Well, they should be on you, dear,' she sighed, her face full of exasperation.

'I was told to get undressed.'

'You leave your knickers on.'

'Well, no one said "Get undressed but leave your knickers on," so I'm standing here about to get frost bite of the derrière.'

'Honestly,' she muttered. 'Fine, go and put them on, then come straight in please.'

'They don't exactly cover much, they're a V-string.'

'A what?'

'A V-string, like a G-string with a fraction more material, but basically my bottom will still be hanging out.' I gave a sarcastic smile to the male hospital staff who raised their eyebrows at my declaration as they passed, giving me the once over.

'I'd still prefer they're on please.' She let the heavy door swing shut and I glared at it, willing her to feel my annoyance through it.

More people were coming up the corridor, so I decided putting my knickers back on, however flimsy they were, was probably the best move. I started my sideways shuffle back towards the changing room, receiving a number of bizarre looks. I prayed that McFitty wasn't about to find me in this state, not that he hadn't seen and touched it all before.

A few minutes later, still not overly impressed that I was flashing a large proportion of leg as well as my lacy thong and bare bottom, I made my way to the room.

Why was it all right to expect me to walk around the hospital like this, yet if I strutted through in a bikini, I'd probably be arrested? As if nothing else could add to my humiliation, I'd just realised that as it was winter and I'd been busy, I hadn't carried out my regular deforestation of my legs. I didn't exactly have Chewbacca's level of growth, but there were definite visible signs of stubble. I was having a whole flashback to my mother's advice that I should never leave the house in unmatching underwear or without having shaved my legs. It was advice I was going to heed from now on.

I was settled onto the bed in front of the huge metal machine with small holes at either end, then supplied with a pair of headphones, agreeing to have music played to help drown out the loud banging I was told to expect.

'You still have an earring in the top of your ear,' the nurse sighed. 'Please remove it, and any other jewellery or piercings.'

'I'm not sure I can. It's a threaded stud that I did up really tightly when it was put in years ago. It never comes out.'

'Well, today it needs to. This machine acts as a large magnet, and the process could also cause the earring to heat up and burn you.'

'What if I can't take it out?' I asked, as I reached up to try and undo it.

'We can't do the MRI, but you're listed as an urgent case, so it needs to come out please.'

After much huffing and puffing on both parts, we finally got it out and she put it in a tray over on the other side of the room.

'Ok, you need to lie perfectly still for the duration. You'll be in the machine for around half an hour. We can communicate with you from the room that you can see through the glass.'

'Ok.' I blew out a deep breath as she pressed some buttons and the bed started to slide me inside.

I quickly made myself as comfortable as I could, breathing deeply as the entrance to the machine passed over my face, far closer than I'd expected. I wasn't claustrophobic, but even I felt a little nervous.

'Jesus, they sure don't make these machines for people with big breasts,' I huffed, my arms squeezing against my sides as I went further inside and my boobs were forced up under my chin. 'Hello, girls. Well, if this damn machine doesn't suffocate me, these huge sexy puppies might.'

'Try and relax, Miss Faulkner, you're not going to suffocate,' a tinny male voice said in my ear.

'Oh crap, you can hear *everything*?'

'Yes. No talking when the machine starts, you need to stay as still as possible,' he said.

'Good thing I don't have trapped wind,' I giggled. It failed to get a response. It seemed the MRI team on duty didn't have a sense of humour.

I was happy to see that after the initial tight funnel neck, the machine opened up a bit, allowing my shoulders to drop, along with the girls. I cricked my neck and clenched my teeth together, ready for half an hour of stillness, when something sparked in the back of my head.

'Ermmm, how big a deal is the whole "no metal in your body" thing?' I asked over the sound of the radio that had just started to play.

'It's serious. You answered no, isn't that correct?'

'Well, I'm not sure. There was an incident with a root canal filling a few months ago. The dentist said he'd lost a piece of the little metal thing they scoop the nerve and pulp out of your root with. He'd already filled the tooth before he noticed it was missing, so apparently it's in there.'

'So you're telling us there's a fragment of metal in your tooth?'

'Possibly, unless I swallowed it, in which case it's hopefully out of my system by now. If not, I'm in serious need of a colonic,' I laughed nervously, to no response. 'Hello? Are you there?'

'Just having a discussion, please give us a moment.'

'Ok,' I called, looking up at the beige ceiling so close to my face. 'This is the *suckiest* Valentine's weekend ever. Like being single each year isn't bad enough, this year I've had my intimate areas invaded by my long-term crush, who hasn't even been to check on me since. I've bottom flashed random strangers, and I've spent the night in the hospital waiting for an MRI, which I might not even be able to have now, thanks to Mr. Wanky and his shoddy tool of torture. And, to add insult to injury, I still can't feel my privates properly, which is making toilet visits rather challenging.'

'Ermmm, Miss Faulkner, just to remind you that we can hear *everything* you say,' the voice said, the unmistakable sound of laughter in the background making me screw up my face. I was so used to living alone that I talked out loud to myself all the time. At least they appeared to have developed a sense of humour now.

'Sorry, force of habit.'

'Ok, Miss Faulkner, we're going to have to pull you out of the machine while we contact your dentist to find out what type of metal was used.'

'Does it make a difference?'

'Yes. Certain types of surgical stainless steel react to the magnetic field, so we need to be sure before trying.'

'I'm all for being sure, pull me out,' I agreed. 'There's no way I want to have my tooth heat up to boiling point, or worse, to end up with my face stuck to the side of a giant magnetic coffin and have to have a maintenance team sent in to dismantle it to get me out, thanks.'

'Quite,' he replied. I'd been seriously considering a whole steamy "patient falls for hot doctor" novel, but after this stay, I was beginning to wonder how any romance blossomed in a hospital. It was far too stressful. And surely once a doctor had seen one naked woman for examination, they'd seen them all. Where was the allure when you knew it all inside out, literally?

'It could only happen to you,' Kitt laughed as I filled him in when he came in to see me during evening visiting hours. 'Did you have the MRI in the end?'

'I did and it was horrible. I mean, apart from the noise, which totally drowns out the music so I don't see the point in them playing it, it was an absolute breeze. What was horrible was the "Well, as we can't be sure about the metal in your tooth, let's give it a go and pull you out of the machine if there's a problem" suggestion. I was on tenterhooks the whole time, thinking that damn piece of metal was about to be sucked out of the side of my face, disfiguring me horribly.'

'So, when do you get the results?'

'I've no idea,' I sighed. 'I can't go home until they've read the scans.'

'I can call in and feed Tibbs and check the litter tray on my way to work,' he offered. I smiled and reached for his hand.

'You're too sweet. She's fine, Quinn's staying to look after her until I come home.'

'Charlie.' I looked up to see McFitty standing at the end of my bed with a clipboard in his hands. 'I have your results. Is this your partner?' he asked, eyeing Kitt curiously, especially where our hands were joined. I saw Kitt giving Guy the once over as well.

'No, we're just friends,' I said, trying to read the unusual expression on both of their faces as I let go of Kitt's hand.

'Very good friends,' Kitt said, standing up and offering his hand to Guy. 'Kitt Fraser, and you are?' he asked.

'Guy Fitton, Doctor,' he replied. I watched as they shook hands, eyeballing each other like gladiators about to do battle. Seriously, what was it with men and their need to have a pissing contest? Neither of them were interested in me, why the show of bravado and posturing? 'I'd appreciate it if I could speak to Miss Faulkner alone.'

'I'd rather stay. I'm concerned about her and want to make sure she's ok,' Kitt said stubbornly.

'She's in excellent hands, *Mr.* Fraser. She's under *my* direct care.'

'That's reassuring to hear, but you only care for her when she's admitted. I'm the one who looks after her in the long periods between,' Kitt replied, neither of them ending the now frosty handshake.

'And I'm the medical *professional*,' McFitty grated out, narrowing his eyes in a sexy display of dominance.

'He can stay. I'd like him to stay, please,' I interrupted. 'You have my results?'

'I do,' Guy said after a pause, releasing Kitt's hand. 'There's no evidence of disc rupture or spinal cord damage, so I'm happy to discharge you. It's more likely a case of bad bruising and muscular tension that's irritated the nerves in that general vicinity. You should regain normal sensation in due course.'

'I can go home? Now?' I asked, my eyes lighting up at the news.

'Yes. I'd suggest taking things easy for a while, no heavy lifting or unnecessary activities that involve bending.'

'Got it,' I said, swinging my legs off the bed. I was desperate to get home and have a shower to get rid of the clinical hospital scent all over me, not to mention get away from the embarrassment of my latest personal encounter with the delectable Dr. Fitton.

'Take it easy, please,' he said firmly. 'Hopefully I won't see you back for some time.'

'Hopefully,' I agreed, as I started shoving my toiletries off the bedside cabinet into my wash bag.

'I'll look forward to seeing you out again one weekend. Maybe I could buy you a drink and you can tell me all about how your writing and that publishing deal is going.'

I looked up at him, stunned, and was sure I heard a grunt of disapproval from Kitt. Had McFitty just implied he wanted to spend time with me? It wasn't exactly a "Charlie, will you go out on a date with me" statement, but I'd take what I could get.

'I ... I'd love that, maybe I'll see you around soon.'

'Soon,' he smiled, showing off that killer smile, which made the girl in the bed next to me sigh. 'Mr. Fraser,' he nodded curtly.

'*Mr*. Fitton,' Kitt replied, emphasising the "Mr." instead of using his medical title. I cocked my head to watch McFitty's sexy backside leaving, then gaped up at Kitt.

'Did he just propose a date? I mean, it's a tentative, casual sort of "let's hang out together if I see you out" proposition, but that's positive, right? Right?'

'I don't like him,' Kitt said, folding his arms across his chest.

'I do,' squeaked the young girl in the bed behind me. 'He's gorgeous. I swear I drool every time he walks past.'

'Do you think that was a casual date proposal?' I asked her.

'I think it was. If you're not going to trawl all the bars in town every night hoping to see him, I will,' she grinned.

'Kitt, can you believe it?' I asked.

'It's not a date if you don't arrange a day, time, or place, Charlie.'

'Don't bring me down, I've had two seriously sucky days. I'm going to pretend it's a proper date and ride on the high of it for the rest of the night. Hell, I might ride on this high for the rest of the year.' I clapped my hands together with excitement.

'Whatever. Come on, let's get you packed. I can take you home and settle you in. We'll sort out getting your car home another night.'

'You're the best, Kitt,' I beamed up at him.

'Hmmm,' he nodded.

'I'll text Quinn and let her know I'm on my way back.'

'Are you ok? You've been really quiet on the drive,' I asked as he turned down my lane.

'Just had a couple of stressful days with Mum,' he shrugged. 'Looking forward to a bit of alone time to clear my head.'

'And I've gone and ruined that by making you visit me and bring me home, I'm sorry.'

'You didn't make me. I wanted to come and see you and I was coming this way anyway. I wasn't going to drive past your house and leave you to find your own way home.'

'Well, I appreciate it. I'll take you for dinner at The Fox next time you're free as a thank you. Plus, it will be good to have a proper catch up with you. You need to offload on me if things are tough. You can always ring me, you know I work late most nights.'

'I don't like to bother you, your work is important.'

'And your well-being is important to me, Kitt.'

He flashed me a grateful smile, which I returned as he pulled up on my drive. He insisted on carrying me to the front doorstep so I wouldn't slip again. Quinn flung the door open before he had a chance to knock.

'It's so good to see you. I've been terrified staying here alone,' she said.

'Why? What happened?'

'That bloody cat, she's stalking me. Everywhere I go, she's there, staring at me like I'm her next meal. I even went to the toilet and felt like someone was watching me, looked down, and she'd climbed into my panties, which were gathered around my ankles, like they were a kitty hammock. I've never been so freaked out in my life.'

'Sorry,' I giggled, 'she does love doing that when women use the toilet.'

'Not just women,' Kitt chuckled. 'I was too embarrassed to say anything, and too scared for my genitals at the time to try ejecting her.'

'That's too funny,' I laughed as Kitt set me down.

'I'll go and get your case, then I'd better get to work.'

'Stay for a coffee, I'll put the kettle on,' I offered.

'Ok, one quick coffee,' he agreed before heading out.

'You are so lucky,' Quinn said as we headed into the kitchen.

'Lucky? After the last two days?'

'Hot doctor, who I still don't like by the way, warming up to you, and a best friend who's in love with you. You get to choose, while I don't even have one guy fighting for me.'

'What did you just say?' I asked as I stalled in my tracks, not sure I'd just heard her right.

'No one's interested in me.'

'Not that. *Who's* in love with me?'

'Kitt, of course,' she said, looking at me as if I was stupid. I blinked a few times as I tried to process her outrageous statement.

'Don't be ridiculous,' I finally said. 'We're friends, that's all.'

'Yeah, right,' she laughed with a roll of her eyes. 'The way he looks at you? The way he looks *after* you, all male protector and swoon-worthy, carrying you inside. Plus, he sent you roses and a card for Valentine's Day. Look, I found them on your doorstep when I got back from the hospital yesterday. I unpacked the box of roses and arranged them, since I didn't know how long you'd be gone.'

'Quinn, you're so far off base. Our relationship is as platonic as yours and mine. Sure, we're close, but no way.'

'Whatever, ignore me, but I know what I know. That man is head over heels for you and you're too blind to see it.'

I ignored her as I went to touch the beautiful red blooms she'd put in a vase, rubbing a petal between my fingers as I inhaled their heady scent. What on earth had made her think that he felt like that about me?

'Your case is in the hall, Charlie. I can take it up if you want,' Kitt said as he appeared in the kitchen doorway.

'Did you send the roses and the card to Charlie?' Quinn asked as she folded her arms across her chest and gave him a curious look.

'Quinn,' I warned. Sometimes I loved her direct approach, but sometimes I wanted to cringe. She had no shame factor at all.

'What? It's just a question.'

'A rude question.'

'I've got to get going,' Kitt said, looking at his watch. 'Let me know in the morning how you're feeling, ok?'

'What about your coffee?' I asked, my face falling. 'I thought you were staying for a few minutes.'

'You know I would if I could. Make sure you don't overdo things, ok?'

'I've got her back,' Quinn said. Kitt nodded and flashed me a smile, then walked out. I hurried after him, giving Quinn a "back off" glare, which made her hold her hands up in defeat as she stayed in the kitchen.

'Kitt,' I called as he stepped out of the front door.

'Yeah?' he replied, turning around to face me.

'Is everything ok? You don't seem yourself tonight and I'm worried.'

'I'm fine, Charlie. Nothing a good night's sleep won't cure. Follow the doctor's orders and don't overdo things, ok?'

'I won't. Come here a second,' I said, too scared of venturing out onto the snowy path again.

'Charlie, I need to go,' he sighed, running a hand up over his face and through his hair.

'Come here, please.'

'What?' He did as he was told and stepped within reach. I threw my arms around his neck and hugged him tightly as I kissed his cheek, then felt his hands curl around my waist. 'What was that for?' he asked, his voice full of surprise.

'Just because. Thanks for being you. Not many girls are lucky enough to have a best friend as good as you, let alone a guy. I really appreciate you and everything you do for me.'

'It's not one sided, Charlie. You bring light and fun into my life and always cheer me up when I need it most. It's a two-way friendship.'

'It's a great friendship,' I said, kissing his cheek again.

'It is,' he agreed, softly kissing my temple before easing me away from him. 'I really need to go.'

'Drive safely. Text me when you get home so I know you're ok.'

'Yes, Mum.' He shook his head with a faint smile playing on his lips before he strode off down my path. I waited and waved him goodbye before shutting the door. When I turned around, Quinn was leaning on the kitchen doorframe.

'Oh *yeah*, just friends,' she smirked.

'Even if you were right, which you aren't, he had plenty of chances just now to say something, seeing how it's Valentine's weekend. Besides, he probably overheard what you were saying about him, as your volume control is stuck at extra loud.'

'It's not easy to admit you love someone when you've been parked in the friend zone for so long. Maybe he's scared in case you don't feel the same. You do go on about Dr. Fitton all of the time.'

'You know what? Instead of trying to twist a beautiful relationship into something it isn't, why don't you make yourself useful and go and make a fire while I do us some drinks. Like you didn't want to talk yesterday, this is a subject *I* don't want to discuss, thank you.'

'Whatever, unbunch your panties, but after years of rejection, I've gotten pretty good at reading guys, and I'm sure about this.'

I sighed as she headed into the lounge, then toed off my shoes and headed into the kitchen to make our drinks and raid the treat cupboard. Hospital food sucked. While the kettle boiled, I picked up the card and headed into the utility room to open it, taking a deep breath before I slid it out.

It was a simple, modern, contemporary design.

I opened it to read the typed inscription.

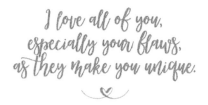

I blinked back some tears of emotion to think that someone felt strongly enough about me to not only send a card and flowers, but to not try flattering me by saying I was the most perfect person they'd ever set eyes on. No one was perfect, as Daphne so often reminded us. Someone who loved you because you *were* imperfect was worth so much more than someone who loved you *despite* you being imperfect. Was this really from Kitt?

I closed my eyes and shook my head. It couldn't be, he'd have said something. We were completely honest with each other. That's part of what I loved about our friendship. While my heart warmed at the thought that my best friend might be in love with me, at the thought of having him with me for the rest of my life, an arctic shiver also ran through my body at the thought of what I could lose if we tried a relationship and it failed. And I was sure he'd feel the same.

No, this wasn't from Kitt. And there was no way McFitty would risk his career by breaking the law to use my address from my medical records for his own purposes. I opened my eyes and smiled.

It was suddenly obvious. It was Daphne. She'd sent them to cheer me up on the worst day of the year for singletons, just like my mum used to do when I was a teenager. I took the card and set it on the island next to the roses and smiled.

Love was love. I was happy to accept it, whoever it had come from.

Chapter Thirteen

Feeling Hot, Hot, Hot
One Month Later – A Friday in March

'HOW GREAT IS THAT view?' I asked Quinn as we dumped our cases and looked out of the patio doors from our apartment in Lanzarote. We had our own terrace, with a small plunge pool down some steps on another level. Our vista took in some palm trees and had a view over the rooftops of the other apartments built into the hill, which sloped down to a shimmering blue Atlantic Ocean that stretched out for miles ahead of us.

'Pretty good,' she agreed. 'And it's great to feel some heat after all the snow back home the last few months.'

'Ok, how about we unpack and go out to get some nibbles and drinks. We could eat out tonight and see if we can find a club?' I suggested.

'Sounds good to me,' she agreed. Her cottage renovations were in their final phase, and I had some down time after submitting my latest novel to my publishers, so we'd decided to have a week away together for some sun and fun. When we went back home, I had a new project to start working on, and Quinn would be getting settled into Honeysuckle Cottage before starting her new job in April.

We headed out as the sun was starting to set, dressed up for a night on the town, and walked down the steep road that led to the main drag of Puerto del Carmen, where there were lots of restaurants, shops, and bars. Even off season, the place was busy, and the gentle breeze that rolled in from the sea was welcome relief in the heat. I smiled as I breathed in the scent of the ocean, thinking of Kitt immediately. I'd messaged him earlier to let him know we'd arrived safely. I'd done my best to convince him to come away with us both. If anyone needed a holiday, it was him. But as expected, he'd refused, saying he couldn't leave his mum for that long.

After some delicious calamari and crispy frites, along with a jug of sangria to wash it down, we ordered some ice cream and cocktails and spent the next hour laughing as we traded more of our dating horror stories.

'Come on then, I'm pleasantly drunk enough to go dancing in this indecent dress,' I told Quinn as we split the bill and I stood up, tugging on the hem.

'You look sexy. You should wear my clothes more often, they show off all of your curves.'

'Because you're about two sizes smaller than me, Quinn.'

'I'd rather have your British "arse" than my flat American ass.'

'Your arse isn't flat, though admittedly, it isn't as curvaceous as mine,' I said as we headed out to walk along the promenade and take our pick of where to go.

'Hang on a second, I want some smokes,' she said, darting into a shop. I gasped in amazement as I followed her inside.

'I had no idea you smoked. I've never seen you with one, and we spend a lot of time together.'

'I started when I was a teenager. I pretty much quit a few years ago, but when I'm out and nicely chilled, I like to have the odd one. You ever smoked?'

'No, I'd probably choke to death,' I laughed.

'Well, when I get you a bit more canned, we'll give you a test drive.'

'Canned?'

'Yeah, you know, sauced, hammered, wrecked, drunk,' she said, handing over her euros to the shopkeeper.

'Canned, that's a new one to me. But you can keep your stinky sticks of death, alcohol is a good enough buzz for me.'

'Whatever, Miss Goody-Two-Shoes,' she chuckled, ripping the cellophane off the packet and dumping it in a bin outside. She flipped the pack open and managed to do an impressive manoeuvre to get one cigarette to stand up without even touching them, before letting it hang from her lips as she flicked the lighter, her hands shielding the flickering orange flame from the breeze. 'Ahhhh, it's been too long,' she sighed as she inhaled, then exhaled slowly, the smoke curling from her lips making me cough.

'Couldn't actually be long enough for me,' I retorted, wafting the vile-smelling stuff out of my face.

'What's the most rebellious thing you've ever done?' she asked.

'I don't know. Does my rather disturbing Internet search history for book research count?'

'No,' she laughed. 'You must have done something bad, like got arrested, done drugs, been kicked out of clubs?'

'No, no, and no. Let me guess, you can tick off all three?' I shook my head as she winked at me.

'Tell me you at least have a tattoo?'

'Nope,' I said.

'Then I'm going to introduce you to the wild side this week.'

'Quinn, I don't need drugs, they're dangerous, and I don't plan on being arrested or kicked out of anywhere. I have a public persona to maintain now, if I want to keep my publishing contract.'

'Doesn't stop you from smoking or getting a tatt,' she said firmly. 'Cautious Charlie is about to become Foxy Faulkner,' she grinned, stubbing out her cigarette as she grabbed my arm and dragged me into a bar that was pumping out some great music.

'I have a feeling I'm going to regret this,' I whined.

A Few Hours Later – Early Saturday Morning

'Sssshhhh,' I giggled, stumbling over one of the plant pots on the patio as we rolled in at four a.m., more than worse for wear. 'I need coffee, then water, lots and lots of water.'

'Liquor coffee? I'm all over that action,' Quinn slurred.

'Liqueur coffee, get with the British programme,' I laughed, plonking myself down on one of the patio chairs to try and focus on the pretty view below, the twinkling lights of the apartments and sea front glistening in the dark. After too many attempts to get the key into the lock, with much accompanying cursing, Quinn finally achieved her goal and pushed the patio doors open and headed inside. The sound of lots of banging and clattering came drifting out, as well as a few more American and British cusses. I was just nodding off in my upright position when she reappeared, bringing a coffee that was more liqueur than actual coffee, but it was nice. When she tried to tempt me into having a cigarette again, I declined and staggered my way through the apartment into my bedroom.

I woke up face down with my lips stuck to the pillow, a banging head, and a dry mouth. I peeled my face off the material, got up, and bounced off the bedroom doorframe before veering left into the bathroom, only to gasp at the state of me. My blonde hair was sticking out at all angles, looking like I'd spent hours backcombing it. I hadn't removed my makeup last night, and my former sexy smoky-eyed look now resembled a bad attempt at Goth makeup. There was crusty drool all over my cheek and pillow creases all over my forehead. I cleaned my face and brushed my teeth vigorously, then stripped off to have a shower.

I winced as I rubbed the shower cream over my hip, and looked down to see why it was stinging so badly.

'Quinn Garcia!' I screamed, shock and horror flooding my veins. 'What the hell did you do to me last night? I have a tattoo!'

I heard the sound of laughter approaching the bathroom door and glared at her through the wood that separated us. It wasn't just any tattoo either. Oh no. I had a small outline of a black heart on the front of my hip, with the word "Kitt" stencilled inside it in fancy font.

'I only suggested getting a tattoo. You came up with that idea all on your own,' she called through the door.

'I don't remember even *going* into a tattoo parlour, let alone having one done, especially not *this*,' I hissed.

'Really? You were all for it when I agreed it would look cute.'

'I'm going to bloody kill you.' I stomped my foot on the tiled floor and aggressively turned off the taps. Wrapping myself in a towel, I stormed over and flung open the door to glare at her.

'What?' she protested, leaning against the doorframe in a brown bikini, with an innocent look on her face. 'It's tiny, and you picked it. It's not like I dragged you in there against your will and forced a skull and crossbones design on your arm, where everyone could see it.'

'I can see it. I can see it, Quinn, and it implies more than friendship with Kitt,' I muttered, pointing down in its general vicinity.

'Hmmm, it does, doesn't it? Maybe seeing it in black and white everyday will open your eyes and make you realise you're not friends anymore. You're more.'

'Off limits topic,' I warned her as I turned right and headed into my bedroom. 'I can't believe you let this happen while I was so drunk I didn't even *know* it was happening. I'm stuck with this for life. And why do you look so fresh this morning, when I feel like hell?' I demanded.

'Because I'm a city girl. I'm hardened to a heavy night, unlike you soft Dilbury-ers,' she laughed. 'I'll put some coffee on and grab you a bottle of water and some pastries for breakfast, they'll help soak up the alcohol. I'm out on the terrace when you're ready.'

'I hate you,' I yelled, as I pulled out a pair of my lacy knickers and my sarong.

'No, you don't. I make you have fun,' she yelled back.

'Fun, I'll give you fun,' I muttered under my breath, seething from every pore.

I slipped on my knickers and tied my sarong around my bust, knotting it tightly to stop it from slipping down, and smoothed my damp hair back into a high ponytail. Grabbing my sun lotion and glasses, I padded barefoot through the open-plan kitchen, dining room, and lounge and out through the patio doors to find Quinn sitting reading. She had her feet up on one of the chairs and there was an array of tasty-looking pastries sitting next to a steaming coffee, glass of orange juice, and a bottle of water on the table next to her.

'Am I forgiven?' she asked, giving me a sheepish look.

'No, that will be sometime *never*,' I retorted, the annoyance still apparent from my tone, which I immediately softened. 'But thank you for this, it looks good. What are you reading?' I asked as I sat next to her and tore off a piece of almond-filled croissant.

'Some filthy book written by this English author you may have heard of,' she grinned, flashing me her screen to show me one of my books.

'I'm explicit. Trust me, there's a difference between explicit and filthy.'

'I'm a pretty good judge of both, with a lot more experience than you,' she scoffed. 'Some of this is *filthy*. I can't believe Daphne reads them.'

'Whatever,' I said, aiming for indifference, but not able to keep myself from smiling. 'You'll be paying for the tattoo removal when we get home.'

'Oh, don't get rid of it, it's super cute. Give it a while and if you really hate it, you could always see if they could alter Kitt to McFitty or fill it in so it's a solid black heart,' she suggested. I gave her a look over the top of my glasses and picked up my juice, chugging it all back to relieve my dry mouth.

After finishing my food, coffee, and the small bottle of water, I was feeling a little more human again, and slathered myself in carrot oil. It was my go-to lotion when I was extra pale as it really deepened my tan, but the damn stuff was so greasy. I couldn't be bothered to get up to wash my hands, so I wiped them on my sarong and used the ends of the knot to get all of the excess oil out from between my fingers.

'Do you have to?' I sighed as Quinn lit a cigarette.

'Are you going to be miserable all damn holiday?'

'It's a horrible habit.'

'Don't knock it until you've tried it. Once you've smoked one, then you're qualified to give unsolicited advice.'

'Fine, give me the damn lighter,' I said, snatching it out of her left hand. She grinned and pushed the packet of nasal torture over towards me, shaking it to make one jump out for me. I whipped it out and stuck it between my lips, trying to emulate her, then grimaced as the paper stuck to my skin.

'I ought to film this. I never actually thought you'd go through with it.'

'Anything to shut you up and make you stop,' I muttered, the cigarette happily welded to my bottom lip, dangling as I spoke. I ran my thumb over the flint wheel to get the lighter to spark, but my fingers were so greasy they kept slipping.

'Wow, you really *are* missing the cool gene,' Quinn chuckled as she watched me try again and again. 'Hand it over, before you take a layer of skin off your thumb.'

'I can do it,' I told her, pushing her hand away. I already felt like the boring class nerd around her, I didn't need her reminding me how "uncool" I was. I smirked at her as I covered my thumb in part of the knotted sarong, struck it again, and the lighter ignited first time. Dangling my cigarette over the open flame, I inhaled and choked. 'Jesus, this is disgusting,' I coughed, slapping the lighter back down on the table.

'Ermmm, Charlie,' Quinn said, her eyes opening wide as she looked at me in horror. I managed to remove the cigarette from my lips, taking a layer of skin off them with it, and tried to hold it the way I'd seen her do.

'What? Am I holding it wrong as well? Maybe I'm starting a whole new cool way to handle the puke-inducing, rank stick that tastes like *ass.*'

'Forget the cigarette, you're on fire.'

'My wit's always at an all-time high when I'm pissed off,' I agreed.

'No,' she yelled, standing up so fast she knocked her chair over. 'You're on fire, actual fire.' She pointed at me, and I looked down and shrieked, dropping the cigarette as my hands flew to the knot on my bust, where small flames were licking and rapidly creeping across the thin material. I shot up, my hands shaking as I started to feel the heat between my breasts, and I desperately tried to undo the knot. The flames were scorching my fingers as I tried, and my heart broke into a panicked canter as I started to hyperventilate. 'Pull it down, pull it over your hips,' she screamed as I felt the building heat on my face.

I tugged at the sides of the sarong and it fell down, coming to rest on my hips. God damn it, why did they have to be two inches wider than my damn bust? All I could see was a mass of orange flames coming from my waist as heat and panic set in, and Quinn started slapping at them with her e-Reader. All I could think of was getting wet to douse them, but we had no water on the table. My eyes darted from the open patio doors over to the plunge pool, trying to decide which was closer. The bathroom won, and with Quinn screaming like a banshee behind me, I took off at a pace an Olympian would have been proud of. By the time I skidded into the bathroom, I didn't need to put the light on. The flames were licking at the underside of my bare breasts as I threw myself into the shower and spun the tap, screaming as the cold water blasted me back against the glass screen.

There was a sizzling sound as the water doused the flames, and I stood shaking under the freezing water, plunged back into darkness. Moments later, I heard a shriek and saw Quinn shooting across the floor past the open bathroom door on her backside, with a washing-up bowl full of water on her lap. She disappeared out of sight, a loud thud coming from my bedroom, followed by a moan and a load of swearing. I felt spaced out, like I wasn't really here or experiencing anything. Had that seriously just happened? The only thing that felt real was the horrible sensation of burning pain in my hands.

'Jesus, love, are you alright?' a strange man panted as he appeared in the bathroom.

I opened my mouth to protest at the intrusion, but nothing came out. Somehow my sore hands found their way to cover my naked breasts as I blinked at him, still not really sure what had just happened.

'Jean, get in here,' he yelled as he turned the light on.

'Is she ok, is my friend ok?' I heard Quinn shout. 'She set herself on fire.'

'Oh God,' a lady said as she joined the man in the bathroom and stared at me. I felt like an animal on display in the zoo. Who the hell were these people? What was going on? Blood was roaring in my ears, there were black spots in my vision, and I felt myself starting to sway on the spot. 'We need to sit her down, she's going into shock. Call an ambulance, then grab a sheet and soak it in cold water to wrap around her,' the lady ordered as she came towards me and smiled, holding out her hands.

'What … what's happening?' I asked, my teeth chattering together uncontrollably. Why was I shaking so much and why was it getting darker in here again?

'Come on, love, take my hands. You've been in an accident. I need to get you lying down as your blood pressure is dropping. My name's Jean, and I used to be a nurse, so you're in safe hands.'

I did as I was told, and heard myself let out a pitiful moan right before everything went black.

When I came back around, I was lying on the sofa in the lounge, wrapped tightly in a cold, wet sheet. Quinn was biting her thumbnail as she stood on one leg and stared at me, while Jean sat on the coffee table, holding my wrist as she looked at her watch.

'Oh God, you're awake. Are you ok?' Quinn asked.

'What's happened? Why do I feel so awful?' I moaned. 'My hands are really stinging.'

'Your hands hurt? How about anywhere else?' Jean asked as she let go of my wrist and turned my hands over to look at them.

'No, just my hands, and I feel really sick and cold,' I said, shivering again despite the heat of the sun reaching through to where I lay. I saw Quinn and Jean exchange a concerned look. 'My sarong … my sarong caught fire,' I whispered, not sure if it was a statement or a question.

'There's not much of it left, a sliver of material around your waist and the knot, that's it,' Quinn said with a grimace as she nodded her confirmation that I hadn't just dreamed the last few minutes. 'God, Charlie, you scared me. The flames were … Jean said you've got some bad burns and need to go to the hospital, we're waiting for the ambulance.'

'I'm fine. Apart from cold and shaking, and how much my hands hurt, I'm fine,' I said, trying to sit up. Jean gently pushed me back down.

'You need to stay lying down for me. Your blood pressure plummeted with the shock of what happened. Your hands will be ok, they've not even blistered. You've just scalded them, see?' she said, holding them up for me to inspect. They were bright red, but so sore. 'Quinn, can you get some tea towels and soak them in cold water? We can wrap them around her hands to soothe the burn.'

Quinn nodded and started hopping towards the kitchen.

'What's wrong, are you ok?' I called.

'I think I broke my toe,' she moaned. 'I filled the washing-up bowl with water to throw over you, but as I ran with it, the water sloshed over the side. I slipped on it and shot down the corridor and stubbed my toe on your wardrobe.'

'Oh no,' I giggled. Jean raised her eyebrows as she looked down at me. 'It's funny. The whole thing is funny. It could only happen to me,' I laughed. I heard Quinn starting to laugh as well, and pretty soon we were both in tears as we guffawed, with Jean looking between us like we were crazy. She wrapped my hands up in the wet tea towels, which made me laugh even harder. Seriously, stuff like this *really* could only happen to me.

'Jean, the ambulance is here. Can she walk or shall they bring the stretcher?'

'Stretcher please, Bob,' she called.

'I'm … really … going to … hospital?' I asked, giggling and gasping for air between words.

'Yes. I'll give Quinn my number, ring us when you've been treated and let us know how you are. We have the apartment upstairs, you're lucky we were so close. Bob thought one of you was being raped, you were screaming so loud, so we ran straight down.'

'Thank you, you've been really kind,' I said, reaching up to wipe the tears of laughter from my eyes.

It seemed like the whole apartment complex had turned out to see what was going on as I was wheeled out on the stretcher and led down the pretty path bordered by cactus and palm trees towards the waiting ambulance, Quinn hopping her way alongside me.

'Seriously,' she said when we were both inside and the ambulance started up, 'you couldn't have waited until the last day of the holiday to have a medical disaster?'

'Sorry,' I grinned, feeling much more like myself and wondering what all the fuss was about, as I felt fine now except for my sore hands.

We arrived at Arrecife hospital and I cried out for Quinn as I was suddenly whisked away down a corridor, leaving her behind.

'I'll find you,' she yelled as the lights on the ceiling whipped past above me.

I was taken into a large room and suddenly surrounded by people peeling off the tea towels and sheet as they spoke rapidly in Spanish. I was getting used to being seen virtually naked in hospitals, but what I wasn't used to was having no idea what was going on. When a man leaned over me, speaking to me in Spanish, I shook my head.

'Inglés,' I said. He frowned and pointed at my stomach.

'Sol? Errrr, this … sol?' he asked. I shook my head, understanding he was asking if I had a sunburn.

'No, feugo, fire.' I bounced my eyes between everyone as they all started jabbering again, and someone appeared with a pair of scissors and made a move towards my hip. 'No, these are my expensive lucky knickers, please don't cut them off,' I protested. 'They cost *fifteen pounds* from Marks and Spencers.'

I was ignored as the tattered remains of my favourite pair were whipped off me and tossed in the trash. I was lifted, turned, tilted, and generally tossed around as they created the most enormous nappy out of bandages and used a big silver safety pin to secure them, then they managed to sit me up to put the dreaded open-back gown on me, before making me lie down again. Moments later, I was being shuttled out of the room and off down another corridor.

My laughter had worn off. The blood pounding in my veins felt as if it was turning to ice as fear set in. I had no idea what was going on, why I needed to be padded like this, or where the hell Quinn was. I was taken into a small bay with six hospital beds, and the staff slid me onto one of them, then disappeared.

A nurse arrived soon after and took my arm, tapping for a vein before she inserted a cannula in the crook of my elbow and attached a drip of clear fluid. She smiled at me before disappearing and leaving me on my own. I finally gave in to some tears. I'd give anything right now for an uninterested Dr. Fitton to come and tell me factually what was wrong, what was going to happen, and when I could go home, or even where Quinn was. After half an hour of frustrated tears, I finally gave in and closed my eyes and went to sleep, hoping when I woke up I'd have some answers.

'Charlie? Oh God, I've been so worried. No one around here seems to speak any English.'

'Quinn,' I called as I opened my eyes and saw her struggling over on a pair of crutches, with her toes strapped up and bandaged. 'What the hell is going on?' I asked, struggling to sit up.

'I don't know. I asked so many times where you were, I gave up waiting and came looking for you. Are you ok?'

'Define ok. I'm wearing a huge nappy, I have no clothes, and I've no idea what's in this drip,' I told her as she plonked herself in the visitor's chair. 'What have you done?'

'Broken my toe,' she grimaced. 'It kills.'

'How long have we been here?'

'Hours. It's late afternoon, you've obviously been asleep for a while.'

'Do you have my phone?' I asked. She nodded and rummaged in her bag and handed it over. I was grateful to see a signal and thankful I'd saved the number for the insurance company in it. When I rang them and explained what had happened, and that we had no idea what was going on, they told me to give them the name of the hospital and they'd ring them for answers. An hour later, they called back to say that I was being kept in for assessment the next morning. When I objected, saying no one spoke English and that I had no clothes or supplies with me, they agreed for me to get a taxi back to the apartment. They explained I would need to go to the English-speaking clinic in Puerto del Carmen the next morning to be checked, then rang the hospital to ask them to release me.

I was unhooked from the saline solution they'd been rehydrating me with and helped off the bed. Quinn burst out laughing as the giant nappy bandage immediately slid off my hips and landed in a heap on the floor, which made me groan and close my eyes from embarrassment. I had to stand with my arms in the air, naked but for the damn hospital gown, as the staff argued in Spanish the best way to wrap me up so that I could walk, and finally we were in a taxi on our way back. Jean expressed her surprise to see us, but sent Bob to collect two large pizzas for our dinner.

She told us to have an early night, asking me to let her know how the appointment went at the clinic the following morning.

The Next Day – Sunday

'Honestly,' I told the dishy English-speaking Spanish doctor as he unravelled my bandages, 'I don't know what all the fuss is about. I feel fine apart from my stinging hands and the underside of my breasts.'

'He's just doing his job,' Quinn said, trying to placate me. She gasped, her crutches falling with a loud clatter to the floor as her hands flew to her mouth when the last of the bandages were removed.

'What? What?' I asked, trying to look down, but my t-shirt clad boobs were in the way.

'Don't look, Charlie, don't look. Oh God, I think I'm going to be sick,' she moaned, turning green as she leaned back against the wall for support.

'I agree, it's best you don't look,' the doctor said. 'I need you to lie down. The hospital, they discharged you?' he asked, sounding puzzled.

'Yes, why? Someone tell me what's going on.'

'You have very bad burns on your stomach and hip,' he said, craning his neck to look behind me at my bare bottom. 'Here, too.'

'How bad?' I asked, looking over at Quinn, who still had her mouth covered by her hands. She shook her head.

'It's like a car crash. I know I shouldn't look, but I can't tear my eyes away. You have an enormous green fluid-filled blister hanging off your side.'

'But I can't feel anything, it doesn't hurt,' I said, trying to decide if I wanted to look or not.

'Burns this deep … they … how you say … kill the nerves,' the doctor said. 'So, no pain. You need to go to hospital.'

'No,' I said, firmly shaking my head. 'I'm not going back there. No one speaks English, please don't make me. Can't I stay here?' I pleaded. 'I'm insured if that's the problem.'

'Charlie, I think we need to go home, get you treated there,' Quinn suggested.

'I totally agree, even better idea,' I nodded as I was told to lie on my right-hand side while he figured out a way to re-dress me, which ended up with me being wrapped in bandages again, with a large white tubular mesh being pulled over the top of them to hold them in place. 'I feel like a Cumberland sausage,' I giggled as Quinn came to squeeze my arm while the doctor left the room to speak to the insurance company.

'You really can't feel anything?'

'Not a sausage. Oh, nice pun by me,' I grinned.

'Well, they ought to take pictures of those gross blisters and put them on cigarette packets as a warning. I'm never touching one again.'

'I think it was more the whole carrot oil and flame combo than the cigarettes, not that I'm going to complain.'

'You were so lucky. Imagine if your long hair had been down, or if you didn't have such big breasts, your face could have been burnt so badly. I'm going to go and see what's happening, find out how soon we can get home, ok?'

'Ok,' I sighed. 'I'm so sorry for ruining your holiday.'

'Our holiday, and to be honest, I'm so shaken up over it all, I just want to get home too,' she said.

A Week Later – Friday

'I'm being moved again?' I complained, as Dr. Fitton came to re-dress my burns and told me that he'd secured a bed at Stoke hospital for me, as they had a specialist burns unit that was better equipped to handle me. We'd landed at Birmingham airport two hours earlier, and an ambulance had been waiting to bring me to Shrewsbury, with Quinn getting a taxi home once I'd been dropped off here.

'Trust me, Charlie, it's the best place for you. You have first, second, and third-degree burns. I'm amazed the clinic over there released you, though lucky for us they did. They mistakenly deroofed your blisters and it looks like you have an infection in this worst section on your side,' he said, frowning as he reapplied the dressings. 'You're dating your friend now?'

'What?' I asked, thrown by his medical assessment. I'd had no idea it was so bad.

'You have his name tattooed on your hip.'

'Oh God, I'd forgotten,' I groaned, covering my face with my hands. 'I was drunk and Quinn dragged me into the shop. I had no idea until the next day. Seriously, that survived the burns?'

'Wrong side of your body, they're all on the left.'

'Great, Kitt will kill me if he finds out. And no, we're not seeing each other. Still just very good friends,' I added. As if on cue, I heard his voice frantically calling for me, and I hastily pulled my dress down to cover everything up. 'Can he come in?'

'I suppose so,' Guy nodded, pulling back the curtain. Kitt raced to my side and pulled me up into a seated position as he hugged me tightly. I returned it, immediately feeling comforted to have him by my side. I felt my eyes stinging, and moments later, I was sobbing. I had no idea why. I hadn't cried since that first day, when I'd been left alone not knowing what was happening in the hospital in Lanzarote. Why was I crying now?

'God, I've been so worried,' he murmured, stroking my hair before kissing the top of my head. 'Are you ok?'

'I am now ... I'm home,' I sighed, burying my face in his neck. Whenever Kitt was around, I felt calmed and at peace. He centred me. Why didn't he make my heart race like Dr. Fitton did?

'Can you give us some privacy please?' I heard Kitt say, in a tone that sounded far more dominant and bossy than I'd ever heard him use.

'I need to check on the transport for her anyway. I'll be back shortly,' Guy said. I heard his footsteps leaving and felt Kitt running a soothing hand up and down my back.

'Deep breaths, Charlie, it's going to be ok.'

'I missed you, I missed Tibbs, and I miss my home. They're sending me to Stoke, but I just want to go home. Please can you see if I can go home?' I begged, dragging an arm across my face as he carefully pushed me back to lie against the pillows.

'If he says you need to be admitted, you need to be admitted, Charlie. What about your parents, do they know?'

'No,' I sniffed, accepting a tissue he pulled out of the pocket of his jeans. 'I didn't want to scare them. Besides, I didn't think it was that serious.'

'It is from what Quinn tells me. Don't worry, she's safely back at Abbie's being looked after, and Georgie's still happy to look after Mrs. Tibbles until you're home. Well, happy is maybe a slight exaggeration. She said she's the spawn of Satan,' he grinned, making me smile. 'That's better. I'm not used to seeing tearful Charlie. You're usually so strong, seeing the humour in everything.'

'I have laughed,' I said, wiping my eyes before honking my snotty nose. 'I promise I've laughed a lot. They had to book a whole row of seats for me so I could lie on my side in the plane, as I couldn't sit on my blistered bottom or have the seat belt on.'

'Really? How are you sitting now?' he asked. I lifted up a cheek to show him the giant inflatable rubber ring I was sitting on to take the pressure off the blistering on my butt cheeks. I giggled, and he chuckled and shook his head.

'And how many people can say that they were stretchered out of a plane through the food loading hatch and whizzed through back corridors, avoiding the hell of baggage reclaim?'

'Not many, I'd imagine,' he smiled, using his index finger to sweep my fringe off my face. 'Except for Quinn too.'

'I owe her another holiday for this,' I said.

'I think the words "I'm never going away with her again, she's a walking bloody disaster" may have been mentioned when she called me from the taxi on the way home,' he laughed.

'I'll convince her.'

'You can be very persuasive, Miss Faulkner.'

'Enough about me and my drama, how are you? How have things been? You look even more tired than when I left,' I said, picking up his hand and giving it a squeeze.

'I'm ok. Better for seeing you and that smile again. It could melt ice, it's so bright.'

'Stop distracting me with flattery. Talk to me.'

'You don't need to hear about me, you need to focus on getting better. I'll cancel work tonight so I can follow the ambulance up to Stoke and make sure you're ok.'

'Kitt, you don't have to do that.'

'I know I don't, I want to. Do you have clean clothes and toiletries?'

'A suitcase full of stuff I barely touched,' I said, flicking my head in its direction.

'Is there anything I can do for you?'

'Well, there is one thing,' I said, biting my lower lip as I looked up at him from under my lashes. 'Something I've been *dreaming* about ever since I said goodbye to you last week.'

'I don't think they allow that in a hospital,' he grinned.

'I'd be prepared to go outside if need be, or in the toilet to do it secretly. I'm *desperate,* Kitt. The ambulance will be ages as it's not an emergency.'

'Fine,' he laughed, pulling out his phone. 'One pepperoni pizza being ordered for delivery now, but I'm warning you, it won't taste anywhere near as good as mine.'

'Of course it won't, but sometimes a girl just has to make do with second best.'

Chapter Fourteen

Like Buses
Four Months Later – A Friday in July

QUINN POURED US EACH a glass of wine while I checked my phone again and frowned.

'He's busy,' she said, as if she was reading my mind.

'For a whole week? He's never gone this long without texting me back. I'm worried about him.'

'There's no written friendship rule of "Thou shalt text back within one hour of receipt," you know.' Quinn slid the chilled glass over to me, the straw-coloured Chardonnay inside never looking more appealing than it did right now.

'I know that, but Kitt always replies straightaway. I was worried after a few hours. This has been days,' I reminded her. I picked up the glass and took a good gulp of the cold, crisp wine before chewing on my lower lip. We'd been friends for eighteen months. I knew his habits, just as he knew mine, and something was wrong. I really hoped things were ok with his mum. Maybe she'd taken a turn for the worse and he'd had to make arrangements to put her into permanent care. That could be why he hadn't called.

'Well, he'll be here with the pizza soon, you can grill him then,' she suggested as she put the bottle of wine back in my fridge. 'I'll clear out if you need me to.'

'I don't want you to clear out. I just want to know what's wrong. How crazy is it that I know parts of him so well, but I don't even know what house he lives in on Falcon's Way. I can't even turn up to check on him.'

'Maybe he wants it that way. Maybe he likes having you separate from his complicated home life.'

'He's here,' I exclaimed as I quickly set down my glass, some of the wine sloshing over the side onto the kitchen island worktop.

'How do you do that?' Quinn asked, a look of astonishment on her face.

'I can hear the car rumbling down the lane,' I said as I ran to the kitchen door. I skidded into the hall and opened the front door, my heart thudding in my chest. Something was wrong, I just knew it. I felt it deep in my bones. We'd become so attuned to each other over the last year or so. I hopped from foot to foot, impatient as I waited for him to pull into the drive, but my frown deepened as I listened to the car engine. It didn't sound like his. I craned my neck around the doorframe and sighed heavily to see an old Ford KA, with so much rust on it, it almost looked brown in colour instead of the aubergine it appeared to have once been.

'Where's Kitt?' I demanded as the lanky late-teen ambled up my path.

'Dunno,' he shrugged. 'He's not been in all week. You Charlie Faulkner?'

'Yes. What's wrong, did he phone in sick?'

'Dunno. I only started there Saturday, never met the guy. Right, I've got two pepperoni pizzas, garlic bread, potato wedges, and two slices of cheesecake, and that'll be–'

'Here,' I said, thrusting the notes at him. I knew how much it was, it was my regular order for me and Quinn on the nights Kitt didn't have time to stop and eat with me. 'So you've no idea why he's taken the week off?'

'No. I just turn up and do my job, lady, not my place to ask.'

'Well, who would know?'

'You his girl or something?' he asked, his brown eyes casting a curious look over my face.

'No, I'm his friend, his best friend.'

'Seems if you were that good friends, you'd know better than me where he was.'

'Can you tell me who I can speak to or not?' I demanded, snatching the piles of food off him and shoving them on the hall console table.

'Can always ring and ask Pete, the boss, if you're that bothered.'

'Well, obviously I am or I wouldn't be asking, would I?' I snapped.

'Ok, ok, no need to take my head off,' he huffed, stepping back and holding his hands in the air.

'Sorry,' I grimaced. 'I just … it's not like him not to be in touch, I'm really worried about him. Keep the change,' I sighed as he started to rummage in his "fanny pack," as Quinn would call it.

'Sweet, thanks,' he grinned. 'Hope this Kitt stays off, if you tip like this each time.'

'It was Pete, you said? The guy I should speak to?' I asked. He nodded. 'Great, thanks, bye.' I quickly shut the door, cutting him off as he was still talking, then swept up the food and hurried back into the kitchen, nearly tripping over a meowing Mrs. Tibbles.

'Well?' Quinn asked, as I shoved the boxes on the island and grabbed my phone. I shook my head and dialled the takeout number, my stomach feeling like it was on a spin cycle as I nervously waited for someone to answer. When I finally put the phone down, I felt tears stinging my eyes. 'What? What's wrong?'

'They don't know, Quinn. He said he needed at least a couple of weeks off and they couldn't tell me any more. I feel sick and frustrated,' I whispered.

'You need to eat. I bet you skipped lunch again while you were writing, it's not good for you.'

'I know.' I let out a heavy sigh and wiped my damp eyes. What else could I do? I had no other way to find him. 'You feed Tibbs and I'll sort the food.'

'He'll be in touch when he's ready,' Quinn said, setting her wine down.

'I know. It's just I don't want to imagine what's so bad that he needs a time out from our friendship and his job,' I admitted as I opened the kitchen drawer and pulled out the bread knife. I hated tearing at the garlic bread where they didn't cut the loaf all of the way through. Kitt always laughed that I had to go over it again myself. 'I mean, he can't even take sixty seconds to send me an "I'm alive, I'll be in touch soon" text?'

'Maybe he went on holiday. If anyone deserves one, it's him.'

'Hmmm.' I couldn't imagine him doing that, not when … 'Owww, God damn it,' I yelled, dropping the knife with a clatter as I clutched my suddenly stinging hand to my chest.

'What now?' Quinn sighed without even turning around, as she scooped Tibbs' food into her bowl.

'I think I just cut my thumb off.' I pulled a face as I looked down to see sticky crimson fluid on my hand.

'No, seriously?' She quickly dumped Tibbs' bowl on the floor, then spun to face me and gasped. 'Oh my God, you're a complete liability. Let me look.'

'It hurts,' I whined, tears prickling my eyes like needles as she grabbed my hand and pulled it towards her.

'Ewww.' She shuddered and grimaced as she looked at it. 'Where's the first aid kit? I need to bandage that and take you to the hospital, you'll need stitches.'

'Can this day suck any more?' I complained.

'What have you done now?' Guy laughed as he snapped on his gloves.

'I think I've cut the end of my thumb off,' I replied, my mood lifting slightly to see my favourite doctor. I'd had a few nights out with Quinn over the last few months, hoping to run into him, but fate hadn't been on our side.

'Was this a ploy to see me again?' he asked as he gently picked up my hand, which Quinn had temporarily bandaged, the snow-white bandage already stained red.

'Well, it's been so long, I figured I had to do whatever it took.'

'Talk about drastic measures.' He flashed me one of his show-stopping smiles and told me to hold my hand in the air as he started to undo the bandages. 'So, how have things been since I last saw you? It seems like this is a record, you've not been back in since your burns.'

'An all-time personal best,' I agreed, keeping my gaze on his chiselled face and those lime eyes. 'My burns healed nicely. I've been left with a really nasty scar on my left hip, but the rest are starting to fade.'

'That's great to hear,' he nodded, grimacing as I winced when the last of the bandage was peeled away and the top of my thumb lifted with it, more blood oozing out. 'Hmmm,' he murmured, then barked some orders at the nurse, who blushed and nodded. Quinn averted her gaze and looked up at the ceiling. She'd never been good with the sight of blood.

'Don't tell me I've cut it off,' I begged, hardly daring to look at it. 'I have to type. How am I supposed to type if I'm missing half a thumb? I need that for the space bar. Do they do prosthetics for digits?'

'I don't think it will come to that,' Guy chuckled, pressing some fresh gauze tightly on my wound to try and stop the blood flow. 'You managed to slice nearly all the way through the tip of your thumb, but luckily you missed the bone and didn't damage any nerves or tendons. Once we've cleaned it up, we'll put some steri-strips on it and a light bandage. Even if it doesn't knit together, this sliver of flesh at the top will dry and fall off and the rest of your thumb will heal underneath. You'll be no worse off, but you were very lucky. Another few millimetres down and it could have been a serious wound.'

'Sorry if we've wasted your time, there was just so much blood.'

'Please stop talking about blood,' Quinn moaned. 'I almost threw up a few times on the way here and it doesn't help that I'm starving, either.'

'Go and get some chocolate from the vending machine,' I suggested. I was pretty lightheaded myself. We'd had to abandon our food to dash here, Quinn hastily covering it to prevent Mrs. Tibbles from wolfing any of it down.

'Great idea,' she agreed as she rushed out, along with the nurse who'd found there weren't any of the supplies she needed left in the drawers. I licked my lower lip as I gazed up at Guy's face, my injured hand smothered in his two strong ones as he held it up. I could feel my chest heaving as I looked at him.

'We never did bump into each other, to catch up outside of the hospital,' I reminded him, waiting for some excuse to come out of his mouth.

'No, we didn't, did we. Well … I'm off duty Sunday night, if you're free?' he said casually, nearly making me topple off the bed I was sitting on.

'You're … you're asking me … on a date?' I said slowly, not sure if I'd just imagined that question, or if it was my hopeful hearing and wishful thinking.

'We never seem to get time to talk about your work whenever you come in. Maybe we could do it over dinner.'

'You want to hear about my writing?'

'I checked you out online, seems like you're doing very well for yourself.'

'I am,' I nodded. 'Since getting this contract, things have gone crazy. I'm going to America next month to do some publicity over there, all paid for by the publishing company. I never dreamed it would happen, but it has.'

'Then it seems like we have a lot to talk about. How about we meet at The Riverside in town, seven-thirty?'

'Great,' I confirmed, my heart doing a series of excited skips. Finally, after months and months of admiring him from afar, it was going to happen. I had a date with Dr. Fitton and by the end of it, I was finally going to kiss those perfect lips of his. There was no way he was ending a date without kissing me. I'd waited long enough.

'Best not to mention it in front of my colleague. It's not really the done thing for doctors to ask out their patients.'

'My lips are sealed,' I confirmed, miming locking them with my good hand. He smiled at me again and nearly made me melt into a puddle on the floor when he gave me a conspiratorial wink.

The Next Day – Fête Day

'What did you do now?' Daphne exclaimed as she spotted my bandaged thumb when I set a load of Abbie's boxes down on the table.

'It was the best injury of my life,' I proudly proclaimed. 'Attack my thumb, get a date out of McFitty. We're having dinner tomorrow night.'

'Charlie, I thought you'd moved on from that obsession with him,' she sighed with a gentle shake of her head.

'Moved on? When did I say I'd moved on?'

'Quinn said that you and Kitt were getting closer.'

'Oh, Quinn said that, did she?' I said, flashing a scowl in her direction.

'Hey, you know my feelings on the doctor. I don't want to see you get hurt,' Quinn shrugged.

'I don't know why both of you can't be happy for me,' I said, flicking my gaze between them. 'You know how I feel about him, how long I've felt like this. I finally have a date with the guy I've been nuts about for months, and you're both making out like it's a bad thing.'

'We just want you to be happy, Charlie,' Daphne sighed as she continued to unpack Abbie's baked goods onto the plates. 'But you've been blinded by lust for this man.'

'There's nothing wrong with finding a man attractive,' I protested. 'That's how most relationships start.'

'There is when that's all you see and you refuse to acknowledge the truth,' Quinn stated as she folded her arms across her chest.

'Shouldn't you be at work? I thought Saturdays were the busiest days for wedding planners,' I huffed, feeling annoyed that she'd been so down on me about the whole thing.

'And miss my first ever Dilbury fête?' she scoffed. 'No way. I booked the day off as soon as I started. This wedding's been planned meticulously. All Heather has to do today is tell everyone where to be, at what time, and if the worst were to happen, I'm on my cell if they need me, or I can pop over there. Anyway, stop trying to change the subject. We were talking about your love life.'

'Maybe we should talk about yours. You and Heath have been flirting with each other for seven months now. Talk about being blind to the truth.'

'This so isn't about me.'

'Well, maybe it should be. So neither of you like Guy. Well tough, as I do. At least I put myself out there. I wasn't so scared that I hid every time I saw him.'

'I don't hide,' Quinn shot back, fixing me with a scowl.

'Yes, you do,' Daphne and I said at the same time.

'Maybe you can lecture me on my love life when you're brave enough to sort out your own,' I challenged her.

'He's over there in the beer tent, dear, making googly eyes at you from afar,' Daphne said, flicking her chin towards him. 'Go and talk to him. You two have pussy-footed around each other for so long, I'm on

175

the verge of knocking your heads together. I'd like to see you all get settled down before my time is up, and at my age, you never know how fast that will happen.'

'I don't date anymore,' Quinn huffed, her eyes sliding over in Heath's direction. 'I have casual hook-ups. Do you really want me corrupting your nephew, Daphne?'

'He's a grown man, he can look after himself. Besides, while you may see him as beneath you because he doesn't have a fancy city job or wear suits like the men you were used to dating in New York, it doesn't mean he's not all man and perfectly capable of corrupting you, Quinn.'

'I never said he was beneath me.'

'And he never will be, if one of you doesn't make a move,' Daphne retorted quick as a flash, making me giggle.

'Don't look at me,' I said as Quinn gave me an exasperated look. 'You know she speaks sense. No one's suggesting you get married and have his babies, but if you don't explore this simmering tension between you, you'll never know if it could have been something.'

'If you're both going to nag me about Heath all morning, then I need a drink.' Quinn spun on her heels and stalked off into the crowd.

'I could shake her sometimes,' I sighed. She still hadn't opened up about what had happened to her in New York to make her so closed off to the possibility of seeing someone again.

'As I could you, Charlie Faulkner. I told you great love isn't built on lust alone. You need a stronger foundation.'

'Don't you start on me as well,' I warned her. 'I don't need all this negativity bringing me down when I'm finally happy.'

'But are you, dear? Are you *really* happy? I mean the kind of happy that saturates your bones and will make you feel warm and comforted for the rest of your life. Or are you fooling yourself into thinking you're happy because you finally got the bright, shiny object that's been on the top shelf and out of your reach for so long? That kind of high fades fast.'

'I don't know what you're trying to say, Daphne.'

'Sometimes we want the new and the shiny because it dazzles us. But it also blinds us to what's been within our reach all of this time. Don't rush to settle for what you think you want, as one day you'll wake up and realise what you've actually lost.'

'You're talking in riddles,' I complained, putting my fingertips to my head and massaging away the headache they'd both given me with their less than enthusiastic response to my news.

'Charlie, can you go and get us all some drinks before the mayhem starts?' Abbie called from the back of the tent.

'Gladly,' I replied, hurrying off before Daphne confused me any more. I was torn between misery because I still hadn't heard back from Kitt and elation because I was just a sleep away from my date with Guy.

'Charlie.'

I stopped in my tracks as the husky voice I knew so well interrupted my thoughts. My eyes quickly scanned the crowd, and I felt my face light up as I spotted him walking towards me.

'You're alive!' I cried as I ran towards him and threw myself at him. Kitt caught me, lifting me up onto his hips as he hugged me back and I wrapped myself around him like a vine. 'God, I've been *so* worried.'

'I'm sorry. Things have just been a little crazy, but I needed to see you,' he breathed, kissing my temple as I buried my face in the crook of his neck. He smelled different. That light, fresh ocean smell of his aftershave was there, but the scent of oregano I was so used to on him as well was missing.

'What happened? Is it your mum?' I asked, pulling my head back to look in his unusually dull green eyes. 'You look exhausted.'

'I … Things have been a bit crazy. Can we go somewhere quiet for a minute? I need to talk to you.'

'I need to talk to you too, you won't believe what's happened,' I said as I slid down his body until my trainers were on the ground.

'What happened to your thumb?' he asked, lifting my hand to inspect the bandage.

'I nearly sliced the end off, but it was worth it. We've taken a step forwards, me and McFitty,' I beamed. I felt so happy all of a sudden. Kitt was back and I knew he'd appreciate how momentous this news was, unlike Charlie and Daphne.

'You've done what?'

'Come on,' I said, tugging at his hand. 'We won't get any peace here. Let's go to mine and I'll make you a coffee and tell you all about it, and you can tell me why you've been missing in action for a week. I've been worried sick.'

'I don't want a damn coffee, Charlie,' he grated out as he yanked his hand out of mine and ran it over his face. 'You're seriously still hung up on that arsehole?'

'Ok, I've had it with everyone being so negative about him,' I huffed, turning to face him as I put my hands on my hips. 'I thought I could at least count on *you* to be happy for me that things were finally progressing.'

'Yeah, because that's me, right? Good old dependable Kitt. Always there in the background when you need him to say the right thing.' He scowled at me, making me take a step back and wrap my arms around myself.

'What's *wrong* with you? This isn't you, Kitt. Disappearing for days, ignoring my messages and calls, and being so ... so ...'

'So what, Charlie? *Angry?* I'm not allowed to be angry? I'm not allowed to step out of the box you've fit me into? Best friend Kitt, always compassionate and caring, taken out to be there in times of need. Well, maybe being the Kitt *you* want isn't what *I* need right now. Maybe I need more.'

'I don't understand what's happening,' I said quietly, scanning his face as I tried to read him. I'd never seen him so riled up before.

'Open your eyes, Charlie. It's been in front of your face all this time and you still haven't worked it out? I'm in love with you. I'm out of my mind crazy about you, and just when I finally get the balls to come and admit it, you tell me you still want *him?*' he bit, glowering in his rage.

'You what?' I whispered, my heart moving into my throat.

'You heard me,' he grunted as he swiped both hands over his face, the sound of his unusual growth of stubble grating against them. 'I love you, Charlie. I'm so in love with you, I feel like I'm living in darkness when you're not around. The only time I can see clearly is when you're at my side.'

'But ... but ... we're friends, *best friends*,' I stuttered, not entirely convinced I wasn't imagining this.

'So friends can't fall in love? Is that what you're telling me? I fought it for so damn long, but I was always fighting a losing battle. I never had any choice in the matter. My heart wanted you from the moment I met you. I really thought lately that you felt the same. You're saying I've read the signs wrong?' He dropped his hands to lock his eyes on mine, making me swallow a lump of rapidly rising anxiety in my throat. I was so confused. I just hadn't seen this coming.

'I ... I ... *Kitt*. You never *said* anything.'

'Because I didn't know how *you* felt, Charlie,' he replied, his voice full of anguish as he held my gaze. 'You were always so insistent that we were friends, nothing more. I didn't dare to hope that you felt the same.'

'But what changed? Why now?' I asked, completely stunned at his reaction. Had Quinn really been right all along and I just hadn't wanted to see it?

'I thought you were seeing me differently since you came back from Lanzarote. I felt like things between us had shifted. I thought maybe ... and I've never been in a position to take it further before ... is it my job?

178

He's a fancy doctor and I'm just the pizza delivery guy, is that what this is?'

'That's unfair. I've never held what you do against you,' I snapped.

'You want to talk about unfair? I'm the one who spends time with you, I'm the one you turn to when you have anything to share, happy or sad. And now you're telling me you want him instead?' His voice cracked as he shoved his hands in the front pockets of his jeans, the frown on his face furrowing his forehead.

'I've always wanted him, Kitt. This can't come as a surprise to you,' I uttered, feeling my heart fragment into sharp glass splinters as a look of hurt flashed across his face.

'You'd think not, wouldn't you?' He shook his head as he let out an oddly inappropriate laugh. 'Call me stupid, I just thought what *we* had ran deeper. That I meant more to you.'

'Kitt, you mean *everything* to me, but I...' I shook my head this time, not sure what to say.

'You love *him*,' he huffed. 'Don't worry, I got the message loud and clear.'

'Love? I never said I loved him, I still barely know him. Come home with me so we can talk,' I pleaded, reaching for one of his hands. He snatched it out of his pocket and ran it through his hair.

'I don't *want* to talk, Charlie. I'm *sick* of talking. I said what I came to say, now it's time for me to leave.'

'I don't want you to go, there's too much we need to say to each other,' I pleaded.

'I don't have anything else to say, Charlie. And I can't hear any more. The more you say, the more I feel like I'm being suffocated.'

'But when will I see you again?' I asked, a spear of pain lancing my heart when I stepped towards him and he stepped back, keeping the distance between us. Distance I hated.

'I don't know. I need time, time alone to clear my head and decide what I'm going to do. I think it's best you give me some space for a while.'

'But … but we're still friends, right?' I asked, desperately scanning his face as I waited for an answer. 'Right? Friends no matter what?'

'I don't know how we can be now. Everything's changed, Charlie,' he said quietly.

'No, don't you say that. Don't you *dare* say that.' I flew at him, fury seeping from every pore, and took him by surprise when I started to hammer my fists on his chest. 'Why did you have to *ruin* everything? We were good as we were. We were *perfect*. Why did you have to ruin it all?'

'Charlie,' he growled, his long fingers wrapping around my wrists and holding them away from him. 'Having me at arm's length might have been perfect for you, but it wasn't working for me. Do you have any idea how it feels to have the person you're in love with so close every day, but always just out of your reach? How it felt to see your face light up every time you mentioned his name or went into detail about one of your encounters with him? I thought it would finally be over, that once I told you how I felt, you'd admit you felt the same way and we could move past this. I can't do it anymore, not now.'

'I never meant to hurt you, Kitt. I love you,' I cried as I looked up at him, but his face was misted over from tears that were filling my eyes. It was like a heavy fog was settling in. It was clouding my thoughts, my feelings, and my vision. I couldn't make any sense out of the confusion blanketing me right now.

'I know that,' he said gently. 'But I thought you were *in love* with me, Charlie. Until I can process that you're not and try and come to terms with that, I can't be around you anymore. I need some time away from you.'

'I don't want to lose you, Kitt, you're my best friend.' I choked on a sob, feeling completely despondent as I felt the sting of tears slowly working their way down my cheeks.

'You have others to fill the void, Charlie,' he said sadly. 'I need to figure out how to fill the voids in my life now, and I can't do that when you're always around, reminding me of what I want and can never have. Just seeing you cry right now feels like someone has sucked my heart out of my chest, it hurts me that much. I can't carry that burden anymore, of feeling pain whenever you do, not when the load's not shared.'

'It *is* shared. I've been so miserable worrying about you this week. Please don't do this, Kitt,' I choked.

'Take care of yourself, Charlie. I hope you get what you want from him, that I've got him wrong, but regardless, if I ever find out that he hurt you, I'll hunt him down and kick his arse.'

'Don't leave me,' I whimpered, gasping for breath as he placed a slow, tender kiss on my forehead.

'You left me first, Charlie. I guess it's inevitable. Someday *everyone* leaves.'

He eased me away from him, then spun around and strode away, his long legs eating up the emerald grass as he disappeared into the happy and oblivious crowds. I tried to call out to him to stop, but I was crying too hard, and when I went to run after him, my legs crumpled, taking me down to the ground with a thud. How could he do that? Just walk away? He didn't see that I felt just as much pain when he was hurting too? I covered my face with my hands as I took a few stuttering deep breaths and tried to calm myself down. I felt someone sit on the grass beside me and place a comforting arm around me.

'What happened?' Quinn asked, her usual brusque tone quiet and gentle.

'I don't want to talk about it,' I whispered.

'What do you need? Some ice cream?'

'Ice cream *and* vodka,' I sniffed as I dropped my hands into my lap. 'And quite possibly a mountain of tissues.'

'I may be bad at advice, but I can meet those demands. Come on, let's get you home and cleaned up, you have black mascara all over your face. Then we can come back when Abbie's stall is getting busy. Plus, we don't want to miss Weston's big proposal this afternoon, do we?'

'No,' I agreed with a heavy sigh. It was a special day for Georgie, although she had no idea. I'd already let Kitt down today, there was no way I was failing anyone else.

Chapter Fifteen

Everything I Wanted
The Next Day – Sunday

'URGH,' I MOANED, REACHING up to rub my eyes with the heels of my hands. I felt rough. Seriously rough. I'd drunk far too much vodka with Quinn last night in an attempt to drown my sorrows.

'Sssshhhh,' Quinn grumbled. 'I was having a nice dream.'

'What are you doing in my bed?' I yawned, stretching my arms above my head and wondering why I felt like my legs were at an unnatural angle. The last thing I remembered was us getting back from the engagement meal and sitting on patio chairs in the middle of my lawn, drinking while we watched the spectacular pink and purple sunset.

'What the hell?' Quinn groaned. I opened my eyes and immediately squinted against the brilliant sunshine that speared them.

'Good night then, I take it?' Georgie's voice called in the distance, the sound of her and Weston laughing making me snap my eyes open immediately. Instead of the white and oak beamed ceiling of my bedroom, I was looking up at a spotless turquoise sky. 'I've never been so drunk that I didn't at least make it to the sofa,' Georgie added.

'What the hell?' Quinn repeated next to me. My head flopped to the left to see her lying on her back, still sort of sitting in her patio chair. Her knees were crooked over the seat with her feet dangling below. She was still clutching her empty glass of vodka to her chest. I giggled as I realised I was in the same position. We'd got so drunk, we'd obviously capsized our chairs and had fallen asleep in the garden on our backs.

'Weston was tempted to come and get you and carry you both to your beds last night, but I said he should leave you,' Georgie scolded.

'Some friend you are,' I huffed as I struggled to get out of the chair. I had to resort to forcing myself into an ungraceful backwards roll off the chair. I landed clumsily on all fours, then flopped heavily onto my side on the grass.

'I'm not the one who kept us awake until the early hours with all the screeching and laughing,' she retorted.

'We wouldn't have been laughing if we hadn't had to listen to your sex noises and attempts at dirty talk drifting out of the open window,' Quinn teased as she floundered, kicking her legs as she tried to get up.

'At least some of us are having sex,' Weston called with a chuckle. 'Even Mrs. Tibbles and Bertie are getting more action than you two.'

'Your dog is having sex with Mrs. Tibbles?' I gasped, struggling up onto my knees. 'Thank God I had her spayed. Can you imagine their offspring?'

'Not with each other,' he laughed. 'Seriously, how much did you both drink last night?'

'Too much,' I groaned, as Quinn said, 'Not enough.'

'Well, we're going into Shrewsbury for a champagne brunch to celebrate our engagement if you want to join us,' Georgie offered, her face peeking over the top of the hedge that separated our cottages. 'Abbie and Miller are coming, Daphne and Jack too. You have half an hour to get freshened up if you fancy it.'

'It was celebrating your engagement last night that got us into this mess,' Quinn said, giving up her struggle and resigning herself to her uncomfortable-looking position.

'No one forced you to carry on drinking when we got home. Honestly, you'd think you'd both be past all this teenage behaviour by now,' Georgie softly scolded.

'You'd think,' I agreed. We were definitely a bad influence on each other. Or rather Quinn was on me. I struggled up onto my feet and smoothed my creased clothes down. 'A big breakfast sounds ideal to soak up all this alcohol. See you in half an hour.'

'You could just bring me some back,' Quinn suggested, her brown eyes pleading with me.

'No way, you're coming too. Grab my hands, I'll pull you up, as Weston's obviously used up all of his chivalry this weekend with his extravagant proposal yesterday.'

'I'll come around and help, give me a minute,' he said.

'No need, I got this,' I told him, positioning myself between the legs of the chair and leaning over it to grab Quinn's hands. I tugged a few times, leaning backwards as I did to lever her up. The chair rose with her at the same time, and we both shrieked as she shot forwards so fast, she knocked me off balance and I ended up on my back in the grass with her on top of me and the chair on top of her.

'Weston's coming,' Georgie laughed.

'Yeah, we heard him yelling that last night, too,' Quinn giggled, making me laugh.

'Oi, you have serious morning breath. Tip your head to the side,' I warned her.

'Like yours is so sweet. Better give your teeth an extra hard brushing, then do a tongue scrape too, if you plan on playing tonsil tennis with McFitty later.'

'Oh my God,' I gasped, the humour rapidly leaving me. For a few blissful minutes, I'd forgotten all about my happiness at my impending date and the agony of my fallout with Kitt. I wasn't sure which emotion I should tune into first as Weston jogged across my lawn to rescue us.

I took a deep breath as I climbed the steps to the entrance of The Riverside pub and restaurant. I felt on edge. I should be walking in on cloud nine. I mean, I'd finally got what I'd been dreaming about, a date with McFitty, so why didn't I feel overjoyed right now? Through the glass door, I spotted him at the bar, dressed in dark blue jeans and sporting an expensive-looking pale blue shirt with white collar and cuffs. There was no doubting he was gorgeous, a total knockout, but as I watched him, I had a horrible sinking feeling.

Everything about his demeanour said just how much he thought of himself, not to mention his blatant ogling of a nearby group of scantily-clad women. His chest visibly puffed with pride as they giggled at one of his jokes, and I saw him take one of their mobiles and key something into it. If we dated, would I always worry about who he was charming when I wasn't around to see it?

'For God's sake, Charlie. He's everything you've ever wanted and he's waiting in there for you,' I scolded myself, throwing open the door and making my way over to him.

'Charlie, hey.' He grinned when he spotted me.

'Hey.' I smiled back in return.

'You look ... not how I expected,' he observed as he ran his eyes over my black maxi dress embellished with a pretty pink cherry blossom design and black three-quarter sleeved shrug.

'What exactly were you expecting?' I asked.

'Less, I guess. But you look pretty.' He leaned in to kiss my cheek.

'Thanks, I guess.' I wasn't overly flattered to think he'd expected me to wear skimpy clothing on a first date. I jumped when his arm went around me and he not so subtly squeezed my backside.

'We can always skip dinner and go straight back to mine,' he whispered in my ear.

'What?' I exclaimed, my eyes bugging out.

'Ah, you're one of those. Like to be wooed first.' He chuckled as he straightened up. 'Ok well, let's keep it down to one course then, shall we? No point delaying the inevitable by stretching the night out with food.'

'Excuse me,' I began, totally affronted that he thought I was only here for sex, but he cut me off by calling one of the waitresses over and asking to be shown to our table. I bristled as I felt his hand squeeze my backside again as he guided me over. He soothed my annoyance for a moment when he showed some manners and pulled out my chair. He helped me into it before taking his seat, but not before I spotted his eyes lingering on the waitress's legs as she bent over to pick up a menu that had slipped from her hands.

'We'll both have the chicken salad and a jug of tap water, please,' he stated in that domineering doctor tone I'd found so sexy in the hospital. Why did it seem so unappealing here?

'Actually, I'm not a fan of salad, as these curves will attest. Can I see the menu please?' It was one thing to have Kitt order food for me, he knew what I liked. Guy didn't, hence the date. I scanned the menu and ordered a fillet steak with brandy sauce and skinny fries, then asked if we could have the wine menu. Our waitress nodded and hurried off to get it.

'You really want to make a night of it here?' Guy asked, his eyebrows raised in surprise.

'Well, I thought that was the point, so we could talk and get to know each other,' I responded, feeling a little confused.

'Ok.' He nodded, leaning back in his chair and steepling his fingers in front of his mouth. 'So, tell me all about your work. Is having a publishing contract really that lucrative?'

'Well, I don't have to watch my finances anymore, which is nice. My earnings have increased dramatically since getting the contract and the marketing push behind me. Don't tell me you're one of those guys who can't handle a woman earning more than him.'

'Not at all. In fact, you can pay for dinner and the wine, that's how down I am with the whole thing.' He gave me one of his smiles, all perfect teeth with sparkling eyes that once upon a time made me swoon. What was wrong with me? It was like seeing it out of the hospital setting made me realise how fake it seemed, like there was no sincerity at all behind it.

'Very funny.' I laughed, not sure if he was being serious or not. 'So how long did you have to train for to qualify and specialise in trauma work?'

An hour later, I was beginning to wish I hadn't asked. All he'd done was talk about himself. How he'd been top of his class, had aced all of his exams, had been captain of the rugby team, drove a Mercedes, had a luxurious penthouse apartment in town. It was like he thought I was an easily influenced youngster who was impressed by his degree and money. Was I really that shallow? Had his job and his looks swayed me?

We weren't having a conversation here. He hadn't once stopped boasting about himself to ask me anything, other than wanting to know how much money I was making at the beginning of the date. Something I realised he'd asked about, casually of course, a number of times before. I was sitting across from one of the most handsome men I'd ever seen, perfect on paper, so why was I wishing I was having dinner with Kitt? Our banter was easy and relaxed. He spoke, I spoke, we laughed between as well, frequently. Neither of us was trying to impress the other, we just … *were*. We gelled. I was really missing him, so much I felt like I'd lost a limb.

As Guy droned on, his eyes occasionally wandering as other women walked past, I realised that I'd spent all of this time fantasising about a perfect date with McFitty, the epitome of one of my swoon-worthy alpha-male characters, and right now I'd happily stuff my napkin into his mouth just to get him to shut the hell up.

'Excuse me,' I interrupted when he showed no signs of taking a breath. 'I'll be back in a while.'

'Oh, ok. Shall I ask for the bill?' he asked, standing as I did.

'Not yet, I'm in the mood for dessert.'

'Seriously?' His face fell immediately.

'Seriously,' I nodded, trying to read his expression. Wow, either he had a real hang-up about women with appetites, which I hated, or he actually was only in this for a booty call. Well, whatever it was, he was going to be sorely disappointed. I loved my desserts and sex was never going to be on the table with him tonight, regardless of how excited I'd been when he'd asked me out. I had no recollection of ever giving him that impression either.

I made my way past the bar towards the toilets, more for a break from Guy's incessant self-love than from the need for a pee. When I spotted a tall, dark-haired guy chatting to his friends in the corner, I did a double-take.

'Kitt?' I called, feeling the depressive atmosphere of this date from hell beginning to lift at the thought of seeing him. One of his friends elbowed him and flicked his chin in my direction as I made my way over to him, only for my stomach to sink when the man turned around and I realised it wasn't him.

'Alright, love?' he asked.

'Yes. Sorry to interrupt your conversation, I thought you were someone else.'

'No problem,' he smiled, turning back to his friends.

I stood there for a moment, trying to work out what was wrong with me. I suddenly felt completely despondent, like the sun had set and was never going to rise again. It was a really depressing thought.

I hurried to the ladies' room, blinking back some tears as I tried to tune into what I was feeling right now. I stood in front of one of the sinks and looked at my reflection in the mirror, my chest hurting with each breath I took. Second by second, the uncertainty started to leave, being forced out by the undeniable truth. A truth so blinding, I had no idea how I'd coped for the last year and a half in denial. I realised who was my waking thought each morning and my last thought at night. Who I turned to when I had news to share, whether it was good or bad. Who never judged me for being myself or had any expectations of me. Who accepted and loved me just as I was. And it certainly wasn't Guy Fitton.

'Charlie, you *bloody* idiot. What have you done?' I whispered to my reflection. I pulled my phone out and went to dial Quinn's number, but at the last moment changed my mind.

'Daphne?' I asked when she answered.

'Oh, thank goodness it's you, Charlie. I was starting to worry that I'd made a mistake in my judgement. Please tell me that you've finally come to your senses?' she questioned, making me shake my head and smile.

'How, how did you know? You and Quinn, you both knew before me.'

'We *all* knew before you, Charlie,' she chuckled. 'It was in the way you talked about him, the look on your face as you did. You'd light up whenever you mentioned him. It was obvious to us all.'

'But you encouraged me with Guy.'

'Because you were so convinced he was what you wanted, and you can be just as stubborn as me when you set your mind to something. Trying to force you down another path would only have made you more determined to prove us all wrong. I hoped that in time, you'd come to realise that you were actually in love with Kitt. And you have, haven't you? That's why you're calling me when you should be enjoying your date.'

'Yes,' I whispered, blinking back a combination of tears of frustration at my stupidity and tears of happiness that I'd finally come to my senses. 'I *love him*, Daphne. It's like a light bulb has turned on in my brain and I can suddenly see clearly. I'm completely head over heels in love with him and I can't believe I didn't even realise it,' I said, admitting it to myself for the first time and feeling my stomach knot with excitement and nerves.

187

'Well, you've never been in love before, Charlie, you had nothing to compare it to. You spend so long writing about perfect men with perfect careers, you were fixated on the one man you *thought* met those ideals, instead of seeing the one in front of you who actually did.'

'Oh, Daphne, what am I going to do? I've lost him now,' I cried, clutching at the sudden blossoming pain in my chest at the thought I might never see Kitt again.

'It's never over until it's over, dear.'

'But I have no way of contacting him. He's been ignoring my calls and texts for the past week, and short of knocking on the door of every house on his street, I don't know how to find him.'

'Ditch that cad and call in on me on your way home. I'll beat the jungle drums, someone will know something.'

'He's not a cad, he's just … he's not *Kitt*,' I stated, my heart fluttering like a newly hatched butterfly testing its wings for the first time at the thought of my best friend and how happy I'd be to see him again and tell him how I really felt.

'Trust me, dear, that doctor's a cad. I know one when I see one. Now, if you can stop at the supermarket on the way home and pick up a box of four chocolate éclairs and a bottle of whiskey, we can celebrate you finally coming to your senses in style.'

'I hope there'll be something to celebrate,' I sighed, worried that my realisation had come too late.

'Have a little faith. And don't be too long. At my age, I shouldn't be eating dairy after a certain time, but I feel like being a little wild tonight.'

'I love you, Daphne,' I stated sincerely.

'Stop buttering me up like a piece of toast and get over here so we can figure out how to tell the man who needs to hear it that you love him,' she ordered.

'Yes, ma'am,' I giggled.

'Ma'am, I'll give you ma'am. I'm still young enough to show you a thing or two,' I heard her muttering before she cut me off.

'I love Kitt. I *love* Kitt,' I repeated, watching my eyes sparkle in the mirror and a rosy glow appear on my face, along with the widest smile I'd ever seen myself sport. 'I love Kitt!' I cried.

'Ok, ok, I get it, you love Kitt. Can I finish my pee in peace now?' huffed a voice from the cubicle behind me. 'I have a bashful bladder and holding it in is killing me.'

'Sorry, I just … I *love* him. I've never said it out loud before. I never even said it to myself. In fact, I've denied it for so long, it's just … oh God, it feels *so* good to admit it. I love Kitt,' I yelled to the ceiling, holding my hands up in the air.

'Seriously, go and find Kitt and tell him and let me pee in peace. I'm going to get a water infection from holding it in,' the girl moaned.

'I am. I'm going to find him and I'm going to tell him, then I'm going to kiss him. I can't wait to kiss him.'

I left the toilets with a spring in my step, my brain frantically trying to work out exactly how I was going to find him to let him know my momentous news. As I approached the table, I saw that Guy was still seated, his back to me as he talked to someone standing at his side. I realised it was his good-looking blond doctor friend, who was holding a pint and had a puzzled look on his face.

'So what are you doing here with the girl from A&E? What's her name? Charlie something?' I heard his friend ask as I approached from the side, unnoticed by either of them as Guy nodded. 'Are you on a date?'

'Sort of,' Guy shrugged, making me hang back, interested to hear what he had to say.

'You just got engaged to Marnie from Paediatrics. Is it off already?'

'Not unless she finds out about this. I can trust you not to say anything, right, Tyler? What she doesn't know won't hurt her. Perfect wife material, but not that great for fooling around with, if you get my drift,' Guy said as I frowned to hear that bit of news. *He was engaged?* Wow, Daphne was right, he was a complete … cad. 'Besides, this girl has been throwing herself at me for months. She's so desperate that she's a sure thing for tonight.'

'Cheeky sod,' I muttered under my breath.

'So you're not interested in her, it's just a casual hook up?' Tyler asked.

'Seriously, you think I'd choose to date someone like *Charlie* if I had another choice? She's a walking bloody disaster. I prefer my women with a bit more sanity. The only reason I gave in and asked her out is she's loaded now, and she's so desperate for my attention that I can have a bit of fun on the side and hopefully get a few quid out of her to clear some of my debts. The car and penthouse didn't come cheap.'

I inhaled a soft gasp. I didn't feel hurt, not now that I'd realised who I really cared about. I was just disappointed that I'd obviously been so blinded by his pretty face and fancy job that I'd nearly let myself be used by this despicable excuse for a man, who appeared to be a cheat and a liar too.

'You know what?' Tyler growled, slamming his nearly virgin pint down on the table. 'I've heard so many rumours about you that I've ignored, not wanting to believe that I could be friends with a guy like that, but I'm glad to finally have the wool pulled from over my eyes, as you've confirmed it for me. You're vain, self-centred, selfish, and egotistical. Thanks for finally setting me straight. You're an arsehole, Guy. Women should be treated with respect, not as cheap commodities. Either you find a way to gently let Charlie down tonight without hurting her or I'll tell Marnie exactly what her fiancé has been up to behind her back. In fact, I still might, both of them deserve better.' Tyler stormed off to the bar as Guy watched him leave, stunned.

I slipped out of his view behind the stone pillar and beckoned over our waitress. After asking a favour of her, and slipping her a twenty-pound note to make sure she did it immediately, I watched her hurry off behind the bar to do as she was asked, looking pleased as punch.

I strode back over to where Guy was sitting with a broad grin on my face, ecstatic that I'd finally come to my senses before even hearing that little exchange take place. How could I have ever been so brainwashed to think he was the right man for me?

'Hi,' I said as I went to stand next to his chair. 'Sorry I've been so long, I just had a moment of clarity while I was in the ladies' room. I've definitely been suffering from white coat syndrome, you know, where your blood pressure goes up when you see the doctor? All this time I thought that dizzy feeling was because I fancied you, when actually it was just the uniform, stethoscope, and fancy medical degree that spun my head. I was lusting over a fantasy, but it turns out that reality is actually a *huge* disappointment.'

'Charlie?' he questioned as he looked up at me, puzzled.

'It took the most *boring* date of my life to make me realise that I'm actually in love with a man who's worth a hundred times what you are.' I picked up Tyler's discarded pint of Guinness and slowly poured the thick brown ale over McDefinitelyNotSoFitty's head, enjoying watching him splutter as it coated him. 'I've just downgraded you from McFitty to McShitty, and for the record, I'd never offer myself to a man who pretended to be interested in me despite my flaws. I'd wait forever for the man who loves me *because* of them. If *that's* insanity, then I'll wear the badge loud and proud. Maybe it's time you looked in the mirror, Guy Fitton, as I see the real you now, and I'm sure your fiancée and the rest of the unsuspecting women of Shropshire will soon, too. There's only so long a guy like you can keep his real persona under wraps in a small town where gossip spreads fast. Thanks for dinner and the champagne. I wish I could say it has been a pleasure, but unlike you, I was brought up to never lie.'

'What champagne?' he uttered as he swept his wet hair away from his face. I spotted our waitress and a friend scurrying over towards us with two uncorked bottles of their most expensive champagne in buckets of ice for him, adding five hundred pounds worth of premium alcohol to the bill I'd just left him with.

I made a hasty retreat towards the exit, winking at an impressed-looking Tyler on the way out.

'Add *that* to your debts, McDick,' I yelled at Guy over my shoulder as I disappeared.

'Sit down, sit down,' Daphne said, gesturing at the sofa as she settled herself into her armchair. She'd already put out some side plates for the cakes and a couple of glasses for the whiskey. 'You look so pretty tonight. So, how did the break-up go?'

'Great,' I nodded as I cracked open the bottle and poured us both a glass. She smiled and shook her head as I filled her in on what Guy was really like.

'I knew it. My mamma always told me to trust my instinct and it's never once steered me wrong in all my years,' she nodded, as I slid one of the éclairs onto her plate and one onto mine.

'I wish my instincts were as good, it would have saved a lot of time and heartbreak.'

'He'll come around when you see him,' she said, quickly picking up the cream-filled dessert. She took a bite, her eyes rolling back in her head as she slowly chewed and savoured it. 'So good,' she sighed, licking her lips. 'Not quite as good as the ones Fleur bakes at French Fancie, but I'd be hard pressed to answer if someone told me I had to choose between cream cakes and sex.'

'It's been so long, I'd have no such problem. Sex all the way,' I said, taking a bite of mine. 'So, how are we going to find Kitt? Now that I know how I feel, I need to share. I'm going to burst if I can't tell him soon.'

'Well, I don't know his address, but I know where he'll be at one o'clock tomorrow afternoon.'

'Where?' I asked, not even surprised she'd managed to find something out. She had her fingers in so many pies, I wouldn't be surprised if she told me she'd been a covert intelligence officer in her youth.

'Put my cake plate down first, I don't want it broken. It's one of my favourite sets.'

'Why would I break your plate?' I asked, though I did as I was told to avoid one of her fierce scowls. She set her own down, leaned over, and grabbed my hand.

'There's no easy way to say it, dear. He'll be at the crematorium.'

'He's dead?!' I shrieked, my heart thudding rapidly in my chest as I shot out of my seat. 'I've just realised I'm in love with him and he's *dead*?'

'No, no, calm yourself down. He's not dead, well not that I know of. But …' She broke off and gave me a subdued smile.

'Oh no. His *mum?*' I whispered, the temporary wave of relief I'd just felt rapidly subsiding as it finally dawned on me what had happened.

'I'm sorry, dear. Knowing you two were getting close last year, I naturally did some snooping to make sure he was good enough for you. Turns out his mum's best friend played bridge with Mrs. Arthur from apartment four. She soon fed back that he was a good man, caring for his mum in her time of need. I rang Quinn after speaking to you tonight and when she said he'd been out of touch and had taken a few weeks off work, it didn't take much for me to put two and two together. A quick scan of the obituaries in this week's papers, then a call to Mrs. Arthur confirmed it.'

'It didn't take *you* much. How did I not reach that conclusion?' I asked as I slumped back down on the sofa. 'I *knew* something was wrong. I can't believe he didn't tell me. Oh, poor Kitt,' I groaned as I covered my face. 'Everything makes sense now. He said he'd never be free to date while she was alive. I should have known when he confessed his feelings on Saturday that he'd lost her.' I could have kicked myself as I replayed some of his statements over in my head. "Everyone leaves," he'd said so sadly, and I still hadn't worked it out. 'I don't deserve him.'

'Don't talk such nonsense, or I'll be forced to cuff you. From what I've heard, he's always been very private when it comes to his home life.'

'He should have told me, I could have been there for him,' I said, dropping my hands into my lap as I shook my head in disbelief. 'I *should* have been there for him.'

'Grief affects people in different ways. If he'd wanted your support when it happened, he'd have asked for it. He obviously needed some time alone. He came to you when he was ready to talk.'

'And I had to go and ruin it by mentioning Dr. Fitton before he even had a chance to tell me what was wrong.'

'Well, all you can do is be there for him tomorrow and each day after that.'

'If he still wants me,' I huffed as I reached for my drink and took a large gulp. 'And I can't just turn up at her funeral uninvited. He said he wanted space. How's me gate crashing a funeral giving him space?'

'Trust me, even if he doesn't realise it now, he'll appreciate you being there and telling him how you really feel.'

'I'm not so sure, Daphne,' I said, grimacing when I incurred one of the scowls anyway.

'Have I ever given you bad advice?' she demanded.

'No,' I admitted.

'Good, then do as you're told. Now stop being selfish and hogging the cake box. Pass it over and get home for an early night so you're ready for an emotional day tomorrow.'

'Is eating another two éclairs at this time of night going to be good for you?' I asked as I did as I was told.

'Since when did anyone only do what was good for them? Sometimes you have to live a little dangerously,' she said, helping herself to a second. 'And no getting drunk and waking up on the lawn again,' she warned. 'He'll need your support tomorrow, you need to be level headed.'

'If I was, we'd have been dating for over a year by now,' I sighed.

Chapter Sixteen

Endings
The Next Day – Monday

I SNUCK INTO THE back of the room, not feeling brave enough to walk up to him, but the undeniable beat of my heart, clammy palms, and fluttering stomach told me that I hadn't imagined my feelings for him. He was dressed in a black three-piece suit, with a crisp white shirt and black tie. It was as if I was seeing him for the first time. Had he always been so handsome? I'd always thought he was cute, but now my love-struck vision had turned him into someone gorgeous and seriously hot.

Honestly though, much as I loved the suited look on men, I just wanted to see him in his white t-shirt, black jeans, and scruffy army boots again. That was the Kitt I loved. This well-dressed Kitt I hurt for, as it reminded me why we were here. Even studying his side profile, I could see the anguish in his posture and on his face.

I bit my lower lip as the service started and kept my eyes off the coffin and on him, waiting for a sign that he needed some support. As the service drew to a close, we all stood waiting as one of the staff pressed some buttons and the coffin slowly started to descend from the raised podium it had been placed on.

People's eyes started to dart left and right when the unmistakable sound of noise started to come from the coffin, noise that sounded not too dissimilar to Mr. Sumo's worst case of flatulence in his heyday. Seconds later, the highly reflective polished wooden lid appeared to start opening. My jaw dropped, and the women in the front row screamed, as the lid flew back and Mrs. Fraser slowly rose up on a rapidly expanding bright yellow and grey self-inflating dinghy. It straddled the podium as it puffed out, while the coffin continued its descent without her.

Pandemonium broke loose. People were yelling and crying, and all I could do was watch Kitt's shocked face as his mum lay there stiffly, totally oblivious to the havoc she'd just caused. I could only assume she'd been lain on top of her favourite rubber boat, to be buried with her, which must have been accidentally set off by the movement of the coffin. All I could think about was how grateful I was that it hadn't catapulted her across the room into the congregation.

Kitt opened his mouth, then shook his head and started to laugh. Small chuckles to start that got louder and louder as everyone else went silent, watching him aghast as he doubled up into a full-blown roar. Part of me wanted to laugh too. I mean, things like this weren't supposed to happen in real life. It was quite funny, but at the end of the day, it was his mum. The shock was going to hit him any moment.

I squeezed my way through the crowd of bewildered onlookers while some of the staff buzzed around the late Mrs. Fraser, trying to work out the most dignified way of making her and the inappropriate dinghy disappear quickly, and the rest tried to usher everyone towards the main exit.

By the time I reached Kitt's side, his laughter had subsided and he was just staring at his mum in bewilderment. I slipped my hand into his and squeezed it hard.

'Come with me,' I said softly. 'You don't need to see this, this shouldn't be your last memory of her.'

He blinked a few times as he tore his eyes off her, then looked down at me and nodded with a blank expression. His green eyes looked glassy, as if he hadn't even registered that it was me. Someone in full funeral uniform showed us to a side exit. I followed the signs for the memorial garden, tugging Kitt along behind me and hoping we'd get a few minutes peace there for him to compose himself. As we entered the small area, which was surrounded by a semi-circular wall with various urns on niches and bouquets of flowers on the ground, I saw a bench. I sat down on it and pulled him down next to me, then gathered him up in my arms. Moments later, he started to sob.

'I'm so sorry, I'm so sorry for everything,' I stated sincerely, kissing his hair as he clung to me tightly, hoping he'd read between the lines that I wasn't just talking about today. We stayed like that for a few minutes, and when he'd finally calmed down and caught his breath, we let each other go. I offered him a tissue, which he used to wipe his eyes, then he blew his nose before taking a few deep, calming breaths. He dropped his head, his elbows resting on his knees, as he stared at the ground. I just sat there with him in silence, not sure if I should say anything more. 'Kitt,' I whispered as I placed my hand on his back, wondering if he'd forgotten I was there or that he had a whole crowd of people probably waiting by the main door to offer him their condolences.

'Why are you here, Charlie?' he asked quietly, with an unnatural coolness to his voice as he turned to face me.

'I ... I thought you'd need me.'

'Maybe I just need some space, like I told you on Saturday,' he said sharply, making me wince at his tone.

'Kitt, please don't be like that. I know you're hurting, not only over what just happened in there or why we're here, but over what happened between us.'

'There *is* no us, Charlie. You made that perfectly clear when you rejected me,' he snapped, a flare of unmistakable anger igniting his eyes and bringing them back to life as he stood up abruptly. I swallowed a lump in my throat at the thought of how much I'd hurt him.

'And I made a *mistake*. I'd spent so long imagining what might happen with him that I didn't see what was actually happening between us. It's you I want, Kitt. I don't want to lose you. We don't need to talk about this now. In fact, we probably shouldn't talk about this now. I just want to be here for you.'

'I can't do this, Charlie. I spent all weekend thinking that maybe I could still be in your life, that maybe I could cope with things just being platonic between us, but seeing you again just reminds me that I can't. I have a chance to start my life over again when I wake up tomorrow, and I don't want to be someone's consolation prize because she couldn't get the guy she really wanted.'

'That's just it,' I cried, tugging on his arm as he tried to walk away from me. 'I did get him. I went on a date with him last night and hated it. Every second I sat there with him, I kept wishing he was you. It took a date with him to make me open my eyes and realise that I'd fallen in love with you, Kitt. It's you I want to be with, not him.'

'What did you just say?' he asked gruffly as he stood with his back to me.

'It's you, Kitt,' I stated emphatically. 'It's *always* been you. I was just too stupid to see it. You're not just my best friend, you're *everything*. I love you. I'm *in love* with you.'

'Jesus, Charlie,' he yelled, shrugging off my hand to spin around and face me, his usually clear green eyes now stormy and wild. 'Why now? Why the *hell* now? Do you see where we're standing?'

'I'm sorry. I know my timing is awful, but I thought it might help if you knew how I felt today.'

'I can't do this right now.'

'I get that. I just wanted you to know that even though you've lost her, you have me. You're not alone. I'm not leaving you, Kitt.'

'No, I'm leaving you, Charlie. I said I can't do this. Right now, being *alone* is what I need. Don't follow me,' he barked. He strode away without even looking back and my heart pulsed painfully as my eyes burned. I wanted to run after him, to throw myself at him, to comfort him and have him comfort me. Most of all, I wanted to kiss him and feel his warm embrace. I'd never wanted anything more, and stopping myself from acting on my desires ripped me in two. I started to sob and wrapped my arms around myself.

He was right. Look where we were. He'd just said goodbye to his mum, someone who'd unintentionally dominated his life for the last three years. What was I thinking, trying to tell him how I felt now?

'Here you are, dear.' The voice made me jump as I dragged my sleeve over my eyes and found a middle-aged lady holding out a tissue for me.

'Thank you.' I sniffed, giving her a weak smile as I took it from her.

'Did you lose someone important to you, too?' she asked. I dabbed my eyes and nodded. I had a feeling that I really might have. 'I'm sorry. It's a hard lesson in life, one you become only too familiar with when you get to my age. But trust me, that darkness you feel suffocating you today will slowly be erased by the bright sunshine that family and friends bring into your life if you let them.'

'I feel like I only just found him,' I whispered as I choked back more tears.

'Did he know how you felt about him?'

'Yes, I guess … I mean … I hope so. I told him, but I'm not sure he believed me.'

'But you said it, that's what's important. While you'll never know if he believed you or not, one day it will bring you peace that you said what was in your heart. When we lose loved ones, the hardest thing is knowing we never told them how we felt. You did that.'

'You lost someone today, too?' I asked, as I forced back the flood of tears I wanted to shed so I could focus on the kind and well-meaning lady instead, who'd totally misunderstood the reason for my tears.

'Yes and no.' She sighed as she placed a bouquet of flowers down in the memorial garden. 'She died recently. I just came for her service this afternoon, but I lost her friendship a few years ago. I said goodbye to her one weekend as her best friend, returned the next and she had no idea who I even was. Thirty years of history wiped out in less than seven days.' She gave me a pained smile as she shook her head.

'I'm *so* sorry for your loss,' I said sincerely, realising this must have been the best friend of Kitt's mum. Thirty years. How did you cope when you lost someone you'd cared for and shared so much of your life with for that long? I felt a deep, gnawing ache at the distance between me and Kitt already, and we only had a fraction of that history between us.

'I never told her I loved her,' the lady continued with a sigh. 'It wasn't the done thing for girlfriends to say that to each other, in case it was misconstrued, but I did love her. A very different love to the one I have for my husband, but love all the same. I carry the weight of not saying it while I had the chance. You'll have more burdens to bear, as you're young and life can be cruel, but at least you've been spared that this time.' She sighed again and looked up the path towards the car park. 'Well, it looks like it's time for me to go. Will you be ok?'

'I'll be fine. Thank you for your wise words. How about you? Do you need a lift anywhere?'

'That's very kind of you to offer, but my husband's waiting for me. Remember, it will get easier,' she said, patting my hand.

I watched her walk away and blew out a heavy breath as I looked up at the expanse of blue above me.

'I wish I'd come to meet you when I had the chance,' I said quietly to his mum. 'Even though you wouldn't have remembered, I'd have told you what an amazing man you raised. I hope I wasn't too late telling him that I love him, and I hope that forgiveness was a trait you drummed into him, as well as kindness and respect, as I don't want to imagine that I've lost him for good.' I took a deep breath and placed the small bunch of gerberas that I'd brought with me on the ground next to the lady's bouquet. I remembered how Kitt had once told me they were his mum's favourites and always made her smile.

I headed home with a real sense of loss, almost as if I'd just attended the funeral of someone I'd known and loved. After throwing myself on the bed and sobbing for an hour, giving in to my self-pity, I dragged myself up.

I changed out of my sombre black clothing and pulled on some shorts and a t-shirt, then headed downstairs to pull back the glass doors that spanned the back of the house, letting the sunlight and summer heat pour in. I wanted to wallow in the warmth, hoping the lady was right, that the bright light would erase the darkness threatening to swallow me whole.

I grabbed a tub of ice cream from the freezer and a teaspoon, smiling to myself. I never understood people who ate desserts with a large spoon. It meant you shovelled in larger amounts in a shorter time frame, and I liked to savour it and stretch out the pleasure for as long as possible.

'Come on, Tibbs, let's go and mope outside in the sun,' I said as she wrapped herself around my feet, rubbing her cheek on my calf as she purred. We padded outside together and I stretched out on the sun lounger with my tub and spoon, Tibbs hopping up to lie at my feet. I exhaled slowly as I soaked up the rays and the tranquil view and tried to let the stress of the morning leave me.

How could I have *finally* fallen in love, with a man that loved me back, only to ruin it all? This wasn't what was supposed to happen.

Romance novels always ended happily. I just had to hope that there were more pages to our story. I swallowed spoon after spoon of ice cream, wishing it would ease the pain I was feeling, but so far it wasn't working.

A loud knock on the door startled me. I shoved the tub of melting ice cream on the ground and flew inside, skidding across the hall to throw the door open. I let out a heavy sigh of disappointment to see that it was Quinn.

'Wow, don't look so excited to see me.'

'Sorry, I thought you were … I should have known, it wasn't his knock. Come in, but it's only fair I warn you that my misery may be infectious.'

'Didn't go so well, huh?'

'You could say that,' I replied, closing the door and turning to face her. 'Like funerals aren't bad enough, the coffin opened on its own and nearly gave everyone a heart attack when the body appeared in a dinghy, then I told him I loved him and he walked away from me.'

'Jeez, good job I brought this over,' she said, brandishing a bottle of vodka. 'Do I need to go and get some ice cream too?'

'Grab a spoon, I have a half-eaten tub outside.'

'I'll bring some drinks out too, you look like you need one. Then you can tell me what the hell happened, because I didn't see this coming.'

I gave her a weak smile and felt my bottom lip tremble. She plonked the bottle down on the console table and pulled me into a hug.

'I'll cry again,' I moaned.

'So cry. Just because I don't doesn't mean I can't handle you getting emotional.'

'I love you, Quinn,' I mumbled, wrapping my arms tightly around her.

'Wow, two hours after being rejected and you've given up on the male species already?' she teased.

'Shut up,' I muttered. 'You know what I mean. I didn't tell him how important he was to me and I might have lost him. I don't want to lose you too, so it's important I tell you how much you mean to me.'

'You're not losing me,' she said as I straightened up and wiped the tears off my lower lashes. 'Friends to the end. I never thought I'd be happy leaving New York behind me, but this little place kind of sneaks its way into your heart.'

'You told me once that you didn't have a heart,' I reminded her, sniffing back the tears I wanted to shed as I flicked my head towards the kitchen and she followed me in.

'Only when it comes to men. They're bloody idiots,' she stated. It still made me giggle to hear her using such a British swear word. She really was settling in to our way of life. 'Anyway, you haven't lost him, Charlie. He's been in love with you for too long to walk away for good.'

'Why did I think it was a good idea to tell him today, of all days?'

'You thought it would make him feel better on one of the worst days of his life, plus Daphne told you to. I'd have done the same in your shoes, she's usually spot on with her advice. She's as wise as she's old. I'm sure he'll come around when he's had time to digest it.'

'You think?'

'I know he will. He's had a rough week. He lost his mum and you rejected him. Throw in a funeral and a damn coffin opening, which you so need to tell me about as that sounds morbidly hilarious, and it's no wonder he was messed up in the head and needed some space.'

'You really think that–' I was cut off by an ungodly howl from the patio, which made us both whip our heads around, only to burst out laughing. Tibbs was streaking around and banging into the patio furniture with my cardboard tub of ice cream stuck firmly over her head. 'That will teach you to steal my food,' I called, making her mewl again as she heard my voice.

'Looks like I need to go to the shop after all,' Quinn laughed as I headed over to rescue my terrified moggie.

'Hey, hey, it's me, calm down,' I said gently as I grabbed her shaking body. I was risking my life by picking her up when she was scared. A happy Tibbs had claws Wolverine would back away from, let alone an agitated Tibbs. I sat on the lounger and held her against my chest with one hand as I gently prised off the tub, which released with a loud pop and a pitiful meow. 'Oh, Mrs. Tibbles,' I giggled. Her head was coated in sticky melted ice cream, which had flattened her fur and made her look like a cream-coloured hairless Egyptian cat. She thrust out a tongue to lick around her mouth and I shook my head.

'Is she ok?' Quinn asked.

'She's going to have a *very* upset tummy in a few hours after scoffing a load of lactose,' I nodded, standing up. 'Come on, you're going to have to wear the gloves and hold her while I give her a bath in the utility sink.'

'Why me?' she uttered, backing away with her hands in the air. 'That cat could star in her own slasher flick, and I kinda like my hands attached to my body.'

'Well, I'm not putting her on her leash and terrifying her by blasting her with a hosepipe. She's a grumpy young sod, but I still love her.'

'You so owe me for this,' she scowled as we headed inside.

For the next half an hour, I forgot my woes as we laughed and tried to evade the angry swipes of her paws as we gave my miserable girl a good bath and then a gentle blow-dry, until there was no sticky residue in sight.

I lifted my head and looked towards the door as I heard a car.

'Oh God, it's him,' I whispered, setting a pristine and fluffy-looking Tibbs down on the floor.

'How can you tell that from the sound of an engine?'

'I just can. I spent nearly every Friday night listening for him, I know the sound of his car by heart.' I shot her a scared look, wondering if he'd come to cut all ties and tell me he was moving back to Newcastle.

'I'm going to go then. I'll sneak around the side of the house. Just let me know what happens either way. I'm sure you won't need me, but if you do, I'll be back within sixty seconds, ok?'

'Ok,' I nodded, swallowing down a burning lump of anxiety. We hugged each other quickly, and she gave me a reassuring smile before heading out onto the patio and disappearing around the corner. I quickly reached up to rake my fingers through my hair before I heard a knock on the door, and my heart started racing. It was definitely him, that was his knock. One loud rap, a pause, followed by two in quick succession, then another pause before a final knock. 'Please don't break my heart, Pizzaman,' I whispered as I made my way to the door.

I hesitated, gripping the handle, knowing that the second I opened the door, everything was about to change. I just had no idea whether it was for better or worse.

'Seriously? The one day I need you to open the damn door in record time and you don't?' his voice muttered on the other side.

'Because today you don't have pizza, or soup, or get-well flowers. Because today I don't need you to take care of me. Because today I'm not sure why you're standing on my doorstep, Kitt. I'm terrified that if I open it, you're going to tell me that you're leaving Shrewsbury, and it might be the last time I ever see my best friend,' I said, dropping my head with a heavy thud onto the oak door. 'Owww,' I moaned.

'Open the damn door, Charlie,' he demanded, a similar-sounding thud vibrating the door between us. I felt sick. I felt more nervous than I had the first time I'd pressed publish and waited for feedback on my debut novel, and I'd bitten my nails down to the quick that night. I took a deep breath and slowly turned the handle, cracking the door open a fraction to peer out. His head was down, his hands braced on either side of the door as he stood there breathing hard and fast, still dressed in his black three-piece suit from earlier, but without his tie. He lifted his head and his green eyes locked with mine, an unreadable expression in them as I scanned his face for a clue as to why he was really here. I jumped back with a gasp as he slammed a palm on the door and forced it open.

'I thought you needed to be alone,' I said.

'I realised I need you more,' he growled, pushing his way inside as I walked backwards, hardly daring to believe that he'd come to claim me. I was scared of finally feeling his lips touching mine, in case that searing need I wrote about so often, that explosion of fireworks, didn't happen.

I gasped as I bumped into the wall behind me and he continued to advance, like a predator stalking his prey. Except I wasn't exactly putting up much resistance or trying to escape. Gone was my sweet and caring Kitt. This was Kitt as I'd never seen him before. A simmering, sexual male in his prime.

I let out a soft cry as he yanked me against his hard body, one hand cradling the nape of my neck, the other firmly in the small of my back. Then he bowed his head and his lips crashed onto mine as the comforting scent of the ocean surrounded me. I felt myself sag against him as my eyes closed against the dazzling eruptions of the most stunning firework display I'd ever witnessed, and I drowned in the sense of his need for me, and mine for him. This was it. This was everything I'd written about and never experienced, but so much better than I'd imagined. I felt tears of happiness rolling down my face as I wrapped my arms around his neck and pulled him even closer, so close not even a page of descriptives of the most perfect kiss I'd ever been a recipient of could come between us.

'Kitt,' I gasped as he broke away, both of us panting for air. We were clinging to each other like shipwreck survivors being rocked by the power of a wild and stormy sea.

'Tell me, tell me again,' he demanded, his eyes searching mine, fretful and enquiring. I tipped my head to the side and reached up to wipe my damp cheeks before gently framing his face with my hands.

'I, Charlie Faulkner, the most *stupid* woman in the world for not seeing what was right in front of her from the moment she met you, Pizzaman, am madly, deeply, and life-alteringly crazy in love with you, Kitt Fraser.'

'I thought you were supposed to have a degree in English,' he replied, a slow smile creeping across his face, causing that set of dimples I so adored to appear.

'*That's* what you take from my statement?' I laughed, holding his gaze.

'Tell me again,' he whispered with hope in his cadence. 'I'm not sure if I'm dreaming.'

'I love you, Kitt. I think I might even love you more than pizza.'

'Pepperoni?' he asked as his smile broadened into an ecstatic grin, one I'd missed so much.

'Pepperoni,' I nodded, smiling back.

'Well, *now* I believe you,' he said, pulling me back for an urgent and hungry kiss before burying his face in my neck with a sigh. 'Is it wrong that one of the worst days of my life has just turned into one of the happiest too?'

'Of course it's not,' I said, softly kissing his neck. 'We take our happiness where we can get it, especially when we're at our lowest. Feel how you want to feel, Kitt. I won't judge you. You did everything you could for her and more. I'm sure she'd be happy to see that you aren't alone now that she's gone.'

'She'd have loved you, Charlie. Although not quite as much as I do.'

'Tell me, tell *me* again,' I whispered, my heart thudding an erratic beat against my chest as I waited to hear those words he'd said when my ears were closed to accepting them. He took a deep breath and lifted his head, holding my gaze as his softened, and I felt like kicking myself. That look had been in his eyes for almost as long as I'd known him, and I'd been so blinded by what I'd thought I wanted that I hadn't even noticed that my best friend was in love with me, or realised what my feelings for him were. But I'd never been so clear on anything in my life now that the light bulb had been turned on.

'I love you, Charlie. You're not just my best friend, you're *everything*,' he murmured, dropping his forehead to mine, and my heart exploded, fragmented, and fluttered to earth like thousands of miniature heart-shaped pieces of confetti.

'Ditto,' I whispered, luxuriating in the warmth spreading through my body at his declaration. 'I'm so sorry. I'm sorry I took so long. I'm sorry for hurting you on Saturday. I'm sorry about your mum. I'm just sorry about everything except how I feel about you. Tell me what you need. I want to help make things easier for you after today.'

'Just be here with me. Just be you. That's part of what I love about you, about us. We've never pretended to be anything but what we are, never hidden any side of ourselves.'

'I beg to differ. I had no idea you were in love with me, or me with you, and I definitely had no idea that my sweet and thoughtful Kitt could kiss like that.'

'That was nothing, I haven't even opened the throttle up yet,' he chuckled.

'Lucky me,' I breathed, weaving my fingers into his hair.

'I think it's me that's the lucky one. I said goodbye to one amazing woman today, but somehow I found another,' he said, his warm hands clutching my face as our eyes melded.

'That means a lot, I know how much you respected her. Please tell me you're not moving back to Newcastle? I don't want a long-distance relationship.'

'I've kind of fallen in love with Shropshire, in addition to you. Now tell me I can forget the platonic side of our relationship and drag you upstairs so I can show you exactly how I feel about you,' he said as he quickly kissed me.

'Are you sure this isn't you acting out of grief?' I asked, the concern I felt evident on my face.

'I'm ok now,' he said with a gentle nod. 'Really. My head said goodbye to her a long time ago. I just needed some time alone this afternoon to let my heart do it and to process what you told me. I want you, Charlie. I want you because I need you, not because I'm using you to forget. Tell me that's ok.'

'Then I'm not going to tell you that. If you really mean it, I'm going to demand it,' I replied, then let out a peel of laughter as he hoisted me up his body and threw me over his shoulder.

'Next time, I'll wear those firefighter's trousers and braces you were fantasising about,' he growled.

'Next time? That's a bit presumptuous, isn't it? We might find we're incompatible and instead of setting the sheets on fire, we could go off like a damp squib.'

'Christ, I hope not,' he grunted as he took the stairs two at a time.

'Me too,' I sighed, curling my hands around his tight butt cheeks. 'Me too.'

An hour later, we lay panting, tangled up in the sheets and each other, both hot messes. My legs felt like jelly.

'Jesus,' he rasped.

'Hmmm,' I agreed, struggling out of his arms to sit up. 'Sorry, but I've got to go. Right this minute.'

'Go? Go where?' he shot back, quickly propping himself up on his elbows, his brown hair adorably ruffled.

'I've got a tonne of work to do,' I said, trying to keep a straight face.

'Are you serious right now?' he gasped, his eyes widening in horror. 'I can't feel my legs, my brain is scrambled, and you're feeling ok enough to get up and go to your office and *work?*'

'Mmmm-hmmm,' I nodded. 'I've got to re-write *every* damn sex scene I've ever published while my memory stays intact, as *hell*, I had no idea it was *that* good.'

'Charlie Faulkner,' he laughed, grabbing me and tackling me back down onto the bed. He rolled over me, pinning my hands to the pillow on either side of my head. 'You nearly gave me a heart attack. I thought you were trying to tell me it wasn't good for you.'

'Hello! That wasn't good. That was … *my God*, I don't have words. You nearly gave *me* a heart attack. I had no idea Pizzaman had so much stamina, or so many moves.'

'Baby, I have so much more to show you,' he grinned, planting a hard kiss on my eager lips. 'And even when I finally hit sixth gear and burn through the fuel tank, I still have a reserve, just for you.'

I screamed with laughter as he let go of my hands and tickled my ribs as he nipped along my jaw, but my screams were quickly dwarfed by a bellow. Kitt leapt off me, his face contorted in pain and his eyes wide with surprise. I sat up, astonished, and stared as he spun around, only to see him swatting at his naked backside, where a furious-looking Mrs. Tibbles was clinging on for dear life as she hissed and growled and tried to bite him.

'She's bloody crazy,' he shouted as I howled with laughter. 'I thought she liked me?'

'Oh Tibbs, of all the times to come and protect me when you hear me scream.' I got out of bed, feeling slightly unsteady on my feet as I went and prised her off him. I gave her a quick cuddle and a kiss as I took her out to the landing and gently pushed her towards the stairs, quickly shutting the bedroom door so she couldn't come back in. 'Owww, that looks sore,' I said, pulling a face as Kitt wiped off the numerous streaks of blood from his pert, and incredibly sexy, backside.

'Thank God I wasn't on my back at the time, with her taking out her anger on my junk,' he said with a grimace.

'Hmmm, thank God indeed. Now do I need to take you to the hospital for treatment? I happen to know a doctor who specialises in being an arse, so he could probably patch up yours very easily.'

'No, thanks,' he huffed, narrowing his eyes at me. 'So I take it I don't have to grit my teeth and tolerate any more damn McFitty references.'

'Jealousy is such a lovely colour on you,' I smiled as I padded over to him and slid my hands up his broad, toned chest. 'No more McNotSoFitty, but I think I just found the *purrfect* McKitty,' I winked.

'Anything's better than Pizzaman,' he grinned, grabbing my backside and lifting me up onto his hips.

'Sorry, Kitt, but you'll always be Pizzaman to me,' I whispered, right before we exchanged a tender kiss and I melted into his strong arms.

'And when were you going to tell me about that sexy tattoo with my name on your hip?' he murmured as he lowered me back onto my bed.

'Oh God,' I groaned, feeling embarrassed all of a sudden as he kneeled over me and traced it with his finger. 'I got it done the night

205

before my accident when we were on holiday. Apparently drunk me knew I was in love with you before sober me.'

'I always thought you were a bit slow,' he teased, dipping his head to kiss it.

'Don't,' I grimaced, trying to pull him back up towards me. 'I have horrible scars down there.'

'You have scars everywhere, Charlie, and I don't care. They make you who you are, and I told you before, I love all of you, especially your flaws, as they make you unique.' He moved his lips across my stomach to kiss the gnarly pink patch on my left hip as my eyes filled with happy tears. He got me. He loved me for me, the whole package, not just what he saw on the outside.

'The card and flowers *were* from you? Why didn't you say anything that night? Quinn asked and I gave you a number of chances to say something.'

'I heard your conversation, insisting so firmly that we were just friends,' he shrugged. 'I didn't want to ruin things between us by confessing they were from me. Are we going to go over old ground for the rest of the night, or can we spend it exploring the new?' he asked as he lifted his head and his soft, adoring eyes met mine.

'New, I vote new,' I nodded as I tugged him back up to my lips.

Chapter Seventeen

New York, New York
Seven Months Later – Valentine's Day

'I CAN'T BELIEVE WE'RE in New York without Quinn.' I was getting a crick in my neck from gaping up in awe at the skyscrapers that towered like gigantic sentinels above the scurrying crowds below. We'd only arrived yesterday and I'd been walking around with my jaw scraping the snow-covered sidewalks the whole time. I just loved it here.

'It would sort of ruin the whole romance part of our Valentine's getaway to have your best friend tagging along with us like a third wheel,' Kitt said as he pulled me closer to him, his arm firmly banded around my waist despite me wearing boots that had been chosen by him for their firm grip in the snow. With my track record of slipping on ice, he was taking no chances of an accident happening here. It was bitter out in the open air, although our brisk walk down 5th Avenue, along with our leather gloves, thick padded jackets, and wool beanie hats, was keeping us warm.

'I guess,' I agreed. I smiled up at him, and he dipped his head to plant a soft kiss on my lips. 'Thank you so much for arranging this. New York is amazing.'

'You're welcome, but I can't take full credit on the romance front. It was for selfish reasons too. What architect wouldn't want to come to a city with so many iconic structures?'

'It's good to see you looking so happy again,' I observed as I slipped my hand into the back pocket of his jeans, my fingers curling around his peachy backside.

'I'm back doing the job I love, with the girl of my dreams at my side. How could I not be happy?' he asked, his eyes sparkling like flawless emeralds as he looked down to hold my gaze. 'So, where are you taking me?'

'I told you it's a surprise. Don't you know the meaning of the word?' I laughed.

'Don't forget we have to be ready for our trip up The Empire State Building later, and we need to get ready for dinner before we leave.'

'You should know by now that it doesn't take me long to get ready,' I reminded him.

'Hmmm. Well, it's not like you have to do a lot to look beautiful. It's hard to improve on perfection,' he murmured, kissing the side of my head as we continued to walk. I felt a warm surge flow through my body at his declaration. I'd never been with a man who made me feel so good about myself, so adored. It was hard to imagine that life could get any better than it was right now.

'Thank you for always knowing what to say to make me feel like the most special girl in the world.' I beamed up at him, my smile threating to crack my face.

'Because you are, baby.'

'Well, it's time I let you know how special you are to me, Kitt. We're here.' I drew to a halt outside the frontage of the exclusive jewellery shop, Havershams.

'Are you planning on proposing to me?' His eyebrows quirked in surprise as a look of what I could only describe as mortification settled on his face.

'Not quite, as I know you believe that's the man's job, but I do have a proposal of sorts for you.' I turned to face him, wrapping my arms around his slim waist as I gazed up at him. Without my high heels on, he towered above me like one of the high-rise buildings that surrounded us.

'What sort of proposal?' he asked, tucking a strand of hair back under my beanie.

'We've been dating for seven months now, Kitt,' I said, pausing for a moment to lick my dry lower lip. I felt nervous, which was ridiculous, as I knew he loved me, but I'd never done this before and it was a huge deal to me. 'Seven amazing months. And it's … well, it's getting harder and harder to say goodbye to you, knowing that I'm not going to see you for a few more nights, so I … What I'm trying to say is that I hate it. I want to wake up with you every morning and go to sleep in your arms every night, to spend as much time together as we can when you're not working. I want you to move in with me, Kitt,' I said in a rush, before I chickened out. 'I know I'm a hopeless cook, and I'm not the tidiest girl in the world, and Mrs. Tibbles still freaks out when she finds you in my bed and leaves you with scars, but despite all of that, I–'

'Yes,' he interrupted with a chuckle. 'Yes, I'll move in with you, Charlie.'

'I had a whole list of reasons why it would be a good idea, to counteract all of the drawbacks, of which there are many,' I said, not sure he'd really thought about all of the negatives I came with.

'I don't need a whole list. I want to be with you too, despite the many war wounds Tibbs is likely to inflict on me. To go to sleep and wake up with you every day is worth any drawback, baby. Just promise me that you won't cook. I'd like to have plenty more years ahead of me to enjoy our time together, and any of your attempts will either kill or hospitalise one of us.'

'You're so cheeky,' I laughed, swatting his arm as happiness surged through my veins.

'I was bought up to never lie,' he grinned as he dipped his head to kiss me again, the spark of electricity I felt whenever he did making me sigh happily. Daphne had been right. There might not have been that elusive crackle when we'd first touched, but falling in love with your best friend was a great, and solid, foundation, and there was no lack of sparks whenever we touched now. 'So why are we here? You want to get me a new fancy key ring to go with my own key to your house to mark the occasion?'

'Something like that. Come on, hats off. It's a posh place and we look like typical tourists who are only going in to gawk.'

I pulled mine off and stuffed it, along with my gloves, into my handbag, then quickly ran my hands through my hair, hoping it didn't look too bad. The security guard gave us the once over with an appraising eye before opening the door for us. We entered a stunning foyer, complete with an enormous crystal chandelier that sent fragments of dazzling white light scattering across the black granite floor. It was so warm compared to outside that we immediately stripped off our coats as we made our way to the security desk. We were signed in and checked for possible weapons, and on clearing their rigorous inspection, we headed into the right wing of the building, where the men's jewellery and all of the accessories were housed.

'Ok, I want to get you a ring,' I told Kitt as I pulled him over to the first display case.

'A ring? I thought you said this wasn't a proposal,' he said with a slightly nervous laugh.

'It's not, but I mean … I guess one day, hopefully, not saying yet, as hey presumptuous much, but one day you might, you know,' I huffed, aware I was suddenly rambling.

'Am I supposed to understand what you're trying to say?'

'I just … you *might* propose one day, and that usually means the man buys his woman a ring and well, if you did, *one day*, you wouldn't get a ring in return. So I thought it would be nice to celebrate you moving in by having a ring. A non-engagement ring. You could wear it on your right hand.' I bit my lower lip as I flitted my gaze across his face, wondering if I'd made a mistake, if I was pressuring him too much.

'A non-engagement ring,' he repeated. The corners of his mouth twitched, like he was trying to stop himself from laughing, before they curled up into that smile I loved, framed by his adorable dimples. 'I'd love that, Charlie. I'm honoured you feel that it's such a special event that you want to mark it in some way.'

'Well, it is. I've never lived with anyone before, let alone asked a man to move in. It's a huge deal.'

'It's a huge deal to me too, and I'd be honoured to wear your ring,' he stated sincerely, making the nervous smile on my face morph into a happy one.

'So, I don't know how you feel, but I kind of see you as a black tungsten guy, to go with your James Dean bad-boy vibe.'

'I have a James Dean bad-boy vibe?'

'Mmmm-hmmm. You're seriously hot in your jeans, boots, and t-shirt, but don't worry, I'll never let on that you're as soft as fudge under that sexy exterior,' I whispered. He laughed and shook his head, and we began to explore the cabinets. When we spotted a slimline one that had bevelled edges and a thin band of stainless steel encircling the middle, the immaculately groomed assistant fetched it for us in various sizes. The moment it was on, we knew it was right. It looked tough, yet sexy at the same time. 'We'll take it,' I confirmed, 'but I want to buy him a watch as well.'

'Charlie,' Kitt protested.

'The ring is a moving in gift. I was always going to get you a new watch as your Valentine's present,' I told him. The strap on his had broken the other week and he hadn't got around to getting it fixed, saying the strap was probably worth more than the watch itself.

'We can get a watch back home, one cheaper than in here,' he whispered in my ear.

'I don't want to get you a cheap one,' I whispered back. 'You deserve a nice one, and I happen to find an expensive watch on a man's wrist incredibly sexy.'

'But they're *so* expensive here.'

'I know we haven't discussed finances yet, Kitt, but I'm making a ridiculous amount of money now. I have no mortgage and everything I need, so it's just building up. Trust me, I can afford to buy you a designer watch.'

'Charlie,' he sighed, swiping a hand over his face.

'Please, Kitt. It will make me so happy to see you have something you deserve, something that tells you just how much you mean to me. You look after me in so many small ways that may seem inconsequential to you, but to me they mean so much more than any monetary value. Let me do this for you.'

'If it will make you happy, ok then,' he agreed, planting a lingering kiss on my forehead.

'Thank you,' I said sincerely, squeezing his hand.

Although I hadn't told him how much money I made from my writing now, I was pretty sure he knew it far exceeded whatever he earned as an architect, even though I knew they were well paid. But I loved that he didn't have a hang-up over it. He was just so proud of how well I was doing.

We ended up selecting a stunning Blancpain Léman chrome watch, with a sleek black face and gleaming chrome hands and dials on a black rubber strap. I nearly swooned to see it on his solid wrist, the new ring on his finger as well. I had no idea what it was about a wristwatch, but it screamed masculinity to me and got me all hot and bothered.

'Stop,' he chuckled as the empty boxes were put into an expensive-looking gift bag and I handed over my credit card to pay.

'Stop what?'

'Staring at me like you want to drag me to bed right now. The look on your face is obvious.'

'Wear that watch every day and I'll always look like this,' I purred. 'In fact, let's forget sightseeing this afternoon and head back to the hotel.'

'No,' he laughed as he rubbed the back of my neck, his long fingers massaging in a way that made my legs turn to jelly. 'While I'm all for spending hours in bed with you, we're here for a limited time. You don't want to regret the opportunity while we had the chance to take it all in.'

'Fine,' I relented, 'but you so owe me later.'

'You can count on it,' he growled, his deep timbre sending a shiver of anticipation down my spine.

Kitt put his arms around me and rested his chin on top of my head as we took in the vistas of a twinkling New York skyline from the 102nd floor of The Empire State Building. The gold roof of The New York Life Building shone like a precious jewel, offset by hundreds of tiny diamond-like lights of the buildings around it and the streaks of yellow and red car lights blurring on the streets far below that seemed to anchor the buildings to the ground. The curved lines of the art-deco Chrysler Building's chrome-look steeple were beautiful, and I'd listened, totally enraptured, to hear the excitement in Kitt's voice as he explained the artistry in the different angles, materials, and varying heights of the structures around us, as seen with his admiring architect's eye. I felt quite emotional to finally have ticked this incredible vista off my bucket list. It was a far cry from the small thatched cottages of Church Lane in Dilbury, that was for sure.

'I can't believe I'm here,' I whispered, the awe in my voice palpable.

'Stunning, isn't it,' he agreed, shifting position to place himself facing me, his back to the view.

'Hmmm, an even better view now,' I murmured as I tilted my head and pouted my lips for a kiss, which he immediately gave to me. I'd always loved Kitt in his casual jeans best, but now and again, when he dressed up in a suit like he had tonight, he transformed into the kind of alpha-male I always wrote about. He was in a graphite three-piece suit, white shirt, black tie, and tan Oxford shoes. The sight of his new watch and ring, offset by the thin strip of his white cuff and cufflinks, almost made me as giddy as when I'd peered down to the streets below for the first time from the open air 86th floor observatory earlier.

'Lust face,' he smiled, reaching up to slowly run his fingers through my loose hair, root to tip, which always made my skin tighten and prickle, hypersensitive to his touch.

'And love, don't forget love,' I reminded him, so happy to see how his green eyes were sparkling lately. Gone were the tell-tale bags of the man who'd had the weight of the world on his shoulders last year. He finally looked like any carefree, thirty-something male who was enjoying his life.

'How could I ever forget love?' he replied. 'The way you look at me sometimes … like I'm all your Christmases and birthdays come at once, it just takes my breath away.'

'Well, you are, Kitt. How many girls get to have it all? Their best friend and soul mate wrapped up in one deliciously handsome, sweet, and caring package? I hit the jackpot when you came into my life.' I felt my cheeks flush with my admission, the slight burn of unshed tears of emotion gathering behind my eyes. 'I've never been so happy,' I added in a whisper.

'Neither have I, which is why I have something to ask you tonight,' he replied as he took both of my hands in his. He took a deep breath, and I held mine, as he slowly dropped down onto one knee, holding my gaze as he looked up at me.

'Kitt?' My voice came out in a hushed tremble, the steady beat of my heart picking up pace as I hardly dared to hope what was coming next.

'I told you once before that I love you, especially your flaws as they make you unique. I've never met anyone else like you, Charlie, and I'm sure I never will. I fell in love with the pizza-obsessed, accident-prone, talented, and creative writer, and there's nothing about you that will ever stop me loving you, not even a schizophrenic Mrs. Tibbles, who loves me everywhere but in your bed.'

'She's protective of her mistress and what she sees as her territory, that's all,' I giggled. 'She loves you as much as I do.'

'I know,' he nodded with a smile. 'I love her too, but I love you more, Charlie. I love the way your nose crinkles when you laugh, the small furrow you get in your brow and the way your bottom lip pouts when you're concentrating. I love how you wake me up when you sit bolt upright in the middle of the night to scribble book ideas down in your notepad and share them with me with so much enthusiasm. I love that you see the bright side to everything, even when you've hurt yourself or you're in pain, which is a not-so-small part of the time. I love how you didn't care that I was just Pizzaman, but you saw Kitt, the man behind the job, and took a chance on giving him your heart. But most of all, I love the way you love me. Wholeheartedly and without reservation. Despite the fact that you're the breadwinner in this relationship, you still manage to make me feel like a man, like you can't live without my support, love, and protection.'

'I can't,' I choked, a few fat tears escaping my lower lashes and tracing their way down my cheeks. 'And I don't want to. I *never* want to, Kitt.'

'Then don't. You asked me to move in with you today, and I agreed, because I want to spend as many seconds as possible with you too. Now I'm asking you a question, because I want to spend those seconds with you by my side as my wife.' He swallowed and licked his lower lip, his fingers squeezing mine tightly as the air hung heavy with anticipation. I even noticed that everyone around us had gone quiet, the excited chatter of the other visitors muted as they waited for this moment to play out with just as much eagerness as I did.

'You haven't actually asked me the question,' I reminded him with a giggle as his face reflected the emotion I was feeling right now.

'God damn it,' he grunted, letting go of my left hand to quickly drag his sleeve across his emotional and watery eyes. 'One look into those gorgeous chocolate eyes of yours and I'm a goner, I lose all sense of rational thought.' He smiled and rummaged in the breast pocket of his jacket and pulled out a ring. My heart stopped beating, my breathing ceased, and time froze for a moment as I saw a delicate platinum band with a large round diamond balanced on the slim tapered shoulders, a rainbow of colours glistening in the faceted cuts that almost blinded me. 'Marry me, Charlie.'

It still wasn't a question. It was an order, in a rare dominant tone from my sweet man. But I didn't care. I'd take Kitt Fraser any way I could get him. Even if he'd been wearing his old pepperoni slice Pizzaman outfit right now, I wouldn't have minded. My answer would still be the same.

'Yes, yes, I'll marry you. Of *course* it's a yes,' I cried. I laughed and sobbed at the same time as his face lit up brighter than the city skyline behind him and he slipped the ring onto my finger. A roar of cheers and whoops went up all around us as Kitt shot to his feet, gathered me in his arms, and spun me around as he kissed me, his lips hungry, urgent, and grateful.

'You won't regret it,' he murmured. 'I'll love you full throttle, I'll never keep anything in reserve.'

'You never have, and neither will I. Oh, Kitt, I'm *so* happy. I wish everyone was here to see how incredibly happy you just made me.'

There was a loud chorus of "Surprise," and I looked away from Kitt's eyes and over his shoulder, then screamed with excitement. Amidst the strangers up on this floor clapping our engagement was everyone I loved from Dilbury. Abbie, Miller, Daphne, Jack, Georgie, Weston, and Quinn. The girls were all dabbing their eyes, even Quinn, though she did her best to do it discreetly so no one would notice. I felt my chest rattle to see my mum and dad standing there with them as well. Dad had his arm around Mum as she sobbed on his shoulder. I think she'd always despaired of me ever finding love.

'You arranged all of this?' I uttered as I slid down Kitt's body and my heels touched the floor.

'I did, weeks ago, so I nearly died when I thought you were about to ruin my carefully laid out plans by proposing to me this morning. We're all going to The Domville now for a private gourmet dinner to celebrate.'

'What if I'd said no?' I laughed, quickly dabbing my eyes.

'Then I'd have looked a prize idiot, but I figured we know each other well enough by now to trust in our feelings and where we were at in our relationship. Did I do ok with the ring?'

'It's stunning, Kitt,' I said, smiling down at it and drinking it in. 'And the fact that you got a round diamond, to remind me of pizza every day, means even more.' I grinned up at him as he laughed and kissed me again, not denying it.

'And I'm moving the ring you got me today to my other finger, it can be my engagement ring too.'

'We're engaged,' I cried loudly, making our friends and family cheer again.

'We are, and it won't be a long engagement. I want to be married and working on a baby Fraser in the next year or so,' he grinned, as we were swamped by everyone, too impatient to wait to congratulate us any longer.

A baby Fraser. My God, I couldn't wait either. Ever since we'd started dating, I'd felt the ticking of my biological clock, an undeniable craving to create something beautiful with him.

'Congratulations, darling,' my mum smiled as she wrapped me up in a hug. 'We're both so happy for you. I knew he was the one for you the first time I met him. The way you both looked at each other was … it was so beautiful to see the love you shared. We couldn't be more thrilled that you're going to become Mrs. Christopher Fraser.'

'Oh my God, forget Mrs. Fraser. I'm going to be Pizzawoman!' I exclaimed, making everyone laugh.

Epilogue

Fête Day
Four Years Later – July

'JESUS, YOU FEEL LIKE you've put on a stone, Mrs. Fraser,' Kitt huffed as he gallantly lifted me over the side of the hot air balloon wicker basket, carefully setting me down before he jumped in and the staff got ready for lift off.

'It's all your cooking,' I protested. 'You're a feeder. I swear you must think the more curves I have, the better.'

'I wouldn't complain,' Quinn said as she took charge of handing out the flutes of champagne. 'How many women get a guy who loves to cook for them?'

'I didn't,' Daphne huffed from the segment to our right, then gave Jack a mock scowl.

'Ermmm, I did,' shouted Abbie from the opposite corner, over the sound of the blast of gas as we started to rise.

'Me too,' called Georgie, smiling up at Weston as he hugged her from behind. 'You just lucked out, Quinn.'

'I don't know about that,' she said, with a faint blush colouring up her cheeks that made me giggle. My self-confessed emotionally stunted best friend had finally thawed. Not only was she dating, she was madly in love, although she wouldn't admit that fact to us all yet. But I couldn't be happier for her.

'Love is a great colour on you,' I told her, knowing I was winding her up, which earned me a punch on the arm.

'Love is in the air,' Daphne sang. 'Quite literally. I love this new annual balloon ride tradition of ours.'

'Me too. Just don't hang over the side of it and lose any more dentures, Daphne,' I warned.

'I don't know, there are some benefits to being gummy,' she winked, making Georgie, Heath, Max, and Jack's faces turn red as everyone else laughed.

'You're incorrigible,' I said as I raised my flute in the air. 'Happy anniversary, Mr. and Mrs. Argent.'

'Happy anniversary,' everyone chorused as we gently rose higher and higher, with Dilbury Manor, the estate, and the village below us bathed in the gorgeous summer sun that seemed to bless fête day each year.

'Joyeux anniversaire,' Fleur added, her rich French accent still sounding so adorable. She'd settled into the village so well. Her bakery business was booming, her moreish creations selling like proverbial hot cakes, and she'd teamed up with Quinn to be her go-to cake girl for all of the Severn Manor weddings or events, which had been a lucrative partnership for them both.

'Daddy, I can't see,' came Jackson's voice, as his head appeared over the edge of his section of the basket, then disappeared repeatedly, as if he was bouncing up and down with excitement.

'Come on then, son, but no wriggling. Mummy will get mad at me if I accidently drop you over the side,' Miller chuckled, as he lifted their nearly four-year-old son up onto his hip.

'Too right I will,' Abbie scoffed as I tipped my champagne into Kitt's flute and quickly set my empty glass down, hoping no one would notice. 'The torture of labour pains are still too fresh in my mind to even think about replacing him.'

'But I thought you were trying again,' I said, confused and rather put off at her assessment. Kitt laced his fingers with mine and squeezed in a reassuring way.

'We are,' Miller laughed. 'But Abbie never lets me forget that she had the rough end of the deal.'

'Rough end? That makes it sound like a momentarily uncomfortable inconvenience. Trust me, if you tried squeezing a bowling ball out of your bottom, that would be a fraction of "the rough end" we women have to face,' Abbie stated emphatically, making me wince at the thought of it.

'Which is why I'm perfectly content with my fur baby, Bertie,' Georgie said.

'What about you, Charlie?' asked Isla as she stood next to Lord Kirkland and Fleur in the section to our left. 'You've been married for what, three years now? Any pitter-patter of little Frasers on the horizon?'

'Well, I …' I felt my cheeks colour up as I glanced at Kitt. He couldn't stop the dimples from appearing on his face as he smiled and gave me a gentle nod of approval.

'I knew it!' yelled Quinn. 'I said you were pregnant. There's no way that tummy you've been trying to hide is from too much pizza. Even *you* couldn't scoff that much!'

'And I said I'd noticed she kept refusing alcohol, which isn't the Charlie we've all come to know and love,' laughed Georgie.

'Hey, I'm not that bad. It's Quinn, she's a bad influence,' I protested. Quinn just shrugged, knowing there was no disputing that statement.

'How does everyone spot this stuff before me?' Abbie huffed, her eyes darting between us all as she tried to work out if they were right.

'Please, you had no idea you were pregnant with Jackson until Georgie and I told you. You're rubbish at spotting the signs. I can't believe I missed it this time. Oh, Charlie, is it true, are you really pregnant?' Daphne exclaimed, her eyes filling with tears.

'It's true,' I beamed. I laughed as everyone cheered and started clapping before bombarding us with questions. 'We're five months along, due in November.'

'Five months!' Abbie spluttered, spraying a fine mist of champagne all over the back of Lord Kirkland, then frantically rubbing the back of his tweed waistcoat to try and get it off. 'You're not even showing. How's that fair? I was the size of a hippopotamus at five months.'

'Oh, trust me, I'm showing. I've just been wearing loose clothes lately.'

'It may be a small and perfectly formed bump, but she's showing,' Kitt agreed as he moved behind me and cradled my belly with his strong hands, stretching my floaty maxi dress tightly across it so there was no disputing the fact. 'Look.'

'Why did you wait so long to tell us?' Quinn asked, the corners of her mouth downturned. The look on her face said that I'd hurt her by not sharing my news with her specifically.

'I'm so sorry, I really wanted to tell you all, *especially* you, Quinn, I promise I did. But I was actually Mum's second child. The first died soon after birth from a hereditary condition she suffered from that affects a baby's development in the womb. I won't go into details, but we only just had the test results back recently to say that our baby was doing fine, so we were waiting for the right time to tell you all. I didn't want to overshadow Georgie and Weston's special day.'

'Please, we stole it as ours anyway,' Georgie said with a gentle smile. 'Officially this is Abbie's special day. Thirteen years of kicking Lady Kirkland's arse in the Dilbury Village Bake-off. Oh sorry, no offence meant, Max.'

'None taken,' he laughed, his attractive grey eyes crinkling in amusement. 'You know our history now, you all do, and I couldn't be happier with the way things turned out.' He cast a soft smile across the balloon and I exhaled slowly and shook my head, so happy for them both.

'I can't take all of this,' moaned Daphne, tears rolling down her face. 'Who has tissues?'

'Here you are, darling,' Jack said, whipping a white handkerchief from the top pocket of his blazer. 'I think you might need it if you're this emotional already.'

'What do you mean, already? Who else is pregnant?'

'Not me!' Quinn stated firmly.

'Nor me, and Weston's booked in for the snip next month, just to be sure,' Georgie said, and the men in the balloon automatically winced, Heath cupping his groin protectively.

'Please, feel free to share the personal details of my crown jewels with all and sundry, Mrs. Argent,' Weston laughed.

'Hardly all and sundry. This is our closest circle of friends in this hot air balloon, we're all practically family.'

'Here, here,' Abbie said, raising her glass again.

'Here, here,' everyone choroused. Quinn quickly put a glass of orange juice in my hand so I wasn't missing out. I beamed at her and kissed her cheek, knowing I was going to have to make up this small betrayal to her soon.

'Well, if I can have your attention for a moment,' Jack called, clearing his throat, 'I have something to say.'

'If it's to announce that there's been no addition to the hashtag turdgate series this year, I for one am happy to toast to my lack of a starring role for once,' Abbie called, making us all chuckle.

'Don't speak too soon,' I warned her. 'There was that incident with a hot air balloon ride once before, and you've scoffed down your body weight in ice cream today.'

'That incident wasn't me,' she huffed. 'Or anything to do with me at all,' she added quickly, her cheeks turning scarlet as she blatantly lied.

'What is it, what's wrong, Jack? Your eye is twitching and you look like *you're* about to fill your pants,' Daphne said bluntly.

'You're a feisty and mouthy one, Daphne Jones,' he chuckled. 'Many a man would run scared from a woman like you, but after seeing action in The Falklands, I'm confident that I can handle anything you have to throw at me. I know I'll never replace David, that he was the great love of your life, but I hope that I've come to live in a small part of your heart, as you do in mine.'

'Jack, what are you trying to say?' Daphne asked as we all listened just as eagerly. 'Spit it out. Patience was never one of my virtues.'

'You're not kidding,' I muttered under my breath, but with her sonar hearing she shot me a disapproving look that made me cringe.

'I never thought I'd find love again after my May passed away. I thought I was old and past it, that the next big milestone would be me knocking on heaven's door, which I almost feel as if I am,' Jack said with a quick look over the edge of the balloon, which sent a ripple of laughter around it. I guessed as a former Navy Captain, he was more used to the ocean than the skies. 'You're an incredible woman, Daphne. You've given me back the love of life that I thought I'd lost when May died. Every day with you, and these young friends and family of yours, brings me joy.'

'You're buttering me up like a hot potato, what's going on? Are you after some action tonight? A bit of the horizontal mumbo jumbo, as Charlie says?'

'Horizontal mambo,' I giggled. 'Though if you're saying jumbo, is that a Freudian slip?'

'Now that would be telling, Charlie Fraser,' she chortled, her cheeks turning pink.

'Honestly, woman, just shut up and let a man speak, will you?' Jack ordered. He was braver than we were with her, he deserved another medal just for that. And how come he didn't get one of her infamous stern teacher looks? Instead he got her soft doe-eyed look that was reserved for when she was feeling extra emotional with her loved ones. 'Some may say at our age there's no point in marriage, but I disagree. I feel like a young teenager with the best parts of his life ahead of him whenever I'm with you. Sadly, my knees are past me getting down on a bended one, so Heath will be my proxy,' he said. Heath immediately dropped to one bended knee as he opened a black velvet Havershams' box to show off a stunning retro square halo diamond ring, which sparkled in the sunlight. 'Daphne Jones, will you do me the honour of becoming my wife?' Jack asked as we all gasped.

My eyes darted around, and other than a small giveaway smile on Abbie's lips, it was obvious that everyone except her and Heath had all been kept out of this loop. The Dilbury rumour mill had well and truly failed us here.

'You're proposing?' Daphne asked, eyeing him suspiciously.

'Yes,' he chuckled. 'Wasn't I clear enough?'

'Whatever for?'

'Because I love you, woman.'

'And I love you, but we're nearly ninety.'

'So? I feel nineteen when I'm with you.'

'And you touch me up like a nineteen-year-old as well.'

'You'd complain if I didn't,' he quickly replied.

'Are you just after me for my view? I know you were always envious that I got the best apartment in the building.'

'It is the best, but I'm not after you for the view,' he smiled.

'I think it's your body, Daphne,' I teased.

'Well, all the men over seventy in the village are after me for that,' she retorted, 'I was quite a looker in my day, I'll have you know.'

'You're still a looker now, and it's not just your body I'm after. Or your money, before you bring that up,' Jack said. 'I just want to make an honest woman of you. Nothing would make me happier in my last few years of life than to be your husband. Are you telling me you don't want me?'

'Get away with you,' she giggled, pushing his chest. 'You know I'm only playing with you. I love to tease. Of course I'll marry you. I'd be so proud to be Mrs. Jack Bentley. David couldn't have chosen a more suitable successor himself, I know he'd be happy for us. Oh, you've made an old lady so ecstatic, you silly fool,' she moaned as she started crying again, setting me off.

Another chorus of cheers and toasts went up as Heath put Jack's ring onto her hand, then held Daphne steady as she gripped Jack's arms and he took her face in his hands and kissed her. I suspected that she knew it was coming, as up until yesterday, she'd still worn her old engagement and wedding rings on her left hand, and they were suspiciously absent today. Nothing got past Daphne, except my pregnancy, it seemed.

'You never told them we were having a baby girl,' Kitt murmured quietly in my ear, before laying a trail of soft kisses down my neck.

'It can wait,' I replied, spinning around to face him. 'Any more happy news and I think everyone will explode.'

'I could explode,' he said, his soft green eyes holding mine captive. 'I'm so happy, baby.'

'Me too. Each year I think life can't get better with you, and it does.'

'Do I get to hug my best friend now and offer my congratulations?' Quinn asked.

'Of course you do. The godmother should always get one of the first celebratory hugs,' I confirmed.

'I'm going to be its godmother?' she gasped, her brown eyes dilating as her mouth formed a perfect circle of surprise.

'Of course, who else would be my first choice?' I said, wrapping my arms tightly around her. 'I'm so sorry for not telling you sooner. If it helps, I've been riddled with guilt.'

'Good, I should hope so,' she teased, hugging me back firmly. 'Please tell me you're not moving away?'

'Why would we move?' I asked, giving her a curious look as we parted.

'You have a two-bedroom cottage. You're going to share your writing cave with a screaming baby?'

'Actually, Kitt's already drawn up plans to add on some extra rooms upstairs and downstairs, and the work will start next summer. But he's having a garden studio built for me in the meantime, which will go up next month, somewhere I can go and write in peace for a few hours a day, with magnificent views down the valley to inspire me.'

'You really thought we'd leave Dilbury?' Kitt asked. 'I can't imagine anyone who moves in, gets to know the villagers, and settles in to the Dilbury way of life, ever wants to leave.'

'I know what you mean, New York was just a place to live,' Quinn agreed. 'Dilbury is *home*.'

'It sure is,' I nodded as we turned to look down at the village we all loved so much. It was easy to forget just how stunning it was when you didn't see the green and yellow fields, orchards, deer, meandering river, or thatched and tiled old buildings all at once.

'Was that you?' Kitt laughed as a loud stomach grumble cut through the peaceful silence up here.

'Of course, I'm eating for two, I'm always hungry. And you know what I'm craving right now?'

'Pepperoni pizza,' everyone in the balloon shouted at once.

'Am I that predictable?' I complained, practically salivating at the thought of my favourite treat once we landed.

'Never, baby. You do something to surprise me every day,' Kitt smiled. 'Not least a whole month of no visits to the A&E department.'

'Oh no,' I cried, clutching my stomach dramatically. 'You had to go and jinx it, didn't you?'

'What, what's wrong?' he asked, his concerned gaze darting across my face.

'Haha, got you!' I teased.

'Charlie Fraser,' he scolded with a laugh as he gently tugged me against him. 'Don't do that to me, I nearly had heart failure.'

'Me too, you just scared me to death,' Quinn stated with a disapproving look.

'I'll always be fine. I married Pizzaman, the kindest, gentlest, and most caring superhero in the universe. He always looks after me,' I said softly as I put my arms around his neck.

'And I always will look after you, Charlie, *always*,' he breathed, before buckling my knees with an explosive and passionate kiss that sent my heart soaring higher than the hot air balloon. I'd spent years writing the perfect alpha males with the perfect careers, so who'd have imagined that after months of pining after Dr. Fitton, Mr. Perfect on paper if not in the flesh, I'd fall for the down-to-earth, sweet and humble pizza delivery guy.

222

Maybe I'd been right all along, pizza really was the best medicine.

The End

Did you enjoy The Best Medicine?

If so, I'd be really grateful if you'd take a moment of your time to leave me a review at your point of sale, and Goodreads, even if it's only a few words. They are so important to me in helping other readers discover my books.

Thank you!

Next Release

I'll be staying in Dilbury for a while, bringing you more romantic comedy tales from the villagers.

Quinn will be back very soon in her own romantic comedy story, *The Wedding Planner (Dilbury Village #4)*.

You can add it to your Goodreads TBR list here:
www.goodreads.com/book/show/35512962-the-wedding-planner

Other Titles by Charlotte Fallowfield

My website contains the most comprehensive information about me, my work, how to get in contact with me, where you can meet me, and how to order signed paperbacks.

charlottefallowfield.co.uk

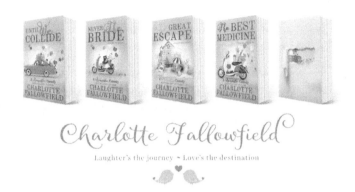

Laughter's the journey ~ Love's the destination

C.J. Fallowfield

Did you know that I also write suspenseful steamy romance as C.J. Fallowfield? *These books are strictly for the over 18's.*

cjfallowfield.co.uk

SEXY, SASSY, EMOTIVE ROMANCE

Newsletter

As well as offering exclusive giveaways every six months, just for my mailing list subscribers, I'll keep you updated on my new releases, including teasers, discounted or free promotions, and any other giveaways that I'm running on my other social network sites. I'll also include details of any events that I'll be appearing at around the U.K. and abroad.

You can subscribe on the following page of my website:
charlottefallowfield.co.uk/newsletter

Charlotte Fallowfield's Book Club

It would be great to see you join my book club. This is a reader group for fans of my work, where I hang out each week to chat to members, share exclusive snippets of my work in progress, answer, as well as set, questions about my books. I also share reviews of any romcoms or chick-lit books that I've read, and love to hear about any other books you have, as I'm always looking out for the next great read. I also do member only giveaways from time to time and offer members the first chance to purchase my limited edition advance paperback copies of releases. To join the group, head to Facebook and use the link below:

facebook.com/groups/517918061877017/

Made in United States
North Haven, CT
24 October 2022

25839153R00124